Americana Adventure Series

Presents

Gaspar

by

Michael E. Vance

Special "Thank You"

To God and my country for Faith, Family, and Freedom;

to my wife for putting up with the long nights of writing; to my children (Connor, Xavier, and Sarah) for their love that inspires me to be a better father; to my Father whom taught me discipline and hard work; to my friends and family that encouraged me to take this leap; to Eric for that blank journal you gave me all those years ago, to my Mother-In-Law for being my first reader and giving me hope.

To my Editor- Gavin – Thank you for all of your advice and insight. I expect big things from you in the future.

This book is dedicated to my Mother.

You were the parent that every child should have. If there were more like you this world would be such a better place. I was blessed to have been able to call you

"Mom."

The legend of Jose Gaspar is true. But it is just that-a legend. For every believer, there is a non-believer. For every tale there is little evidence. Many documents make the claim that he was a real person and pirate but there is no verified historical record of him. I leave the truth of his authenticity to you. Seek out your own answers. Tell your own tale.

Most of the historical facts in this story are true. However, this story is purely fictional. "Faction" if you will-a fictional story with factual references. Any similarities to character names or descriptions are purely coincidence. Many of the locations are real and I invite you to learn more about them because amazing things are all around us at every step. We just need to stop sometimes and take a moment to appreciate them.

I hope you enjoy reading this story as much as I did in writing it. By making history fun and entertaining we not only can have a good time but we can learn a lot about ourselves, where we come from, and what we are capable of doing in this world. But most importantly, just take yourself and your kids outside and explore this amazing country. There is so much to see all around us that you won't be disappointed. And who knows? You may just be inspired to write your own story. Good luck and God Bless.

Chapter 1

Gulf of Mexico, 1821

The warm, gulf, sea spray wet the open bow of the buccaneer ship "Floriblanca." With every rolling wave, the massive wooden ship crashed down into the trough only to race up its crest again. As the stiff hemp sails tacked into the summer breeze, the Floriblanca picked up speed. Sprinting out of its secret berth- a hidden palm tree lined cove- the sheets filled with wind and the sleek wooden ship headed out towards its prey. A large merchant vessel just northeast of the harbor, had lost its rigging and was now floating helplessly adrift. Making no headway, the fat heavy ship was too tasty a prize for the Floriblanca's Captain to pass on.

The rudderless merchant ship sat deep into the sea, too deep for just any trade ship. Obviously, weighted down by heavy gold or rum filled barrels the Floriblanca's crew suspected. Too delicious a treat to let go even if just days before, the old pirate captain had sworn he was getting, "too old to plunder, too tired to set sail, too rich to be richer." No, not for this old seadog, the sight of that merchant ship was like blood in the water. This was an easy meal for the most feared shark of the seas. This prey was too tempting- no predator could pass up- no matter how stuffed its belly already was. This was Captain Jose Gaspar's chance to finish his ever lucrative 40 year swashbuckling career with a smash.

"Manuel… haul in the sheets. We are coming to port," - Captain Gaspar yelled to the boatswain on deck. "Haul in the sheets," the crew repeated. "Raise the main and ready the starboard (right) side," the Captain followed. "Starboard aye," echoed the crew.

Captain Gaspar could taste the saliva building in his mouth. The rush of seawater seemed to course though his veins. This is what he does. This is what he has always done. No treasure hunter had seen his level of success and no pirate could match his ferociousness in battle. When others would flee, he would attack. When others would trade, he would take. These were the lessons he learned from his youth growing up in the poor city streets of Barcelona, Spain.

Short in height but stocky in build, he was often picked on by other kids. Instead of suffering through the slings of their taunts and teases, Gaspar reveled in the sharp pain of flesh against his club like fists. A misplaced word or even a harsh look from a passerby could switch the charming young man into a rabid brawler in an instant. His notoriety on those broken stone streets grew rapidly and soon the young Jose Gaspar became known as Gasparilla- the outlaw.

As a young man, Gaspar found himself out of the favor of the Royal Spanish Courts. He was forced to make a decision to either serve in the Spanish Navy or go to jail. For many young men, at that time, the idea of jail was actually preferred over years of sea service-but not for Gaspar. The seas were where the angry young man discovered himself. He was born for it. The freedom of the sea gave him peace and its bounty gave him purpose. The lust for wealth, eventually led Gaspar to desert the military life for a life of piracy- a life that would span over four decades at sea and take the pirate to every corner of the ocean world. He knew every trick, every local custom, and always had a place to hide out when he needed to make a quick escape. He was respected as much as he was feared because his actions- right or wrong- were always met with results. He had stolen more bounty and fought more battles than any man that came before him. And now, like blood to a Great White, the Captain could smell the beautiful, wide hulled, oak covered, brig lifelessly adrift in the gulf just two points off his bow.

Coming up fast on the distressed ship, the Floriblanca eased its sails just a bit to slow its approach. The pirate ship was unusually fast for its size. Lesser sailors often misjudged her capabilities but not the Captain. He handled her as if she was an extension of himself and the two sailed as one. The white capped saltwater splashing the bow slowed to a smooth racing current down her beam. The pirate crew waited with glee as they stood on the deck with grappling hooks and sabers in their hands. The Floriblanca made its approach, upwind on the port stern of the motionless vessel. It was in perfect position for attack as it had done so many times before. And just like so many times before, the restless buccaneers aboard were bursting with anticipation as they gracefully sailed towards their target. Captain Gaspar stood at the helm and took in a long deep breath of salt air. This was the part of a pirate's life that he was going to miss.

Suddenly Gaspar noticed some rapid movement on the drifting ship's decks. The merchant crewman raced about not in frantic fear but in disciplined order. The turnbuckles snapped tight and the brig's top square sails quickly filled with wind. She was coming about, turning fast and opening her port hatches. The Floriblanca's crew was astonished as they watched the distressed vessel move into attack formation with absolute precision.

Captain Gaspar watched the vessel turn around and knew he had been played… but he was not afraid... he was never afraid. Not when the brig showed her broadside of 14 guns; a heavy load that would weigh down any ship much the same as precious gold or rum. Not when those iron barrels aimed low at the Floriblanca's waterline. Shots from that angle meant there would be no chance for negotiations. Either she was going down, or the Floriblanca was. Not when the merchant ship's pennant dropped and raised the Stars and Stripes of the United States. And not even when the Captain realized that the distressed wolf in sheep's clothing was the feared pirate hunter U.S.S. Enterprise. The Captain was not afraid… But then again the Captain did not fear death.

Built at a Baltimore, Maryland shipyard in 1799, the U.S.S. Enterprise was a decorated and seasoned ship of war. She had fought and won battles from the Mediterranean to the Caribbean and no privateer or pirate ship had ever faced the Enterprise and won. The Floriblanca's fate had just been sealed.

Marine rifleman, in their red cotton jackets spread out on the yard arms like ants swarming out of their mound. Cannons lit, the Enterprise opened fire in a hellish cloud of smoke and flames. The thunderous barrage of iron hit the Floriblanca sending massive chunks of wood and even crewmen into the dark blue sea. The Marines with their black powdered long rifles picked off pirates with rapid and deadly accuracy. Starting with the boatswain mates and then the deck hands, the Marines were killing the crew of the Floriblanca from the top ranks down. Captain Gaspar would have been their first target, they even had their best sharp shooter, a 21 year old long rifle from Kentucky, scanning the decks for him, but the Captain was no longer on the flying bridge.

The ships passed each other port to port (left side to left side) and in a few short moments of deafening cannon and musket fire the battle was over. The Floriblanca quickly began to list, or lean, to its port side. The hull had been breached, and she was taking on water fast. As the Enterprise was coming around for another pass, the Floriblanca slowly came to a stop and sat lifeless in the gulf sea-dead afloat. Once the greatest pirate ship of the sea- now the Floriblanca, was just moments away from being another wreck on the ocean floor.

The eerie silence of the ravaged ship was interrupted when a wooden hatch suddenly slammed open on the deck with a rattling crash. A sweating, blood soaked, Captain Gaspar climbed out from the galley stairs. He had disappeared shortly after the first shot from the Enterprise ripped through the giant oak timber of the main mast. The shot from the main cannon had almost cut the Floriblanca's mast clean in half.

A young Private aboard the Enterprise had been tasked with the one in a million shot. "Take down the main mast or we lose Gasparilla" were his orders. A challenging order for any sailor but this teenager was ready. He had practiced for this moment for months. It would be the shot of his life and he was salivating for his opportunity. Sweat on his face, he didn't dare wipe for fear of losing focus. His eyes were fixed on his target as the Floriblanca was coming into range. Hot, loud, sweaty, cramped quarters, the Private was bent over in a painfully crouched position for several minutes… holding… holding. His legs ached and quivered pleading with him to stand up. The fuse was a 2 second delay that he had to time perfectly for his shot. The ships were passing opposite each other in an open rolling sea, the cannon deck was filled with smoke when suddenly the 18 year old private shouted "FIRE." The room around him erupted in a deafening thunder of rapid explosions. His eyes burned with sweat and hot soot but he pained to keep looking at his target praying that he had not missed and then he saw it. It was a hit.

The ships past by each other and the barrage of cannon and musket fire stopped for a moment of agonizing silence. Even the wounded seemed to hold their screams in anticipation of the attacks outcome. But the Private knew already that his shot was priceless, and it was only a matter of moments before everyone else would know as well. The mast stood for a moment but the weight of the sails was more than enough to finish the job and bring the giant timber with all of its rigging down on the deck and into the sea. With a snap and a long cracking sound, the mast, sails, and a thousand pounds of oiled hemp rope splashed into the gulf from 80 feet above the deck. The Floriblanca swung back hard to its starboard side. The weight of the mast and its sails nearly rolled the ship until the last of the great oak's splinters severed and the massive wood pole broke free. Shooting like an arrow straight down into the deep dark blue water, the mast quickly disappeared, and the Floriblanca rocked back to its previous listing port position. The violent rocking motion actually sent one of the few surviving pirates 30 yards out to sea because his hands were too soaked with blood to hold on to the foremast.

Barely able to stand, the Captain pushed himself up from the deck hatch. His right leg was attached to his knee by a few strands of ligament and some blackened skin. The opening cannonball shot, from that teenage Private, had struck the mast ricocheting and splintering on impact. A chunk of the fiery iron ball ripped through the Captain's shin as he had stood at the helm. It nearly took his leg clean off and in an instant the great Captain knew he was facing his final moments. However, he had one more task to complete before his time was up.

Bracing himself as straight as he could, the Captain took out a piece of cloth that he had retrieved from his stateroom. In the dizzying moments of battle it wasn't the ship he was concerned with or even to find a doctor to remove what was left of his leg, but the piece of cloth from his stateroom-that was all that mattered to the Captain now. Holding the hemp cloth in his hand the Captain bellowed, "Gomez… come here boy."

A young child, no older than 10 years of age ran up to the Captain. He had been hiding in the scuppers, staying low from sniper fire during the attack. Even children aboard a pirate ship were fair game when it came to deadly justice. Gaspar leaned over to whisper into the child's ear and then he handed Gomez the bloody cloth from his pocket. A moment later, Gaspar hobbled up to the bow and looked out across his beloved ocean. He wrapped an anchor chain around his waist and raised his sword high above his head. Taking in one last long deep breath of moist salt air he shouted out towards the approaching Enterprise,

"Gasparilla dies by his own hands… not his enemies."

And then the last of the great buccaneers dropped into the ocean with the heavy metal chain dragging him to the crushing bottom of Davey Jones' locker.

Chapter 2

Jacksonville, FL Courthouse, 2012

Gabriel Fletcher was standing in front of Judge Davis once again. The young boy had been here many times before and he knew the procedure. Just as before-he had filed the paper work and pleaded his case. Now he was just waiting for his "DENIED" judgment, yet again. But this time something was different. The Judge seemed to ponder his decision a little longer. Concern was now showing on his face where before it was just dismissal.

Judge Davis had a deep baritone voice that seemed to come from the pit of his stomach. His booming bass tone echoed throughout the nearly empty courthouse and it demanded attention. "Mr. Fletcher" he said. "In light of your persistent returns to my courthouse and your most recent dispute with Mr. Skillings - your legal guardian - I'm reconsidering my previous rulings."

Sitting on the bench across the aisle from Gabriel was Tony Skillings, a large overweight man with sweaty skin, who was at the time Gabriel's Foster Parent. He stood up and glared at Gabriel with venom. The deep bluish red bruise around his eye and the large plaster cast on his leg was proof that Skillings had recently met his match in the much younger Gabriel. Skillings had started the fight, as he always did, but it didn't go his way this time and Gabriel proved to him that he would not take the abuse anymore.

"Even though you are only of the age of 15 this is your 8th time in this courthouse seeking legal emancipation," the Judge stated. "It is obvious that your current situation-as with the others- is not a healthy environment for you. Yet you portray yourself in this courthouse before this Judge with dignity, confidence, and respect. You have defended yourself primarily without legal representation so I know you are of exceptional mental ability. Given your young age it is against my normal judgment, however removing your age from this process I see no other reason to reject your plea for legal emancipation."

A sigh of relief began to swell up in Gabriel's throat while an obnoxious outburst came from across the room. Pounding his fist and shouts of threats came from Skillings as he couldn't believe what he was hearing from the Judge.

"Are you kidding me? This brat kid is going to walk free? Look at my face! Look at my leg- he broke my leg!" Skillings cried out at the judge and then he turned his anger to Gabriel. "You wait until I get my hands on you… you little…"

The CRACK of Judge Davis's gavel brought the chaos to an abrupt halt. "Order! Mr. Skillings," Judge Davis boomed. "I will not tolerate outbursts in my courtroom and your reaction has only validated my decision." Judge Davis looked towards Gabriel and with gentle but impartial eyes said, "Mr. Fletcher- you have not been dealt a fair hand in your young life. You have the sympathy of this court. Life is not fair-but the rule of law must be and in this court it will be. You are here by free to go as an independent citizen. Good luck with your life and I hope to not see you back here again do you understand?" Gabriel couldn't speak but he was able to softly nod his head. "Very well, this court is adjourned."

The gavel cracked one more time as the Judge rose to return to his quarters and just like that Gabriel was free to live his life-at last. He stood still for several moments at his table trying to take in the fact that he was now free. When it suddenly hit him, he dropped to his knees in rejoice because God had finally answered his prayers. Tears did not quite come to him- they never did- even though his eyes begged for them. Instead every muscle in his body relaxed and the tormenting scream of frustration in his head, after years of suffering, was suddenly quiet. The cold shackles of his bondage were now off and freedom covered over him like a warm blanket.

Gabriel had lived with great pain and terrible loss over the last 8 years, more than any child should suffer. But he never made excuses or lashed out with hatred in his heart, instead he found peace in his challenges, courage in his fear, and strength in his struggles.

"God has a plan for everyone Gabe," his Father had once told him, "some suffer more because they can take it but no one gets more than they can handle. It's how you handle that pain that will lead you to something greater." Gabriel had suffered more already, by the age of 15, then most due in a lifetime but he never forgot those words. Through the fear, the pain, and the loneliness of his short life Gabriel had found courage, strength, and peace to move forward. And now after so many years, the nightmares were over. His countless prayers had been received with the slamming of a wooden gavel. He was finally free, and it felt good.

The shouts of his now former Foster Father began to ring in his ears as the irate Tony Skillings was escorted past the quiet kneeling boy. Gabriel couldn't help but feel a slight sense of pleasure when he stood up and stared down his former abusive legal guardian. "Take care of that leg now, Mr. Skillings." Gabriel couldn't help but smile and offer a dismissive wink at the miserable man. As Gabriel turned to walk out, the last vision he would ever have of Tony Skillings was one of three armed officers dragging him through the courtroom doors into a contempt of court holding cell. "Perfect," Gabriel whispered to himself.

Chapter 3

Florida Gulf Coast, 1821

Juan Gomez, the 10 year old cabin boy that had received Captain Gaspar's last order, was finally on dry land again. A small wooden boarding boat had ridden the surf and beached itself into the sugary white sand of the Florida coast. The name U.S.S. ENTERPRISE was painted on its weathered hull.

Indentured into the sea-life at the age of 6, Juan never was comfortable aboard boats. He had spent the last 4 years aboard the Floriblanca and he hated every minute of it. The lure of adventure and treasure was nothing compared to the sickening rollercoaster of the sea or the terror of vast blackness that constantly slept beneath his young feet. Moments of peace and calm would be shattered by the summer rains and hurricane wind storms. Not to mention the life of a cabin boy was hard enough to survive but add to that the frightening reality of the sea and little Juan Gomez could not press his toes deep enough into the hot dry sand.

Off into the distance, behind the sharp leaves of a Saw Palmetto tree about a hundred yards away, a small telescope peaked out from the shaded dune.

"What can you see?" a high pitched voice whispered. "It's the Enterprise skiff alright." Raúl replied with a snarl. "I see Vasca, Soto, Moreno… and the boy Gomez."

Juan Gomez was the first off the skiff; he was one of only four survivors from the doomed vessel Floriblanca. The buccaneer ship that now rested at the bottom of the sea. The other three men followed him with ankle shackles and wrist irons clamped tightly together to prevent their escape.

As he lined up next to the other survivors, little Juan could feel the bloody cloth that was handed to him by Captain Gaspar just before he dove into the sea. He could only wander what it said as it pressed against his chest thru his shirt pocket. Ensign Mitchell, a tall strapping young officer in a blue wool uniform, bent down to look Juan in the eyes.

"I'm going to take these men to prison. They will be tried for piracy and hung until they're dead." Grabbing a hold of Juan's painful wrist irons and twisting the metal deeper into his raw skin, Ensign Mitchell wanted to make his point crystal clear. "If I ever see you on a pirate ship again, I will bleed you like a pig and feed you to my dogs! Do you understand?"

With both eyes wide with fright-Juan could only nod his head-yes.

"Then get out of here boy and don't ever let me see you again." The Ensign removed the irons from his wrists, turned away from little Juan, and returned to his work arresting the other pirate sailors.

With a deep sigh of relief, as his shackles clanked to the sandy ground, Juan let out a long breath of air from his lungs. A sigh of relieve that seemed to have been held in him ever since he was clutched out of the debris filled water and taken prisoner aboard the Enterprise. The moment of relief came over him like a ray of sunshine. He was free. No longer in shackles as a prisoner of the United States, he was free to go. He was no longer a servant aboard a pirate ship with little hope of growing old. He was free. But the warm feeling of relief was soon replaced with a cold sense of loneliness as he began to walk away from his former shipmates and the sea that had been his home for the last 4 years.

Since he was 6 years of age he had been on that ship. He had been told what to do, when to do it, and how to do it for even the most basic of his daily activities. He lived a tight schedule. A detailed daily plan guided him thru every moment of his day.

Time aboard ship was kept thru the use of ringing bells. When a 30 minute hourglass would turn a bell would ring telling the time. At 2 bells, during the Morning Watch, it was to the Captain's cabin with a wash cloth and hot water at 5 AM. sharp.

Juan's breakfast was finished soon after because the Captain's breakfast was to be promptly ready by the sound of 3 bells or 530 AM.

Clean the Captain's stateroom, empty the bed pan and make the bed by 4 bells (6 AM.).

Then it was above deck to learn line handling, chart work, celestial navigation, and of course deck scrubbing.

Lunch was a loaf of bread, if you got lucky, and dinner was rung in at 4 bells (6 PM.) but that was because the bell pattern would repeat itself for every duty watch. Dinner was during the Dogwatch, the hours between 4 PM. and 8 PM. They called it the Dogwatch because during that time Sirius, the Dog Star, would be the first star in the night sky to be seen.

The Captain's turn down service by 8 bells at 8 PM. and then a little free time before lights out at 4 bells (10 PM.) during the First Watch.

Usually Juan would have duty during the Mid-Watch of 8 bells at 4 AM. but sometimes when the older sailors had been maneuvering the ship all day he would have to go on watch at midnight. There was nothing Juan hated more than finally getting to sleep only to be awoken, two hours later, to go back to work. Sadly, that was his life aboard ship it was all he knew.

The days were long and hard but there was an uneasy comfort in consistency. The life of a cabin boy aboard a privateer was difficult and extremely dangerous. But Juan was thankful for some of his time aboard the Floriblanca. Captain Gaspar was always fair to the boy. He was firm when discipline was needed but equal in praise when awarded. The Captain made a point to teach the boy the ways of the sea and pass on to him his extensive knowledge of his beloved ship.

Most cabin boys were not strong enough to do the ship's work they were simply cheap labor to be at the beck and call of their Captains to clean or fold clothes as needed. But Juan was unusually strong for his age and Captain Gaspar treated him as an equal member of the crew. Equal in pay of the ship's bounty and equal in the reward of the Captain's knowledge. In fact, Juan often worked harder than most of the crew and this did not go unnoticed by the Captain.

If there was one way to get on the Captain's good side it was through hard work and Juan had that in spades. But there was something more to the relationship of Captain Gaspar and young Juan Gomez. If there was such a thing as a soft spot in the treacherous heart of Jose Gaspar it was for the young Gomez. Claiming no children of his own, the Captain admired the boy's work ethic and dedication. "Had I had a son- he would have been a worker like Juan," Gaspar often thought to himself. And for the young Juan, that feeling of respect was as close to love as the boy had ever known.

As a child, no one wanted Juan. His own parents gave him to the Captain for a mere month's wage of silver. But the Captain treated him with respect as he did with all the crew. The Captain taught him, disciplined him, and kept him accountable. The Captain gave him purpose and responsibility. The Captain was the father that Juan never had. Now the Captain was gone and Juan had nowhere to go and no one to turn to. Once again, the little boy that no one wanted was left alone… until he heard a noise coming from behind some sea grass along the palm tree lined beachfront.

Chapter 4

Jacksonville, FL- present

It had been nearly a year since young Gabriel Fletcher had been granted his independence, 8 months and 12 days, to be exact. He had spent the previous 8 years bouncing from one foster home to another. Years of fear, abuse, and heartbreak had all come to an end with one slam of a Judge's gavel. Now free, with each new day his spirits soared. Food tasted better, smells were sweeter, sleep was more restful, it had been years since Gabriel had woken up and not been sore from the previous night's beatings. Now he woke up every morning with smile on his face excited for what each new day would bring him.

But "freedom isn't free" as Gabriel had often heard from his father and that fact was never more apparent than when he had to head off to work because now he had bills to pay.

Gabriel often thought of his father throughout the day especially when he would walk to his job at the local Jacksonville Library. Thoughts of his dear father would flood his mind with each step. He was very young when he last saw his dad but he still remembered the camouflage uniform of olive drab and green. The colorful patches, that covered his father's large broad chest, seemed to blend together in a beautiful patchwork of tiny ribbons.

Gabriel never knew what they meant, but he remembered his father saying- "they are for a job well done. When you do a job Gabriel-you either give it your all or you fail and there are no rewards for failure."

Tall and strong, Jake Fletcher was a large man who seemed to block the light from every doorway he walked through. But when he would pick up his young son, his hands were as soft as the boy's favorite Star Wars pillow. Gabriel always felt safe and loved when his father would hoist him up into the air and give him a great big hug. Especially when his father had just returned from a long deployment he would hug him hard and toss him high in the air and then of course offer a toy for Gabriel's excited little hands.

Over the years, those moments of flying thru the air and squeezing his father's leg as tight, as he could, would always bring a smile to Gabriel's face. No matter what pain he might have been experiencing at the time, those memories would keep him company. He loved his father and his father loved him. Unfortunately, the same could not be said about Gabriel's mother.

Monica Fletcher was a beautiful young woman, perhaps too young. This may have led to her eventual depression. Probably didn't help that her husband was gone for long periods of time leaving her with a rambunctious baby boy. She was closer to a child herself then a woman when she married Jack Fletcher. Both just 17 years old when they graduated high school and Jack went on to enlist in the Navy.

Fearing the loneliness of separation, as young lovers often do, they rushed down to the little white chapel in town and got married. They were happy for the first year but Jack was moving up the chain fast which meant long times apart from his bride. Monica began to long as well, not for her husband, but for the life she felt was slipping away from her. This yearning for her past life became painfully obvious when she began to feel the kick in her side that was soon to be her newborn son- Gabriel.

Buying baby clothes or storing up on diapers was never a choice Monica's friends had to make. They were living the life of young college students. As they were partying and trying to find a man, Monica was expecting to soon be raising a man.

Never physically abusive to Gabriel, Monica was abusive with distance. When Gabriel was five and playing his first year of soccer, he remembered the 2 mile walk home because his mother forgot to pick him up. He had waited over an hour on the cold wooden bench after practice. He passed on several offers from his friend's parents for a ride because he knew his mother was just running late. Eventually, he came to the conclusion that she was not coming and that would not be the last time he would make the long walk home. There were moments when she was attentive but they were few and far between.

Only when his father was around would things feel normal and happy. But even those times were becoming infrequent. His father's time home was less about playing cops and robbers in the backyard and more about arguing with his wife in the kitchen. Even at the young age of 5, Gabriel knew his parent's marriage was on rocky ground.

It was during this last fight that Gabriel heard his father say "This will be my last deployment."

Not sure what that meant, Gabriel knew by the sadness in his father's eyes that it was a decision that was not easy to make. Unfortunately, that sad face was one of the last times Gabriel ever saw his father again. Later that day, Gabriel and his mother stood there in a sweltering hot parking lot, just off the St. Johns River, at Jacksonville Naval Air Station. They waved "goodbye" to a large battleship grey C130 cargo plane as it raced down the black tarmac. Deafening with its roar, the massive four engine beast lifted off and disappeared into the dark rain filled clouds of the Florida sky.

A few weeks later, it was the uniformed officer at the door that brought Gabriel's mother to fall on the floor. A message from a "Grateful Nation" did little to comfort the sobbing boy or the mother that was already drifting away from him. Soon after the news of his father's death, it was prolonged stays with family members that Gabriel would remember. Overnight sleepovers with friends from Church became more frequent. The frightening nights alone in his house would happen again and again until the fear of the dark was almost comforting to the young boy. It became a game to him. He would hide in the closet only to jump out into the room screaming and flailing his arms around as if he were fighting a dozen monsters. Of course he always won. But they would put up a good fight, especially the tall blue-haired creature with the yellow eyes. Darkness no longer scared him, he became comfortable in it and the loneliness became his only friend. Then one day, it was his turn to fall crying to the floor.

One sunny Thursday morning, the uniformed Child Services worker took his hand and walked young Gabriel away from a home that he would never see again and a quiet mother, sitting idle in her kitchen never turning to look back or say goodbye to her son as he was walked out of her life.

Chapter 5

Florida Gulf Coast, 1821

Too drunk to sail that early summer morning, several of the Floriblanca's crew had been left ashore by an angry Captain Gaspar in order to "dry up." When the Captain's first mate struggled to wake Raúl and the rest of the main mast's crew, it was the Captain that sent them off of the Floriblanca's decks. Afraid he would lose his chance on the fat bellied merchant ship adrift at sea, Captain Gaspar had no patience for a drunken crew that had no discipline.

"Get off my ship and await your punishment you lazy lot," the Captain roared at the sleeping hammocks. "Your lack of discipline has cost you your share of the loot. When I return, prepare to face the crack of my whip!" hissed the Captain.

Who would have known that the Captain's punishment would eventually save the lives of the disorderly crew? Raúl and the remaining pirates watched in horror from the sun bleached shoreline as the Enterprise opened fire on their floating home, sinking the Floriblanca.

Now, young Juan Gomez standing on the hot beach sand heard the whispers calling out to him from a patch of sea grass along the base of a large sand dune.

Juan knew the voice immediately… Raúl! Raúl Vargas was a nasty man. His gift for line handling and seamanship had kept him aboard the Floriblanca for years; but his lack of discipline, respect, and general absence of cleanliness, were the reasons he had been passed over for First Mate countless times throughout his long career. When he was sober, no crewman could best his knowledge of the sea. But when he had tasted the ship's grog, it usually led to a lashing at the Captain's hand. Juan had never liked Raúl. From his early days aboard the Floriblanca, Raúl had gone out of his way to pick on and frighten the little boy. Eventually, Juan had learned to ignore the crude man but every once in a while Raúl still managed to get under his skin. Now, Juan knew he would have to face this crude man one more time but hopefully it would be his last.

"Come here boy," Raúl barked over the whistling sea grass. Reluctantly, Juan walked over towards the hidden voice.

"Behind the sand dune by the palm tree, out of sight of the Enterprise," Raúl ordered.

The small skiff with Ensign Mitchell had pushed off the beach and was crashing back into the surf. Its new course was the Enterprise some 300 yards off shore. Having sent the last of the Floriblanca's crew to the local Port Authority, the Enterprise's small boat was returning to the mother ship. One last glance from Ensign Mitchell towards the small boy was fruitless as the young Cabin Boy had disappeared behind the windblown sand dune. All the young Ensign could do was hope that his mercy on the boy would lead to a long happy life for the child.

Approaching the swaying palm trees, Juan saw the 3 pirate scallywags hiding in the shadows motioning to the boy to come over.

"What did the Captain give you boy?" Raúl questioned. "Nothing, he was shot in the leg and had to leave the main deck," Juan responded.

With a quick flash of light that reflected from the swinging sword, Juan immediately felt a sharp blade under his chin. "Don't lie to me you little brat. I saw him hand you something. What was it?" Raúl demanded. Only when his head had turned away from the knife at his throat did Juan see the long telescope in one of the other pirate's hand. He immediately replayed the situation in his head.

Huddled under the shady palm trees, the motley crew would have discussed their pending punishment at the Captain's hands. Perhaps one of them may have even discussed the notion of another attempted mutiny. They had tried once before about a year ago but when the First Mate failed to return to the ship with the Captain, they knew he had been killed and their hope of mutiny had died with him. When the sound of the first cannon shot hit the shore. Juan imagined their despair as they watched their life's memories and treasure get blown away by the superior classed Enterprise. Distraught over the loss of their ship and all the secrets that she kept, the crew saw their money and the countless bounty the Captain had hidden disappear in a moment.

But then, through the worn walnut handle, brass trimmed fittings, and salt sprayed lens of the telescope, would come a glimmer of hope in a small piece of cloth given to the boy by a desperate Captain. Juan could now see the scenario perfectly clear and even while facing the pending danger, perfectly calm. Exactly the same way Captain Gaspar had seen it in his final moments.

Removing the blood soaked rag from his shirt pocket, Juan handed it to the vile Raúl.

"Here-this is what the Captain gave me," Juan answered.

Reaching into his pocket and pulling out the bloody cloth, Juan held it up to the pirates. Quickly grabbing for the cloth like rabid dogs over meat, Raúl cast a menacing glare to the other men as they began to crowd in on him. As if to say "back up or be prepared for a fight," the frenzied look in Raúl's eyes was all that needed to be said and they each backed up a step. Even Juan found himself straining to see what was on the cloth but he feared not getting too close to Raúl's anger. The cloth was rolled out in the palm of Raúl's hand and there it was in all of its simplicity- the map to Gaspar's treasure.

Hidden off the ship in a secret location, the treasure of Gaspar was a thing of legends. Over the years after so many successful raids, the crew, in quiet circles, often talked about the Captain's immense treasure. How much gold he must have or precious jewels that one could only imagine. Some talked about the Rio de la Paz or Peace River and its fresh water flowing south into the bay as a likely spot for the hidden treasure. Others believed he kept it on his private island Captiva. Named for the countless prisoners Gaspar had held captive there over the years. It was also a favorite port of his because many of those prisoners were beautiful young affluent women who on their lavish trips across the ocean had fell prey to Gasparilla. The ship's crew often dreamed of seeing Gaspar's treasure and what value it must have been. The Captain's final "redemption" he would call it, the treasure of all treasures. No one knew how much had been hidden or to what value it would be worth, but now finally whatever amount it was, it was in the rowdy crew's grasp.

The map was a rough sketch of the Florida coastline. Inked in charcoal, obviously in a frantic rush, a dashed-line snaked up a large river and ended with a blackened "X" near an almost backwards bend in the river.

"Here, we are here," Raúl pounded on a starting point at the edge of a blood stain. "It's only a few miles from this very spot, just up the river at Snake Bend. We could make it before nightfall."

The men begin to cheer and shout for joy as they rushed off in the direction of the river but Raúl quickly stopped in his tracks. He turned to the boy and addressed him. "If you say anything of this to anyone… I'll find you when you least expect me to and finish this cut all the way through." With a flick of his wrist, Raúl slashed his blade across Juan's face. The gash cutting along his cheek reached the bone and blood began to pour immediately into his mouth. A scream leaped out of Juan's lungs before the pain even hit him.

"Say anything-ye' die, follow me- ye' die!" and with that Raúl took off in a sprint to catch his fellow pirates. Juan stood there for a moment with his hand on his jaw trying to stop the bleeding. However, watching the pirates race off in the wrong direction like a band of clueless fools brought a smile across Juan's swollen lips.

"Run fools. Keep looking for that treasure. Just as the Captain knew you would," Juan laughed.

The young boy started jogging in the opposite direction of the crew. He no longer felt the drain of the day or even the sting from the cut in his face as he picked up speed running along the powdered sand. He knew something that Raúl and the others did not know; something that the Captain whispered into his ear at his final moment.

"Go to the Old Beach Church. Find the King on the cross and ye' will find your treasure," the words echoed in his ear. "Give this to anyone that gets in your way and trust no one," the Captain then pressed the torn bloody cloth into Juan's hand. Juan was thankful for the wisdom of his Captain. It was that wisdom that Juan had learned from during his time aboard ship and that had kept the treasure safe for so many years. And if he was going to survive this, young Juan thought to himself, he would have to be just as wise.

Chapter 6

Jacksonville, FL- present

Gabriel Fletcher walked into the Jacksonville library and began his usual weekend routine. The friendly wave to Ruth the elderly volunteer that worked in the used book store at the top of the stairs. He gave a quick nod to Jim, the security officer that never seemed to mind standing in the same spot for hours on end. An enthusiastic wave to the young children sitting in the semi-circle being home schooled by the pony-tailed lady. And then there was his old friend Miguel.

Miguel Mendoza was pushing 90 years of age and had worked at the library since the early 80's. He was a gentle man with stark white hair and always had a friendly smile. He had introduced himself to Gabriel, on Gabriel's first day, and quickly took the young boy under his wing.

"Good morning Senor," Gabriel offered his normal greeting to his dear friend. "Como estas amigo?"

Miguel's normal wide toothy grin was non-existent. Gabriel could immediately sense something was wrong with him.

"Not too good my friend. Last night, I ran into someone I knew many years ago and I need to talk to you." Miguel said quietly almost as a whisper. "Of course, how can I help?" Gabriel responded sensing something serious.

Miguel's eyes darted around the room in a frantic sweep of the area. Satisfied the room was safe, Miguel answered. "Follow me."

The elderly man took one more glance across the almost empty library floor, walked past Gabriel, and headed towards the back conference room. Gabriel stood for a moment trying to take in the situation. He had just shown up for work on a normal Saturday morning like he had many times before but now his heart was in his throat. The look on his old friend's face had made Gabriel's blood run cold.

Entering the large conference hall, Miguel did another quick survey of the room. It wasn't until he peaked behind the brown rolling temporary wall did Miguel feel comfortable enough to speak.

"I saw a man yesterday. A man I have not seen in many, many years." Miguel lamented. "I am afraid my past has finally caught up with me and I do not have a lot of time. I have always considered you a friend and a person that I can trust. I need to ask a favor of you but before I do, you need to know the seriousness of this situation."

"Of course Miguel, anything for you, you know that." Gabriel tried to comfort his concerned friend.
"No, my friend, you have no idea what favor I request of you. I fear that I have put your very life in danger and for that I am so sorry." Miguel pleaded.

Gabriel's pulse again started to spike up in his chest. He was starting to sense that this was no run of the mill favor to ask. This wasn't a "can you cover my shift this weekend?" or "I need to borrow a few dollars" type of favor. This was something more-something that hinted of actual danger. Miguel was always bright eyed and smiling with Gabriel. He was such a happy and easy going man that Gabriel wondered if perhaps his friend was playing a trick on him. But this was real this was not normal behavior for Miguel. This was something Gabriel had never seen in his friend before. He saw fear… deadly fear.

"I cannot talk long. I fear you even being here with me is putting you in danger. You have no idea the type of man I saw yesterday." Miguel continued. "I hate to have to put this burden on you so soon. I had hoped to have more time to prepare you, but there is no time anymore. I have always considered you like a son to me and I need to pass on a great family secret to you."

Reaching into his front pants pocket, Miguel pulled out an elaborately ornate gold ring. Gabriel took a quick glance at it in his friends hand as he listened. The sides were engraved with a strange detail that at first appeared to just be a design feature, like a Celtic band, but oddly different. Almost like a strange language, the detail was actually a series of letters but the writing had no order to it. The curving letters wrapped around the band but didn't make out any words. What normally would have been on the face of the ring would be a center stone of some kind. But the stone had been replaced with an engraved image. The image was of an 18th century, three masted, tall-ship sailing in the sea. The ship was cresting a wave, about to crash into the trough, with the bow pointing up high out of the water. It appeared to be moving fast with water splashing up the bow and the square sails filled with air. The engraving was beautifully decorated with even the tiniest of details that Gabriel could make out at such a brief look. He wanted to look closer at it but Miguel was talking and Gabriel felt he needed to pay attention and not be rude to his friend.

"This ring is the key. It holds the secrets that you will need to find what you seek," Miguel whispered. "Never let this out of your possession and never trust anyone with it."

Miguel handed the ring to Gabriel and the weight of it surprised the young man. Gold by itself is very dense and soft, as a metal, it is normally combined with other metals like steel or zinc to give it strength and hardness. The worn down etching on the sides and the startling weight to its size led Gabriel to assume that it was at least 8 oz. of pure gold. An amount worth thousands of dollars.

"I will give you more information soon. I don't mean to be vague, forgive me. The answers to your questions I honestly do not know. This is what was passed on to me and now I pass it on to you." Miguel continued. "When I was a boy, my Father gave me this ring and said those very words to me. I spent many years of my life trying to find the secret but I was not able. That journey introduced me to some very bad people, and I decided that the secret would be safer if I were to disappear. So I started a new life here."

Gabriel was trying to take all the information in as fast as it was coming at him. He wanted to remember every word from Miguel's mouth because this was obviously no joke. Miguel was scared and Gabriel began to feel a little afraid as well.

"Those people from my past have finally found me and it is time for me to pass on this secret to you in order to keep it safe again. My name is not Miguel. My real name is Jose Juan Gomez." The old man paused for a moment as if to take pleasure in saying his full name for the first time in decades. "My great grandfather was Juan Gomez, he was a cabin boy aboard a pirate ship many years ago and this is his ring. He was entrusted with a great treasure that has never been found and this ring is the first clue to its location. I was forced to change my name for protection from the men that still seek it. The men I saw yesterday. And you need to know that this danger is for real."

Ok now Gabriel was scared. Everything he thought he had known about this man Miguel was now a lie and he has just been told that his life was now in grave danger. Gabriel's mind was spinning. It took every ounce of mental capacity to stop the ringing in his ears and focus in on what Miguel or Jose was saying.

"Forgive me for placing you in this situation. I had hoped to have more time. The Lord never blessed me with children but I have loved you like a son. I want you to have this ring but understand that it is your decision to discover its secrets or not. All that I ask of you is that if you do not want this journey that you, in time, pass this ring on to another that is as worthy as you. This secret has been in my family for almost 200 years and now I give it to you."

Squeezing the ring into Gabriel's hand, Jose kissed Gabriel on the cheek and quickly turned to walk away.

"I will give you more information soon but this is all I can give you for now. Good luck."

The elderly man formerly known as Miguel now raced out of the room and disappeared down the hall leaving Gabriel stunned and barely standing. With his whole world twirling around him, Gabriel was trying to fixate on everything that had just happened. Jose's every word replaying in his head and the fear of danger swelling in his throat. However he couldn't seem to dull the sense of adventure that was also now pulsing through his racing heart.

Chapter 7

Jacksonville, FL- present

The morning could not come fast enough. Gabriel had barely fallen to sleep when his alarm went off at its usual time - 5am. Normally, he would jump out of bed and begin his morning workout routine of push-ups, sit-ups, and pull-ups but not this morning - no today was different. Today was unlike any other day. Today was truly a brand new day filled with all sorts of new possibilities.

Holding the heavy gold ring in his hand, Gabriel had not put it down since Miguel or actually Jose had given it to him yesterday morning. He pulled it out from under his pillow. He could remember every scratch and wear spot on the ring's surface. Gabriel had studied every line and curve of the ring. The deep golden color enhanced by the dark filled edges of the engravings. The skill and craftsmanship was fascinating to observe. It must have taken months to complete with the most patient and skilled hands. Even the cannon portholes could be seen clearly on the embossed tall ship. Gabriel could count all seven circles along the ship's starboard side but he needed to use a magnifying glass if he wanted to see any cutting marks. The portholes were so tiny Gabriel wondered what blade or knife could have been small enough to make the precise cuts. The care and patience, not to mention dexterity, that was given to the ring was absolutely remarkable. There was a band around the sailing ship that at first Gabriel thought it was just a detail for decoration. But as he studied the ring closer he began to see letters in the circling crest. He had written them out to see if there was any meaning behind them.

MVKTZXDARSTNFSKTZXDARXDRXV

He didn't see any immediate answer to the letters. Not sure where they began or where they ended, the letters were encircling the ship. He knew it wasn't just a decoration but he would have to wait to work on that clue. He returned his focus back to the writing on the band of the ring where he did see a possible pattern in the letters.

Sitting on the small nightstand next to Gabriel's thread bare single mattress, was a flattened oval piece of Silly Putty and some yellow paper notes with scribbled writing all over them. The Silly Putty had been laid out flat there were some raised images on the surface. During his observation of the ring, Gabriel had noticed that the letters on the band didn't make any sense when he tried to read them. He thought that perhaps it could have been written backwards, but it still didn't make any sense so he decided to make a cast of the ring to see if he was missing something. He had wrapped the ring in the Silly Putty and when he unfolded it and laid it out on the table, he noticed that the letters were a little clearer but still didn't make sense. It took him about an hour to put them together and break the code. A simple code really, once he figured it out thru some trial and error. It was called a cipher, Caesar's shift cipher to be exact. Often used by the legendary Roman Emperor Julius Caesar to keep his orders secret.

Caesar would often mix up the letters in a message and only the receiver of the message would know how to read it. Usually a General in the field would be given a number that would change periodically to make it more difficult but that General would then be able to decipher his Emperor's message. Today it's pretty easy to figure out but back 2,000 years ago this system was virtually unbreakable. Even 200 years ago, when the ring was made, education was very limited so understanding the Caesar's shift cipher would have been a tough task for almost anyone.

Gabriel had remembered reading a book about ciphers and knew eventually the funny letters on the strip of Silly Putty would make sense. He wrote out the letters of the alphabet and gave each letter a number A-1, B-2, C-3 and so on. He then wrote out the letters that had been imprinted on his Silly Putty.

KTIAKTZXK RG OYRG JK RG SAKXZG

After some time and several other attempts at breaking the code, Gabriel decided to try the Caesar's shift. It is a process of elimination with 25 letters there are 25 possibilities, but Gabriel tried one particular number and happened to get it right the first time. Having studied the ring to such detail as he did, he knew the only number that was given on the ring was the number of portholes of the ship's guns- 7.

He shifted the alphabet down 7 spaces and wrote it out again. Writing it underneath his original alphabet the new one started with “A” under the letter “G.” “G” is the seventh letter of the alphabet. “B” was next under the “H” and “C” was under the “I” but when the letter “T” finished under the “Z,” Gabriel continued with “U” back at the beginning under “A.” When he finished the alphabet shift, Gabriel wrote out the letters that were above the letters given on the ring. A smile came across his face as the words began to come alive in a language he knew how to read-Spanish.

ENCUENTRE LA ISLA DE LA MUERTA

Gabriel had studied Spanish over the years. He once lived for a few months with a family from Puerto Rico when he was 8 years old. They had a small boy that Gabriel tried to become friends with but couldn’t talk to. The parents only spoke Spanish at the home so Gabriel spent hours on end studying and reading everything he could about the language. He practiced it at every opportunity available. Gabriel was only with the family for a few months but he became fluent in the language and it sparked a passion for other languages as well. He never knew who he would meet or have to live with so he just decided to learn as many languages as he could to always have a friend no matter where he would end up. The little boy and Gabriel did become friends but like everyone in Gabriel’s life he was soon a distant memory as Gabriel was forced to move on to yet another foster home.

The decoded message written out on the yellow paper was clear as day to him but offered a very vague clue for Gabriel.

"Find the Island of the Dead,"

Gabriel spoke out loud to himself. His heart was racing but his mind was lost in thought. What did it mean? What was there? Where is the Island of the Dead? Would that name show up on a map? With each step closer the path seemed that much further away. So engrossed with the ring's secret, Gabriel lost track of time and suddenly realized he was late for work.

Thirty minutes later and breathing heavily, Gabriel ran up the library front steps and swung open the double pained glass door. Hoping no one would notice his tardiness; Gabriel quickly slowed his pace to a fast walk and nodded once again to Jim the ever vigilant security guard- who still did not seem to move. Making his way back to his work area, Gabriel was scanning the rooms looking for his friend now known to him as Jose. Not completely unusual for Jose to be late on a Sunday morning, the man was in his 90's and Sunday's were always slow days, the library was only open until noon anyway. An issue that seemed to always bother Jose, "working on the Sabbath is not right," he would say. Gabriel would often join Jose at Church after work on Sundays. It was a small, quiet, but peaceful Church just down the road. Gabriel enjoyed those moments with his friend. But something didn't feel right to him now. Remembering the fear that was on Jose's face, a sudden chill shot up Gabriel's spine when he noticed that his friend was nowhere to be found.

Two agonizing hours and four unanswered phone calls later, Gabriel walked out the library door and was on his way to Jose's house. The long walk through the Jacksonville suburbs gave Gabriel time to second guess himself. Was he jumping to conclusions? Was this all one elaborate practical joke? Was the old man, formerly known as Miguel, losing his mind? Ancient secrets, pirate ships, mysterious gold ring, it was just too wild to be real. Why was he wasting his time walking to his house? The old man just forgot again. It had to be a mistake but… flashing lights… police cars… yellow tape around Jose's house… that for sure was real. Gabriel's instincts had been right. Something was terribly wrong, and it appeared to be coming from Gabriel's dear friend's house.

Chapter 8

Tampa, FL- present

Nathan Gale hated getting up early on the weekends especially when it was to attend his twin sister's cheerleading competition. He would rather be watching his favorite Discovery channel Shark Week recaps or passing the next level of Gears of War on his Nintendo DS. He would even rather clean up his room just so he could avoid the horrific wall of noise from 100 screaming teenage girls. The loudest and most spirited of the bunch was his annoying and pestering twin sister Lisa.

"Mom Nathan's touching me," Lisa shouted from the back seat. "I am not," Nathan responded.

The radio volume in the sky-blue minivan quickly increased, drowning out the arguing kids. Mrs. Gale gave a jovial smile to her husband who was ignoring the arguing kids as he sat behind the steering wheel and tried to zone out on the road.

"We are almost there can you two please behave for one more minute?" Mrs. Gale pleaded. "Fine but I'm not clapping for her. I don't care if she wins. I hope she loses," Nathan barked. "That's a terrible thing to say you little twerp. You wait until I get…"

"KIDS," Mrs. Gale cut off Lisa before she said anything she would regret. "Quiet! We are here. Get out of the car and behave or else." Mrs. Gale ordered.

Scientists say that nothing ignites the memory of the human mind quite like the sense of smell. The 40 million olfactory receptors in the lining of the nostrils are capable of identifying up to 10,000 different smells. And as amazing as the nose is, right now, Nathan Gale wished his allergies were still stuffing him up. Almost every weekend, for as long as he could remember, he had spent at various ballparks across the state and to Nathan they all smelled the same. The steam off of the black asphalt parking lots, the downwind whiff of stacked up garbage, the oily odor of fried corn-dogs and baked popcorn, and worst of all the saturated stench of body spray to try to mask the pungent smell of hundreds of sweaty teenage kids. The smells were all the same even though the parks were all different. Nathan hated spending his precious time baking in the Florida sun. But since he didn't play sports, he was forced to sacrifice hours of his life clapping in support of his annoying twin sister.

Lisa Gale was a gifted competitive cheerleader and her sport took her and the family all over Florida. Even though she was only 5 minutes older than Nathan, she liked to act like a much older sister. The two used to be very close, as most twins are, but like so many young kids peer pressure always seemed to raise its ugly head. Lisa was a very popular, outgoing, athlete. Her brother Nathan was not, in fact, he was quite the opposite. And that didn't always go well with the circle of friends that Lisa ran in.

"Good luck Lisa hope you do well," Nathan sarcastically mumbled. "OK thank you I will," she responded in her typical bubbly voice unaware of his sarcasm.

"Oh there he is," Lisa took a few steps but then stopped cold in her tracks.

About 20 yards away, almost in slow motion, Roger Woods strutted towards the siblings. As Lisa's heart began to race, Nathan's began to run cold. "Hi Lisa," Roger said. "I'll be cheering for you." His words were like fingernails on a chalkboard for Nathan. "Maybe when you finish we could go get something to eat?" Roger asked. "I'd like that a lot" she responded. A cough leapt out of Nathan's mouth.

"Lisa, I thought we had dinner plans already," Nathan interjected. "Oh that's right," she remembered. "I'm sorry. We have dinner with some family friends tonight, maybe another time? Can you call me?" she pleaded. "Of course, I would like that" Roger answered with confidence. And with that Lisa was off and across the field leaving the two boys waving in unison. The pleasant smile across Roger's face was quickly replaced with a scowl directed squarely at Nathan.

"You don't like me much do you, you little jerk?" Roger asked. "No not really." Nathan responded. "What did I do to you?" Roger questioned not really concerned for the answer. "I see you at school and I see you stabbing people behind their backs. You use people and then discard them like trash. Nothing is important to you except for what you want. I may not always like my sister and we fight most of the time but even I wouldn't wish you on her."

"Well you listen to me then Nathan. Your sister is the hottest girl in school and I'm going to date her. It only makes sense. Every girl in school wants me. I'm the coolest kid in class and if you don't put a good word in for me I'm going to break your neck."

Nathan was playing it cool but deep down inside he was starting to feel the shakes of fear move up his leg. Roger is over 6 feet tall and 220 pounds. He is the captain of every sporting team he plays on and he plays them all. He is a high school senior and he could crush Nathan if he wanted to too. In fact, Nathan feared it was only the crowds of parents in the stands that were keeping him from doing just that.

Nathan summoned every ounce of courage he could, "Sorry Roger. I would rather take a punch then let my sister date a creep like you." Blood began to rush through a vein in Roger's forehead as he leaned into Nathan's line of sight.

"Because you are Lisa's brother, I'm going to let that go. But my patience is running out. Tell your sister what a great guy I am and get her to go out with me or I'll give you much more than just a punch. I'll pound you into the ground!"

Roger paused for another second to hold his glare at Nathan and then backed away. As he strutted off down the well-worn dirt walkway between the over towering steel bleachers, Nathan could hear his beating heart pounding over the thunderous cheers from the fans sitting above him. A deep sigh of relief came fast, but it was replaced quickly with a dreaded fear of what his future would entail. He thought about the boy that crossed Roger last year at school and that vision was still seared into his eyes. It was a beating that Nathan would never forget.

He was Junior that had enough of Roger Woods. The boy was big and a good athlete but didn't like Roger's arrogance. Finally one day he had heard enough from the pompous school star and he stood up to the bully. Roger was surrounded by his teammates and the fight only lasted a few moments. It was a valiant effort but the young boy stood no chance. He tried to lunge at Roger but each time he did, one of Roger's friends would shove him off balance. Roger had easy pickings at the distracted target. Of course it was the boy's word against the most popular kid in school and his 8 teammates. No one else had come forward to refute Roger's claim that he was jumped by the boy. Nathan was too scared at the time and just a freshman. He felt it wasn't worth sticking his neck out for someone he didn't even know. But not stepping forward to tell the truth was a constant reminder of his shame. The junior eventually had to switch schools due to the non-stop teasing and Nathan never forgave himself. Since that bloody day Nathan never liked Roger and when Roger took an interest in Nathan's sister, he knew he would one day have to face him. But the sight of that boy's beating made Nathan choke at the thought.

Chapter 9

Jacksonville, FL- present

The sweeping ancient oak trees lined the street in a beautiful canopy of green foliage and grey Spanish moss. The quiet neighborhood that saw little excitement was now ablaze with flashing red and blue swirling lights. Neighbors stepped out of their comfortable living rooms to take a look at all the commotion going on at the old Mendoza House.

As Gabriel ran up to his old friend's home he was stopped by a police officer stringing up a yellow tape barricade.

"What's going on? What happened?" Gabriel pleaded. "Sorry kid but can't talk about it, it's an ongoing investigation." the Officer replied.

"Investigation? Where is Miguel?" Gabriel still thought of his friend as Miguel, the name he had used for the last year and not Jose Antonio Gomez. Just then the front door of Jose's house opened up and two paramedics pulled out a stainless steel table rolling on dirty grey wheels. There was a large black plastic bag lying on top of the table secured with three nylon straps spanning the table's width.

"Is that a body bag? Where is Miguel?" Gabriel's worst fear was starting to be realized.

"Sorry kid, can't talk about it but you have to back up and make room for the gurney," the police officer ordered.

The metallic vibration was piercing to Gabriel's ears as the steel table gurney rolled down the paver walkway. The same sandstone paver walkway Gabriel had spent three weekends, this very summer, working on because tree roots had raised the old concrete path and Miguel kept tripping over it. His eyes were fixated on the passing large plastic bag when the metallic ringing in his ears was suddenly interrupted by a hissing voice beside him.

The officer that had halted Gabriel was now taking a statement from a tall thin man. The thin man with pale white features and dark sunken eyes looked as if a skeleton had come to life and was giving a statement just a few feet away from Gabriel. Large knot-like bumps surrounded the thin man's joints as his long slender fingers pointed to the body being rolled into the awaiting ambulance. What startled Gabriel out his trance was not how this man looked but what he had said.

"My brother was a kind good man. I don't know who could have done such a terrible thing to him. I had just spoken to him the other day, and he said nothing of any danger. Everyone loved him no one wanted him hurt," the thin man stated.

Gabriel heard this statement like a car crash. He had seen Miguel, or more recently the man formerly known as Miguel, almost every day for the past year. He had spent countless workdays and weekends with his friend. Not having a family of his own, Gabriel had leaned on this kind man for friendship and guidance.

Gabriel had been in Jose's house dozens of times and had long late night conversations about life and every other topic he could think of but never once had Jose ever mentioned a brother. Granted Jose had kept his name secret from Gabriel all this time as well but he had also recently told Gabriel about dangerous men that had found him. Something just didn't feel right.

Gabriel started to look around at the crowd and suddenly a rush of fear shot up his spine. The crowd was fixated on the ambulance and the house. People were taking pictures and talking on cell phones as they called loved ones with this breaking story. But two men on the far side of the yard were not looking at the ambulance or the house. These men, both dressed in black business suits similar to the thin man's white shirt and black tie, were looking at the crowd. They too were filming the scene, but they were not filming the ambulance or the body; they were filming the spectators and the camera was now slowly panning towards Gabriel.

Trying to not make any sudden moves, Gabriel turned his face away from the oncoming camera and started to make his way through the crowd. Moving slowly but deliberately, he cleared the three rows of bystanders and started to walk down the sidewalk without turning around. Perhaps his careful movements were too careful because his actions sparked the interest of the thin man who was just finishing his statement to the police officer. Motioning to the two men across the yard, the thin man started to walk after Gabriel. The thin man had cleared the crowd of people and began to pick up his pace. With Gabriel's back in sight, the thin man continued to increase his speed. Just a few yards away, the boy turned down the next street and disappeared behind a white washed wood paneled house. Jogging now, the thin man was just steps away when he raced past the corner of the house and started to call out to the young boy. But to his surprise, the boy was nowhere to be seen. He was gone. The pale man looked far down the street and back around the house but the boy had just vanished. A toothy smile spread across the thin man's pale lips, "Could you be the one?" the words hissed from his mouth and hung in the humid air.

Chapter 10

Out of breath and exhausted, Gabriel opened the door to his small apartment and fell on the floor. He had jogged the 4 mile run back from Juan's house many times before but never averaging a 6 minute mile. That was a record for Gabriel but one that he wished had not been brought on by fear.

He had heard the footsteps behind him as he walked away from Jose's house but it wasn't until he caught the thin man's reflection in a car side view mirror that he knew he was in trouble. Passing by the 2005 silver Toyota Sequoia on the street next to him, Gabriel saw his pursuer gaining on him and made his way closer to the wood paneled house. He waited until he turned down past the white washed building out of sight for a moment when he began his sprint. The first 30 yards were raw explosive speed but it was the dive behind a pair of shrubs in a neighboring yard that was brilliant. Hiding down low and under the thick brush cover, Gabriel got a good look at the thin man when he jogged around the house and stopped, obviously stunned at the boy's sudden disappearance. The dark black eyes and pasty skin, the faded and well-worn black slacks with a crisp starched white shirt made the man look uncomfortably out of place and time in the laid back Florida lifestyle. He watched the pale thin lips whisper something but he was too far away to hear it and couldn't quite read them either.

Gabriel had waited a good twenty minutes in the cool shaded dirt before he made a break for it. Not wanting to be followed, he made sure the coast was clear and then proceeded to run as fast as he could. Weaving in and out of small backstreets using alternate routes over fences and sometimes even backtracking, the normal route home was one long road and two left turns but this time Gabriel was not taking any chances of being followed.

He had not been home 30 minutes when the doorbell rang. How did they follow him? Did they have his photo and address already? A moment of panic was soon followed by relief when Gabriel saw the large brown freight truck pulling away from his apartment complex. The traditional double tap on the truck's horn gave Gabriel the signal that all was clear. Opening the door, careful not to open too wide for fear of being spotted, it was a large flat cardboard box that had been delivered and was now leaning against his wall luckily still in arms reach. He didn't have to step out of his apartment, but the width of the box required two hands to lift and maneuver. About the size of a wall poster, the box was not too heavy but a little cumbersome to fit through the doorway.

Locking the door and flopping down on his well-worn couch, the rush of the chase had just started to come down when Gabriel's heart raced again as he started to read the label.

"To: Gabriel, From: Miguel." Gabriel still struggled with that name now knowing his dear friend's real name was Jose. It was surreal to receive a package from someone that had just died hours earlier. The friend he had known for the past year. The friend he had worked with and visited at his home. The man, that was so gentle and kind, that Gabriel looked to him as a father figure and mentor. Now that man was gone, murdered in his own home, and the very life of the man that Gabriel thought he knew so well had just been turned upside down and inside out in less than 24 hours.

Gabriel took a deep breath and began tearing into the package the very package that possibly was the reason for his dear friend's death.

Chapter 11

Florida Gulf Coast, 1821

Even in the bright light of the hot Florida sun, the Old Beach Church was still a spooky place to be at but at this time of day, with the sea breeze howling and the last rays of light setting for the night, it was absolutely terrifying. Little Juan Gomez gingerly stepped over the barely standing Church fence. The sun bleached picket rails that surrounded the Church yard had not seen any care for many years. Still upright in some sections but mostly leaning towards the ground, the simple little Church seemed to be one stiff breeze from falling over.

"Go to the Old Beach Church. Find the King on the cross and ye' will find your treasure," those were the last words spoken into young Juan's ear from his father figure the dreaded Pirate Buccaneer Jose Gasparilla.

Juan had rarely attended Church himself but having spent his young life afloat, he had heard many frightened sailors praying. Whether it was a prayer for safe travels, protection from a summer storm, preparing for battle, or just prayer to pass the time, sailors are a particularly spiritual group. Juan had heard their prayers at many times refer to the King of Kings or the King on the cross. He felt confident that the Captain was referring to Jesus. According to their prayers, Jesus was the Son of God who had been crucified on the cross in a place called Golgotha in Jerusalem. All Juan had to do was find a cross at the Church with Jesus on it and he would find his treasure. However, upon entering the falling down Church Juan soon realized it would not be so easy.

A cypress wood planked wall slanted towards Juan as it hovered over what must have been the alter table at the front of the Church. All the Churches or Chapels that Juan had seen before had a cross on the front wall at the center of the aisle seats. But now all that was left was a faint outline on the wall. Juan began to panic.

"It's gone! Did it fall to the ground? No, it is not there." Juan spoke out loud. "Did someone take it? Is it in the wall?"

Juan ran his hand along weathered curling wood planks. Looking for any loose boards, he realized the wall was only one plank thick. There was no secret hiding spot behind it. He looked for any writing or etching in the wood but he did not see anything. He spent the next several hours scouring through every nook and cranny of the rickety wooden chapel but again, he found nothing… *nothing.*

He must have fallen asleep at some time in his search because now the morning sun beaming through a knot hole in the wooden wall woke up his crusty eyes. Stiff from sleeping on the floor, Juan stretched out his limbs and took in his surroundings. After hours of feeling his way through the mess of wooden debris, last night he could have walked around the chapel blindfolded. But this morning, in daylight, the Chapel was like a whole new world to him. The shadows were gone and the bright warm sun lit up a whole new Chapel to what he had struggled to see in the dark. The long collapsed stairwell that used to spin its way up to the second floor choir seats. The crooked center aisle could clearly be seen to have once been straight and quite nice. Ornate etchings of intersecting lines in the shape of a cross were carved into each pew seat showing a great care from one craftsman's work. The walls were bare wood with slight stains of candle smoke about every 6 feet down the length. Obviously, at one time candle sticks once lit the way for those seeking salvation. The Chapel in daylight was an all-new experience for Juan, unfortunately the outcome of his search was the same - nothing.

Another few hours of searching and it was time for Juan to give up. He was tired and hungry and there was no place else he could search. Defeated and exhausted, he walked out the back side of the Chapel. He could feel the full heat of the noon day sun on his swollen and aching cheek. Was this the wrong Church? Could he have been too late and someone found it by accident? Did Raúl and his crew somehow beat him to it?

Not really sure where he would go, Juan just decided to start walking south when he caught a glimpse in his right eye. A stark white square stone, peeking out from the thick sea grass, sparked the child's curiosity. As he turned to take a better look he noticed another stone, and then another. There were dozens of little, white, stone plaques popping out from under the green grass.

"Morrison, Joseph 1789. Clark, Benjamin 1788. Smi… Smith, K…" Juan struggled to read the worn off name on one of the white headstones.

It was a small cemetery only about 40 feet wide by 40 feet long. It was enclosed by a still fairly sturdy split rail fence, the kind of fence ranchers would use to keep their cattle contained in or out of an area. Juan counted 37 headstones some had multiple names on them so he guessed about 50 total graves under his feet.

Most sailors took their time off to drink, sleep, or do anything that would not resemble work. But not Juan, the young boy had taken every chance to grab any written material that he could. Whether it be a name on a sea trunk, a note from the Captain, or God willing sometimes even a book, the young boy was now thankful he had taught himself to read as he continued reading off of the white stones.

"Beloved father… Rest in peace… KING," Juan stopped mid-sentence as his heart pounded in his throat. "King, Sarah 1809, King, C 1783, King…" Juan stopped again.

Looking closer, Juan realized there must have been an entire family of King's buried in this area of the Chapel cemetery. He saw no less than 8 King names on separate headstones and one broken stone with only a "K" showing. They were scattered throughout the graveyard. There was no order to them, no pattern to the dates carved on them. They appeared to be just placed in the ground along with all the other names. Their stones were no bigger or prominent then any others. Most likely just a family in the Church named King. They offered up no clues. There was no order. The headstones didn't make sense, but they had too.

"What where the chances of this?" he thought to himself.

Frustrated with the Captain's vague orders, Juan knew something was close. His heart wouldn't let him leave but he couldn't figure it out. What did the Captain mean-King on the Cross? There was no cross here. Cursing the hunger growling in his stomach and kicking an old tree stomp that stung his toe, Juan let out a scream of frustration. But suddenly, Juan noticed some movement across the graveyard ground. With the rising sun, a shadow crept ever so slowly through the grass and over the various white stones. An unusual shadow, one that immediately grabbed Juan by the spine and made his hair stand up, he climbed on the rickety fence to get a better look at the whole graveyard.

Earlier in the morning, Juan had taken notice of a flag pole at the front steps of the Chapel. He noticed it at once because he recognized the thick solid oak timber of what was once a ship's mast sticking out of the ground. But what made him pause was the relative newness of the pole compared to the rest of the dilapidated Chapel. Pausing only for a second, he never gave the flagpole another thought-until now. Following the mysterious shadow cast from the flagpole high above the broken down Chapel, Juan watched in amazement as a small cross, the symbol of Christianity, at the peak of the mast about 20 feet above his head cast a shadow that crept across the small graveyard.

The sun reached its noon zenith and a smile spread across Juan's face. With his heart racing, the boy did everything he could to wait patiently and watch. Until finally, the cross shadow stopped, just for a moment, square on the center of a large grayish white headstone engraved with the name "KING." Juan had found the King on the cross… or so he hoped.

Chapter 12

Jacksonville, FL- present

Gabriel, lost in his thoughts, was sitting quietly on his threadbare couch trying to understand what had just happened to him over the last 24 hours. He had learned that his longtime friend Miguel was not the man he thought he was. Miguel, whose real name it turns out was Jose, warned him that his life was in danger and that there was little time. Then Jose suddenly dies mysteriously and a creepy man tried to follow Gabriel from the crime scene. It is all capped off with a strange package sent to Gabriel's home from his now dead friend Jose. It was a lot for the young man to process but a few long deep breaths and he was ready to open the large brown box. With a rip of the thread lined paper tape, he reached his hand into the cardboard box.

The grainy, teak, wood frame was what Gabriel found first. A beautiful handcrafted picture frame with lavish scroll work slid out of the box. The detailed carvings were definitely handmade and obviously very old but it was the picture, the frame surrounded, that took Gabriel's breath away. What must have been dozens of different species of wood were meticulously carved into tiny shapes. Like a jigsaw puzzle, hundreds of these different wood cutouts formed an amazingly accurate and lifelike picture. Painstakingly each wood grain gave texture and depth, each color change was perfectly shaded to give dark and light tones to the picture. There were no painted colors or pencil strokes just tiny pieces of various woods carved into a mesmerizing image. Developed in the early 16th century, Marquetry as the technique is called was used for furniture designs and picture artwork. The process of using cut out pieces of wood veneer to create lifelike images of intense detail takes years of skilled craftsmanship to develop. This picture was as accurate and lifelike as any painting or mural that Gabriel had ever seen.

The image depicted two men sitting at a small wooden table. They were raising their wine glasses to each other celebrating a "toast." The wine sommelier, a heavy set man with a long apron, stood behind them waiting to fill their glasses again. They were in a basement or wine cellar with large steps climbing up behind them. Two large circular shapes that looked like giant wine barrels rested behind the men. They appeared to be in a basement with no candlelight but the image was bright and happy not dark and gloomy. It was jovial picture of good times and friendship. But what were they celebrating? What were they trying to tell Gabriel? What was Jose trying to tell Gabriel? Is this the clue? He could only stare at the picture and allow his imagination to run ramped.

After a long while the picture, although amazingly skilled and beautiful, did not offer any great answer to Gabriel's questions or offer any obvious clues. He looked deeper in the box and saw a folded piece of paper flat against its side along the box wall. Gabriel unfolded the heavy cotton fiber paper and paused, he knew these were the last words of his dear friend. His heart was pounding in his chest. It was written not on a modern printer with ink jets or dot matrix laser printing but with an old fashioned typewriter. The worn black ink ribbon gave a ragged edge to each letter's stamping. There was something warm and comforting to this letter that Gabriel had never felt with the current cold sterile modern printed type he usually read.

-Gabriel, forgive me for placing you in this dangerous situation. I wish that we had more time but unfortunately, we do not. I believe that I am coming to the end of my life and it is important that I pass what I know on to you. You now hold in your hands the key to perhaps one of the greatest treasures ever lost. If you choose to pursue it, you must know that with great reward comes great danger.

In the youth of my life, I began my journey with great excitement and enthusiasm. But I quickly realized that I was not along in this quest and the others involved were very dangerous people. This danger was too much for me and I became the man you knew as Miguel Mendoza. But at one time, I was known as Jose Gomez, the great grandson of Juan Gomez. It is this family line that brought me this picture and the secret that it keeps. It is also this past life that has caught up with me and now I must pass my secret on to you. If you choose to pursue this path, as I once did, God speed and good luck. It is a journey like no other. Captured Princesses, untold golden fortunes, adventure, deception, and danger await you. And if you choose not to I, most of all, will understand. However if you decide not to make this journey all that I ask is that you pass this picture and the ring on to another person as worthy as you. And that you give them this piece of knowledge that has taken me my life to discover.

"Tampa is the port,"

I was never blessed with a family of my own but I often prayed that you would look to me as a father because I have always considered you as a son.

God Bless you-

Jose Gomez.

It did not take long for Gabriel to make up his mind. He considered the warning of his dear friend and he had witnessed the reality of that danger in his friend's untimely passing. He knew the coincidence of the two was too much to be just that. He felt in his heart that his friend had been killed by the very men that Jose was warning him about and those same men would now be after him. He considered going to the Police but for generations this secret had been kept in Jose's family and perhaps there was a good reason for that. Now this secret has been placed into his hands for him to solve and he couldn't possibly just give it away to the authorities. This burden had been placed on his shoulders and it was his to bear.

Early the next morning he moved out of his apartment. Jacksonville had always had some hard memories for him so there was no hold up there and the funeral would be too dangerous to attend so sticking around wouldn't make much sense either. Being chased by a creepy Ghost Man at Jose's house yesterday, Gabriel knew that he could not attend his friend's funeral. The Ghost would probably be there again. He would send flowers and a unanimous note instead. It wasn't an easy decision to make, especially since Jose had very few friends and Gabriel had none. In fact, had he gone, Gabriel most likely would have been the only visitor. The thought of his only friend being laid to rest with no one in attendance made Gabriel's heart sink but he knew that if he were to complete the quest that Jose had given him, then he had better start making tough decisions.

A single duffel bag packed, his new framed picture carefully covered in a bed sheet under his arm, lights off, and Gabriel walked out of his apartment forever. He didn't know what he was going to do but with the ring in his pocket and his mysterious new picture he knew his journey would begin in another city across the state. A journey that, to Gabriel, was as much an adventure to a new world as the very "land of flowers" itself was to Ponce de León in 1513 when he landed on La Florida. An exciting new world was to be discovered by this young man seeking adventure and fortune while at the same time facing imminent danger. Like the explorers of the past, Gabriel was driven by his beliefs. He believed in himself. He believed in his friend's loyalty. And he believed that around every dark corner in life there is always a light at the end of your path. You just have to be willing to risk everything to get there.

Chapter 13

Tampa, FL- present

The morning fog was lifting and beads of dew were starting to slide down the window pain in front of Nathan Gale's face. As his head leaned against the cold metal window frame of his school's yellow bus, Nathan tried to ignore the rambunctious kids sitting in the faded green vinyl benches around him. He didn't mind taking the bus to school but there were those times when he had wished he could put up with his sister's mindless babbling about boys, popularity, makeup, girls in her clique and the girls not in her clique. It drove him insane. His mother seemed to be indifferent to Lisa's constant texting and chatter in the morning but Nathan would rather face the 30 plus kids on the 10 mile bus ride then deal with his one self-indulged sister. He and his sister had always been close growing up, twins often share a special bond, but something about school seemed to make her intolerable to him. And it all started last year when they were freshmen.

It was that first week of high school when Roger Woods, a junior, noticed his beautiful sister. Roger told his buddies about this stunning freshman and Lisa quickly became the most popular girl in their class and soon the school. There was no turning back for Lisa and there was no room for her less than cool twin brother. Nathan was OK with being the less cool sibling he didn't even mind being second to a boyfriend… but Roger? Anyone but Roger.

Out of the corner of Nathan's eye, waking him from his near slumber, he noticed a young boy running along the sidewalk beside the bus. His initial thought was that maybe the boy had missed the bus stop, but that was before he saw the jogging shorts and sneakers. A backpack was strapped down tight on his shoulders and the boy was jogging faster than Nathan could sprint on his best day at gym class. The bus caught up with the boy but it took longer than it should have to pass him. He must have been running over 10 miles an hour. A quick glance up from the road gave Nathan a glimpse of the boy's face and their eyes caught each other briefly. The boy was barely breathing hard a little sweat on his forehead but no tension in his face or skip in his stride. He was bounding like a deer with barely any effort at all. Nathan noticed the boy's backpack as the bus finally passed.

It was a tan bag not your ordinary colorful Jan-Sport school bag. It had more pockets than usual and a lot of straps and clips across the back. It looked like an old military pack but this boy couldn't have been older than 17, too young for him to be a soldier. Nathan had to assume he was a student running to school. He was baffled by the idea of walking to school let alone someone who was running to school. Who would choose to run to school? But then again, Nathan thought, who would choose to take a hot crowded bus when an air conditioned car was available.

Nathan thought about the boy runner for the next 5 minutes until the large yellow school bus squeaked and hissed to a stop in the school parking lot. Nathan stepped off the bus with the mass of other students but as they turned left towards the school house, Nathan turned right to look back at the road. He knew it would be pointless to look for the boy. Obviously he would be miles behind the bus but not that far, not far enough for a normal everyday kid. There was something different about that runner and being different was something that Nathan could relate too.

Chapter 14

Jacksonville, FL- present

Pasty white fingers pressed down on the clear glass face of the Ghost's cell phone. With each number pressed a slight phone vibration raced up his boney finger, each vibrating jolt was like a shock of adrenaline for the Ghost's lifeless heart. After the third ring, a raspy heavy voice answered the call.

"What did you find?" the heavy voice asked. The Ghost's high tenor hissed back. "No one was at the funeral but I think we have a name. A boy that Jose worked with at the library this past year has not shown up for work all week. No one can find him." "I'm paying you to find him," the voice on the phone quickly interrupted.

"Yes sir, we will get him. If he is here, we will find him." "Don't waste your time," the thick voice replied back. "We must assume Jose gave this boy the map." "You think he will try to find the treasure?" hissed the Ghost.

"Wouldn't you?" replied the voice on the phone.

"If he does have the map and the ring, I believe he is coming to us." The thick heavy voice smiled into the phone with excitement. "You won't find him because he is already here. Do you have a name?"

The Ghost's throat quickly choked a bit as he struggled with an answer. "We don't have a full name yet."

The pause on the phone was deafening.

"The name he went by was not the name on is job application. When we looked deeper it seems as though this boy has bounced around a lot in the state system. He has had multiple last names that will make him difficult to track. His listed known address was vacant, no known parents, always paid for things with cash, no known friends other than Jose."

"What do you know?" the aggravated voice spit through the phone.

"Gabriel," the Ghost answered with a slight panic in his voice. "His first name is Gabriel… at least we know that."

After a long pause the heavy voice on the other end of the phone replied-

"Find him."

The SLAMMING of the receiver exploded into the Ghost's ear and then was quickly replaced with the digital hum of disconnection. However, the point had been made and the Ghost was well aware-find the boy Gabriel or suffer the deadly consequences.

Chapter 15

Florida, 1821

Young Juan Gomez stood in the Old Chapel Graveyard with his mouth open. At his feet was a sun bleached stone with the name "King" engraved on it. The noon day shadow, from the Cross on the chapel flag pole, was square on the stone face. This had to be it. Juan thought to himself as his heart continued to pound in his chest. The new ship mast pole was placed in a chapel yard that no one ever came to anymore. This had to be the work of Captain Gaspar. The Cross affixed to the top of the massive timber in perfect location to cast a shadow across the tombstone name King.

"This must be it," Juan blurted out and fell to his knees. He wasn't sure if it was official or if he was even doing it right but he bowed his head and to the best of his ability tried to pray.

After a few moments of thanks and pleas for guidance, Juan began to look at the weathered headstone. He started to dig around the edges and noticed that the stone only sunk in the earth about 3 inches. After some effort Juan could barely squeeze his fingers underneath the heavy stone. It was a tight fit but he could start to work his hand around the perimeter. It was hard work, especially in the brutal afternoon sun, but after about 30 minutes and some bloody scrapes, he had cleared all around the stone and could see every side of the massive cube. He needed to rest but he couldn't waste time. He was too close to stop.

His blood was running hot through his body and even the aching pain of his hands and back would not slow him down. Sweat poured down his face and his hands were slick with blood. He wiped his hands clean on his pant leg and reached down to grab a strong hold of the stone. Bracing his feet in the fresh dirt close to the stone, he straightened his back and bent his knees down low. Taking in a deep breath Juan held it in his lungs for a second almost as a countdown then released the pressure in his chest as he tried lifting the stone. His fingers tightened and strained while his legs began to shake as they pushed down in the soil. Every muscle in his arms and back stretched under the tension of the stone. Blood raced into his face, his eyes began to bulge, and his mouth let out a scream.

Just when he thought his joints couldn't hold any longer, he felt the stone move. He didn't have any more strength to try again it had to be now. Juan gasped another gulp of salt air and thrust his back up towards the sky. For one moment, Juan thought his arms might rip off his body and his torso would shoot up through the sky like an armless cannon shot. He was about to quit just as the stone moved from its perch and rolled over on its side. He collapsed to the ground and gasped for air.

It took a moment to recover. His body heaved for precious oxygen and his muscles quivered and shook. His fingers were in such pain he couldn't straighten them out. They were stuck in their hooked gripped positions.

He rolled to his side and wanted to get up but couldn't, he was too weak. But then he saw it. Looking up at the bottom of the stone, Juan noticed a canvas bag jammed into a carved out hollow compartment inside it. In that moment, all the pain in Juan's body disappeared when his hand reached up and felt something inside the dirty oily canvas sack.

The bag had a musty smell to it. It had been under this rock for a long time. The bag had been soaked in an oily pitch that was common for ship sails. It was a mixture of tree sap, whale oil, and wood ash. It kept the hemp sails flexible while also making them waterproof. Obviously, Captain Gaspar knew this would be in the ground getting wet and he didn't want whatever was inside it getting ruined. When he untied the leather strap around the pouch neck and opened the bag he saw the top of a rolled up piece of parchment. Unrolling the parchment, Juan noticed that it was actually a very thin piece of lamb leather. The edges were a little cracked and rough, obviously, it had been unrolled and rolled again many times. But the image pressed into the smooth leather was as clear as the day it was drawn.

It was a map. A map that had been drawn by the old Captain himself. Ornate with details down to the last sandy bottom sounding, that only the highly skilled hand of an expert sailor could draw. The coast line looked flat and level with lots of plant life not the rocky cliff lines that were common among the islands in the Caribbean. There were long sand bar islands that reached out far into the sea and protected a deep wide harbor. The harbor inlet had frightening drawings of giant sharks, water snake monsters, land dragons, and an eight-legged creature from the sea with arms that wrapped around a helpless ship.

Many sailors feared these monsters, as they were often drawn into maps, and would sail for safer waters whenever they saw them along their charted paths. But Juan knew better. He had often watched Captain Gaspar laugh at the colorful characters during their chart work sessions together. The Captain himself would at times add an extra arm or enlarge the mouth on one of the creatures. Juan used to think that the Captain was just wishing for doom and asking for the monsters to attack but he eventually realized that in fact, the Captain simply knew they did not exist. The Captain didn't fear them and soon neither would young Juan.

By the looks of these water creatures, the inlet on Captain Gaspar's map would be the most dangerous stretch of water that Juan had ever seen. Obviously, the Captain wanted to scare away any run of the mill sailor that may come across this map should it fall out of the Captain's hands. But what was most interesting to the young boy was that there were no markings of any kind about the harbor itself. Away from the harbor there were names of locations that Juan recognized and actually knew quite well. The large point of Cape Romano, the numerous islands in Punjo Bay, the fast flowing Delaware River were all clearly labeled and recognizable but the harbor was nameless. This was never the case on any map Juan had ever seen. Any distinguishable features that were in the area would always be labeled for reference. Any town or village would have been named. Territories that belonged to Spain, or France, or even the America's were always marked but not on this map. From the mouth of the bay into the harbor there were no markings other than depth soundings and a series of unusual circles along the shoreline. But there was one marking that immediately caught young Juan's eyes. One that stood out and made his heart race, a large black "X" scratched on a small island at the mouth of the harbor. Juan knew that "X" must mean the very treasure itself. Gaspar's fortune was his to find and this map would lead him to it. Usually there would be a Compass Rose on every map giving the basic cardinal directions of North, South, East, and West but there was no compass to be found. This alone would make any chart virtually worthless. But with the names of some locations labeled, the map could get away without it. However, given that the harbor was nameless it would still be very difficult for anyone to find. But to Juan this map was far from worthless, to him it was priceless and he knew just where to go.

Juan had spent the last 5 years on the Floriblanca as a cabin boy and rarely spent a day without knowing where the Captain was. He had sailed into every port and every harbor from Spanish Mexico to the French Canadian territories of the north. Every chart and map he had ever seen was always well labeled and marked but not this one. Not the one that was now in his tired dirty hands. The harbor that contained the black "X" at its mouth had no reference point or discernible detail yet; Juan knew the area and knew it well. Juan realized that the Captain didn't just want anyone to find his treasure, should he not make it back, he wanted Juan to find it. All the chart work and time spent working with the young boy; Juan was being prepared to find it if tragedy should strike the captain. This chart in particular, this harbor alone Juan remembered the Captain making him draw it over and over again until the young boy could retrace it in his sleep. With no names in the harbor it could be one of thousands the Captain had explored, but to Juan it was only one and he knew it well.

Standing in the church graveyard as he looked at the map, Juan was still holding the musty canvas bag when suddenly something heavy sparked his interest; Juan turned it over and let the contents fall out.

It was a beautiful gold Cross necklace. An obvious symbol of Christianity, the Cross was encircled by a band of gold that touched the outer edges of its four endpoints. Along the band was a series of precious gems and in between the gems were a series of numbers engraved into the gold. The center of the Cross had an opening in it almost as if a large precious stone had been removed and left a void. The solid gold chain that was attached to the Cross alone weighed at least a pound. It was priceless and young Juan knew that this was just a piece of Captain Gaspar's vast treasure trove. His mouth watered with anticipation of what else would await him on that treasure filled island. Still stuck to the waxy leather pouch was something else that Juan noticed.

A large gold ring dropped into his dirty little hand. It was a beautifully engraved ring with etched words that Juan did not understand. However, he could make out with no problem a large engraved tall-masted ship and its seven gun ports. It was the ship he had known as home for the last 5 years. The ship that now sat at the bottom of the deep. It was the Floriblanca.

Chapter 16

Tampa, FL- present

The first day of school is never easy. New faces, new classes, old flames and new opportunities are around every corner. Finding homeroom class and where to sit at lunch are always top priorities. Naturally, kids group together and form cliques… The sport cliques with the cheerleader supporters, the smart kid cliques, the strange and odd kid cliques, the rich kids, the poor kids, the geeky kids, kids who play music, kids who group together but want to be left alone cliques… all of these social groups and many more take time to form but are generally solidified within the first couple of weeks of school. So for Gabriel's first day, he knew it would be even more difficult to fit in given that school started four months ago.

However, Gabriel knew the routine. He had always been the new kid. His years in the foster care system never let him stay in one school for more than a couple semesters. He knew how to answer the Principle's questions before he or she even asked. Gabriel could explain his situation briefly with just enough detail to answer the questions but leave little more than needed to be discussed.

He knew that the address he gave would take about a week to verify and that would be plenty of time for him to find an apartment and a job to pay for it. He knew the YMCA that he was currently staying at would suffice until then. But he also knew that it was critical to get registered in school as soon as possible because that was the one stipulation Judge Davis gave him when he was given his freedom- "Stay in school or come back to this courthouse." That was an order Gabriel would never take lightly, he had prayed and worked too hard and too long to go back into the system.

So with his new registration in hand, Gabriel approached the tan painted classroom door, took a deep breath, and reached out to the worn and flaking chrome plated doorknob. As soon as he opened that door he knew the questions would start to fly, so he took a moment to prepare himself before entering Mr. Orsos' packed history class.

The room fell silent, it always did, and everyone's head turned to stare at the stranger in the doorway. This was always the worst part no matter how many times he had been there before. Gabriel offered a brief "Hello" to the teacher when he handed him his official papers and then his eyes began the frantic search for an open chair. The back of the room was packed, it always was, but he found a lone chair about mid-way up the aisle to the right hand side of the classroom. Near the window, it was the first open seat Gabriel saw. He could feel the eyes on him and he just wanted to sit down… fast. He made his way up the aisle and quickly took his seat flush faced he tried to look calm and comfortable.

The questions came fast, just as Gabriel knew they would. He made sure to answer them quickly but not too abruptly. He didn't need to go off into any long tangent to explain his past. It was better to answer as if nothing had ever been wrong and everything was perfectly normal. He would act as if he was happy with coming to this new school and he looked forward to meeting everyone.

He knew this was unlikely but deep down inside there was some element of truth to his last thought. It had been years since Gabriel had made any friends at school. He tried to be a likable guy, and he was usually welcomed but just as he would get close to someone tragedy would strike and he would have to start over. Only in the last year living on his own, had Gabriel had any stability. However, even then his only friend was a ninety year old man that had just died in a very mysterious situation. Nothing was normal for Gabriel but he had grown comfortable with the normalcy of abnormality.

Where are you from? What do you like to do? Pretty standard stuff for a new kid in class but one question however did always choke Gabriel up. No matter how hard he tried to prepare for it or pretend it didn't matter, it always got to him. "What do your parents do?"

"My Father died in Iraq… six years ago. He was a Marine and a good father."

Thankfully, this was enough of an answer. It was complete enough that no one seemed to follow up with any more questions and awkward enough that no one would continue to ask about his Mother. Class resumed and Gabriel started to breath normally again.

As he looked around the class some kids stared back at him but most couldn't care less and looked down aimlessly into their schoolbooks doodling to pass the time.

However, towards the back of the room a few seats to Gabriel's left, there was one boy that seemed to be more interested in this new kid than most. Nathan Gale watched Gabriel take his seat and was about to go back to his doodling when he noticed the worn and tattered tan colored backpack. The unusual military style bag stood out to him as he recognized the boy he had seen earlier running to school. No longer in his gym clothes, Gabriel had changed into jeans and a collared shirt, but that same kid that was racing a bus was now sitting two rows away from him.

Nathan watched Gabriel and could sense his uneasiness as awkward as it is to be the new kid and not part of the norm. The sense of being alone and different from the pack was all too familiar to Nathan, so he felt a strange bond to this new kid that he had never even met.

Chapter 17

The redness of his flushed face was beginning to go down as Gabriel was starting to settle into his new seat when something suddenly struck his ear in Mr. Orsos' history class.

"The early Constitution of the United States failed to provide equality to all people." Mr. Orsos continued. "That is why over the years, this Constitution has been required to change and adapt with modern times."

Gabriel could feel the blood rush back into his face. His heart began to beat faster. He looked around the room and hoped that someone would raise a hand and question this statement. Was this a test? Was Mr. Orsos challenging the students? He seemed to continue on as if nothing was said out of order. Gabriel didn't want to raise his hand on the first day. Not in a new school with strange faces, he never wanted to be that kid. But his mouth blurted out before his mind could stop his hand from climbing awkwardly and instinctively halfway up.

"Sir, could you explain that?" Why did he say anything? He should have just let it go. Gabriel thought to himself. However as the class room snickers became deafening to Gabriel's ears he didn't want them to think he was just the new kid trying to be funny. He had to show them that he was serious because he was. Gabriel had a legitimate question this wasn't a prank. He thought about waving off the comment for a moment but something just didn't sit with him and Gabriel couldn't help himself. "I don't understand your statement. What do you mean the Constitution failed to provide equality?"

With a sense of aloof, Mr. Orsos answered with a smirk. "Well class, let us see if we can answer the new boy's question?" "Go ahead Mr. Fletcher, explain." Gabriel had to word his question perfectly. Nerves could not fluster him or he would be forever known as the new kid that sounded like a moron on his first day.

"Well sir, by definition equality means equal. Therefore how could the Constitution provide equality unless it was a supreme governing authority? I thought the Constitution was a set of rules that dispelled over reaching government by providing individual rights under a uniformed set of laws. With individual rights and self-responsibility there are no equal results for everyone only equal opportunities. It provided for adjustments over time through the amendment process but by no means would I consider the Constitution a failure. Its core principle to provide our God given rights of life, liberty, and the pursuit of happiness has been the most successful system in the history of the world."

The stillness in the room was unsettling but Gabriel felt he had answered the best he could and the long pause was promising… unless of course the class suddenly broke out in laughter. But they didn't. Mr. Orsos was thinking about his answer. Gabriel's confidence began to rise. But then Mr. Orsos spoke.

"Well that was a well worded attempt but unfortunately you just demonstrated your severe lack of understanding to the Constitution. Perhaps your previous school did not cover the subject but I assure you your thought process is off the mark." The awkward feeling of nervousness was quickly dissipating to anger. Gabriel had no problem being wrong, but he hated being dismissed. If you can prove me wrong then do so but don't dismiss me for asking a question, he thought to himself. The stares of the kids around him disappeared from his peripheral and Gabriel's focus zoomed in on Mr. Orsos.

"Would you care to explain sir? Where is my thought process off its mark?" Gabriel replied. The contempt for this follow up question was obvious not just to Gabriel but to the rest of the class as well when Mr. Orsos answered.

"Well, even though we have previously addressed these topics in this class, I must ask are you familiar, from your previous school, with the 3/5th's clause or perhaps the separation of Church and State clause within the Constitution? Or do we need to go back and start our classes from the beginning?" Mr. Orsos said with a smug grin.

"I am aware of those topics but I don't see your point." Gabriel shot back.

"Of course you don't." Mr. Orsos smirked. "Class, allow me a moment to step back and inform this young Mr. Fletcher about what you already know." Mr. Orsos walked towards Gabriel attempting to stand high above the young boy still in his seat. "The 3/5th clause stated that early black Americans were to only be considered as 3/5th a man so that their vote would be less in numbers then successful white men, obviously not treating them with your definition of equal opportunities. The same goes for the separation of Church and State clause in our first amendment. It was supposed to protect us free citizens from the inequality of religious persecution but the Constitution does not adequately protect us from the churches of intimidation or political influence even to this day. Should I go on Mr. Fletcher or do you need more examples?" Mr. Orsos finished feeling confident even proud of his answer.

Gabriel was stunned by this teacher's ignorance. But it was his arrogance that really set Gabriel off and now he was ready for the fight.

"Mr. Orsos, I have done my reading as well. In fact, I have done a lot of reading and please allow me to disagree with everything you have just said."

The kids in the room were wide awake now and not completely sure who to root for but this was quickly becoming the best class ever.

"Article 1 section 2 of the Constitution does state that the whole of all free persons receive one vote in the House and all other persons, excluding non-tax paying Indians, receive 3/5th of a vote. This would be adjusted every ten years due to enumeration of the census poll." Gabriel took a breath.

"So you have read the Constitution?" Mr. Orsos snickered.

"I have," replied Gabriel. "I have also read the Federalists papers and the words of Frederick Douglas, a freed slave, who was perhaps the most prominent thought leader and a dear friend of Abraham Lincoln in the Civil War era. And all of these writings point to the fact that the 3/5th's clause was a compromise that would eventually ensure the freedom of the slaves in America."

The students in the class sat in silence as they watched this new kid school their teacher.

"The southern states refused to ratify the Constitution because they didn't have the population to out vote the northern states. They wanted to count the slaves as voters even though they deemed the slaves as property. The northern state representatives wanted the slaves to be freed in order for them to be given a vote. This forced an impossible stalemate that was only settled when the 3/5th clause was presented. The founders knew that over time as the northern states population grew, so would their votes. The southern states would eventually have to free their slaves if they wanted to gain more votes or the South would suffer from the impending majority loss to the Northern abolishment states all together. The 3/5th clause was the death knell for slavery in America and it was written into the Constitution for that reason." Gabriel took another breath.

Mr. Orsos was beginning to look uneasy and started to shift in his stance.

"Your second point was that of the separation of Church and state." Gabriel began his assault again in rapid succession. "Nowhere in the Constitution do the words Separation of Church and state appear in any way including the First Amendment. It actually says: Congress shall make no law respecting an establishment of religion or prohibiting the free exercise thereof." Gabriel recited.

"The term Separation of Church and State first appeared January 1st, 1802 when then President Thomas Jefferson replied to a letter from the committee of the Danbury Baptist Association. The Committee was concerned that the local governing authority of Connecticut was starting to push its influence on the Baptist Church. Jefferson in a personal letter replied to the committee and stated that this would never happen due to the First Amendment establishing a wall of separation between Church and State. However, many years later, this term has been used in various court cases to establish the supremacy of government over religious freedom in complete reversal of its original meaning. This was never Jefferson's intent nor the intent of the Constitution."

The class erupted in applause not because they so much understood everything that Gabriel had just said but in the passion and conviction in which he said it. They had never seen anyone stand up to Mr. Orsos and certainly no one had ever attempted to out debate him.

Mr. Orsos was speechless for a second as he tried to gain his composure and quiet the class down. He was taken aback by Gabriel but he wasn't about to claim defeat.

"Well said Mr. Fletcher, but you can't deny that Mr. Jefferson was a strong voice for less religious influence within the Constitution. He believed that the government should provide equality and not allow the Church's influence to disorient the Constitution. This is why he referenced the First Amendment in his coining the phrase Separation of Church and State. He felt that it was the government's role to provide equality for its citizens and that's why the Constitution limits religious influence."

"I'm sorry but you're confusing me. At first you declared the Constitution as a failure for equality but then you say it's a success in limiting religious freedom with the First Amendment thus promoting equality. All things being equal, why do you have the right to limit my freedom if I don't have the freedom to defend my right? It's not equal if I have to give up what is mine so that others may take what they don't have. Who are you or who is the government to tell me what is right or wrong if it is not declared in our Constitution which the government ironically pledges to uphold?"

"Well I…" Mr. Orsos struggled to find the words fast enough to stop Gabriel's onslaught.

"I also find it interesting that you think Jefferson had such an influence on the Constitution given that he was never present at the Constitutional Convention." Gabriel was firing all pistons now. "In 1791, Jefferson was the Ambassador to France. He was not even present at the Convention. If you want to talk about the Constitution or the First Amendment and its intent, perhaps you should reference the most active speaker of the Convention and actual writer of the Constitution Gouverneur Morris from Pennsylvania or perhaps you should look to General George Washington who presided over the convention. Maybe, Fisher Ames from Massachusetts who physically wrote the First Amendment. I believe you choose not to look at these original legitimate resources because you found a narrow group of words that could be twisted to satisfy your agenda. You chose to reference a letter that was written

11 years after the convention trying to claim that it supports your belief of government superiority over individual liberties. Even though the fact is, that Jefferson wrote the letter to explain the Constitutional limits of government in matters of the Church's liberties," Gabriel finally took another breath.

"The Constitution promotes equal opportunity for all under the law. How we choose to use those opportunities does not promise equal results. But it is this equally protected choice that is in fact our freedom."

The room was silent for a second as Mr. Orsos tried to look unshaken but the deep swallow in his throat spoke volumes.

He had finally decided on what he would try to say to the class when the bell pierced the silence and saved him from total humiliation. Every kid bolted out of their chairs before the last note was rung and the epic debate of the new kid and the teacher was quickly sent to the lunch room table conversations of history. Gabriel had not noticed anyone else in the room for the last several minutes. His focus was laser-like on the teacher at the front of the room, but the shrieking bell startled him from his trance. He knew that he was poking the bear that would control his grade in this class but when it came to this subject Gabriel was fearless. He had lost a Father for this country and as a result a Mother as well. To Gabriel there must have been a reason for that, so U.S. History and Constitutional studies have been a passion for the boy. The more he learned the more he loved and even with the scars of this country's history he knew that America was exceptional. Gabriel never backed away from standing up and speaking out in defense of the country he had learned to love so much.

To the boy that had lost everything, he also knew much had been given and for that Gabriel was thankful.

Chapter 18

Florida Coast, 1821

Juan's little legs could walk no more for he had barely slept in three days. In those last three days he had survived a viscous naval attack and watched his beloved Captain go down with the ship. He had been taken captive and then released by American sailors only to be slashed and threatened by rogue pirates from his old crew. He had taken clues, given to him from Captain Gaspar, to the Old Church and had found the secret map, a gold Cross, and the Captain's gold ring. Needless to say, it had been an eventful few days and now Juan just wanted to get back to a town where he could find some food and a place to rest his aching body.

The town of Tarpon, named after the hard fighting fish, lived up to its name. It was a rough area with little traffic from land lubbers. A large population of Greek settlers had come to these waters because of the rich sponge diving the corral coast offered. Similar to their native waters in the Mediterranean, the clear water and rocky bottom shores were perfect for collecting sponges from the cold depths. Most of the town's people were welcoming to sailors but only if they brought lucrative spoils from the high seas. Juan had been there once before with the very wealthy Captain Gaspar and remembered liking the place. But now there was no Captain Gaspar and no money to be spent. Juan quickly realized his visit to Tarpon this time would be very different.

Walking along the town's dusty limestone road, Juan ran up to a local merchant, "Please sir, do you have any food or water? I can work for it."

The man sputtered something in a language that Juan could only assume was Greek and shrugged the boy off.

Several more attempts and all to the same result. Juan was standing in the middle of the street along the docks hoping someone would help him but no one came to his aid. He was so hungry he contemplated using his gold ring for a bargaining chip but knew that would only lead to a quicker death then starvation. This was a tough town and sailors often came here to spend their money on drink and brag about their found treasure. Most of them left with nothing and those that had the most sometimes never left at all. For a young boy like Juan to be walking around with such a gold ring he would never stand a chance. No, Juan decided he would have to resort to a different less appealing approach. He would have to steal it.

The smell of roasted lamb suddenly filled his nostrils. Wafting down the street from a small window on the north end, the cooked lamb made Juan's mouth water. He started to walk the cobbled path towards the charred meal when he suddenly stopped. Out of the corner of his eye, Juan saw three large men exiting a dark saloon when a familiar raspy voiced caught his ear.

Slowly turning his head, Juan watched Raúl and his henchmen covering their eyes from the bright afternoon sun. In that moment, Juan didn't think he just ran.

As their eyes were adjusting to the bright noon sun, Juan hoped he had just enough time to run and hide before they spotted him. He was wrong.

"Look there he his!" One of the men barked out. Juan knew they would be running after him but all he could hear was his own feet racing across the wooden boardwalk in front of the local barber shop. Ducking under locals and hoping over railings, Juan pushed his body to the limit. His size allowed him to move quickly through tight spaces but his little legs were not long enough to match the long strides of the men chasing him. He had to find a place to hide fast. Racing past a large wagon cart, the lead horse raised up in its bridals at the flash of a little boy darting in front of him. Juan used the large cart as a cover to change directions. Spinning in place he was now heading back towards Raúl and the other men. He would have to time this move perfectly. A dangerous move he had seen once before on the Floriblanca.

A few years back, Captain Gaspar was trying to escape from a large British war ship. Well out of his class, the ship was much more powerful and would have easily taken the Floriblanca if not for the quick decision of Captain Gaspar. Using the Floriblanca's speed and maneuverability to its advantage, the Captain sped through a narrow channel of key islands to lose sight of the war ship. In a move that seemed like suicide to the crew, the Captain came about, dropped his sail and lowered the top mast. Running with the current and not under sail the Floriblanca slowly drifted back through the channel. Knowing the channel was too shallow for the war ship to travel in it would be forced to move out into the deeper water. This put the island's tree line, which was now taller than the lowered mast of 40 feet, in between the passing vessels. Blinded to the Floriblanca's movement, like two ships passing in the night, both ships were no more than 200 yards apart and in broad daylight but completely invisible to each other. Silence was critical, no commands were given, only the beating hearts of the crew could be heard as they slowly drifted back along the island's mangroves. The crew's breath was held for several minutes as the Floriblanca quietly came out of the passage and entered into the open water. When the British war ship was nowhere in sight, the collective exhale alone was enough wind to fill the sails and push the ship back out to sea.

Juan remembered the cold courage of Captain Gaspar in that maneuver and was trying to find it in himself as he stood up straight and slowed his run to a confident walk. Blending in with a small group of merchants walking along the storefront boardwalk, Juan fixed his eyes on Raúl and his men. He knew that he only had one shot at this and he could not miss. His life depended on it. Timing his walk with the people around him, who seemed oblivious to his near presence, he spotted a tall wooden lamp pole along the street's sidewalk. Directly in the line of sight of Raúl, the pole might just be wide enough to hide him, he thought. Raúl had to stay on course and not change speed. Juan needed to pick up his pace and move to the left about two more feet away from the pole. He bumped into the crowd of people next to him but not enough to cause alarm or knock him off his path. He barely even noticed. Juan was transfixed on the pole between him and Raúl. He had to time it perfectly.

Suddenly Raúl stopped. Too fast for Juan to react in time; he took one extra step and prayed Raúl didn't see him. Now standing motionless, Juan slowly slid his foot back behind the shadow of the pole. Raúl and the men had not seen him. All three men and little Juan were now standing in pure stillness only 10 feet apart from each other. The men were looking in every direction they could but completely hidden by the round cypress pole between them stood their silent target.

"Hold… hooold," Juan kept telling himself. "Do not panic, don't run… they haven't seen you yet," He tried to convince himself that he was ok even though his heart said "RUN".

The raspy voice carried over the noise of the street to Juan's ears. "I don't see him. At the corner spread out and find him. He couldn't have gone far," Raúl gave his men their orders and then started to walk again.

Juan took his first step in what seemed like forever. His muscles were twitching, and he thought for a moment he would lose his balance and tumble but his foot landed and his body moved forward. Keeping the corner of his eyes on the men, Juan didn't want to turn around and make a false step but he couldn't help straining his neck a bit to keep the men in his sight.

"It worked," Juan thought to himself and almost said it out loud. He walked a few more steps until he was off the boardwalk and back on the limestone pebbled road. One more glance behind his back and Juan could see the men splitting up and going on their separate ways about 50 yards from him. They were not looking back at him and Juan never looked back again. He took off through a narrow pass between the buildings and ran as fast as his little legs could move. He hoped to never see Raúl and his men again. Unfortunately, in his heart he knew Raúl, and he knew that Raúl would never stop looking for him. But for now, today, Juan was free and that's all he could ever hope for.

Chapter 19

School Library- Present

"That was pretty cool what you said in Mr. Orsos' class," Nathan Gale spoke out to Gabriel.

Gabriel, who was sitting with his nose in a book, was startled by the interruption. Jumping back in his chair, Gabriel responded. "I'm sorry what did you say?" "That was cool what you said to Mr. Orsos in history class. Was it true?" "Was what true?" Gabriel was confused. "What you said about the Constitution and Thomas Jefferson?" Nathan answered.

"I wouldn't have said it if it wasn't true… Why are you talking so loudly?" Gabriel questioned. "This is the school library. You are supposed to be quiet here." Nathan laughed. "Look around this place. No one comes here. I had to search the entire school before it dawned on me that you might be in here being new and all and not really knowing anyone."

Gabriel looked over his carpet covered half-wall out across the empty cubicle covered library room. He was right. Aside from the old lady behind the counter, the library was completely empty. "That's sad" Gabriel commented.

"Not even geeks like me come here during school I just figured there was no place else to look," Nathan chimed. "A lifetime of information at your fingertips and no one wants to learn it," Gabriel lamented. "That's what the internet is for. No one reads books anymore," stated Nathan. "I prefer books. They don't edit as quickly. Slow to change." Gabriel said.

"What's your name?" Nathan asked.

"Gabriel Fletcher," Gabriel responded. "Yours?" "Nathan Gale, sophomore." The two boys shook hands. "I'm a sophomore as well. Transfer student from Jacksonville," Gabriel smiled. "Well you must be a history buff then. What are you reading? I'm more of a math guy," stated Nathan. "You sure schooled Mr. Orsos in U.S. history and you claim to not be hiding out here so you must be studying something right?"

"Do you always talk so fast?" Gabriel replied.

"Pretty much. Even when I was young, it used to drive my family crazy especially my sister. She hated it. She's a sophomore here too. We are twins." Nathan breathed.

"We don't always get along well. She got all the cool popularity traits, and I just got the brains. But every once in a while she can be cool too, except when Roger comes sniffing around. He's the most popular kid in school. Roger is the captain of every team, good at everything, and he hangs out with the coolest kids at school. He's been trying to go out with my sister for a year now but my parents won't let her. She's only a sophomore, and he's a senior with a car. But I overheard her in the hall the other day tell a friend she might sneak out soon to see him."

"Do you ever stop talking?" Gabriel blurted out. Nathan looked surprised. "I'm sorry but you're making my ears hurt." "Sorry… I have a tendency to go on and on." Nathan continued. "Sometimes I don't even know I'm doing it. This one time at dinner I started talking about a show on TV and my Father…"

Nathan looked at Gabriel's face. "You're right. I'm sorry. I do talk a lot," he apologized. "I don't mean to be rude." Gabriel responded. "It's just that I'm used to more quiet conversations with myself."

"I understand, my mistake, just wanted to say hi." Nathan began to step back and Gabriel felt bad that he had snapped at him. "How do you like it here?" Gabriel questioned. Leaning back into the conversation, Nathan responded.

"It's ok. I mean if your with the right clique or a good athlete, maybe one of the good looking kids you can fit in better but even if you're not it's not that bad."

Gabriel didn't respond. He could tell by Nathan's answer how Nathan felt about himself. Nathan was a good looking kid but he often hid his face with downward glances as if to hide from other people looking at him.

He was actually a pretty tall kid with a good size frame but with no apparent muscle tone or definition, Gabriel knew sports were not his thing. Judging by how hard Nathan had tried to find some new kid to this school, chances were that Nathan didn't have too many friends himself so the right clique was out of the question. Popularity, Gabriel thought, was not Nathan's thing either.

"That's good to hear. I hope I like it." Gabriel smiled. "I think you will." Nathan responded. "So what are you studying?" Nathan asked. "Oh nothing really, I was just trying to look up something for an old friend." Gabriel tried to downplay his search. "Well, maybe I can help. What's it about?"

"Nothing really, I can't even seem to get started it was just something I was curious about." Gabriel replied. "Seriously, I don't mind. I can help you search. Two heads are better than one. That's what my Dad always tells me. (Impersonating his Father) Two heads are better than one. Work with your sister, we all know she needs the help. When I got glasses, he said four eyes are better than two. Can you believe that? My Dad is cool and all but sometimes he can be… I'm talking too much."

"I appreciate it but I was just about to leave. I've looked through all the books I can find in here and there is nothing on my subject. You really can't help me but it was nice meeting you."

Gabriel got up to leave but his notes were exposed for a split second from under his book as he picked them up. Nathan noticed them, "Tampa, Pirate, Treasure, captured Pri…" Nathan read aloud.

"Look it's just a hobby for a friend forget you saw anything." Gabriel replied with annoyance. "What was that last line?" Nathan ignored him.

"I don't want your help." replied Gabriel. Looking up at Gabriel's face, Nathan saw that he was touching a nerve with his new found acquaintance. "It was nice meeting you. I hope to see you around but you can't help me," Gabriel started to walk away.

Nathan watched Gabriel walk off in anger as a smile spread across his face. "If that last line said captured princess… you're looking for Captain Gaspar."

Gabriel stopped cold in his tracks and spun around to face Nathan smiling from ear to ear. Gabriel was stunned, "Excuse me."

"You heard me. You're looking for Captain Jose 'Gasparilla' Gaspar. Now do you want my help?"

Chapter 20

The last ten minutes had been a blur to Gabriel. He barely remembered a thing about his conversation with Nathan except the name Jose Gaspar. Gabriel had a been given an ancient secret from an old friend just before he died and then was forced to flee his home from the men he believed had just killed him. He had moved to Tampa to seek out this secret and had spent countless hours researching questions to no answer. And then comes along Nathan, this complete stranger he had just met and in an instant had given Gabriel his first actual solid lead. But it wasn't true… was it?

"I thought Captain Gaspar was a made up legend. A mythical pirate created by a marketing firm to bring tourist to Florida." Gabriel was walking down the school hallway between the cafeteria and senior lounge with Nathan at his right.

"So you knew about him?" Nathan responded. "Not really. I read something about him in my search but there were no actual accounts of him. No records, until the early 1920's, ever existed and I need to go back further to the early 1800's." "Why?" Nathan questioned. "I can't tell you why but I need to find someone prior to the fictional pirate Gasparilla.

"Listen." Nathan stopped their walk to address Gabriel. "In mathematics you have quantifiable fact.

Tested and proven laws that explain all the natural wonders of the world. Physics, astronomy, astrology, and even evolution can be explained thru mathematics. Undeniable facts all of them, but can you explain what caused the big bang? What placed the stars in their alignment and gave them motion along their orbital paths? What stories do the star's patterns tell? What gives evolution life? There are recorded historical facts that we all can see but there are also facts and stories that we may never know. The question is what do you believe? Myth, legend, folklore all can be written off by some people as just stories. But I happen to believe that every great story has some hint of truth. Even if you can't prove it, that doesn't mean it didn't happen." Nathan took a moment to judge Gabriel's reaction. "I would like to help." Nathan pleaded.

Gabriel thought about his answer for a moment, "I don't have a lot of friends. Actually, I don't have any friends. But if there is one thing I know, it is how to read people. If you don't mind, I could use your help." The boys shook hands and smiled at their new friendship.

A voice suddenly called out from across the courtyard. "Nathan, where have you been? I've been waiting for half an hour." Lisa Gale shrieked

"That's my sister, Lisa. She is 6 minutes older than me but sometimes she acts like my Mother," Nathan mumbled to Gabriel.

As Lisa stormed down the walkway and up to Nathan, she quickly cooled down when she noticed the handsome boy talking to her ever late brother. She had never seen him before but he was tall and strong looking with rugged facial features that made him look mature for his age.

"I've been looking for you for 30 minutes." Lisa tried to hide her anger. She didn't want to show her uncool frustration with her little brother to the new good looking boy. "Lisa, this is Gabriel. Gabriel this is my sister Lisa," Nathan responded.

With a sincere smile and introduction, Gabriel spoke first, "Hi Lisa, it's nice to meet you. I'm sorry your brother kept you waiting but it's my fault. I'm new here and he was just being nice. I had some questions, and he was helping me out. I didn't mean to make you wait."

Lisa really didn't hear a thing Gabriel said. She couldn't stop looking at his strong gorgeous eyes. Her mouth spoke but she wouldn't remember what she said.

"Hi. It's nice to meet you. Let's Go Nathan." She hated her response but it was too late to change it. "What are you doing tomorrow night Gabriel? You should come over for dinner. My Mom always cooks too much food and she would love to meet you." Nathan asked.

"Nathan, don't be a loser! He is not going to want to hang out with our parents for dinner," Lisa blurted out.

Hungry and alone Gabriel didn't want to look desperate but he could use a good meal and Nathan could use some cool points. He stayed confident in his response.

"Actually, I would love to come over. It would be great to meet some new people in town and I appreciate all of your help Nathan. If it's ok with you, Lisa?"

She wanted to scream. Not only was she acting like a child in front of this gorgeous guy but now he was asking her if she would let him come over. Her face was getting redder and her hands began to sweat. "Of course it's ok. Why wouldn't it be? We would love to have you over. I'll tell Mom you're coming." Lisa rambled.

"Thank you," Gabriel responded "I'll see you tomorrow." His eyes looked at hers with confidence and a twinkle of playfulness. All she could do was smile back at him too nervous to think straight.

A few more awkward smiles and the twins were on their way to the parking lot. Gabriel watched them walk off and smiled to himself. It had been a long time since he made friends at school. It had been even longer since he sat down for a family dinner. The idea covered over him like warm jacket and he felt normal for a moment. But soon the heavy gold ring in his pocket reminded him that his life was anything but normal and he quickly dropped back down to Earth. Once again, he was alone to walk back to his home and get back to his research. But Gabriel wasn't alone; he was being watched. Off in the distance, on the other side of the courtyard jealousy raged in Roger Wood's head.

Roger had watched how Lisa looked at this new kid from afar. He saw her eyes light up and sparkle as she spoke to him. Her bashful smile and longing gaze were like knives thrust into his back. She didn't look at him like that. She had never looked at him like that. Roger was the most popular kid in school and any girl would love to go out with him. He had dated most of them and the ones he had not were not worth it to him. But now, the one he had spent the better part of a year pursuing had just crushed him with a simple look at some new kid in school. Roger never lost. Roger wasn't going to lose her and Roger was going to make sure this new kid never gets close to his girl again.

Chapter 21

The sweet cigar smoke wafted up into the dark musty room from the bar below. It was an elegant room with dark stained wood walls, ornate ceiling patterns, and detailed crown molding trim. The noisy patrons enjoying their happy hour drinks below were oblivious to the room just above their heads. And for the few that might know of the second floor office room, none were aware of the sinister man that owned it.

A tap on the door and a sudden rush of smoke filled the air as the heavy oak door opened. "Excuse me sir, but I wanted to let you know that we have taken care of what you asked for," Hissed the tall thin man with pale ghostly features.

A deep raspy voice seemed to come from every angle in the room. It wasn't until the worn brown leather chair started to turn around that the Ghost knew where the sound had actually come from.

"Well done. Now we wait until our fish swims into the net."

The chair turned and made a slight squeak as its position changed. A heavy set large man stood up and sucked in a deep gulp of air that took a long time to fill his massive lungs.

"Can you feel it? After so many years, can you feel that we are this close to finding my treasure?" the large man said with excitement. The Ghost smiled his toothy grin, "Yes sir. We are close. I will find this boy Gabriel. The map will be yours soon." "I can taste it," gnarled the large man.

A phone ring pierced the conversation.

"Find him and you will be rewarded beyond your wildest dreams… now go" the large man dismissed the Ghost and turned towards the phone. Sitting back in his leather chair with a heavy thud he answered the ringing handset.

"This is Santos."

A brief pause forced Santo's to look at the phone number but it was not listed. Then the silence was broken.

"What is the status in Minnesota?" An old breathy voice came though the receiver. The man's voice sent chills down the large Santos' spine. With the recent excitement, Santos had forgotten about the task he had been given some time ago from his employer. An important mission that needed the most careful of hands had been specifically assigned to Santos and he had fallen behind on it. The recent revelations of the Gaspar Treasure had Santo's salivating for days. He had forgotten to do his job.

"Sir, I have not yet looked into Minnesota. I have had a recent discovery here in Florida that has taken my upmost attention." Santo's tried to sound confident. "I am your utmost attention," replied the old man on the phone. Santos could almost feel the warm breath through the receiver. "Forgive me Sir, I promise to give Minnesota my full attention just as soon as I can. But this is a personal favor to me and my family. I have finally, found a lead to the lost treasure of Gaspar,"

Santo's cringed in anticipation of the old man's response.

"Gaspar's Treasure? The very treasure that has eluded you and your family for 200 years? That treasure is more important than my work? Please help me understand your grave disobedience for a folk legend." The old voice was noticeably aggravated.

"It is no legend, my lord."

"Do not interrupt me. My patience is wearing thin. You are chasing a fool man's dream. What proof do you have?"

"We found Jose Gomez, sir."

A brief pause silenced the angry voice and then a reply.

"Really?" The voice on the phone suddenly took a softer tone. "What did you discover?" "Unfortunately, he refused to talk. Even to his death, he refused."

"He's dead?" The angry voice returned.

"Yes, sir. But this is why we are so close now. He gave the secret to another and we are on his heals we just need a few more days and it will be ours." Santos held his breath hoping his plea had worked.

The old man on the phone took a few seconds to ponder his response and then decided to let it play out.

"Ah my friend, of course, I understand. The lost family treasure is an attractive prey. Consider this my gift to you for your loyalty. Pursue your treasure and find glory for your family. I will take care of Minnesota and the rune stone myself. You find Gaspar's treasure and don't forget to repay your old friend with some heavy gold for my kindness. I hope to hear from you soon," the old voice faded.

"Thank you my lord, I will repay you for your generosity and look forward to serving you again soon," Santo's lied. "I know you will," the old voice clicked to silence.

Hanging up the phone, Santos' politeness turned to anger.

"How dare you treat me that way you old fool? You collect artifacts for your guilty pleasure, to be decorations in your pompous house. I have spent my life trying to right this wrong to my family and I don't need your approval to do what I must do. How dare you be so kind to allow me my quest? You may think you own me now. I may just be another cog in your machine of thieves but one day, I will have my revenge and I will take your collection as well as your life. I swear it," Santo's raged.

Chapter 22

Gabriel had spent the day at the Tampa Museum looking over some old journals and history books. It was a peaceful morning another beautiful sunny day in Florida. Gabriel was looking from his desk, in the research room on the second floor, out though the large glass window. He watched some kids circling around a fishing pole waiting for a bite. Simple pleasures he thought to himself. Boaters were cruising up and down the Harbor Island Channel as the channel's current was flowing out so some of the smaller boats were struggling to motor up the strong waters. Gabriel had to laugh at one poor man who must have been a new owner of a 20ft sailboat. The novice was working hard to sail up wind and up current instead of dropping the propeller and motoring on. However, even with the struggling lines and frustrating effort, Gabriel had to think that on a day like this even a bad day on the water was a pretty great day overall.

His research had brought him a lot of great insights about the history of Tampa but not much on the famed pirate Gaspar. The museum had wonderful displays on early native Indians and even short movies that detailed the arrival of Spanish conquistadors like De Leon and Narvaez. Their exciting stories about the search for gold and the fountain of youth kept Gabriel's attention for hours.

The miniature buildings and replica of Tampa's Ybor City historic cigar culture was also fun to read about. He had learned about the Tampa Banana Docks that were made famous for their extensive trade with Cuba and the islands in the Caribbean. Formerly trading valuable goods such as tobacco, fruit, cattle, and labor, now the docks are home to several very active cruise lines. The U.S.S. Victory, a World War II frigate, is a floating museum and could be seen from Gabriel's window as it welcomed visitors aboard its historic decks. He enjoyed his quiet research as he marveled at the city's sunny beauty.

Gabriel truly loved history because it told us so much about the present, ourselves, and where we come from. The lesson's we have learned and the lesson's we forgot. The mistakes of our fore fathers as well as their amazing achievements always seemed to inspire Gabriel. But he mostly loved history because no matter where he went or where he was history was always all around him. He just had to stop and look for it.

While looking over some Brook Brothers professional photographs, Gabriel spotted something that he had seen before. It was a beautiful black and white photo, taken in 1955, showing the Sulphur Spring water tower. The tall white medieval looking tower stood high above the tree lined River Park. Completely alone the tower seemed to stand out of place on the page of photos.

Gabriel had seen the tower a few weeks ago on his bus trip into Tampa. He had no idea what it was there for and why would a tower that seemed to belong to a story like Rapunzel would be shooting up high into the Tampa Sky.

He read about the water tower and its history in the area. He flipped through other amazing photos and articles when he came across an article from a journalist named McKay. Published in the early 1940's, the article talked about ancient Indian mounds that were discovered in the areas surrounding Tampa bay, including the Sulphur Spring area where the tower now sits. The article struck an interest with Gabriel because very little recorded history with Tampa started before the mid 1800's. As the young American nation was forming, most northern settlers avoided the wild and untamed "swamp" land of Florida. Florida had actually been in dispute and fought for over the previous 300 years by the Spanish, French, and English. Rich in other resources but lacking in gold, the land had been traded between the countries for centuries. Eventually, after the First Seminole war in 1818, Andrew Jackson had broken the back of the Native Indians and the now viable American colonies purchased Florida from Spain in the Adam's-Onis treaty of 1819.

But legend had it that Gaspar sailed the seas around Florida from the late 1700's to early 1800's and yet there is little to any historical structures or landmarks from that time in the Tampa area. Except for the mounds that Gabriel was now looking at in a drawing from D.B. McKay. A 1940 Tampa Daily Times article stated that the mounds were an accumulation of shells, sand, and bones that were piled up over hundreds of years. They were large trash piles that also doubled as burial chambers for the dead. The tallest and largest mound would usually be home to the Indian King of that area and he would build a home on top of the mound to overlook his kingdom. McKay had suggested that these mounds also served a second purpose that of an ancient calendar.

He suggested that the mounds were organized out in a pattern that would point to the cardinal directions North, South, East, and West, as well as could highlight the most important days of the year-the equinoxes. The summer and winter equinox's, where the Sun would reach its highest peak, told the natives that it would be time to harvest or plant food. The article ended without any more proof other than the writer's theory but to Gabriel it was completely plausible. He had studied other ancient cultures, and he knew the importance of calendar dates to those civilizations. The Mayans, the Incan's, the Egyptians, even the early Israelites, all had an amazing knowledge about the solar system and its importance to their survival. It made only sense that the Native Florida Indians would also contain this knowledge. And since Gabriel, was striking out on his research of Jose Gaspar, it was the only historical evidence he could find from that time.

He packed up his books and folded his notes, waved to the museum assistant and started to head home. He needed to get ready for his dinner at Nathan's house tonight. He was looking forward to a family dinner like the one's he remembered from his early childhood. He knew that there would be the uncomfortable questions about his past but that was ok. Nathan and his sister didn't seem to be judgmental and he felt comfortable with them in a way that he had rarely ever felt. The various kids that he had lived with over his past years had never felt honest and true like Nathan had to him. The foster homes, even the ones that weren't so bad, never really felt genuine. This felt genuine. Dinner with Nathan's family felt right, and he was looking forward to witnessing what he had always dreamed of having- a real family.

Chapter 23

The tour was everything Gabriel had dreamed of. The collection of family photos on every wall in the house. The photos of Lisa and Nathan for each of their birthdays were in plain view for all to see. The family vacations at the beach, the happy photos of playtime in the yard were like the images in Gabriel's head that he had dreamed of for so long. Of course there were the awkward toys still lingering in their rooms. They should have been packed up years ago for much younger twins but they had still given nostalgic pleasure to the kids. However, with the new seemingly much more mature boy now standing in their house, the toys were quite embarrassing-especially for Lisa.

There were the posters on the wall of the ever popular Bieber-mania that lined Lisa's room and the fighter jets that plastered Nathan's. There was the poor choice of bold room colors that gave the twins individuality and the pile of dirty clothes that were rapidly stuffed under their beds to give the illusion of a clean room. Everything that made normal kids- normal was there for Gabriel to see but it was the photos that Gabriel focused on and the memories that he would never have that

"I hope you don't mind my sister's messy room. All of those clothes and heaps of make-up she uses to cover up her piggy face and fat ankles," Nathan chuckled. "Shut up you loser. At least I don't still play with my 7 year old dolls," Lisa responded. "They're not dolls, they are G.I. Joes." "You dress them up and play with them, they are dolls," Lisa argued. "Uniforms and battlefields are not dressing dolls you cow," Nathan snapped.

Gabriel had heard enough and started to laugh. "Guys stop it. You sound like little babies." The siblings separated into opposite corners of the room. "Both of you sound ridiculous. The whole time I've been here you have done nothing but argue. You're both wrong."

Turning to address both of them separately, normally the siblings would roll their eyes to a scolding but for some reason Gabriel's stare commanded attention.

"Lisa you are a stunningly gorgeous girl with a beautiful face but your attitude sucks. Stop worrying about what other people think and be happy with yourself. Nathan you are not a loser. You have a remarkable mind and I expect you to do great things with your life but you lack confidence in your ability and that makes you spiteful."

The twins had never heard a kid talk like this before not even their parents used words like that.

"What are you a shrink?" Nathan joked. "No but I'm an excellent judge of character. And it pains me to see so much potential being squandered with this bickering." Gabriel answered. "You think I'm beautiful?" giggled Lisa.

"Kids, dinner is ready!" a shout came from downstairs.

"It's what brother's and sister's do to each other. It's just teasing," Nathan pleaded. "Don't make excuses," Gabriel replied with a smile. "Enjoy your family; you're blessed to have one."

The comment was fleeting but Nathan heard it and it struck a chord with him. He remembered Gabriel's introduction to history class and his soldier Father who was killed. He wanted to ask about Gabriel's Mother but before he could ask, the kids raced down the stairs towards the savory smell of lasagna.

"He thinks I'm beautiful," Lisa kept thinking to herself. The thought made her body feel warm all over. She was so lost in thought she ran right into her Father.

Lisa and Nathan's parents were pretty much what Gabriel expected. Mid to late 40's, well dressed, and both full of smiles and courtesy. Gabriel could tell that Lisa got her looks from her Mother. Mrs. Gale was an attractive woman who moved about the house with ease and grace. Mr. Gale was a little rough around the edges. He tried to fit into the corporate world with the shirt and tie from his work but he wore it with the disdain of a man who would rather be working with his hands. A very muscular man he must have been a great athlete in school Gabriel thought. Nathan got his height and size from his Father but missed out on the confidence.

Dinner got off to an awkward start when Gabriel paused to bow his head and pray. The Gale's took notice and felt like they should join in but it was so far removed from their standard practice that they didn't know how to do it. So they just smiled and waited. The awkwardness continued when the questions started.

"So Gabriel what do your parents do?" Mrs. Gale chimed in.

Gabriel had a lot of different answers for this one. It just depended on the situation but he didn't want to lie to these nice people. So he decided to tell them the truth. He tried to smile and put on a happy face. He didn't want to ruin their nice dinner.

"Well unfortunately my Father was killed in Iraq. He was in the Marines and died around 2005. Not exactly sure when. His body was never found." "I'm so sorry, I didn't know." Mrs. Gale tried to deflect the awkward moment. "You must have a remarkable Mother to raise such a strong boy. What does she do?"

Gabriel smiled and paused. No way around it now, so he took a deep breath and tried to just get thru it.

"Actually Ma'am my Mother left me soon after my Dad died. I bounced around from foster home to foster home for about 6 years. Some were violent, some weren't so bad. My last home was so bad however, that I was finally able to gain my independence and I've been living on my own for the last year," Gabriel thought it was better to just get through it- just rip the Band-Aid off.

"It hasn't been easy but thank you for your kind words. They must have done something right. There were some good times early on as a child and those memories keep me going." Gabriel returned to his meal.

Mrs. Gale began to tear up as she stared at Gabriel and then to her children. The twins looked to their parents for a response not knowing what to say. But it was the Father, Mr. Gale that spoke first.

"Your Father was a true hero you should be very proud of him." Gabriel smiled and nodded in agreement. Lisa spoke up she just had to ask. "So where do you live?"

Gabriel was still living at the YMCA but he had put a small deposit on an apartment yesterday so one little white lie couldn't hurt.

"I actually have an apartment down on Cypress. It's not much but it's mine." Gabriel continued, "I got a job at a restaurant down by the marina. It doesn't pay much but we split the tips and I can cover my rent."

"I'm impressed, a job and a place at your age. I can't get these two to clean their rooms." Mr. Gale tried to make it lighter. "Dad, Gabriel is a whiz at history you should ask him a question." Nathan spoke up trying to change the awkward tension that was now in the room. "Really, that's great. Why are you so interested in history?" Mr. Gale responded.

"It started at an early age I guess. My Father used to read to me about great historical battles and famous warriors. Tales of the Spartans at Thermopylae and Great American Revolutionaries were my bedtime stories. When he left for the last time he gave me his Marine Corps Service Manual, a U.S. History book, and his Bible. He told me that all of life's problems could be solved in those books so I just read them constantly. I didn't really have any friends growing up but I could always find a good book and live through a great story." Gabriel finished. "History just seemed to stick with me."

Mrs. Gale couldn't take it anymore. Her emotions were starting to overflow, and she asked to be excused from the table. She wasn't yet out of earshot, just in the other room, when the tears started and her sobs were heard by the others. A quick reassurance from Mr. Gale kept his children from chasing after her but Gabriel felt he needed to tell her something.

Gabriel said "excuse me" and stood up from the table to pursue Mrs. Gale.

She was standing in the kitchen with her arms crossed staring out into the back yard. Her face was red and swollen. She had tried to wipe her tears away but it just made her makeup streak down her face. The tears were still there. Gabriel approached her cautiously.

"I hope I didn't upset you. I didn't mean to ruin dinner. It's excellent. Thank you by the way." She turned to look at his innocent brave eyes. Her mouth began to quiver.

"It's not your fault. You didn't do anything wrong." She started to turn back to the window but then suddenly reached out and grabbed him into her arms. Hugging him with her whole body she sobbed into his wide broad shoulder.

"This isn't your fault baby… You did nothing wrong."

Gabriel's first reaction was to free himself and push her away but he stopped and let her hold him. After a moment he began to hold her back and suddenly his eyes started to tear up as well. For the first time in as long as he could remember, Gabriel began to cry. Not tears of fear, or anger, not tears of sadness, or loneliness but finally tears of joy.

The Father he lost the Mother that left him the countless years of loneliness seemed to pour out of him all at once like an eruption of sadness escaping from his heart. A smile spread across his face as he finally, after so many years, began to feel love pouring back into his soul. He held her tight, like a child does to a parent's leg. But this was not his family, she was not his mother. However, her compassion and warmth made Gabriel feel close to her and he just wanted to hold on to her as long as he could.

Mrs. Gale just kept repeating: "This is not your fault. This is not your fault."

Chapter 24

That night had been the best night of sleep Gabriel had felt in years. He didn't realize just how much emotion he had built up since his world came crashing down with the loss of his parents years ago. He had always put on a brave face but there was something about being with a family that brought out a deep sense of loss in him. A dream to be normal, like the other kids who just seemed to take it all for granted. A warm safe place to call home and someone that would always be there for him. Gabriel had always wanted those things but never felt they would be a reality until last night when the loving embrace of Nathan's Mom crashed in on him like a tidal wave. The rest of the dinner went on without a hitch and the late school night was capped off with a Buccaneer's win over the Carolina Panthers. Gabriel found a mutual fan of the pewter pirates in Mr. Gale who had rooted for the team since their founding in 1975. With a good win and a long good-bye, Gabriel said "thank you," and made his way back to his cold empty apartment. But the small apartment didn't seem to be so cold or empty anymore. Left over lasagna filled his refrigerator and memories of laughter with a kind family filled his heart.

The school day came early, and it seemed to drag on forever. Gabriel sat on the edge of his seat waiting for the class bell to ring. Before the last chime sounded he was off his seat and out the door. Walking past the grey lockers covering the hallway wall, he barely could move past the mass of kids darting back and forth in front of him. As they laughed and yelled for each other to talk about the most recent class gossip or other pressing issues, Gabriel stayed focused on the door at the far end of the hall.

It was a non-descript metal door with a narrow window on the upper right side just above the handle. The pale yellow color blended the door with every other door in the entire school but this one was different. This one was the entrance to Gabriel's sanctuary from the dullness of the classroom and the chaos of the hallways. It was the door to the Library.

Logging on to the library computer, Gabriel quickly selected several books and then returned to his seat. Just as he was starting to lose himself in the second chapter of his first book, Nathan raced up behind him.

"How's it going?" Nathan always spoke loudly.

A little startled Gabriel responded, "Good, I got some books on Jose Gaspar and I'm pursuing your lead. Still have my doubts but I've got nothing to lose at this point."

"Tell me what you know and I'll help you look thru some of these other books," Nathan offered. Gabriel was resistant. "I don't know. I don't have much and I'm a little uneasy getting you involved in this. My friend warned me about some possible dangers and I don't want you taking any risks," Gabriel replied.

"Don't be crazy. I'm just reading some books on a mythical pirate from my home town of Tampa.

Besides, Gasparilla is like a week away." "Gasparilla?" Gabriel questioned.

"Yeah it's a big parade that celebrates your boy Jose Gaspar's invasion into Tampa Bay. Every year the city lines up on Bayshore Drive, gets dressed up like pirates, toss beads, and drink a lot of alcohol. It's a great party."

"I've never heard of it." Gabriel stated. "But I still don't think you should get involved. The man that gave me this information, I believe was murdered by some people from his past. And they want what I have. I don't want you or your family in any danger."

"Gabriel, I can't imagine the life you have lived. I know you're used to doing things on your own but I've had tough times too you know. I'm always second best to my perfect sister. Why can't you be more like her? She has so many friends and you…" Nathan paused. "I don't have many friends and I would really like to help you."

Gabriel thought hard for a moment. He weighed all the possibilities of something going wrong but he could sense something in Nathan's voice. Physical pain definitely hurt, this Gabriel knew too well, but emotional pain was always much worse. Emotional pain sticks with you long after the bruises of physical pain are gone. Nathan needed to be a part of something, plus Gabriel could use the help.

"Ok, but you do as I say and if I tell you to stop you listen. Ok?" Gabriel demanded. "Great thanks." Nathan smiled as he flipped open a book from Gabriel's table.

The two friends spent the next hour scouring over numerous history books. However, between the warmth of the carpeted cubicle and the silence in the room, Nathan's eyes began to grow heavy so he needed to talk to wake himself up. "Where did you get the phrase captured princess from?" "It was in a letter I was given from my old friend. He referenced her when he told me about the mystery."

Barely listening to his friend, Nathan in his semi-delirious state sarcastically spotted a word that he thought would be funny.

"Hey did you know Itimpi was the Tocobagan Indian word for 'near it?' I'm sure I'll use that someday. You never know when you need to speak Tocobagan to someone." Nathan joked to Gabriel but Gabriel didn't seem to get it. His response was too serious to be going along with it.

"I read that too. Historians disagree with how Tampa got its name. Some say Itimpi was just a misspoken translation about a nearby village and became the name others say it was Tanpa which means 'fire sticks' the name the Calusa tribe gave this area."

"I'm going with Tanpa that sounds more like it." Nathan gave up on his attempted joke.

"Yes but that's a Calusa Indian word and the Calusa's lived south of Tampa Bay. It was the Tocobagans that lived in the Tampa area. Why wouldn't they have named it?"

Nathan looked at Gabriel, who still had not lifted his head up from what he was reading, and had to laugh at his seriousness. What was supposed to be a joke went over like a lead balloon and Nathan had to chuckle at

Gabriel. This kid was intense he thought to himself as he returned to his own reading. Suddenly, Nathan spotted something.

"Here it is, Isla de Muerta. That is what you said right?" Nathan asked.

Gabriel took the book and scanned down rapidly to the line.

"The anchorage of Gaspar's crew was believed to be called the Isla de Muerta near a protected harbor off the Florida west coast but the location was never revealed." Gabriel read out loud. "What does Isla de Muerta mean?" Nathan asked. "Island of death," responded Gabriel without hesitation.

A little surprised Nathan turned to Gabriel. "You speak Spanish?"

"I speak Spanish, French, Italian and some basic German. My Cantonese is shaky but I can read it ok." Gabriel didn't look up to see Nathan's mouth drop in astonishment.

Pulling a folded piece of paper from his pocket, Gabriel spread it out on his table. The paper's scribble marks and erased lines made it look like some sort of homemade crossword puzzle. But the bottom line had the letters that spelled out, Isla de Muerta.

"What is that?" asked Nathan. "It was a code. It took me awhile to figure it out, but it's actually quite simple. It was just a basic Caesar's shift. I arranged the letters and came up with Isla de Muerta." Gabriel began writing the book's passage down on the worn paper.

"But where did the letters come from?" Nathan asked.

Gabriel paused trying to decide if he should answer.

"It was from a ring, a gold ring that was given to me by my old friend. It had some other letters and engravings on it. But this was the only thing that I had deciphered so far." Gabriel answered. "Can I see it?" Nathan quickly responded.

"No... Not yet" Gabriel wanted to show him but not now. Nathan was disappointed but understood that Gabriel was not one to trust easily. Looking over Gabriel's right shoulder, Nathan noticed the little old library lady getting up from her seat.

"Don't look now but your old friend Mr. Orsos is taking his shift as the librarian now." Nathan stated.

It was recommended that each teacher volunteer for shifts at the library. Hardly any of them ever chose to do it. But given the fact that he was a history teacher, Bill Orsos felt obligated to volunteer for most of the shifts that were not filled. Unfortunately for him, that meant that Bill Orsos would spend most of his free time in a place that he despised.

Now walking towards the two boys, Mr. Orsos was anxious to see what they were doing. The boys quickly started packing up their things. "What are you two doing?" Mr. Orsos asked. "Nothing sir, we were just leaving," Nathan answered. "Mr. Fletcher right?" Mr. Orsos asked.

Gabriel nodded.

"I enjoyed our class discussion the other day. I think we will have an exciting year together. I hope you're more willing to listen next time then to just shout out sound bites." Gabriel wanted to fire back at the ignorant teacher but this was not the time or place. He swallowed his pride and just smiled it off.

"I'll look forward to your class next week sir. Thank you, but I have to go now." Gabriel smiled and moved passed the teacher.

The boys started to walk away when Nathan whispered over to Gabriel.

"Gaspar would have taken him to Isla de Muerta," Nathan joked. Gabriel shot him a quick glance and hushed him with a "Shhh."

Mr. Orsos watched the boys leave and then with his ever nosey personality walked over to the library computer. Easily deleting a search from a young girl who had just entered the library and an earlier boy who was looking for a book on magic spells, Mr. Orsos came across a series of searches with the tags of:

"Gaspar, Gasparilla, Floriblanca, Florida Pirates, Florida Treasure, and Isla de Muerta."

"Well, well, well, what are you up to Mr. Fletcher? Could you be the one they want? I guess it's time I make a visit to my new very wealthy friends." Mr. Orsos grinned as he quietly spoke to himself and began keying in the phone number that a strange, thin, pale man had recently given him.

Chapter 25

The following day was Saturday and Gabriel loved to get up early on the weekends and explore. Walking along the concrete boardwalk of the Hillsborough River in the downtown area, Gabriel gazed across the rapid flowing river waters. He admired the beautiful old drawbridge that stood at attention like a centurion guarding the river banks. With its countless graffiti painted names of all the college crew teams that scuttle down the river during the winter training months, the bridge is not just a historical landmark but a social one as well.

Down along the riverfront past the giant colorful Children's Museum building, Gabriel breathed in the dry air and smiled up to the bright sun on his face. It was an early Saturday morning and Gabriel had just finished his usual weekend run- five miles with some pushups and sit-ups to break up the monotony about every 1/2 mile or so. It gave him time to clear his head and make his body ache in a good way. Working out had always been an escape for Gabriel. Sometimes in his life when everything was racing out of control the one thing that he could take command of was his body and he treated it with discipline and respectful punishment. Today was his light day; his usual weekday routine was much more intense.

Cooling down as he continued to walk along the river walk, Gabriel smiled at the children playing in the grassy plaza. He watched the frolicking dogs that insisted on sniffing and simultaneously barking at every other dog around. Continuing south to the outdoor auditorium, he took a moment to stretch out his tight legs on the cement steps. It was an open seating area that gave him a great look at the beautiful old H.B. Plant Hotel that is now the University of Tampa's main building.

Built in 1891 by Henry Bradley Plant, a railroad magnate that wanted to make Florida the next great tourist destination, the hotel still stands as a magnificent architectural piece of art. The Moorish revival style building features sweeping red brick arches, 6 stainless steel onion-shaped minarets, and 3 domes spread over 6 acres of land. The interior rooms and hallways were covered with Plant's personal collections of artifacts he and his wife had purchased from all over the world. With a railroad at its front door, the hotel brought some of the world's most wealthy and influential people south to the land of the lost known as Florida.

Some of those famous attendees were the future Prime Minister of England Winston Churchill and the 20th President of the United States Teddy Roosevelt. Roosevelt had stayed there with his Rough Riders to stage the invasion of Cuba during the Spanish American War. The Hotel also watched another famous President pass by its gaze as John F. Kennedy did in 1963. Visiting Tampa, the young President's motorcade, the longest domestic motorcade of his presidency, passed along Grand Central Avenue in front of the Plant Hotel.

As he reached out to a jubilant crowd of Tampa fans it would be only four days later in another motorcade where the President would tragically die in Dallas, Texas. A memorial statue stands on the Hotel Campus grounds facing the old Grand Central Avenue whose name was later unanimously changed to Kennedy Boulevard.

Gabriel turned East down Kennedy Boulevard and began to make his way through the downtown high rises. Relatively quiet on the weekends, most employees that work downtown live in the suburbs of Tampa, which leaves the normally hectic sidewalks practically empty. Gabriel felt an urge to travel a different route then he had last time he was here. He always had an ever curious mind. He loved looking for new places and enjoyed travelling into areas that he had never seen before. He usually followed those urges and was always happy when he found something new that he had never known was there.

It wasn't long, just a few blocks past the waterfront hotel and tall bank buildings, that he noticed a large square brass marker on the side of the street. Gabriel had seen several of them over the last few weeks and knew exactly what it was once he saw it. Checking for oncoming traffic, he crossed over two street lanes and hopped up on to the sidewalk. He began to read the green tinted metal plaque before eventually stopping a few feet from its base.

Gabriel stood silently and began to read from the plaque: "Near this site… once stood a large temple mound dating before the time of Christ… 50 feet high… top decorated with temples and residences of Indian chiefs. The Fort Brook Soldiers, in the 1840's, used a tall Gumbo Limbo tree growing on the crest of the city-block long mound as a lookout post."

Interested by this new find, he then proceeded to look around at the surrounding area. Covered in concrete and gravel with a few scattered trees sticking out of the sidewalks, Gabriel tried to image the tall shell mound that once stood in this very spot. Was the great Gumbo tree there where the multi-level parking garage now stands? Or perhaps that empty lot over there? He continued to wonder. The plaque talked about the Indian Mound that was replaced by the Military Fort. Most likely it would have been closer to the water, Gabriel suspected as he walked around the large square parking garage to see to what proximity it was to the river. The Fort most likely would have stood at the mouth of the river so Gabriel continued across the street to the Large Convention Center. He couldn't be certain about the locations but he could almost feel the past surrounding him as he walked slowly along the concrete walkways.

Closing his eyes and standing in the sunshine at the great steps of the Convention Center, Gabriel imagined the smells and tastes of the early 19th century. Campfire smoke and the smell of searing beef enveloped him. The taste of baked beans and cornbread wet his tongue. He could hear the horses that were penned up in the village and the sound of chopping axes that were milling some needed wood. The scent of black gunpowder filled his nostrils as he imagined the soldiers practicing their aim on the target range. But then his mind slipped back even further.

He imagined a simpler time when there were no wooden buildings or split rail fences. More native and untouched, the wagon trails were replaced by small footpaths in and out of the dense forest. Animals scurried under the bushes as Gabriel imagined himself walking along the dirt trail. The land was dense with trees and shrubs but one large tree seemed to stand high above the others. The Gumbo Limbo tree with its peeling reddish bark seemed to erupt from the large sandy mound high above the palms and saw grasses. The large mound, that was the center point of their culture, was now teeming with native Indians alive and vibrant in Gabriel's mind.

Kids were racing each other and playing in the sun. Women with their long black hair were working on preparing the food and gathering supplies for their families. The men with their strong tanned and tattooed bodies pulled hard on their nets that were heavy with fish from the river. Several older men stood on the outside edges of the nets with their spears and bow and arrows quickly snagging any fish that managed to get away from the enclosing trap. Smiling and cheering loudly they brought in their great haul of fish. They waved and shouted out to their Cacique or King as they thanked him for this great blessing of food. The smell of smoked fish and venison filled his nostrils as his mind continued to wonder. Gabriel imagined the King as a large man, much bigger than the others, but with a gentle and pleasant smile as he waved back to his people. The King was standing high on top of the mound that had become his home and in fact the village temple. Shaded by the large

Gumbo Tree, it was a perfect location for the warrior King to see all around and far beyond his kingdom.

Gabriel enjoyed tranquil moments like that, he always had, but this one felt special for some reason. Something deep inside his mind was searching for an answer and Gabriel had a feeling that it was close, very close, but it wasn't ready to be told just yet.

A sudden short "honk" from a blue Ford sedan, woke Gabriel out of his daydream. The Sedan was trying to turn around in the parking lot and the strange boy standing alone in the center of it was in its way. With a quick smile and wave of acknowledgment, Gabriel jogged to the side of the lot but suddenly stopped frozen in his tracks. Across the river bank from the convention center parking lot, Gabriel could barely believe what he was looking at. He put his hands up to block the bright sun from his eyes because he must be seeing things but he wasn't. Plain as day and big as life no more than a few hundred yards away on the opposite river bank was the unmistakable tall square masts and long keel of a… giant pirate ship.

Chapter 26

The swim would have been quicker but Gabriel decided to run back across the bridge to get to the other river bank. Under the convention center, down Channelside Drive and across the Platt Street Bridge, Gabriel was moving at a fast pace. At the top of the bridge he spotted the distinctive Jannus Memorial Park, with its historical marker of the world's first commercial airline flight, on the east bank in front of him.

Normally, Gabriel would have stopped to read the plaque affixed to such a neat looking memorial. But he had seen the monument in a magazine on Tampa aviation during his bus ride from Jacksonville and already knew its tale. Hard to miss, situated on the Hillsborough River banks in the downtown area, the monument was nearly ten feet tall. Carved of stone, the memorial was pilot wing emblem with a metal propeller in its center protruding straight up in the air. It was a fitting memorial to the bravery and courage of pioneering aviator Tony Jannus and his paying passenger Abrem Pheil who, with a winning bid of $400, made that inaugural flight. The memorial marked his landing spot of the historic first scheduled commercial flight in the world. The flight from St. Petersburg to Tampa took about 23 minutes in the Benoist XIV "air boat" as it crossed the bay. But that quick flight, on January 1st 1914, was the beginning of modern commercial aviation.

Turning left and heading south from the Platt Bridge Gabriel slowed his pace and fixed his eyes on the tall ship. The long black iron hull stretched over 160ft along Bayshore Drive. It had a striking white stripe that was painted down the entire length and completely wrapped around the bow and keel.

As Gabriel moved closer to the ship the shadows cast by the tall masts, each over 100 feet above the deck, stretched clear across the street behind him and on to the sidewalk over 50 yards away. At the stern of the ship, Gabriel looked at the elegant gold gilded scroll work along the quarter deck railings. Just below the railings were colorful multi colored glass panels that enclosed what would be the captain's cabin. As Gabriel looked closer to the colorful glass squares on the stern, he noticed the golden scrollwork seemed to come together between two whales facing each other. In between the opposing large sea mammals the scroll work seemed to be forming letters, perhaps the ship's name. Gabriel focused in on the swirling letters and suddenly the air burst into his lungs as he gasped at the reading. The ship was called the "Jose Gasparilla"

Now running back along the length of the ship towards the bow Gabriel saw the name painted on its hull again. "Jose Gasparilla." He looked at the bow of the ship and its beautiful golden mermaid figurehead just below the bowsprit.

Figureheads on vessels date back to the Egyptians who would use carvings of holy birds on their ships for protection. The Vikings would often use the image of dragons and monsters to strike fear into their enemies. The Romans would use centurions to symbolize valor and bravery in battle. Birds were often used to imply mobility for early European ships and even America's Tall Ship, the U.S. Coast Guard Cutter Eagle, has a golden eagle under its bowsprit to symbolize America's freedom and strength. For many years, this form of ship identification was used because most early sailors could not read and these characters allowed them to identify not just other ships but their own as well. For even more early superstitious sailors, women on ships were considered to be bad luck and therefore usually not often welcomed aboard, ironically however a naked woman figurehead was believed to be able to calm the sea storms and pacify the sea gods. Because of this long held historic superstition, mermaids are a very common figurehead on sailing vessels and this tall pirate ship was no exception.

Stepping back away from the ship trying to take in what he had just found in broad daylight, Gabriel thought to himself-what is a pirate ship doing in downtown Tampa? Then out of the corner of his eye his heart skipped a beat when he saw a beloved favorite of his- another marker. Gabriel loved reading historical and descriptive markers, he always had. This ever inquisitive nature had opened him up to a life of knowledge and he could never pass one up. This maker was tall about 8 feet off the ground and the pole was capped with a wood carved scroll with the name Jose Gasparilla engraved into it in bold letters. His eyes raced to finish the reading to appease his whirling imagination.

"This vessel named for Jose Gaspar a gentleman Lieutenant of the Royal Spanish Navy, who achieved great fame as a pirate headquartered on Florida's Gulf Coast. As leader of a mutinous uprising, Lt. Gaspar seized command of the Spanish war-sloop Floriblanca in 1783. Known as 'Gasparilla', he captured and destroyed thirty-six or more ships in twelve years of piracy; a career ended with an attack upon a U.S. Navy warship disguised as a merchantman. He was drowned when he leaped into the sea to avoid capture."

The marker went on to talk about how the ship was owned by the Ye Mystic Krewe, an affluent social group in the Tampa area. They had hosted the Gasparilla parade thru the streets of Tampa since 1904. The parade Nathan was referring to the other day. This ship, the Jose Gasparilla, was the main attraction as it brought marauding pirates and scores of their beads and coins to adoring spectators. They would capture the city mayor and steal his key in order to take over the city for a day. This was the second ship of its kind used for the parade. The original was decommissioned in 1951 because it was no longer seaworthy but this ship, the Jose Gasparilla II, was commissioned in 1954 and it is the only commissioned specific pirate ship afloat in the world today.

Gabriel didn't know what to think. Was this just a tourist attraction? Or was there something more here? If the legend is not real, why would such great lengths be taken to keep it alive for over 100 years? An entire city, millions of spectators cheering and routing for a fake pirate that never existed, it doesn't make sense. The ring, the warning, the clues, obviously his old friend believed it. He believed it so much that he passed its secrets on to Gabriel. Secrets, Gabriel thought, that may have cost him his life. Not to mention the men that may be responsible like the ghost who tried to follow Gabriel just a few weeks ago. Real or not? Gabriel was dealing with people who believed. And they are willing to do anything to find the treasure. Gabriel knew he was holding the key to that treasure and even if he didn't quite believe it yet- he knew he had better start believing or he might meet his old friend sooner than he wants.

Chapter 27

The Hula Bay was a popular bar and grill during the weekdays but Saturday nights were by far the most hectic. Situated on wooden posts buried deep into the crushed shell covered bay floor, the deck of the Hula reached out over local marina waters of the bay. Dozens of boat slips were filled with gorgeous yachts of all sizes and shapes of big. Sun seekers coming in from the long day of fishing and other weekend activities were looking to share some good food and cold drinks. Lunch was always a little hectic but happy hour was a chaotic blur.

The Hula Bay sits on the Eastside of Old Tampa Bay just south of the Gandy Bridge. The view is relaxing and casual while the sunsets can be breathtaking. The who's who of Tampa drive up in fancy exotic car- Jaguars, Mercedes, the occasional Ferrari but the real money arrives in the private yachts.

Gorgeous white hulled sea yachts with perfectly scrubbed teak decks line the floating berths. Shiny chrome and polished brass gleam in the setting sunlight while ship crews hustle to tie off and coil lines once the thunderous motors finally stop churning up the bay bottom. White linen pants with silk Bahamas shirts are the fashion of choice for men and for the lady's flowing sundresses with sparkling sandals are common place. For Gabriel Fletcher it was a steam soaked t-shirt and coveralls that reeked of lobster butter. His blue jeans were stained from every possible food substance that had come in contact with his body while the wet denim clung tightly to his legs.

His sneakers hydroplaned across the slick concrete floor with just the bare minimum of surface traction keeping him from slipping flat on his back. The normally cool outside was colder than normal even for this late January evening but the grill's kitchen, like always, was every bit as hot and humid as an August summer day.

"Gabriel, take five," a welcomed shout came from the stewarding supervisor.

The dry cool breeze was like an ice bath on Gabriel's soaking body. His hot soaked shirt quickly turned cold on his sweaty skin but it felt great to his overheated body. Most of the stewards turned left towards the parking lot smoking section but Gabriel preferred the fresh salt air of the marina.

Looking up at the platform deck, Gabriel watched the restaurant patrons eating their meals and laughing off the hard week. A young couple sat at their table trying to settle their children down in order to not let the screaming ruin their one nice evening out from the house. The single people sat by the bar and tried to not be single anymore with pick-up lines and generous gestures. An old man sat by himself at a table he had sat at a few years ago when he came with his wife on their anniversary. But two years later and a lost battle with cancer, the man now sits alone with just the good times to keep him company. Gabriel watched the man for a little time and could sense his loss. It was the eyes that always told truth about loss. The distant stares that no smile could hide. It was a loss that Gabriel himself had lived with for years. No matter how hard he tried to move on and cover it up, the loss of his parents was always on his mind just behind his eyes. Suddenly a shout came from down the boardwalk.

"Hey Gabriel, what are you doing?" Nathan bounded down the wooden pier. "Hi Nathan, what brings you here?" Gabriel responded. "I'm here with the family. Actually, I knew you were working tonight and begged my Mom to come here for dinner. I wanted to talk to you about something I found out about Gasparilla."

Nathan was breathless with excitement and wouldn't let Gabriel say another word.

"Juan Gomez was on the Floriblanca!" Gabriel listened with interest but already knew what Nathan was going to say. "I found an article written about a guy named Juan Gomez who was on the ship and lived down on Panther Key just south of here near Charlotte Harbor. He lived to be like a 110 years old." Nathan continued. "He used to talk about Gaspar's treasure and how he had seen it first hand as a cabin boy on the Floriblanca. Do you know what that means?"

Nathan waited for an answer. Gabriel didn't respond. "The story is true!" Nathan exclaimed. He was a little surprised at Gabriel's lack of enthusiasm. "Did you hear me?" Nathan asked. "I did and I appreciate your enthusiasm but what does that tell you?" Gabriel replied.

Nathan paused a moment to answer but then gave up, "I don't know but they talk about the treasure being buried up the Peace River. It was split up into six different treasure chests and…" Gabriel cut him off.

"You're right Nathan. That is what the legend says but there is more to it. That information is what a lot of people know. Juan Gomez lived through three wars and one day was found floating dead near his fishing boat taking the treasure's whereabouts with him. I believe there is some truth to that legend but there are pieces missing that must be added."

Gabriel was about to tell Nathan about the ring and the message on it and how seeing the great pirate ship yesterday had sealed his commitment to focus exclusively on Gaspar further when he noticed Roger Woods walking down the pier towards him. Lisa was at his side and looked beautiful in a floral dress that was now pressing hard against her athletic body from the brisk sea breeze.

"Did he come with you?" Gabriel asked. "No." Nathan snapped. "He heard we were coming to dinner and like a tick he latched on to my sister and asked if he could come. I promise you, he's the last person I wanted to come with us."

"What's up Gabriel?" Roger asked smugly. "How do you know me?" Gabriel responded. "Are you kidding after your class with Mr. Orsos? You're the talk of school." Roger stated. "I think it's pretty cool what you did to Orsos that jerk of a teacher. I would have done something like that too if I had him for class this year but I'm glad someone finally shut that guy up."

"Well I was just pointing out where he was wrong. I didn't mean to shut him up." Gabriel responded. "Yeah well no teacher would dare talk to me like that or I would have put him in his place too." Roger said with brashness. "Those who exalt themselves will be humbled and those that humble themselves will be exalted-Mathew 23:12." Gabriel quoted but Roger was too arrogant to get the point. "I welcome truthful debates in class, honest questioning, and accountability, are the only ways to learn," Gabriel continued.

"Everyone was wondering who the new guy is." "And I told them your name," Lisa jumped in enthusiastically.

"That's right. Word in school is you're the new guy that people want to get to know." Roger continued. "I was wondering if you wanted to come to my party tomorrow night. All the cool kids are going to be there and it's going to get crazy."

Gabriel paused to be polite but his answer was already made. With a large smile on his face, he responded. "Thank you very much but I really can't. I have some things I need to take care of." Lisa jumped in "Oh you must come! It will be great! You'll get to meet all of my friends and some really nice kids."

"Yeah you should go Gabriel. I would." Nathan spoke up.

Roger snapped a look at Nathan and his nice demeanor suddenly changed in an instant. It was a flash of a look that most people would probably not notice. But Gabriel saw it and Nathan felt it.

Gabriel watched Nathan recoil back from Roger's glare and he could see the years of intimidation on Nathan's face. He turned back towards Roger and the smug look on his face, Gabriel had never felt accepted or part of the "in" crowd and that was ok with him but it didn't sit well with him when others were made to feel inferior.

"I was planning on hanging out with Nathan here tomorrow night. We were going to see some old teammates and cheerleader friends from my old school but I'll come if he can go." Gabriel turned to see Nathan's smile sweep across the shy boy's face.

"That would be great!" Lisa exclaimed before Roger could answer. Her heart was pounding in her chest as she gazed at Gabriel's piercing blue eyes. Even in the popular arms of the senior captain next to her, Lisa was excited by the opportunity to have a few more moments with Gabriel. A party with friends would be a great opportunity to get to know the handsome new boy. Roger was not happy but had to give in to Lisa's enthusiasm.

"I guess that would be ok." Roger answered and then turned towards Nathan. "But don't you embarrass me you little twerp." "Roger, please leave him alone." Lisa pleaded. Roger didn't like being told what to do, even if it was Lisa, but he chose to bite his tongue-this time.

Gabriel broke the tension, "Great! Then I'll see you all tomorrow night. I'm sorry but I have to get back to work. My break is over. I really appreciate it Roger thanks. Nathan I'll meet up with you tomorrow before the party."

With a gracious nod Gabriel gave one more stare at Roger as he walked past the arrogant boy. Gabriel had known kids like Roger all of his life. They prey on the weak to make themselves feel strong. Gabriel couldn't stand kids like that but this wasn't the time or place to say anything. He decided to walk it off and go back to work. There would be another time to put Roger in his place. With kids like that they would eventually get what they deserve and Gabriel was very patient.

Chapter 28

The next evening was a cold winter night. The moon was clear and bright and the air was dry but calm. It was a perfect night for a high school house party even if that house was full of upper grade kids and you were the least cool kid in school. But Nathan was still excited to be going and didn't care if he didn't fit in.

Lisa was pumped to have her Mom's car for the night, not so much to have her brother take control of the radio but that was the small cost for her independence. She could barely contain herself. Her excitement grew even more when the white Toyota Camry pulled into the small apartment complex on Cypress Ave. She couldn't tell what was more thrilling, going to the biggest party of the year in her own car or picking up the handsome new student she had just recently been smitten with. There was just something about Gabriel that she couldn't grasp but it was exciting… he was exciting.

The apartment was a small rundown building with no street lights anywhere. A dark canopy of oak trees covered the already gloomy parking lot but the Spanish moss hanging from the trees gave the whole scene a very spooky feel. This was definitely one place she would not tell her Mom that she had been too tomorrow at breakfast.

Gabriel walked out of the second floor and bounced down the rickety stair case that looked like it would collapse at any moment. Even with the frightening backdrop, Gabriel just seemed to glow with confidence. He walked towards them without a care or fear in the world. He was wearing a simple black t-shirt with a worn in pair of jeans. Not the brand name labels Lisa was used to but he made it look like a million bucks. She just thought he was gorgeous.

"Hey guys," his smile brightened their fearful faces. "You live here?" Nathan asked with questionable concern. "Yeah, right there in room 203. I'd invite you up but we're late and I have no furniture to sit on anyways."

The car sped out of the parking lot faster than it should have and was on its way to the party. It was only about a 10 minute car ride but it just as well could have been a world away. The mansions that lined the streets were the biggest Gabriel had ever seen. His entire apartment could fit in most of the garages and there would still be room for their Mercedes.

The houses on Bayshore Drive overlook the water on Tampa Bay and they were some of the most expensive properties in the Sunshine State. Amongst them all, Roger Wood's home was perhaps the biggest.

The party was already spilling out on to the sidewalk and down a side street that bordered Roger's property. Kids could be seen all over the yard and the music was heard from several blocks away, not uncommon for a Sunday night on Bayshore during football season especially when the Tampa Bay Buccaneers were playing. Most of the kids grouped around the back pool area but there were so many that everywhere you looked you could see someone.

"You made it!" a familiarly annoying voice spoke out from the front door. "I'm glad you came." Roger continued. "Lisa you look amazing!"

Roger was wearing a fitted purple shirt and tight jeans that showed off his muscular physique. He was a large young man who spent a lot of time in the gym and he wasn't afraid to show off his hard work. With each arm movement the sleeves on his Polo shirt seemed to constrict his ever flexing muscles. Standing up straight and puffing his chest out, Roger took a strong stance tensing every fiber in his body as Lisa walked towards him with her brother and Gabriel just a few steps behind.

"Thank you Roger." Lisa acknowledged.

Taking her hand Roger guided her into the doorway. He made a little room for Gabriel but completely cut off Nathan forcing him to stop and wait for the path to clear before he could enter.

"You have a great place Roger." Gabriel offered.
"Thanks, my folks do well but I could use a little more space. Maybe when they give it to me I'll knock out a few walls and add some more rooms to make it a little more comfortable," Roger answered but never looked back at Gabriel.

Before Gabriel could reply Roger was off with Lisa in his tow and disappeared in the crowd. "What a jerk." Nathan stated. "Can you believe how spoiled this guy is and now he just runs off with my sister? Man I hope he keeps his hands off of her I can't stand him."
"Lisa's a smart girl I'm sure she can take care of herself." Gabriel replied.

"You don't know her at all do you? That's the same girl that dropped two classes just so she could have 8th period off to change her hair and clothes so she could watch the boy's lacrosse team practice. She is boy crazy, and she has her eyes set on the biggest jerk of them all, Roger Woods."

"Come on I'll grab some food. We need to talk." Gabriel said.

After a few moments waiting for the line to clear at the kitchen, Gabriel grabbed some chips and two sodas. He bypassed the massive amount of liquor bottles that covered the table and settled for two luke warm Coke cans. The boys found a quiet table outside the pool area and away from the party noise. Settling into a few sips of his drink and a bite of his chips, Gabriel cleared his head and began to focus on his treasure quest.

"Ok you're right about Juan Gomez. He is connected to the legend. I'm not sure how but I think the legend is true in that he carried the secret with him from Gaspar's ship. But it doesn't take place in Charlotte Harbor up the Peace River. I believe the treasure is here in Tampa Bay."

"Why are you so sure?" Nathan replied. "The article I read, said that Juan Gomez had spent his entire life living on Panther key in Charlotte Harbor. He spent every day of his isolated life searching for it. Why would it not be in Charlotte Harbor?"

"I was given some information from my friend before he died. He gave me some items that have clues on them and he told me that Tampa is the Port. I can't help but believe him." Gabriel finished. "What items?" Nathan asked. "A gold ring with some engravings on it and a large wooden picture," Gabriel answered. "Can I see them?" "Maybe when we head back but I really need to keep them safe. I think he died trying to save them and he sent them to me. I can't lose them. But I don't know how they fit into the puzzle yet."

A voice pierced threw the crowd and startled the two boys. "What's up ladies?" Roger Woods confidently strolled up to the boys from the shadows behind the house. "Are you having fun at my party?"

"It's great, thanks again." Gabriel responded. "What did you do with my sister?" asked Nathan. "She's talking to some friends. I thought I would come over and hang with you guys for a second. Maybe get to know you a bit."

Gabriel noticed several other boys beginning to close in around him. He started to count them and take notice of every detail in his surroundings. Roger's demeanor quickly changed to anger when his buddies encircled Nathan and Gabriel.

"You look like a pretty big guy I was wondering if you ever played Lacrosse." Roger patted Gabriel on the shoulder. "The season has already started, but I thought maybe some of my teammates could give you a little tryout."

Three in front of me with two at my back and one on Nathan's side- Gabriel thought to himself as he scanned the scene.

"You see this is my school and I make the rules and rule number one is don't make me mad and you two have made me mad." Roger gleamed with confidence.

Trying to buy some more time, Gabriel spoke up. "I think you mean La Crosier," as he continued to read the boys that were now closing in around him.

"What did you say?" replied Roger now distracted just as Gabriel had hoped. "La Crosier or Bishop's staff. It was a Jesuit missionary in the 1600's that first documented the Native American Indian game. He thought the curved sticks they were using looked like a bishop's staff called a Crosier. The curved bishop's staff or Crosier often had a Cross on top of it. Those that carried it carried "the Cross" or in French- la Croix. Lacrosse was the eventual translation of- la Croix, meaning the Cross. For Centuries Native Americans had used the sport, they referred to as "the little brother of war" instead of actual war to settle their disagreements. The games often went on for days and many players died playing but it was better than war" Gabriel finished.

Annoyed at the history lesson, Roger interrupted, "I don't know what you're talking about but you're about to get your butt beat in."

Nathan was having a small heart attack. He had been picked on before and even beat up before but never by a group of kids. Even if he could find the strength to fight one off how could he fight against 5 guys? He had never been so afraid in his life but he knew he couldn't leave Gabriel. Gabriel was his friend. No matter how bad the beating would hurt, he couldn't run from his friend. So he just had to brace himself for impact. Gabriel continued to read the surrounding players. Who would strike first? He thought to himself. Roger was still talking and talkers do just that-talk. He sounded tough but he was leaning back from Gabriel. He was waiting for his friends to do the dirty work. He would egg them on but would be the last to fight. He was the bully and bullies like to intimidate. He wanted to see fear in his opponent's eyes. He wanted them to feel whatever pain he was feeling, most bullies do. All bullies want to humiliate, but not all bullies want to fight, Roger was afraid and Gabriel knew it. He could read it in the bully's eyes.

The boy on his left was just as nervous as Nathan. His eyes were looking from side to side hoping someone would stop this. He was praying someone would walk up and put an end to this before it got out of hand.

The boy on the right was ready to fight. His eyes were wide and fixed on Gabriel. His breathing was fast and his fist was clenched. He would be Gabriel's second target.

The two boys behind him were hard to see so he would have to rely on hearing their movements but it was the boy on Nathan's side that Gabriel knew would strike first.

Gabriel had noticed the boy earlier as he moved into position. Stepping away from the pack he wanted to start the violence. He chose the side by Nathan because a shot to someone's head from their blind side would make a highlight for any You Tube video and this guy was excited with adrenaline. His heart was racing and Gabriel could even see him lick his lips a little in anticipation. He would be Gabriel's first hit.

Gabriel had been in fights his whole life. He had learned to read people and could anticipate their moves before they would act and with lots of practice it didn't matter the size or number of fighters in the fight the outcome was usually the same.

Suddenly, the boy on Nathan's side made his move just as Gabriel had predicted. But Gabriel was ready. A quick jab over Nathan's shoulder surprised and stunned the attacker. It wasn't hard enough to knock him out, so he may still be dangerous, but Gabriel could tell by the way the cartilage crushed under his knuckles that the boy just got a broken nose. No matter how big you are, a smashed nose will bring down anyone.

Number two was next; just off of Roger's right side but Gabriel quickly thrust a side kick to his knee and the boy crumbled before he even got close. His season was over from a torn meniscus and ligament tear in his knee cap. Coach would not be happy with that one.

The third boy got close with a swing from behind but Gabriel's reaction was too quick. Gabriel responded with two jabs and a right cross that probably cost the kid some teeth. The boy next to him was able to get a hold of Gabriel for a brief second but with a foot stomp and return head butt, that boy will be in a lot of pain- after he wakes up.

Gabriel could see that Roger was already beginning to walk backwards away from the fight but before Gabriel could follow him a piercing thud hit the back of his head. Gabriel had underestimated the boy on Roger's left. Perhaps blind loyalty made him do it but the kid who didn't want to fight in the beginning got the best shot on Gabriel. It was a hard hit but by the size of the young athlete, Gabriel knew it wasn't fully committed. The kid had pulled his punch. Probably trying to save face with his friends by getting into the fight, but he didn't want to be there. Gabriel decided to go easy on him.

The stars were still in Gabriel's eyes and the pain was pretty bad but he wasn't mad at the kid. Peer pressure is difficult to stand up too and this kid just didn't have enough courage to stand up to his friends. Gabriel forgave him by deciding to teach him with fear instead of his fists. Slowly turning his head and acting as impervious to the hit as possible, Gabriel asked him in a cold calm tone.

"Is that all you have? Why don't you go get some more friends and I'll let you have another shot."

The frightened boy looked at his friends lying on the ground knocked out or crying in pain. Three of them taken down in a matter of seconds and his supposed friend Roger was nowhere to be seen.

"I'm sorry, man. I'm sorry," pleaded the kid while he ran off as fast as he could.

Nathan couldn't believe what he had just seen. Who was this kid that just took out the entire starting Lacrosse team in ten seconds and barely got a scratch on him? His heart was in his throat, he couldn't talk. His eyes were wide open with fear and his lungs were starting to hyperventilate. Gabriel stepped over one of the kids writhing in pain as if he was just strolling thru the park. He turned back towards Nathan and smiled without much more than one short breath.

"I think we should get Lisa and head back. I don't think we are welcome here anymore." Gabriel smiled.

Chapter 29

Flopping down to stretch out on his cold tile floor, Gabriel was nursing a bag of ice on his swollen hand. His head was still pounding from the lucky shot from the boy on the left but it was his hand that hurt the most. The skin was swollen to the point where his knuckles were almost gone. Like little chubby sausages, his fingers no longer looked like his. They were bruised and stretch smooth with no creases. They weren't broken but hurt too much to try to open up. So Gabriel was forced to keep his hand in the same fist-like gesture as it was at the last punch. Even when you "win" in a fight- both parties "lose" to the pain, he thought to himself.

Nathan and his sister had been arguing for most of the drive back but their anger had seemed to cool when they entered into Gabriel's dilapidated apartment. It wasn't much of a room but the fact that it belonged to a sixteen year old boy and there were no adults anywhere around gave the cramped one bedroom space an open air of awesome. Lisa's phone rang again for the 100th time in 20 minutes so she stepped outside the room out into the dark stairwell for privacy.

"Is she still mad at us?" Gabriel asked. "No, I think she is more embarrassed than anything." Nathan continued. "Roger convinced her that his friends were out of line but that we should leave before anyone else gets hurt. She is afraid that Roger and the upper class will ignore her now." "What does she see in him?" Gabriel asked. "I don't know. She knows I can't stand him but that doesn't seem to matter to her. She likes being popular."

Nathan grabbed a drink out of the fridge and chose to change the subject.

"How did you learn to fight like that?" Gabriel looked over to his friend and smiled. "It was Plato that wrote, 'Necessity, who is the mother of invention.' I didn't learn fighting by choice. It was something I had to do to survive. I wish I never had to fight because no one really ever wins."

"But you're great at it," Nathan interjected. "Fighting is easy when you're pushed to it?" Gabriel corrected him. "Instinct takes over and your desire to survive becomes fierce, but it's talking out of a fight that is great that's the hard part. My hand is killing me and those guys are going to need doctors and for what… arrogance, pride? We would all be a lot better off if we could have talked instead of fought."

"If you don't like it so much why do you train for it? Those moves don't just come from instinct. You've practiced." Nathan argued.

"Si vis Pace, Pera Bellum" Gabriel responded. "Excuse me?" Nathan questioned.

"It's Latin. In the 5th century a Roman author Vegetius Renatus wrote: If you want peace, prepare for war. My Father used to say that to me when he would go to work. But if you must know it's not about the moves or punches, it's about the anticipation. I knew who was going to throw first, and I was anticipating it."

The front door opened up and Lisa walked in. "You guys are so lucky that Roger is cool about all of this," she blurted. "He was going to call the cops on everybody and imagine what Mom would have said if you got arrested."

"How do you know?" Nathan ignored his sister and remained focused on Gabriel. "You look for signs, body language, things that are shown but not necessarily said." Gabriel continued. "It's not about words but actions."

Gabriel looked up from the floor and started to stare at the only piece of art in his completely bare apartment. The wooden picture that his friend Jose Gomez had sent him seemed to be staring back at him. Something started to spin in his head and he was no longer talking to Nathan but his focus was now on the picture. "It's about seeing what is there but not always in plain sight." Gabriel stood up and walked towards the wall. "It's not always the most vocal or most obvious person that is the most dangerous but the one with something behind their eyes…"

His train of thought seemed to wander off as he lifted the picture from the wall hook. Lisa and Nathan stared as they watched the strange trance like movement of Gabriel. He picked up the frame and stared closely at it as if he was reading the wood grain itself. Then he turned the picture over and began to trace his finger along the back edge.

There was a plain piece of thinly cut oak that covered the entire backing of the picture. It appeared as though it would ruin the intricate wood cutouts if it were to be removed. The aged wood was dry and almost brittle but the screws that held the backing in place were still shiny almost new.

He had looked at them before but didn't think to take them out and ruin the picture. Even the carved out triangle shaped hole that he hung the picture on had been studied under a bright light with a magnifying glass. But the screws had never crossed his mind until now. Gabriel thought back to Jose's last words in his letter.

"The picture and the secret it keeps," "of course," Gabriel blurted out. "How could I be so blind?"

Gabriel ran off for a second only to return with a small multi tool screwdriver. He quickly removed the first two screws and was on to the third by the time Lisa and Nathan stood up to see what his excitement was about.

Finally with the fourth screw out, Gabriel pried out the tool's tiny knife and carefully slid it into the wood backings crease. It was a tight fit. The knife blade left a small indent as it was forced into the separation. But after a few seconds, Gabriel was able to pry the backing up and get a finger nail under it. Taking a deep breath he lifted up the backing and removed it from the frame. He cringed at the thought of hundreds of tiny hand cut wood inlay pieces falling out of place like a crumbling jigsaw puzzle. But nothing seemed to be sticking or falling to the floor. Carefully he handed the sheet of oak wood over to Nathan never taking his eyes off of the exposed picture frame.

And there it was, lying peacefully in place on top of a second oak wood backing, a rectangular folded up piece of parchment paper. Gabriel could hear his heart beating loudly in his chest. Yellowed and brittle it took several minutes to unfold it-carefully and without damage. It had to have been old. Ancient perhaps, paper was not made like this anymore and Gabriel had only seen similar papers in museums.

"What is that?" Lisa broke the tension.

Gabriel smiled and answered, "The key to Gaspar's treasure… his lost map."

Chapter 30

The map was extremely frail and brittle. The edges were torn and cracked. The fold lines were deep and hard to pry open. It had been folded and refolded in the same shape many times but it had lain unopened for a long time and when Gabriel tried to open it even the slightest "creek" made his heart skip a beat. The fear of tearing it made him pause with each movement.

It was an ornately hand drawn map with meticulous detail. The coast lines were clear and sharp with every jetty, inlet, and depth range drawn out. The land mass was covered with bundles of palm trees and various animal drawings. Alligators, black bears, and armadillos were placed all over the land area while giant sea creatures and various other monsters leapt out of the sea. The sea creatures were gathered in front of a large waterway that appeared to be a protected harbor but it had no name. In fact, there were no names anywhere in or around the map at all.

"It's interesting how the map is folded." Gabriel finally spoke out. "That's it! You just found a 200 year old treasure map and you're interested by the way it's folded! Are you crazy?" Nathan whispered. Afraid his very breath could damage the fragile parchment. "What about names? There are no names anywhere. What are we looking at?" Gabriel studied every inch of the precious map with amazement, as he carefully unfolded each section, yet the question Nathan raised was a good one. What exactly was he looking at? He had to wonder himself.

The parchment paper had been folded in such a way that the outer sides were folded in on the center. Like wrapping a present, the outside ends were folded in forming a crease square in the middle. The map was an outline of a harbor. Centered on a large body of water with some barrier islands at the mouth, the coast line curved up into a gentle point like a horn on what appeared to be the north end but with no compass rose they couldn't tell. Along the shores were multiple rivers, estuaries and several strange rectangular shaped little boxes at the water edge but no names to tell what they were. Where they villages? Homes? Farms? The shapes were all different sizes and in no particular order other than they were all along the coastline.

Gabriel folded back the last piece of the map and his heart leapt into his throat. "An X," shouted Nathan. He couldn't whisper that one.

There it was, Nathan was right, under the last fold was a dark black "X" Amongst several barrier islands and at the mouth of the bay, a black charcoal marking in the shape of an "X" was on the tip of a long narrow island.

There was no compass rose on the map and the pictures of creatures were all in different directions even the words that could be found were in various positions including upside down making the map difficult to even determine which direction was north.

Normally, the map legend would have the meanings of symbols, distance measurements, or location names to help the reader understand what they were looking at. This map had none of that. However, there was a written journal that read:

"El día dos de abril, del año de Nuestro Señor 1812. Encontré mi redención en una fuente vibrante entre los nativos al norte de la gran bahía. Le di recompensa al gran **c**acique nativo con los respons**a**bles de veinte ocho. Para el pequeño rey de los jefes de siete, a la gente de las cuca**r**achas **l**as cabezas de cinco, y para la gente de las agua**s** turbulent**o**s que le di las cabezas de tre**s**.

5 días más tarde, a 2 minutos antes de la medianoche, bajo los ojos de mi amada princesa, enterré mi gran fortuna que nadie volvería por miedo a la muerte."

Reading out loud in Spanish first, Gabriel then translated it to English for the excited twins.

"On the 2nd day of April, the year of our Lord 1812. I found my redemption at a vibrant spring amongst the natives north of the great bay. I gave bounty to the great native Cacique with the heads of 28. To the little king the heads of 7, to the people of the cockroaches the heads of 5, and to the people of the turbulent water**s** I gave the heads of 3.

5 days later, 2 minutes before midnight, beneath the eyes of my beloved princess, I buried my great fortune where no man would return for fear of death."

"Look up there." Lisa interrupted.

She was pointing to the top left corner where some words written in long hand were so faded that they were almost unreadable. Gabriel noticed some charred marks on the edge of the map around the faded words. He gently turned the map over and realized the darkened dirty parchment was in fact slightly charred. It was considerably darker on the backside of the map than the front. Gabriel had assumed it was due to exposure, but it was actually black smoke from an ancient heat source.

"Invisible ink, very cool," Gabriel said. "What do you mean?" Nathan questioned. "Secret messages were often written in invisible ink. It's an ancient practice that goes back thousands of years. Any carbon based liquid can do, usually lemon juice or white wine. You can't see it after it dries but if you heat it up the carbon burns and the image reappears. It looks like someone in the Gomez family over the years discovered it and opened the first clue." Gabriel answered.

"What does it say?" Lisa asked. Gabriel leaned in closer and began to read.

"En la Isla de Caldez en el Puerto de Carlos... enterré mi amado... bajo la piedra quemada, cien pasos al este de la gran tumba de conchas."

He then repeated in English.

"On the island of Caldez in the Port of Carlos… I buried my beloved… under the burnt stone, 100 paces to the east of the great tomb of shells,"

Gabriel finished and looked to Lisa and Nathan with a wide grin. "Do you know what that means?"

"Useppa Island!" Gabriel and Nathan answered in unison. "Lisa you're driving let's go!" Nathan shouted as he grabbed his jacket and headed towards the door. "Go where? Where's Useppa Island?" Lisa questioned. "Charlotte Harbor" cried Nathan, "Let's move."

Gabriel stood up but then suddenly stopped himself. "Wait… before you go I want you to know that this could be dangerous. If you don't want to go I understand but if you do then you will need to know everything," Gabriel continued. "There is something else."

"What else is there?" Nathan asked. Gabriel pulled out the heavy gold ring from his pocket and held open his hand for the others to see. "This."

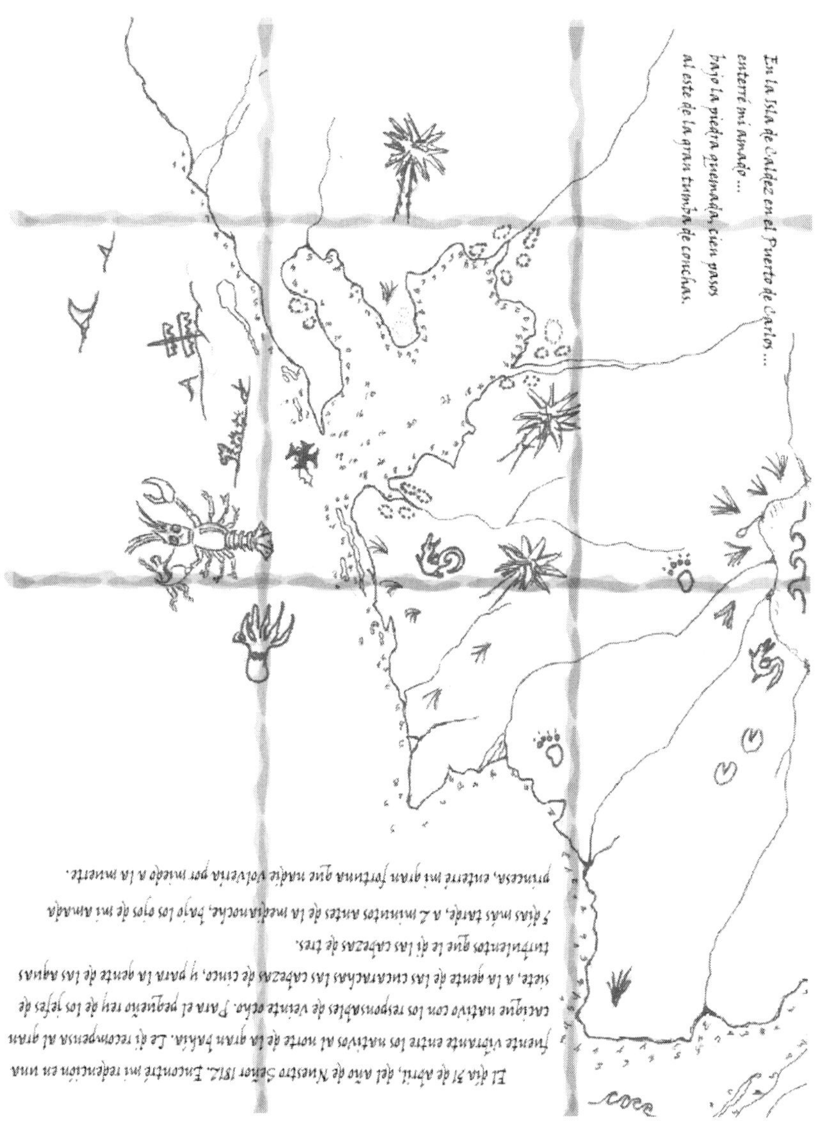
En la Isla de Caldez en el Puerto de Carlos...
enterré mi amado...
bajo la piedra quemada, cien pasos
al este de la gran tumba de conchas.
El día 31 de abril, del año de Nuestro Señor 1812. Encontré mi redención en una fuente vibrante entre los nativos al norte de la gran bahía. Le di recompensa al gran cacique nativo con los responsables de veinte ocho. Para el pequeño rey de los jefes de siete, a la gente de las cucarachas las cabezas de cinco, y para la gente de las aguas turbulentos que le di las cabezas de tres.
5 días más tarde, a 2 minutos antes de la medianoche, bajo los ojos de mi amada princesa, enterré mi gran fortuna que nadie volvería por miedo a la muerte.

Chapter 31

A loud thud from the heavy wood door echoed across the great hall as it was shoved opened. Soon the sound of hard leather shoes tapped back and forth as two men walked along the long granite tiled hallway. Giant stained glass windows that stretched from the floor to the ceiling gave the space an almost Cathedral appearance. It was a beautiful piece of architecture, as far as large buildings go, but this was a house which made it feel cold, dark, and evil.

After a brief walk the two men entered into an even grander round greeting room area. Detailed crown molding hand carved out of Brazilian Cherry wood capped off the high reaching ceilings. The walls were covered with ornate recesses filled with precious pieces of art. A dealers dream if only they were for sale and not a personal collection.

The shrill voice of the Ghost spoke out, "Sir, sorry to interrupt you this late at night but this man refused to…" Before he could finish a short potbellied man stepped out from behind the thin pale Ghost.

"Good evening Mr. Santos. My name is Jim Orsos and I think I have some information that you might like to hear." Loud and boisterous, the high school teacher was enjoying his new false sense of importance.

The Ghost looked up to a large man standing in the door way. With a nod from the large dark figure, the Ghost was ordered to back up and let the sniveling man talk. Seeing that he now had the floor, Mr. Orsos' confidence grew.

"It was brought to my attention a couple weeks back that there would be a substantial reward for any information concerning a boy looking into the pirate Jose Gaspar," Orsos continued. "This boy had taken some property from a very wealthy business man in this area and any information should be offered to my friend here," Orsos motioned to the Ghost who didn't acknowledge him.

A deep raspy voice filled the room, "You were supposed to call." The Ghost began to speak but Mr. Orsos cut him short.

"Oh, I prefer to speak in person when I'm talking business. I insisted in fact. I wouldn't take no for an answer." "It better be worth it," the raspy voice of Santos answered.

"It is." Mr. Orsos confidently continued, "I have a new student in my class. He arrived a few weeks back just before I heard of your request. Annoying little brat who thinks he knows it all. Likes to cause trouble in my class and…"

The deep grunt from Santos was enough to make Orsos get to the point. "He was looking through a long list of resources in our school library. He checked out some journals about lost pirate treasure in Florida, nautical charts, and a few books on Jose Gaspar. I would argue that this is the thief you are willing to pay for." Orsos finished very pleased with himself.

"Is that all?" Santos boomed. "You interrupt my evening with this? A school boy looking up pirate stories days before the entire city erupts with a parade celebrating pirates. You are out of your mind coming here and annoying me." Santos turned to walk away while the Ghost grabbed Mr. Orsos' arm yanking him almost out of his shoes.

Mr. Orsos cried out. "He said something about the Isla de Muerta."

This stopped Santos cold in his tracks. He turned and looked to the Ghost as both men recognized the importance of that last statement.

"What did you say?" "His friend, another boy, mentioned going to the Isla de Muerta." Orsos' voice cracked a little stunned at his fleeting confidence and new uneasiness.

"What is this boy's name?" Santos asked. "Gabriel…. Gabriel Fletcher," Orsos said with a dry mouth. A giant smile crossed over the leathery skinned face of Santos. "Oh Mr. Orsos you have been of great importance tonight. Thank you. My friend here will take you back to your house and reward you very handsomely for your help."

Mr. Orsos' heart stopped panicking, and he too began to smile. "Thank you. Thank you very much, perhaps we could…"

Santos was already out of the room before he could finish.

Moments later, Mr. Orsos was still feeling pretty good when he walked out of the giant stone castle. Even when he got into the Ghost's car he was still feeling confident with himself but when the black Audi turned south on Interstate 75 instead of north panic began to build in his body. Perhaps he made a mistake and got lost or new of a quicker route Mr. Orsos chose not to speak up at first. He was so excited about his future wealth he didn't want to be bothered right now he just wanted to think about what he would spend his new fortune on. However 10 minutes into his 10 minute ride home he could wait no longer. He had to ask what the creepy pale man driving the car was doing.

"I think you made a wrong turn back there we are heading the wrong way." "We're not heading to your house just yet. We need to stop and pick up your reward," the pale thin lips spoke in a whisper voice. "Great! I can't wait." Mr. Orsos' concerns foolishly disappeared.

The Ghost's thin pale lips arched into an evil smile.

The black Audi finally pulled off the interstate and with two quick left turns it made its way onto a long windy road. About two miles into it, the windy road pavement ended and the unmistakable bumps and vibrations of a dirt road began. Another mile or two and the car finally stopped on a dusty dark trail deep into an overgrown wooded area. The smell of the swamp was as thick as the mosquitoes that were dancing in the headlight beams. The Audi's headlights shined on a concrete building about 50 yards away. As the men got out into the darkness, the sound of chirping crickets and flying bugs whizzed in Mr. Orsos' ears. The blood thirsty mosquitoes wasted no time attacking the two men as they approached the small brick building that stood behind a tall chain link fence. The fence was about 10 feet high with razor wire at the top and it seemed to run for about 100 yards each way until it disappeared into the black forest.

"What is this place?" Orsos questioned with a shaking voice. His fear had returned a long time ago. "The safest place in the world to hide gold," the Ghost answered. Orsos smiled with excitement, "Gold!"

As the Ghost opened the gate, Mr. Orsos looked up into the night sky and was amazed at how bright the stars were. "They don't look like that in the city," he mentioned. "No they don't. Push that button on the wall and it will open the storage door," the Ghost ordered.

Mr. Orsos noticed a red pressure button on the wall but didn't see a door. He thought perhaps it was along the far side hidden by the shadows. He pressed the plastic knob as he was told to and was startled by the piercing sound of a loud fog horn. His reflex was to cover his ears and turn to the Ghost to see what was going on. He was confused as he watched the Ghost walking back out through the tall chain link fence. The Ghost closed the gate door behind him and began to lock the gate with a padlock.

"What are you doing? What's going on?" Orsos screamed. The Ghost didn't reply but just stood there staring at the frightened man. "Answer me you freak! What was that noise?"

The Ghost smiled and then whispered to the scared man, "A dinner bell."

Just then off in the distant, splashes started to sound out in the darkness. Into the pitch black woods Mr. Orsos strained his eyes to look and listen at the ever increasing number of splashes. A few at first then more and more, louder they seemed to be growing in volume and speed. Dozens of them he had counted until he finally saw the first of the bright yellow spots reflecting in the darkness.

Dozens of pairs of yellow eyes lit up in the Audi's headlights as the car backed away and drove off down the dusty road. One final tap of the car's brakes lit up the swamp in a hazy red glow. To Mr. Orsos horror, the glow illuminated hundreds of alligators crawling out of the water up onto the short bank in front of him. His back up against the locked fence he could see them getting closer until the car turned and he was again blanketed in complete darkness.

The muffled grunts of the beasts got louder and louder until the noise of scaled tails sliding across the grass seemed to be surrounding him. Panic raced through him as he tried to climb the metal fence but when the piercing crunch on his leg pulled him to the floor, all he could do was scream. Unfortunately for Jim Orsos, in the Florida swamps no one could hear his screams.

Chapter 32

The drive towards Charlotte harbor had gone fast. Normally it would have taken about an hour, the kids made it in 45 minutes. Lisa was driving while Nathan and Gabriel sat restless and giddy in the backseats. Under the harsh, bright, car dome light, the boys were scouring over every inch of the frail map trying to unlock its secrets.

Gabriel knew that the water level around Useppa Island had risen several feet since the early 1800's. This meant there was a good chance the buried treasure was under water now so he decided to make a quick stop on the way. Gabriel had made an acquaintance at work, a young dishwasher with long pony tailed hair named Jacob. The young man had often talked about his weekend SCUBA diving trips around the bay. He was hesitant at first to lend Gabriel his gear but when the striking young Lisa stepped out of the car his hesitation turned to high fives and the kids were quickly on their way again.

"So the map and the ring go together to solve a 200 year old treasure mystery?" Nathan still couldn't get his head out of the clouds from all the excitement.

"Yes, but let's not lose sight of the fact that my friend was killed for these things and whoever did it will probably do it again if they catch us," Gabriel stated. He took a moment to see the impact of his statement, but there was none. The excitement in the car was too high to be concerned about life and death issues.

"What clues does the ring give?" Nathan looked closely at the ring under the car's bright dome light. "There is some writing along the band, only on the outside. A picture of a pirate ship sailing through a storm."

"A Barque." Gabriel corrected. "It's a Barque sailing vessel. We don't know if it's a pirate ship. But we know it's a Barque because of the three masts and their sail configuration."

"Ok… it's a Barque." Nathan agreed as if he understood what Gabriel was talking about. "It looks like some markings around the bezel but… are those letters around the center? Any idea what those are?"
"Not sure about the letters around the top but I figured out the writing on the band that's where I got 'the Island of Death', la Isla de Muerta, from."

Gabriel pointed along the ring's edge as his fingers rolled back along the letters. "They were engraved backwards and with every other letter alternating upside down but when I rolled the ring along a flattened out hunk of play dough, the code was easier to decipher by using a Caesar's shift of 7 spaces. I got that number from the portholes off the Barque image. Encuentre la Isla de Muerta. Find the island of death."

Nathan had to look at Gabriel and wonder just what this kid was talking about. Who knows this stuff and why? He thought about how Gabriel just blurts out things that no normal person would understand but to Gabriel it seems to make perfect common sense. All

Nathan could do was to seem to agree as if he understood and just go a long with it.

"Ok, so the tomb of shells has got to be the Calusa mound on Useppa Island," Nathan added. Pleased with his homework Gabriel responded, "So you read the articles I gave you? Good work." "Thanks I actually never thought I would use it but I guess I was wrong. So what's the burnt stone?"

"It's probably a..." before Gabriel could finish Lisa jumped in.

"What are you talking about? What is a Calusa mound and how do you know about this?"

Nathan answered, "The Calusa Indians inhabited southern Florida for thousands of years. Calusa was their word for shells. Shell people if you will. They were called this because they used shells for everything: tools, weapons, cooking pots, even garbage dumps and burial chambers. They would dig large holes in the ground and then cover their garbage or dead people with shells. The shell piles would grow bigger and bigger until they became these giant mounds some 30 to 40 feet tall."

"How do you know this stuff?" Lisa yelled in frustration.

"The library. It's pretty cool; you should check it out sometime." Nathan replied with a smile.

"So the legend goes that the Pirate Gaspar was very fond of women. So much so that he kept many of them on an island near the Florida coast. He kept them as slaves or captives. Hence the name Captiva Island in Charlotte Harbor." Nathan was starting to even impress himself with his new found knowledge.

"Charlotte harbor gets its name from a translation of Carlos. Named after the son of the King of Spain, Carlos was the vicerore of Spain at the time. The Conquistador Ponce De Leon named the beautiful bay, Bahia de Carlos, Carlos Bay in his honor. It was later changed by the British to Charlotte in respect to King George III's wife. But Caldez's island in the harbor was where the legend takes a dark turn."

Gabriel jumped in, "Jose Caldez was a Cuban fisherman who first settled on a small island in the bay around the early 1800's. It was a fishing island with a small house on it but it later became known as Useppa Island. According to legend Useppa is a mistranslation of Joseffa the Spanish Princess."

Nathan can't wait, "She was the most beautiful woman around and she was captured by Gaspar. He fell in love with her instantly but she didn't want him. He tried and tried to make her love him but she refused and he became so angry that he beheaded her and buried her on the island of Caldez or as we know it today-Useppa Island." Very proud of himself and almost out of his seat, Nathan waited to her Lisa's response. "So you want to find a 200 year old lady's head?" Lisa managed to deflate the boys' enthusiasm in one breath. "Yes, but when you put it like that it's not so cool." Nathan responded flatly.

They parked the car on Pine Key just a few blocks north of the local marina. Moving the scuba gear to the edge of the bay Gabriel told them to wait by the canal on the side of the road until he got back and then he was off running down the dark road towards the marina. About 20 minutes later, a small single engine boat could be heard in the distance and eventually coasted up the shoreline. As the outboard Yamaha 80 engine shut off, the boat drifted to a slow stop right in front of the waiting twins.

"I don't want to know how you got that boat do I." Lisa answered her own question with a slight smile. "It's better that you don't know. But I'll return it in one piece I promise. Load the gear we've got to get moving."

The kids pushed off and lit up the engine. It only took a few minutes to get out into the channel and then they turned south heading down the current towards Useppa Island.

Chapter 33

It was a cold bone shivering night on the water but it was the vast darkness that put a chill down Lisa's spine. She was a city girl. Her excitement came from going out with the girls and chasing boys. Shopping for clothes and talking on the phone with her best friend. But now she found herself racing down a lost treasure in the middle of the ocean in a stolen boat under the pure darkness of night. As frightened as she was it was also strangely exhilarating for her. The occasional glance back at the handsome boat captain didn't hurt her excitement either. Her nerves were on total alert but Gabriel looked so comfortable at the helm. It just seemed to suite him so well, it seemed natural to him. His confidence calmed her uneasiness.

"We should be getting close," Nathan barked. "My cell phone GPS has us coming up to the island. It should be on our left."

Moments later, there it was. Appearing through the darkness, the large black island was quickly coming into sight. The sounds of the white water surf were loud as they splashed along the rocks that surrounded the islands edge. A seasonal fishing mecca, Useppa Island is a private island for the well-to-do's and the coming ups of society. Some of their home lights could be seen sparkling off into the distance on the north end of the island. But it was the dark side of the island that Gabriel was heading for, the dark uninhabited side that had been protected from developers. Protected because ancient remains of the lost Calusa Indians were found here many years ago, this part of the Island was protected by the National Park Service. Unfortunately, most of the once great Calusa Tribe's Capital that covered the island is now buried under mega mansions and seasonal get-aways. But fortunately for Gabriel, what was protected by the park service happened to be the highest burial mound on the island and it was just coming into his sight.

"There it is; the burial mound of Joseffa." Nathan thought to himself.

But the smile on his face quickly turned to concern as his body started to shake uncontrollably. Even in the cold night air his hands and face started to sweat. He started to shout out to Lisa and Gabriel but he became dizzy and just fell to the floor of the boat. Seeing Nathan fall to the deck, Gabriel turned off the engine and jumped to his friend's aid.

"Nathan! What's wrong?" He yelled. Grabbing Nathan's head he tried to lift him up and sit him straight but Nathan was heavy and almost all dead weight. Even though Nathan always thought of himself as weak, the boy was 6ft tall and almost 200 pounds. In a rocking, slippery, wet Jon boat, the heavy body was almost all Gabriel could handle.

"Lisa, give me a hand. Help me sit him up." He yelled. "Hold on." She replied calmly. "Let me get my purse." "Your purse? What's wrong with you?" Gabriel snapped.

"Just a second," she responded.

Grabbing a small red box from her purse she pulled out a tiny syringe and removed a plastic needle cap. Calmly she leaned over to her brother and stabbed the syringe right into a pinch of flesh on his stomach.

"Give it a second or two," She ordered. "He has diabetes."

Turning to her now semi-groggy brother, "You probably didn't eat anything today with all of your adventure did you- you little twerp? Leave it to your older sis to take care of you. Don't you forget you owe me one now?"

Nathan opened his eyes and began to smile. Diabetic since he was 8 years old, it wasn't uncommon for Nathan to experience high blood sugar. But stress, exercise, and adrenaline can cause one's body to burn up sugar faster than normal. Compared to Nathan's typical structured routine of a day, the events of this evening had caused his body to burn faster than normal.

The insulin shot he took at dinner is normally fine to cover his food intake. But since his food was burned up quicker than normal tonight that insulin shot had nothing to work on so it drove his blood sugar too low and Nathan was going into a hypoglycemic state. Deadly if not treated quickly, Hypoglycemia is when the body's sugar levels in the blood are too low and the body has nothing to burn for fuel. Luckily for Nathan, everyone in his family carry Glucagon shots with them just in case he has an episode. This was from a lesson they learned a long time ago when he first was diagnosed.

Nathan had been a laughable outgoing child just like all the other kids in school when he was younger. But in the 3rd grade he had gotten sick with a bad case of the flu and all of that seemed to change for the young boy. A few weeks after some bed rest and a lot of soup he began to lose weight. He was constantly thirsty and always running to the bathroom. He had refused to eat anything because he didn't feel good. When his Mom took him to the Doctor it was there in the office when he had his first episode similar to the one just now in the boat. He dropped to the office floor and began to shake. His Mother screamed for help when one nurse, who still cares for him today on his follow up visits, rushed to his aid with a Glucagon shot and brought him back. Ever since then the family has been diligent in learning about Type 1 diabetes and carrying all the important tools to help Nathan with his disease. Every family member lives with the disease but unfortunately, in this case, the one with the disease is the worst advocate for it. Nathan often doesn't carry his insulin shots or glucose tablets. He never likes talking about it with those around him and his personality has become withdrawn and reserved ever since his diagnoses. All the while his twin sister has blossomed with others kids and become the most popular girl in school.

The bond between the twins is strong. Even though they fight and argue most of the time, Gabriel could see the love between them as Lisa held her brother in her arms. Nathan hated being different from other kids but to Lisa he was still just her brother and she loved him for it.

With a long hug and a kiss on his sister's cheek, Nathan was back to business.

"Are you going to be ok?" Gabriel asked. "I'll be fine for now but as soon as we get back I'll need to check my blood and get something to eat." Nathan responded. "Ok. You scared me you know. I never leave a friend behind so if I have to drag your butt back to land let me know now so I can start swimming. Lisa can stay here to do the diving."

"Excuse me." She laughed.

A quick final check of his gear and one last look to the now clearly visible shell mound, Gabriel felt this was as good a place as any to begin his dive. A smile spread across face as he leaned backwards over the boat and with a sudden splash disappeared into the black gulf water.

Popping up a second later to fix his mask and blow into his regulator he gave a quick thumb up and then sank back into the abyss.

"You scared that guy?" Lisa joked as she watched him disappear underwater. "Is he scared of anything?"

Chapter 34

"Never leave a friend behind," Nathan repeated. The thought of being Gabriel's friend was a good one for him. And even though he was in complete darkness in the middle of the freezing nowhere, he was happy.

Nathan always felt different from the other kids. No one else had to inject needles into their stomach 4 times a day. When other kids inhaled their Halloween candy or devoured their birthday cakes, Nathan had to measure and read the ingredients of everything that went into his mouth. He had to calculate the amount of insulin his body would need just to have what other kids took for granted so joyously. He remembered as a child being great at sports. Like his father, Nathan was tall and strong for a young boy and he was always the best on his team. But after he got sick, his parents saw sports as an additional risk. They tried to get him involved into other "safer" activities. His love of sports eventually diminished. He hated being different. He never thought it was fair. He was bitter that life had been unfair to him but then he met Gabriel and realized that perhaps life wasn't as hard on him as he had once thought. And now that boy whom Nathan so admired considers him a friend, the thought put a smile on his face.

The gulf water in February was about 64 degrees but to the twins it was as good as ice water. Even through the metal hull of the boat, their toes were numb. The breath from their mouths drifted up in the air like little white clouds as they huddled close together. In their excitement to find the treasure, the kids had failed to think about the jackets they had in the car and now the freezing gulf wind was ripping through their shirts and piercing their skin like tiny sharp knives stabbing their bones.

After a few moments, a light seemed to flare up from under the water. It was from the small flashlight that was in the SCUBA bag along with a dive mask and regulator vest. When Gabriel was putting the gear together Nathan had asked him how he knew what he was doing with the equipment.

"Saw it in a movie," was all that Gabriel would say.

The light seemed to dance back and forth across the bottom of the bay. About 15 feet down and directly west of the great Indian mound Nathan hoped that Gabriel was right. One hundred paces they guessed would be about 300 feet so they lined up their boat and had dropped a small Danforth anchor over the side. Gabriel had figured that with past hurricanes and tidal rises that what used to be fairly shallow water or even land was now deep underwater but if properly weighted and undredged the treasure could still be there.

Still huddling together for warmth, the twins stared up into the vast darkness of the sky amazed at how bright each and every star appeared to be. Beautiful sparkles of light blanketed the world like they had never seen before. Old classroom illustrations that had long been forgotten started to make sense as the two siblings tried to make out constellations. The new names the children made up for them had caused the two to shake with hysterical laughter. “Fat Muffin Man, Twinkle Guy” Lisa snorted with “Bumpy Bumpy Fish Boy” which led to even more uncontrolled laughter as the twins sat waiting in the cold steel boat.

Gabriel had said that the air tank would be good for about 30 minutes but if he could control his breathing it would last for about 40. Looking down at his watch, Nathan could tell it had already been 35 minutes since he last saw his friend and now the light, that was once bright under their boat, was a distant glow under the surface. Nathan was starting to worry.

Underwater in the sand churned bay, checking his regulator, Gabriel was now coming up to the little red line that marked his air limit. He was soon to be on borrowed time. Even at 10 feet, a diver could suffer from the “Bends” if he didn’t ascend properly and properly meant slowly over time. However, time was something that Gabriel was quickly running out of. Just then a large shape caught his eye about 3 yards to his left.

Not too far from him a big white block in the sand stood out on the horizon. The turbulent water made everything cloudy and bright from his light but this rock seamed to stand out from the sandy bottom profile. As he got closer he could see that it was definitely not where it was supposed to be. This lone rock in the middle of a fast flowing channel was out of place with nothing but sand everywhere else around it. He had to control his breathing hard now because his was starting to get excited and he knew his heart was racing.

He reached out to the rock and brushed away some of the sediment causing him to pause a second until he could see again. It was a smooth stone with slimy grass and barnacles on it, but what startled Gabriel was a rusty piece of metal that was just under the surface buried in the sand. It looked like a chain link. It wouldn't budge as he pulled on it. It had been wrapped under the rock. Gabriel took a grip of the rock and with all of his strength pulled it towards him. As it rolled over, an unwanted gasp of air shot out of his mouth when he saw blackened burn marks on the bottom of the stone. Hammered into the blackened stone was a metal rusted spike that had several chain links attached to it. Gabriel was now able to pull the chain up easily, unfortunately, too easily. He knew his excitement was short lived when the last link of the chain came up with nothing else on it.

Like the fisherman and the one that got away, Gabriel sat there on the bottom of Useppa channel with a chain that had nothing on the end of it. Even though the chain had rusted solid and was 200 years old, it was still intact. The chain links, at one time, were over an inch thick. Whatever got off the end of this line was cut off.

Despair soon turned into a smile as Gabriel thought about someone finding this chain just has he had now some 200 years earlier and what treasure had that person found. His smile quickly faded when the needle of his regulator stopped deep into the red. Not sure exactly what that meant or how much danger he was in but he knew he had to start ascending now and fast.

"It's been over 45 minutes. I don't see the flashlight any more, something is wrong," Nathan said.

"We need to call the Coast Guard or something." The twins were frantically searching the water's surface looking for any sign of life. The last 5 minutes they had spent yelling into the water and slapping its surface in hopes of getting Gabriel's attention. But there had been no signs from the young diver. Minutes seemed like hours and the joy of what was once a fun adventure was now turning into a tragedy.

Just as the realization of watching someone disappear in front of you and possibly die, bubbles erupted off into the distance.

"Over there" Lisa shouted.

About 60 yards away in the distant darkness the sound of air bubbles rushing to the surface were coming hard and fast. Nathan started the engine as Lisa pulled up the small Danforth anchor and the twins hurried the small boat over to the spring of air in the water. Careful not to get too close with the propeller, Nathan coasted the boat just a few yards off of the erupting ring of bubbles. Again moments seemed like hours as the twins waited when suddenly Gabriel's head shot out of the water and gasped for precious air.

The frigid night air stung his mouth and lungs but Gabriel didn't care. He was alive. About 15 feet from the surface he had run completely out of air and had to force himself to push out every ounce of oxygen in his lungs. The veins in his neck and face bulged out in pain but it was his only hope of expelling as much pressurized oxygen from his bloodstream as he could. To hold his breath and keep that air in his blood could have been deadly. As pressurized oxygen climbs up to atmospheric pressure on the surface it expands and can cause serious damage to one's arteries and heart. It's called the "Bends" and it can kill, but not for Gabriel-not tonight. Pushing to the point of blacking out, his body had almost been out of precious oxygen for over 3 minutes and then with one supernatural kick, he surfaced and filled his lungs with that wonderful chilled air.

Chapter 35

The car ride home was long and mixed with emotions. The crash one's body experiences after such an adrenaline rush is expected to make you feel down even tired, but combined with the disappointment of no treasure-that was just painful. Adding to that pain, the twins were trying to think of excuses to give their parents since it was already an hour past curfew. And Lisa was waiting for that phone call from her Mom to come in at any moment. However Gabriel was in high spirits and couldn't understand why the twins were not feeling his enthusiasm as well. He rambled on about the underwater adventure and the thrill of finding the burnt rock with the chain bolted into it.

Nathan just assumed Gabriel's hyper activity was the beginnings of hypothermia because he saw no reason to be happy but he listened to him talk anyway.

"Don't you see? It was there," Gabriel continued. "We found the rock. I think it was an anchor stone of some sort; maybe a ballast weight from a sailing ship but it was the rock for sure. It was blackened and charred on the bottom where the chain was located."
"But there was no treasure!" Nathan interrupted.

"But there was," Gabriel snaps back. "That chain, even though it was rusted, was still thick and heavy I couldn't break it if I tried. Whatever was at the end of it had to have been cut off." "You said it was an anchor chain right?" Lisa asked.

"Perhaps?"

"Well then, how do you know that it didn't just break off from a ship and sink to the bottom? Maybe it never had a treasure attached to it at all? Or maybe the Captain tied the treasure to the chain with some rope and it has broken free to be lost forever?" She continued.

"I don't know," conceded Gabriel. "But I believe we are close and we just need to keep looking. Someone knows what was down there and we just need to keep trying." Gabriel refused to let their disappointment ruin his excitement.

The white Toyota Camry pulled into Gabriel's apartment complex and the tired and disappointed twins said their good bye. With any luck their parents would still be asleep but they both had sinking fears that their parents would be waiting for them to return way past their curfew. Even if they were awake, Nathan thought, he couldn't care less he was so tired he just wanted to get home. Lisa was already in the back seat closing her eyes. She wouldn't make it home awake. Nathan pulled out of the parking lot with one final wave to his new best friend.

As the white Camry sped out onto the street, it passed a black Audi on the side of the road under the shadow of an old tired oak tree. After a moment, a dark figure appeared in the driver seat of the black car and the blue light of a cell phone illuminated the driver.

The pasty white skin and deep dark sunken eye sockets gave the appearance of a blue skeleton in the driver seat. The long boney fingers reached out and dialed some numbers as he placed the phone to his ear. Soon the thick gravelly voice on the other end answered "Hello," the Ghost in his whispery hiss responded, "I found him."

Chapter 36

July 4th 1920. Panther key, Florida

A small wooden boat drifted along a winding channel that cut through the mangrove lined keys. Out past the sandbar where the wind picks up across the water, a tiny sheet is hauled up along an 8 foot mast. Now the little wood boat is making close to 6 knots in a perfect trim on a gorgeous Florida morning. After about 30 minutes of smooth sailing, the old leathery hands of the boat's skipper drops the sail and throws his handmade hemp cast net out into his favorite fishing hole. Like he has done so many times before over more years than he can remember, the skipper takes in the fresh sea air on what may be the most perfect sunrise his dark brown eyes have ever seen.

The man's strong tanned back can still pull in the heavy fish laden cast net that most men, a third his age, would struggle to do. Never afraid of hard work and isolated from the mainland at his home on Panther key, the skipper's lifetime of self-reliance has made him a formidable body at an age when most everyone he has ever known have long since passed away. He takes in a deep breath of salt air and smiles up towards the awakening sun. A genuine smile, a welcoming smile one that is truly happy with this life on the sea. His grin was so big that even the bone deep scar that slashed across his cheek, a wound the man suffered from when he was just a child, could barely be seen past his gleaming white teeth.

He took in the cool morning breeze and smiled at his good fortune of fish so early in his day. The speckled mullet pushed hard against the hemp knots on the net but they were no match for the strong net or its handler.

Unfortunately, the Skipper's good fortune was about to change as he watched the morning sky begin to turn to a reddish yellow color high in the upper clouds. As every sailor knows "red skies in the morning a sailor heads warning," a sudden chill raced up his spine. Looking towards the open sea for any sign of an oncoming storm, the skipper noticed something behind him. Off in the distance he heard the splashing of a large sailing vessel. It was not long before the vessel was just a few dozen yards off his stern. In another time, the skipper's instinct would be to turn his small boat into the wind and try to outrun it but those days were long gone. His days of running are over and the solitude of life on the key has made him appreciate the rare contact of other sailors in this area. He stood up tall to greet his visitors and reached up high in the air to wave, again illustrating his strength and remarkable balance in such a small unstable boat.

"Good Morning, great day to be on the sea don't you think?" The Skipper's good natured welcome quickly turned to concern when his greeting was met with the jackal like smile of the large vessel's Captain.

"Well, Well, Well, if it isn't our long lost friend." The Captain called out. "Do I know you? You are far too young to be from my past Sir," The old skipper questioned. "No, you do not know me. But I know you Mr. Gomez and I'm sure you know my name," the Captain answered. The skipper responded, "You must be mistaken. My name is not Gomez."

"Don't lie to me old man." The Captain's smile turned to rage in an instant. "Your name is Juan Gomez, the last of the Floriblanca's crew, and you are the keeper of Captain Gaspar's treasure."

Taken back by the statement, the skipper had not heard those names in half a century. "Gaspar? Floriblanca? Those names mean nothing to me my boy." The skipper was lying.

"Don't test me Gomez! Perhaps my name is a name that you will remember." "And you are?" "Vargas… Raúl Vargas, the second, named after my Grandfather. I believe you knew him."

The sound of that name sent Juan Gomez staggering backwards falling hard on his back. The impact on the boat forced a wave of cold salt water over the bow.

"You knew my grandfather, and he died looking for you. So I have spent my entire life dreaming of the moment when I can set right what you have wronged."

Rolling to his side and grasping at his chest, Juan Gomez leaned over the side of his boat towards the sea. Suddenly, Raúl leapt on to the small boat, and a violent lift of the bow flipped Gomez back into his boat's hull. The weight of Raúl forced the small wooden dingy to stick up out of the sea- bow first. The early morning catch of fish were sent wiggling and bouncing back into the frigid water. Still grasping at his chest, Gomez's hand slid under his shirt collar to pull out a chain necklace that was wrapped around his neck. Removing the chain over his head, Gomez reached his arm back in an attempt to throw the necklace deep out to sea. But before he could let it fly, Raúl was on top of him blocking his arm with a violent collision. The two men began to struggle on the rocking boat.

"You're strong old man. I'm going to enjoy this. I only wish my Grandfather was here to see you die!"
"You will never find the treasure. I have hidden the clues and you will fail just like you he did."

A few heavy punches to Raúl's ribs left him stunned and out of breath. Gomez recoiled his fists to strike again but the much younger man quickly took control of the fight with a sudden kick to the old man's side sending him crashing back into the bottom of the boat.

Ripping the necklace from Gomez's hand, Raúl smiled down at the gasping old man. "I know this necklace is just the first piece of the puzzle but from here I plan on paying your son a visit. He's in Boston correct?"

Gomez screamed with everything he had and landed a solid punch to Raúl's jaw. At the age of 119, Juan Gomez could still pack a punch. So much so that Raúl will be missing some teeth for the rest of his life but it still was not enough for the old man to escape.

Grabbing the fishing net, that just a few minutes ago had made Juan so very proud, Raúl wrapped it around Juan's neck and pushed the old man over the boat's side into the cold gulf water. Holding him underwater for what seemed like forever, Raúl was surprisingly exhausted by the time the old man finally stopped struggling and succumbed to the sea.

Standing up in the old man's homemade wooden boat, with one hand on the mast for balance, the other hand raised up to the cheers of the men back on his vessel Raúl's dream was coming true. His outstretched hand was holding a heavy solid gold chain with a beautiful jewel covered gold Cross at the end of it. The gold value alone, with today's prices, would be a fortune but the secrets that the Cross would hold were priceless. And now, after nearly 90 years and two generations of searching, it finally belonged to the descendants of the Floriblanca's old deckhand Raúl Vargas.

The large duel mast vessel turned downwind and sailed past Juan Gomez's simple fishing boat while Juan was still submerged half way under his boat. It is said that you live the life of a pirate you are doomed to die as a pirate. For Juan Gomez, he had spent the majority of his life trying to repay for the sins he had done in his early years. But even his past had come back to haunt him. However, if there was any justice to the life of Juan Gomez, the boy that was forced into piracy and lived with those sins until his death. He chose to live his life free. He chose to live his life in peace. He lived on the sea and died on the sea, fighting with his last breath. It was a good life, a free life, a sailor's life.

Chapter 37

Tampa, FL- present day.

Bayshore Drive, on the second Sunday of February just like every year, was heavy with thousands of costumed pirates. The annual Gasparilla Parade is an event that is sponsored and re-enacted by the Ye Mystic Krewe. While the Krewe is dressed up in their costumes, they invade the city of Tampa to capture the key to the city on their pirate ship the "Jose Gasparilla." The same tall pirate ship, that Gabriel had found a few days ago, was now streaming from head to toe with signal flags and confetti explosions. Hundreds of costumed pirates were walking the decks of the ship as it pulled into the Harbor Island channel shooting of the ships cannons and firing their muskets into the air. Dozens of other Krewes, representing various social groups in the city, were driving down the parade route as well in their floats tossing out beads and coins to screaming fans. As the parade progresses down Bayshore Drive, the pirate ship docks and ceremoniously captures the Mayor of Tampa in order take over the city for the day. It has become a Tampa tradition and each year thousands of people from all over the country take the opportunity to act like a pirate.

The Ye Mystic crew is an ever expanding collection of well-connected families and affluent business people in the Tampa area. Generations of family members and business types are connected through a social network of who's who in Tampa. Over the years similar Krewes have developed within a common model of social structure. Get together and pay some fees, have a common theme, maybe do some philanthropic or community service good deeds, and then a once a year come together and party like pirates. There is the Krewe of Neptune, the Krewe of Hillsborough, The Krewe of the Rough Riders named in memory of the 28th president Teddy Roosevelt who camped in Tampa on his way to Cuba during the Spanish American War. The Spirit of Cigar City Krewe and many many more spread for miles along the parade route.

However, one Krewe has been around almost as long as the original one but hardly a word is ever said about them. Yet they are more connected and more well-funded then all of them combined. They have members from the fields of politics, medicine, engineering, banking, marketing, sports teams, and most importantly school board members. Like the ever unfortunate Mr. Orsos, a history teacher from a local high school whose missing persons search was just called off with the discovery of a mysterious suicide note in his top desk drawer. This Krewe has tentacles that can reach every corner of not just the city of Tampa but the entire state of Florida and across the Nation.

As Santos Vargas stands up, at the aged oak wood podium, to address the members of his Krewe the banquet hall erupts with cheer and confetti. Several hundred Krewe members have joined together to start the party early and listen to their leader kick them off for another year's celebration. The large marble stone room echoes with delight as the revelers have been enjoying the early morning food and open bar. Santos takes a few steps up to the podium and is reminded of his life long journey to reclaim what, he believes, is his family's rightful heritage. Stolen from his great great grandfather Raúl Vargas, the story of Gaspar's treasure and the betrayal of Juan Gomez, was never far from Santo's mind. Never forgotten was the name Raúl II and how it was spoken with such reverence in his family circles. How Raúl II had found the gold Cross and killed the man that had wronged their name. And no matter what success Santos could achieve, no amount of money or power would ever amount to that sincere praise that Santos craved-until now. So close to his grasp the water in his mouth was sweet with anticipation. He couldn't wait until his web would catch his prey and today was that day of celebration, but before he could act he had to address the crowded room of drunken ignorant pawns.

"Today my fellow Krewe members we take a step towards making history."

The crowd erupted in cheers.

"Today we set right a course that was changed many years ago. Today we will not just let Tampa know but in fact the world will soon know that we… the Last Krewe of the Floriblanca are the true heirs to Gaspar's treasure."

The crowd screams in delight and gives a collective "arggh" in praise, not aware of the real meaning behind Santo's words. To them it's just an act, part of the show, for the thousands of screaming fans that now line the streets of Bayshore. After a few moments the cheers die down and the drunken costumed pirates stumble out of the building and on to the streets of Ybor city.

They will quickly make their way down Central Street where their floats wait for them. To them Santos' speech was in reference to every years' collection of plastic beads and tin coins that litter the streets at the end of the parade. The coordinated pirate invasion is their chance to live the life of a pirate for a day and enjoy a city wide party but to Santos it is much more. As the descendent of pirates, his family name is at stake and his legacy within that name is vital to him. The lost treasure of Gaspar will be his. Nothing will stand in his way. Especially, those two young boys who he has just learned are walking along the parade route.

A subtle nod from Santos to the Ghost, who was standing in the back of the room next to two large men in buccaneer outfits, sends them off to the streets. The web had been cast and now the spider just had to wait for his prey.

Chapter 38

It had been a few days since their night in the water at Useppa Island. The boys had not seen each other much over the last week. It was test week at school and Gabriel had to work a lot of hours at the restaurant ramping up for the weekend. Thankfully, he got the day off and was happy to spend the day at the parade going over things with Nathan. Although Nathan had lost some interest, discouraged with the outcome of their recent unsuccessful hunt, Gabriel however, was more committed than ever to his quest and it was just a matter of time before he got his next lead.

The boys walked down the sidewalk, along the seawall, and tried to enjoy the parade. But every costumed pirate, all hundred thousand of them, was a vivid reminder of how close the treasure was to them and Gabriel could not stop thinking about it.

The boys were trying to walk in some form of a line but they were constantly sidestepping overly excited pirates. Barely able to look up from the crowd, they crossed in front of some of the most expensive and amazing homes in Tampa. Homes that started in the millions of dollars, passed by the boys without even so much as a glance from them; they were deep in their conversation and deep in avoiding drunken pirates. Even the brown stone home of Roger Woods, the house of their attack the other night, passed by their eyes. They were at the parade but their thoughts were someplace else.

"So you still think the treasure exists?" Nathan questioned. "I know it does. Whatever was on that chain had to have been cut, even with the rust it was too thick to just break off and it was a clean break," replied Gabriel.

"Ok Gabriel. I believe you. Let's keep looking." The friends smiled at each other for a moment and then continued to walk along the party filled street.

"While you were drowning the other night I took a long look at your ring and those letters around the top again." Nathan looked at Gabriel to see his reaction but there was none he was too deep in thought. Gabriel suddenly spoke from memory.

"MVKTZXDARSTNFSKTZXDARXDRXV"

Surprising Nathan he thought to himself Gabriel was listening and had an incredible memory.

"The letters around the ring's bezel, I can't find any correlation with them." "But did you notice the repeating letters?" Nathan responded.

Gabriel halted abruptly in his tracks, forcing some followers to grumble under their breath as they were quick to move around the boys.

"Impossible! I've studied that ring for weeks; I never saw a repeating sequence." "It's there." Nathan interjected. "It wasn't easy to see but when you look at as much computer code as I do you tend to pick up on things like that. It was KTZXDA. But that's all I know. I can't make any sense of those letters."

Gabriel bounced the letters in his head for a moment. "KTZXDA reordered, ADXZTK, ZXTKDA, DAKXZT, those don't make any sense it has to be a code or cipher." "Or a coincidence to another dead end." Nathan suggested. Gabriel looked at Nathan with sympathy. He knew the frustration Nathan was feeling, but he believed in his heart they were close. He needed to make Nathan believe it too.

"Ok so let's back up and take a look at what we have? Let's take another look at the ring and the map. Maybe there is something we are missing. It doesn't make sense to have a treasure map with a harbor that has no names or a clue with no answer. There must be something else."

It was a hot dog food cart that crossed their path and made the boys stop for a second giving them a chance to look around at the sea of people screaming and laughing. With each and every new float that moved down the parade path, showers of beads rained down on the crowd. It was one handful of purple colored beads that soared thru the air landing across the street that Gabriel followed with his eyes and forced him to gasp.

Off in the distance, just a glimpse, a moment and then he was gone but it was him. Gabriel would never forget the pale skin and sunken features of the man that chased him in Jacksonville. Like a phantom, the Ghost was there in front of him just on the other side of the road but then disappeared in a blink of the eye. Just a moment but their shared instant was long enough for the two to make eye contact, and those black lifeless eyes of the Ghost sent chills through Gabriel's spine.

"We have to go… Now!"

Gabriel grabbed Nathan's shoulder turning him right into two giant men dressed in buccaneer outfits. Not unusual attire given the parade but these men were reaching out to grab the boys. Gabriel instantly knew they were not just partiers, they worked with the Ghost. With a sudden duck and spin, Gabriel was able to avoid the reach of the man on the right but Nathan was not so fast. Gabriel took a quick step and leaped into the air, driving his foot down into the back knee cap of the man on the left. With a scream of agony he let go of Nathan sending the startled boy backwards into the street. The man on the right was back with another attempt on Gabriel's arm. He got a hold of Gabriel's wrist and his grasp felt like an iron handcuff. His strength was too much for Gabriel to break free. This giant could toss the boy like a rag doll if he wanted too but now he made the mistake of trying to get Gabriel's other hand. Gabriel saw his opportunity.

The human body has over 200 bones in it. Some are big and powerful bones but most are actually small and narrow, many of the smallest ones are in the hand. Small and numerous bones with multiple joints and hinges give the human hand articulation beyond any other animal on the planet. But unfortunately for this gigantic pirate, the marvel of the human hand also hurts beyond belief when one of those little fingers is bent backwards until it snaps in half. No matter how strong or big you are a ripped apart little finger will force anyone to double over. This was the moment Gabriel needed to escape. Taking hold of the giant's finger, Gabriel tried to rip it off.

Nathan had hit the floor pretty hard and some good Samaritans were reaching down to help him up. Everyone was there to have a good time and even strangers were happy to help someone who had fallen to the ground. Unfortunately for one young man, who was just trying to help, he was violently jerked back away from Nathan by a large man in a buccaneer outfit holding a now dislocated knee. Nathan pushed back away from the limping monster sliding his butt across the street into the path of an oncoming parade float. The float looked like a giant octopus eating a pirate ship wrapped in its tentacles. It was a sight to see, even for Nathan who had to take a second and register the surreal vision. His pause was interrupted when Gabriel's arm hooked under his shoulder and ripped Nathan up to his feet.

Both boys were now standing in the middle lane of the closed off street with walking pirates and parade floats rolling towards them. Along the parade route were metal barricades that lined the street to keep people safely away from parade floats and marching feet. Just a head of the boys, behind the oncoming floats, was a long stretch of those barricades. Gabriel decided to race into the oncoming traffic in hopes that the two men attacking them would be forced to run behind the crowd of people and get held up by the barricades.

Running south on Bayshore during the Gasparilla parade with large floats, marching bands, and thousands of Krewe members heading towards them was not a wise decision. But to Gabriel, it was the only way for the boys to get away from the attacking men. There were several police officers walking the parade route nearby but they were looking into the crowd from the street and didn't see the boys race passed. The police officers had noticed a fight begin to break out, and they began to rush toward two large men dressed as buccaneers, one of them was limping on a hurt leg. They were pushing some bystanders down and it was getting out of control. Several police officers raced past Gabriel and Nathan choosing not to stop the boys because their priority was now a fight breaking out along the parade path.

A few more dodges and fast leaps from side to side with an occasional profanity laden comment from a walking Krewe member, and the boys made it to the barricades. They leaped over the metal railing and landed on the southbound lane that had been closed for participants. Pleased that they had escaped, they turned around and found themselves face to face with the yellow toothy grin of the Ghost.

Gabriel started to make a move but the metal barrel of the Ghost's gun was hard to miss as it was jabbed into his ribs.

"We finally meet, Mr. Fletcher," The Ghost hissed. "I have someone who would very much like to meet you."

Chapter 39

Sitting outside the finger-smudged glass window of Burger King play-area, Lisa and her best friend Tara were just finishing up their chicken tenders and diet Cokes.

"You should see him Tara. He is amazing," Lisa exclaimed. "He dove into this freezing water and was like a gorgeous teenage crocodile hunter. Calm and cool, never any fear and always so polite… sort of strangely too polite. He always says, sir and ma'am with everything. He even called me ma'am once when I asked him if he liked our school. I said do you like school? And he said, 'Yes ma'am, I do.' Can you believe it? Weird… but so cute."

"Does he have a good body?" Tara finally gets a word in to ask the only question that she cares about. "Does he? Tara, he got out of the water soaking wet and when he took off his vest I could see."

"Hi girls!" A familiar voice interrupts them from across the parking lot. "Oh, I didn't see you there, Roger what are you doing here?" Lisa blushed.

With his red BMW behind him, a gift from his parents on his 16th birthday, Roger was casually walking towards the girls. Wearing a loose fitting button up shirt with a light leather jacket and black trousers, Roger was always dressed up for any occasion and he always looked good. However, the butterflies that normally dance in Lisa's stomach when she sees him don't seem to be there anymore. In fact, she was a little disappointed that it was him walking up to her and not Gabriel.

"What are you all up to?" Roger asked with a wide grin. "Just hanging out-girl talk," Lisa answered.

"Good, then Lisa do you mind if I talk to you. Tara could you give us a minute?" Roger was nice to ask but it was more of an order then a question.

Tara got the hint and with a quick smile to Lisa, she was off for a refill and another table.

"I wanted to talk to you about the other night." "Roger, it's really ok. It's not a…" Before she can finish he continued on. "I really think your brother and his friend need to watch themselves at school. Some of the guys have been talking about the fight and I'm worried about them." "What do you mean-fight? They were jumped by those guys." Lisa exclaimed.

"Well, their story is that your brother was talking trash and then when they confronted him his friend Gabriel just started throwing punches."

"That's a lie!"

"Listen I wasn't there I showed up too late to stop it so I don't know. I believe you. Some of those guys have got some real tempers but they stand by their story, which means that I'm concerned for your brother. I can keep an eye out for him and try to talk to some of the guys. I'll do my best to keep him safe but please just ask him to try to keep his mouth shut for a bit. He's a great guy but sometimes he just say's things."

"I know he can sometimes mouth off but he didn't start the fight I'm sure of it. He and Gabriel told me." "It's ok. I think I can calm them down and keep things cool. I'll talk to them and see what I can do. I just want to keep Nathan safe." "Thank you, Roger. That means a lot to me."

She was compelled to reach out and give him a hug. Not so much a hug of passion but more of a hug of gratitude. She often got mad at her little brother but would hate to see some older kids bully him. She held Roger and could feel the warmth from his body on her shoulders. It felt good, and she did have feelings for him but again her mind drifted off to Gabriel. She couldn't help but think what it would feel like if he were the one holding her.

For Roger, the plan worked. Of course everything he had said was a lie, but he had to do it. He could sense some attraction between Gabriel and Lisa and that was unacceptable. As far as his teammates coming after her brother and Gabriel that was not the issue, two were on crutches, one had his mouth wired shut, and the other was forced to wear a side brace to protect his broken ribs. The last thing those guys wanted was to confront Gabriel again. A sinister smile of chemically bleached teeth flashed on Roger's perfectly tanned face, his plan was working just fine.

"Do you want to go somewhere tonight? Maybe catch a movie or just take a ride in my car. I would love to spend some time with you. I just feel like we are both so busy that we never get a chance to… talk." It was a cheesy line even for Roger but he really could sell it with those big brown eyes of his. Lisa bought it.

"Sure, I'd like that. Maybe a movie, say around 7pm?" Roger looked deep into her eyes and with every ounce of sincerity that he could pretend to muster. "You just made my day."

The two smiled at each other and talked a little while longer but were unaware of the watchful eyes staring at them… her to be precise. Across the parking lot and beyond the drive up lane sat a dark figure quietly staring at the unsuspecting teens. The shadowy man whose job it was to watch and follow this young girl- as if his life depended on it because in fact it did- had not let her out of his site for the past several hours. When you work for Santos Vargas, failure is not an option. He would follow this girl into the gates of hell if he had to because he would rather face eternal flames then Santos Vargas. So he just watched and followed until the phone call would come and then he would pick her up and take her to see the devil himself.

Chapter 40

The car drive was very short and even though the windows were blacked out, Nathan was pretty confident they were in Ybor City. He knew this area well. Nathan had lived in Tampa his entire life and he had always enjoyed the diversity of the area. The beaches, the casual suburban districts, and even the touristy places that brought people from all over the world to enjoy what Florida had to offer but it was the Ybor City area that he had a special affection for.

He had always enjoyed the collaboration of early 1900's Italian, Cuban, and Spanish immigrant influence in Ybor's culture. Historically known to the world as "Cigar City," Ybor became the largest cigar manufacturing city of the 20th century. Immigrants flocked to this area from all over the world to try to make a better life with the American dream. The cultural diversity is still represented from the simple wooden "cigar homes," that once housed the factory workers, to the colorful brick paved shopping district of 7th Ave. The local food also takes on flavors of Cuban, Italian, and Spanish ingredients but it is a taste that is uniquely Ybor. The large brick factories that used to dominate the landscape, when the cigar industry was booming, are now somewhat dilapidated and abandoned.

But it is these run down giant structures that used to capture Nathan's imagination the most.

He would often wander what secrets those giant structures could tell. What stories they most hold within their brick walls. Some of the luckier factories have been renovated to hold some law offices or other business suites, a couple have been saved for Florida landmark preservation groups, and one was even renovated by the Church of Scientology before they too moved on and returned the building to vacancy. Just a few miles from the Bayshore Drive waterfront, Tampa's historic Ybor City revolved around the nearby shipping docks. It was the lifeblood of the area and Nathan could still smell the dense salt water air from inside the car. He knew they were still close to the bay.

The car parked in an underground garage, a large room with white stone walls. A few modern plumbing and air condition pipes were running along the ceiling of an otherwise very old building. The concrete floor covered most of the ground but some vehicle wear spots had crumbled the smooth surface and exposed the red brick rectangles of the older original garage flooring. The room was musty and damp with the toxic mixture of the black Audi's exhaust fumes and ancient stale air. As they climbed out of the car, they found themselves now standing in front of the Ghost.

"Mr. Santos is excited to see you. He has waited a very long time for this. I hope you enjoy it." The Ghost hissed. "I hope we don't disappoint him." Gabriel replied. "Oh you won't I can assure you." "We can't wait." Gabriel tried to sound as cool and confident as he could but inside he was panicking.

A dark spiral staircase towards the back of the garage was leading up to another floor. Unlike modern staircases of today that often rotate to the right in a clockwise fashion, this one rotated to the left, counter clockwise, which was more common in ancient times. Stairwells in Medieval castles were designed this way when the weapons of choice were swords. Since most people are right handed, invading soldiers would be forced to either swing their weapon with the left hand or lose precious power because they couldn't strike from over their head. To their advantage, the soldiers who would be defending from the higher position could strike down at full force with their stronger right hands giving them the upper hand. Although the building was definitely old, it was not from those days. However, Gabriel thought to himself whoever designed this place must have been a fan of history.

The staircase landed on the second floor and the concrete steps gave way to a pewter and red colored carpet. The dank musty exhaust smell of the garage was replaced with the sweet smell of lingering cigar smoke and Spanish Cedar. The walls were lined with deep mahogany wood and up lighting sconces that framed out beautiful painting reliefs of the great Spanish explorers. Ponce de Leon's landing in St. Augustine; Narvaez meeting the Tocobaga Indians, various old nautical charts with ancient shipping trade routes, and official charters of Spanish domain, Gabriel was trying to look at each one but was getting rushed down the hall by the Ghost. If he had more time he would gladly spend all day looking at these pieces of art. In that moment the fear of being kidnapped disappeared in his mind as he looked to the artwork with delight, Nathan was not so impressed and the fear was already very real for him.

"I see you are a fan of history." A graveled voice called out from a room at the end of the hall. Gabriel spun his head forward to see a large, olive skinned man, with coal black, hair standing in the center of the round room. It was Santos. The vaulted ceiling, that must have been at least 20 feet high, made the boys feel small as they walked up and stood at the edge of the great circular space.

"I too am a fan of history, especially when it comes to setting history right," Santos continued. "I have something I would like to show you."

Santos turned and took a few steps towards a small table along the back wall of the rotunda. Reaching for a dark Acacia wood covered box, Santos picked up the box carefully and with reverence opened it. A small gold latch was lifted and the top was raised up to show off a soft red felt lined interior. Santos reached into the box and pulled out a long gold chain with a solid gold Cross at the end of it. The Cross was polished gold that seemed to light up the room with a warm glow while dozens of stone jewels sparkled dancing light throughout the room. The jewels were inlayed around an outer circle that created a halo encircling most of the Cross. There was a cutout right in the center of the Cross but it was empty with no jewel or stone in it, just an open hole. The Cross itself was about 4 inches long with a 2 inch intersecting piece. Touching the outer ends and the top of the Cross was the perfect circle that met about halfway down the long center line. Inlayed along the curve of the circle were the beautiful polished jewels, some red, most were blue with a couple green ones intermixed, and one very black onyx at the foot of the Cross. In between the jewels were markings of some kind, but the Cross was too far away for Gabriel to read it.

"My great-great grandfather Raúl Vargas was a sailor on the pirate ship Floriblanca. He was a crewman for Captain Jose Gaspar. I believe you've heard of that name." Santos didn't wait for an answer.

"When the Captain sank in the deep, he took the secrets of his buried treasure with him, or so Raúl first thought. That was until a young cabin boy named Juan Gomez was given the secret during the Captain's final moments. Raúl witnessed the Captain give this boy a map. But the map turned out to be part of a trick. The cabin boy then took the treasure for himself and my great-great grandfather spent the rest of his life looking for it."

Gabriel was frantically looking for an escape but he found himself gradually paying closer attention to the Santos story. Perhaps there was a clue in the mad man's talking that would help find the treasure and perhaps save their lives. But he also had to find a way out of here and fast.

"Maybe Gomez already found it and spent it on a bunch of stuff?" Gabriel offered.

"He was a fool!" Santos snapped. His disgust for even the name Gomez was obvious. "He was a fool not capable of solving the mystery. That treasure was meant for my family-for me" Santos took a deep breath to calm himself down.

"But he got close once. In 1848, a hurricane was moving up the gulf and Raúl had cornered Juan at the south end of Long Key. But before he could get him, Juan escaped on a small fishing boat by sailing right out into the eye of the hurricane. The storm ripped apart the entire area making new islands and leveling some old ones. Maps had to be changed because the area was so devastated. That barrier island of Long Key was cut in half at John's Pass during that storm. Madeira Beach and Treasure Island were once connected. Did you know that?"

The boys shook their heads in response.

"It was because of that storm, the 'Great Gale of 1848', that the treasure was finally lost. Raúl and his men barely made it out alive and he knew Juan couldn't have survived in that boat. So, he was forced to suffer the remaining years of his life anguishing over what was his but now was lost."

Santo's paused to take a sip of aged rum from his glass and breathe in a long puff of cigar smoke. As the grey smoke poured back out of his mouth, he continued.

"And then one day an article appeared in a local newspaper about a man living on Panther Key in Charlotte Harbor. A man that was over 100 years old and had lived his entire life on the sea from his days as a scout in the Seminole war, as a soldier for the Civil war, and even all the way back to his childhood when he was a young pirate cabin boy. It talked about the adventures and life of Juan Gomez, the last of the pirates. They made him out to be some gracious and humble man, a man that would help others around him and had committed his life to service. Even telling the story about how some fishermen were stuck on Pass-a-grill beach one day with no fresh water when old Juan came to save the day. He had remembered the location of an old artesian well that had been buried during a storm. He dug it out at great expense to himself and provided water to the stranded sailors. Oh they made him out to be a great man. But my family knew different. My family knew the real Juan Gomez."

Taking another puff of smoke from his cigar, Santos continued. "Raúl unfortunately died a few years before the article but his Grandson, Raúl the second, knew the story very well. He honored his Grandfather by taking his revenge. He went to Panther Key to kill Juan but when he found him, he also found this."

Santos held up the golden Cross.

"Juan had found a piece of the treasure and Raùl the second knew there had to be more. The treasure was still alive and waiting to be found. Raúl the second had reignited the Vargas' legacy and once again the treasure of Gaspar would be rightfully ours. Unfortunately, old man had already passed his secret on to his family and even at the cost of his life he would not give up that secret. We, the descendants of Raúl Vargas, have been searching for it ever since. And that search is what has brought us together here today."

"You killed an innocent man. Jose Gomez was my friend and a good man," Gabriel responded.

"Jose Gomez was not an innocent man," Santo's rage could not be hidden. "He was as guilty as Juan himself that lousy cabin boy. He refused to give up his secret, and he deserved to die. I knew he had passed the secret on to someone else, someone close to him, just as it had been passed on to him. It was just a matter of time until we found you. You the son he never had. You the boy that he trusted with his most valued possession and you the one that would do what he never could do."

The memories of the gentle man Gabriel knew as Jose Gomez flooded back into his mind. It hurt to think of his friend's life being taken from him but Gabriel took comfort in hearing how much he meant to Jose. Jose was like a father to Gabriel and now the man that killed his friend wanted to ruin his memory as well. Gabriel's sadness began turning into defiance.

"You have something that belongs to me and I want it back." Santos broke Gabriel's thought.

"I'm not sure I know what you mean," Gabriel replied. "Don't lie to me!" Santos roared as the room echoed with his thunder. "I know about the map. My family has been searching for it for 200 years and I know that cowardly old man Jose Gomez gave it to you before I had him killed."

Nathan gasped at the admission. He had never actually seen a killer before and that cold fact was now realized right in front of him. His fear was justified, he was being held captive by a confirmed killer. Not someone you see on TV or in a movie, this was real and this was real danger. Nathan's heart was now almost audible across the room as it beat in his chest.

Gabriel found his anger growing with Santo's comments and he was now furious. He loved Jose. For a child that had never known friendship or kindness past the age of 5, Jose was a father figure to him. The nervous blood that had been swelling up Gabriel's neck and flushing his face was quickly cooled with his new resolve.

"Why did you have to kill him?"

"Because he wouldn't give me what I wanted. Don't think I won't do the same to you. Now give me the map." Santos took a large step towards Gabriel but Gabriel refused to flinch. "I don't have it."

Enraged Santos stepped forward again and violently grabbed Nathan who was standing silently by Gabriel. Now holding Nathan by the throat he began to lift the boy up off the ground with one hand.

"I'll hang him here until you give it to me."

Nathan's face was already bulging with swollen red capillaries around his blood shot eyes. Struggling for air, all Nathan could do was wiggle and make grunting noises. He wanted to swing his fists at Santos but his will to survive overcame him and all he could do was grab the thick wrists of his captor to hold his weight up. The strain on his neck from his body weight was already starting to make him blackout.

"Ok," Gabriel couldn't hold out any longer watching his friend suffer. "I'll give it to you but I don't have it here." "Where is it?" Nathan was now turning blue. "My apartment closet under the back carpet, there is a tear in the carpet there that you can lift up. The map is under it. I can take you there."

"No need," Santos grinned. "I know where you live." Nathan dropped to the floor and gasped for air.

Turning to the Ghost, Santos ordered, "Lock them up until I get back."

The large man glared back into Gabriel's eyes, "And if you're lying to me. I will come back and finish the job with your little friend over there." Santos turned and raced out of the room leaving the boys to the Ghost.

"Come with me," the Ghost hissed, "I've got someplace special for you."

Chapter 41

The room smelled like Pine Sol and the burning sting in his eyes told Gabriel that ammonia was present as well. It had to be a cleaning closet. The boys tried to run their fingers along the cold ceramic tile walls, in hopes of finding a light switch, but it was difficult because their hands were bound with plastic zip ties-compliments of the Ghost. After a few minutes of searching it was Nathan who felt something tap the top of his head when he moved across the center of the room. Pulling down on the little nylon string a single incandescent bulb fired its filament and lit up the room.

The boys were in a pastel covered pale blue 8ft by 8ft cleaning closet. There were some dirty mop buckets and a small rinse sink along the wall. Some common household cleaners were on a small shelf just above Gabriel's head. There were no windows to break and the air vent was too small to climb out. The boys quickly realized that if they were going to get out, they were going to have to go through the heavy wood door that was now locked behind them.

Gabriel turned his back to Nathan, "Against my back in my pants, hooked to my belt, grab my hawk."

"I'm sorry. You want me to do what?" Nathan questioned. "My hands are tied, I can't reach it but he didn't search us for weapons."

"You have a weapon?"

"Just grab it," Gabriel ordered.

Nathan reached out his bound hands and lifted up Gabriel's shirt revealing an odd rectangle shaped plastic cover. He grabbed the cover and pulled it towards him, a long handle began to slide down Gabriel's back. A metal handle about 13 inches long was fixed to the end of the plastic cover.

"What is this? It looks like an axe." "That's exactly right," Gabriel removed the cover revealing a curved sharpened blade and pointed spike on the back, "a tactical Shrike to be precise. It was my Father's tomahawk."

The RMJ tactical Shrike was a modern version of the historical and effective weapon of the ancient Indians. Forged with 3/8th inch chrome-moly 4140 steel and flamed hardened to basically cut through anything, the Shrike was virtually unbreakable. A favorite tool for forward line military personal, the Shrike could dig, hammer, cut, and if necessary in close combat-effectively kill.

"A soldier, serving in Afghanistan, came across some rubble in a destroyed Humvee vehicle. He found my Father's rucksack with a letter to me and this tomahawk inside it. It took him 6 months to find me but one day he just showed up at my door and gave it to me. He said that it actually had saved his life in battle but that it belonged to me. It was his duty to return it to honor my Father's sacrifice."

Nathan turned the heavy axe-like weapon in his hand and could tell by the scrapes and scratches that this tool had some stories to tell. He noticed an engraving on the head of the blade.

Si ves pacem, para bellum.

Gabriel saw Nathan trying to read it and answered his question before he even asked.

"If you want peace, prepare for war." "I told you that was my Father's favorite saying. He served in the military so that his family could live in peace."

After a pause to remember his Father, Gabriel snapped back into the situation. He took the tomahawk and quickly sliced through Nathan's plastic handcuffs. Soon his were removed as well and he turned his attention to the door. With a few quick hard swings and one heavy foot kick, the tomahawk ripped through the door's lock and the boys found themselves in an empty corridor. Nathan began to run to the left but Gabriel went right.

"Where are you going? This way takes us towards the garage we can find an exit." Nathan stated. "We can't leave. We need that Cross." "What?" Nathan gasped before he quickly lowered his voice. "Are you insane? We can't go back there?" "Listen, that Cross could be the missing piece that we need. The map, the ring, they don't make sense. What if that Cross is the answer? It has to be the missing clue." Gabriel argued.

"But what about our life, is that worthless?" Nathan pleaded. "You see what they are capable of doing." Gabriel replied, "Do you think they will let us go? They know where I live, probably you too. Are you going to be safe at home? Your family? Your sister? No, we have to get it and solve this thing now. It's our only way."

Nathan reluctantly agreed and the boys were once again racing down the hall trying to not make too much noise. A few turns and a minute later they were back at the great round room and luckily, so far, had not been spotted.

The wooden box containing the gold Cross was still sitting on the mahogany table. Gabriel grabbed the box, removed the Cross and placed it into his khaki shorts pocket. Nathan's head was peeking out the door, keeping an eye on the hallway, hoping that no one was coming.

Something suddenly caught Gabriel's eye across the room along the floor board. The highly polished and lacquered wood floor showed years of layered wax giving the surface a very reflective gloss shine, except for one spot. Almost impossible to see, if not for just the right angle of spotlight glare off the floor, a scuff mark in an arch like pattern extended out from the wall about 90 degrees. Walking across the room to take a closer look, Gabriel saw a tiny black line perfectly hidden along the seam of two marble slab base boards on the floor. The tiny black line continued up the wood trimmed wall towards the ceiling.

"A door!" he nearly shouted. "Here a hidden door."

Nathan ran over to him and struggled to see what he was talking about but then plain as day, there it was. A perfectly shaped rectangle right around the wood wainscoting concealing what had to be a secret room or even better a secret passage.

"We've got to find the handle." Nathan started to scan the wall with his hands gently pressing every square inch of the wall in hopes of a pressure latch. Gabriel turned and scanned the room for something he could use and then he saw it.

Santos, in his rush to find the map at Gabriel's home, had left his cigar, still lit on the table. Gabriel gently blew on the glowing end of the Tabanero Churchill forcing it to flare and smoke up. With the lit end now smoking steadily, Gabriel passed it along the wall. The hot smoky air bellowed up the wall in a steady flow until Gabriel saw the smooth flowing smoke dance into tiny swirls.

"Here, look here, a draft." Gabriel put the Tabanero down and strained his eyes to look at a dark soiled spot. From past years of oily fingerprints on the polished white marble, a tiny thumbprint size smudge covered a button about the size of a push pin. Pressing on the darkened spot a silent click could be felt though the wall. The wall began to rumble and then slowly slid open with an air rushing hiss. It was black behind the wall, pitch black, and the boys had no idea where it lead to but they knew couldn't stay here so they stepped into the darkness and prayed for a way out.

Chapter 42

Santos' silver Cadillac Escalade was parked at an angle taking up two spaces in the already crowded apartment parking lot. Out of the car and up the crumbling stars, Santos was now standing in front of the paint peeled door of apartment 203.

It only took one kick of his massive size 16 shoe to open the dry rotted tan colored door that led to Gabriel's room. After a moment to take in the bare walls and furniture less space, his eyes settled on a wood inlayed picture resting on the floor and leaning against the wall. It was the only piece of art in the room but Santos didn't question why it wasn't hanging on the wall. He failed to understand the pictures significance to the very treasure he was searching for as he made his way towards the closet.

The empty apartment was not surprising given Gabriel's financial situation and lack of parents but something started to bother Santos. Two young boys in search of an ancient treasure, on the quest of their lives, and there was nothing in the entire apartment. No books, charts, or maps, no compass or surveying gear, no shovels or tools of any kind, Santos' blood pressure began to rise.

He walked towards the closet in the bedroom, stomping heavily across the linoleum, and ripped open the louvered panel doors. Santos looked to the back corner of the closet at the carpet but saw no tear or space. He grabbed the carpet threads and began to yank on the still glued carpet. Finally the carpet tore back across the closet bottom and before it could even roll back to the ground, Santos was racing out of the door back towards his car.

The cell phone was on and the Ghost's number was dialed before Santos even opened his car door. "Yes, sir" the Ghost hissed on the other end of the phone. "Get those brats on the phone. I'm going to take them to feed the gators myself."

With an agreeing and hiss like "Yes" from the Ghost, Santos' waited on the line to hear back from his henchman. A moment turned to a minute, and then another minute, and then after three minutes of waiting Santo's finally heard a voice on the other end of his phone.

"Sir, we have a problem. The boys are not here. We are searching the property but they are not where I left them." The Ghost could almost hear the boiling blood shooting into Santos' eyes as he waited for a response. After an agonizing second, Santos spoke, "Find them or you will beg for a quick death that I will not give you." "Yes Sir." The Ghost took a deep swallow and then pressed the phone's "Off" button.

Chapter 43

The heavy wood door closed behind the boys just as they heard the Ghost's footsteps getting closer. In their rush, they slid into the narrow passageway without looking where it led before the door slammed behind them and locked them in darkness. Now they found themselves feeling along the exposed wood studs and itchy insulation that backed the hallway wall and its priceless works of art.

Sliding one foot behind the other and a hand on each other's shoulder, they started to make their way single file down a narrow path. They stopped cold in their tracks when they heard the screams and orders begin to echo on the other side of the wall. The Ghost had just discovered the two boys missing, and they knew at once, by the tone of his voice, that getting captured would be a death sentence. They continued to move cautiously along the passage way between the narrow walls. At one point, Nathan was forced to hold his breath for at least a minute in fear that the man, just inches from him on the other side of the wall, would hear him breath. They both stood there in silence and waited with sweat beading down their faces until the man on the other side of the wall began to move. They couldn't tell which way he went or how far away he was but they had to keep moving. They had to keep going, and they had to go now even if they didn't know where they were going.

The two boys continued along their path running the length of the wall until the tight narrow space seemed to open up just a little.

Still in pitch blackness but with a little more room to move, Gabriel could sense they were in a different part of the house. An older part, not remodeled by wood and fiberglass insulation, but made of metal and cold brick. Sliding his feet along the floor and straining to capture any possible light in his now dilated pupils, Gabriel's foot stopped at an opening on the ground. Dropping his foot down a few inches and landing on a step, Gabriel and Nathan soon found themselves creeping down into a cold empty void in the floor

The descent lasted for about 30 feet, Nathan guessed, and then it leveled off. The floor was covered with little rectangular shapes that felt like bricks. Most likely the red brick pavement that is so common around Tampa's old historic areas. Nathan was so focused on his senses within his blind silence that he could almost feel every uneven bump and seam of the floor through his rubber soled sneakers. He wished he could see to be sure. But at least they were on flat ground and not still descending into the dark abyss, this gave a little comfort for the boys. The walls were thicker and they no longer could hear the men scurrying on the other side of the drywall. This made them feel a little safer to start breathing again and pick up their pace at the expense of some noise. They marched on for several minutes until they came to a fork in the tunnel. Feeling a trail of water descending past his feet, Gabriel decided to turn left in hopes of following the water to an exit.

"I bet we are underneath Ybor City," Nathan whispered, "I know we are not far from the docks I can smell the sea thru these tunnels. We have to be in Ybor."

"Why do you say that?"

"I took a tour here one time with my Father and the guide said that in the early 1900's, Tampa Bay was one of the busiest ports in America. Ybor became a hotspot for cigar manufacturers with tobacco imports from Cuba. During the prohibition time, cigars, alcohol, gambling and the mob were all around this area and they developed a series of transport tunnels and hidden escape routes underground."

"Like we are doing now?" Gabriel added.

"Yeah, at the time I thought it would be cool to see but now that I'm here I have to admit it's pretty awesome. I can't believe I'm using old mob tunnels."

"Well, I'm happy that your happy," Gabriel turned to smile at his friend but it was pointless in the dark tunnel. He couldn't even see his own feet in front of him.

The last 30 minutes seemed like an eternity. The boys were so focused on each and every short step they forgot to talk to each other and were forced to let their imagination and pulsing heartbeats to keep them company. Occasionally the entire space around them would rattle and shake, forcing them both to stop as if they may have caused the quake. Nathan assumed it had to be a large truck or vehicle above them which meant that they were close to some roads.

"Why do we need the Cross if we don't have the map anymore?" Nathan finally spoke out into the empty darkness. "Who says we don't have it?" Gabriel's voice was further away than Nathan expected forcing him to pick up his pace and catch up. "You told Santos where to find it. I'm sure he has it by now." "The map is not there. I hid it in my school locker with the ring."

"Man you're good, even I believed you. I would hate to be around Santos when he finds out you tricked him." "Let's just hope we find it before he finds us."

"Up here I think I found something." Gabriel pushed his arm up into a circular space in the ceiling. His fingers felt some jagged metal rungs from an old rusted ladder that ascended upwards into the hole.

"They at least go up. Stay here." Gabriel pulled himself up and climbed to the fourth rung using only his arms when he could finally get his feet on the ladder. The ladder was holding but it creaked and cracked like it wanted to pop off the wall and take Gabriel crashing to the floor. About 20 feet up, the ladder was still holding when Gabriel stopped at a metal plate blocking his path. He pushed with all of his might but it didn't budge. Just when he was about to give up and descend back down, he felt a hinge a few inches behind his head. Grabbing his tomahawk Shrike, Gabriel began to strike the large metal bracket. Sparks, from the colliding metal blows, gave a welcomed flash of light to Nathan standing on the floor some 20 feet below. Like a strobe light in a dance club, flashes of brightness lit the room and gave Nathan blinding snapshots of his surroundings.

Much like his imagination had shown him, the tunnel they were in was about six feet tall and 5 feet wide. The walls and floor were covered with red rectangle bricks stacked on top of each other. Nathan recognized the triangle shaped logo of the Southern Clay MFG. Company that was common on many of the bricks that paved the streets throughout Tampa. Early 1920's he thought to himself, about the time of Cigar City's heyday. These tunnels were old but very few people have ever seen them before. The thought brought a smile to his face with each flash from above.

A few more hard strikes and the hinge gave way. The heavy weight of the metal plate swung open, breaking free, and dropped to the brick floor with a deafening metallic crash. Nathan narrowly jumped out of the way avoided the death blow from the heavy metal plate.

"We're in." Gabriel yelled down to Nathan who then began his climb up. Not as graceful or clean as Gabriel, but Nathan was quite impressed with himself for actually making the climb up. His adrenaline was still pumping hard when he reached the landing and found Gabriel slamming his shoulder into a wall. The boys found themselves in a small square room about the size of a phone booth. The room had a concrete floor, but the walls were bare wooden studs framing up some modern drywall and wiring.

Nathan looked back down at the hole in the floor they had just climbed out of. He could see cracked cement around the opening in the smooth concrete floor. As if a thin layer of cement had been poured over the hatch in the sub flooring, the secret hole would have been invisible to anyone looking for it.

"It's nailed pretty well but I can smell food behind it. I almost got it."

With one more violent thrust of his body, the wood studs gave way and Gabriel erupted out of the wall and into a bright lit room. He slammed hard onto the tile floor with a crash of wood, stucco, and flesh. Covering his eyes from the stinging light that was now flooding his vision, he could hear a collective gasp of people and rattling silverware all around him. When his vision slowly began to return he could see tables of people sitting down for lunch. Gabriel could make out a man standing over him with a black apron and a pitcher of Sangria.

"Is this a restaurant? Where are we?" Gabriel asked. "What are you doing here?" the man in the apron asked. "Sorry, my friend and I got lost." Nathan needed to allow his eyes to adjust to the light that had suddenly filled the tiny room. The bright light stung his eyes and forced him to stop in his tracks. But after a moment, he quickly climbed thru the gaping hole and grabbed Gabriel's arm to lift his friend up. "Come on we have to go."

Racing past the startled waiter, who had just watched his bus station explode, the boys ran across a banquet space and thru a spacious garden that sat in the center of a beautiful restaurant. A few odd glances came towards the running boys but most of the patrons just continued enjoying their meals completely unaware that this duo had just escaped captivity from a century old tunnel beneath their feet.

The boys slowed down their pace when they saw sunlight through a large glass window. The bar of the

Columbia Restaurant that sits on 7th ave. and 22nd street has been a stable in Ybor City for over a hundred years. The mirror that has been hanging on the wall since the time of Teddy Roosevelt caught one last glimpse of the boys in its reflection as they ran out onto 22nd street and disappeared around the corner.

Chapter 44

It was a cool afternoon outside the Veteran's 24 movie theater, but it wasn't the weather that was giving Lisa the chills. She had not heard from her brother in hours. She knew he had gone to the Gasparilla parade with Gabriel. But when she covered for him with their Mom around 5pm she thought he had just lost track of time, now it was almost 7pm and she was worried. She paced back and forth in front of the large matinee staring at her cell phone pleading with it to ring. She constantly was checking her phone's bar status making sure there was a strong signal, the signal was fine, but she was not.

People started to make their way into the lobby for the 7pm movie. She saw some friends from school, two young lovers out on their first date, and a group of kids with nothing to do but hang out; unfortunately the one person she was dying to find was nowhere to be found. On her last glance towards the parking lot she saw Roger's car pull into a space and knew he would be there in a second. She had no idea what she would say but knew she couldn't watch a movie now while her brother seemed to be missing.

She argued with herself, questioning whether or not she was being paranoid. Her little twerp of a brother was probably just nose deep in a book or watching TV completely unaware of the hell he was putting her through. He must not be paying attention to his phone again or more likely he was just ignoring her. Perhaps she was just nervous about her date. What would Gabriel think if he and her brother came up now and Roger was here? If only Gabriel were here maybe she would feel warm and calm again. Her panicked mind was all over the place and she couldn't focus. A tidal wave of mixed emotions was pouring through her but she knew something wasn't right. They say twins have a special sense about each other and right now she had to focus because she sensed something was wrong.

Roger walked up with a giant smile and seemingly not a care in the world… just as usual. He was genuinely happy to see Lisa, especially since she was wearing a snug fitting outfit that showed off her striking figure, but he was also keenly aware of the two shapely girls walking in front of him. He couldn't help but to take one last glance before turning his attention back to Lisa.

"Wow, you look great Lisa. Are you ready to go in?"

She hated to do this but had no choice.

"Hi Roger, I'm so sorry but I can't stay. I need to go." Roger was startled, "What do you mean? What's wrong?"

"It's my brother. I haven't heard from him in hours and I'm worried. He and Gabriel went to Gasparilla and they haven't come back."

Frustrated at her answer, Roger tried to hide his anger. "Look I'm sure they are fine. They probably just had too much fun at the parade and lost track of time. I was there earlier, and it was crazy. They are just having fun and we should too."

"I don't think so. I've been calling his phone, and he is not answering I even called over to Gabe's apartment and there was no answer. I'm really worried."

All Roger heard was "Gabe's apartment" the words were like knives stabbed into his back. No one had ever stood Roger up for a date before and given her feelings for Gabriel this was unacceptable to him.

"Gabe? You mean Gabriel? What's up with you two? Do you like him or something? I thought we had something special between us and all you talk about is this Gabriel guy." "That's not what I said Roger. I said I'm trying to find my brother who is missing."

He had heard enough. No one, not even Lisa, tells Roger "no." "Your brother's a loser. He's probably just hanging out with that other loser friend of his, the jerk you so affectionately call Gabe!"

Turning his back to her, he began to walk away but decided to play one more card. "Look I thought we had something together Lisa. I thought you were different from the other girls. I really wanted you to get to know me. So if you want another chance, let's skip the movie and you can come with me in my car and we can spend some quiet time together."

Tears began to swell in her eyes she was so mad at him. "You can just keep walking you jerk. I can't believe I ever liked you. Have fun with yourself tonight, you seem to be the only one you care about anyway."

She turned away from the arrogant senior and stormed off towards the parking lot. She never looked back at him. She was so mad at herself for ever liking a jerk like Roger Woods. As she got closer to her car, she slowed her pace down and started reaching for her keys. The car's lights flashed and the alarm "beeped" when she unlocked the doors. She looked down at her phone again and started to dial Nathan's number for the 100th time when her mouth was slapped shut and her arms were strapped to her side. The phone fell to the ground, the green call button still waiting to be pressed. She couldn't see her attacker but her first thought was it was Roger. However when she was lifted off the ground and carried towards a large black sedan, her fear was now even more frightening.

She couldn't see the drivers face, only his leather gloved hand on the steering wheel, as she was thrown into the back seat. She tried to scream with all that she had to Roger or anyone that could help her but when the door slammed behind her she knew it was no use. The pressure percussion on her ears, when the car door closed, was almost painful. The car was soundproof. Lisa was in real trouble and she knew it.

Chapter 45

The streets of Ybor city were getting dark now as night was sweeping in. Gabriel and Nathan had moved a few blocks down from the Columbia Restaurant. They had moved down 22nd Street a little ways but every car that drove by them felt like it was one of Santos' men. So they decided to camp out in a parking garage by the rail tracks on 6thAve. to lie low for a bit.

As the sun dropped below the last of the city's rooftops, it was officially dark now. The boys felt safe enough to venture out and make their way down the 6th Ave. train track. Gabriel thought they should still try to stay out of sight but time was wasting and they needed to move faster. They hopped from timber beam to timber beam as they walked east down the train tracks towards downtown. Nathan knew there was a cab station not too far up on Cass Street about a 20 minute walk from where they were.

They took a few steps off the tar soaked rail studs and slid down the small shoulder hill of white stones to a level grassy parking lot. The boys walked passed a fence and onto a small sidewalk lined street. They were tired, hungry, and walking on fumes, neither of the two talked much and both just wanted to get out of downtown. Gabriel wasn't aware of the large red brick building next to him but when he walked into the back of

Nathan he was forced to look up and see what made him stop.

Nathan was standing idle in the middle of the sidewalk staring at a double pained dungeon like metal door. It was built into the brick building and encased by a tall archway that was at least 12 feet tall. The name La Tropical was written on the door handle, in a large ribbon-like custom metal design. The title was written with fluid cursive script, a throwback look to hand painted advertising, much different than the modern block looking logos that are so common today. It was warm and friendly but very much out of place. The glass window next to the door said the building belonged to a law firm and the office equipment that could be seen through the glass panel confirmed it.

"What are you looking at?" Gabriel asked. "This door, that name I've seen it before. I read about La Tropical."

Nathan walked past Gabriel back along the sidewalk looking up the outside wall of the tall brick building. Almost Cathedral like in its size the building was the tallest in Ybor City, yet Nathan had never really looked at it before. Gazing up the steep brick surface about two thirds of the way up Nathan could make out some white painted bricks from another era. The brightness of the name on the building had faded but Nathan could still make out the words, "Florida Brewing".

"So this is where the brewery is. La Tropical was the beer of Ybor in the early 1900's. This used to be the brewery." Nathan smiled at his find. "They built a brewery on top of an ancient well that had been used for hundreds of years by the Indians in this area. The water was so pure and full of minerals they said it was a gift from God. They actually made sacrifices to it." He took a breath.

"During the civil war, Union soldiers would carriage water from here and bring it to Fort Brook. This building was actually the first beer brewery in Ybor City. It was built, by Mendez Ybor himself to have beer for his cigar factory workers."

Nathan was pleased with his recently acquired knowledge.

"I can't believe I remembered that from one of those books you had me read. That's pretty cool. I had read about it but couldn't figure out where it was. I've driven by here a thousand times and I had no idea this place was here."

Built in 1912, the Florida Brewery and its popular brand La Tropical was a staple for the Cigar workers of early Ybor city. Built by heads of three local factories, they decided to provide quality beer to their employees. The brand grew and expanded into other markets but the economic downturn of the 1930's decimated the cigar industry and put a slow end to the beer brand.

"You learn something new every day, my Father always said. Never really thought about it much but I guess he was right. Come on, we've got to go." Nathan finished but Gabriel didn't move.

The wheels in Gabriel's head were spinning fast. He was weighing all the possibilities and looking at every option he could think of in a matter of seconds. He was so deep in thought that it was on Nathan's third attempt with a poke in his arm that woke him from his trance.

"What are you doing? Let's go."

Gabriel still didn't move but slowly began to speak. "Nathan, do you know what you just did?"

Nathan's blank response answered the question. Gabriel turned with a giant smile on his face, "I understand the map."

Gabriel took off passed Nathan, in a full sprint, up the block and over to Florida Avenue. It was nearly a quarter of a mile of shear adrenaline that allowed Nathan to even get close to catching up to Gabriel.

"Slow down," he pleaded. Gabriel dropped down a gear to allow Nathan to catch pace with him. "What do you mean you understand the map?" Nathan squeaked out the question between gasps of air. Gabriel didn't lose stride and could still talk as if he were walking in the park.

"The map isn't of Charlotte Harbor at all. It is Tampa. The map is a fake. Or at least, it's misleading. It's a combination of the two, a false door. My friend told me it was Tampa all a long but I couldn't figure it out until now."

Nathan was too out of breath to ask a question to continue the conversation. He was forced to agree and just try to run with Gabriel. With all that he could muster he tried to sound as in shape as possible but the best he could do was a breathless, "Well let's go."

Chapter 46

Orange Grove High School was built in the late 1990's to house the ever expanding population of the Tampa Bay area. Orange Grove was an "A" rated school with good facilities and a clean campus. It was built on the outskirts of several new housing suburbs so it had taken a few years for businesses to develop around the area but now the once lonely school building sits in the middle of a popular shopping district.

The school housed a little over 1000 students, not the largest school in the county but a good size. Their academic scores were up to state requirements and they usually had a high percentage of students go on to attend college each year. There was a robust extracurricular program that offered a lot of different options for students with very diverse interests. Like the school newspaper editor that had recently received national recognition for her excellence in local journalism. The sports program had always been competitive, even in the early years of the school they won several championships across multiple sports. But over the last four years their sports teams have had a great run of success largely in part to a standout senior named Roger Woods. The music and art programs were good and for the most part the student body seemed to get along with each other. Gabriel had been very pleased with the school that he was now attending. He knew how blessed he was to go to a good school because he had not always been so lucky in his past.

The gymnasium was a tall tan block building with large paneled windows, one of which had just been pried open. The gym was sitting adjacent to and more importantly connected with a covered hallway to the main campus building.

Now inside the window and down the bleachers, the boys were running across the wood parquet basketball court. Gabriel crossed his fingers in hopes that the double hinged door at the entrance of the gym would be unlocked. He was in luck, it was. Pushing the break bar with a loud clank and turning left they continued running down the hall. The corridor looked totally different, almost creepy, without the bright neon lights and scores of screaming children lining the hallway. For the first time in two years, Nathan noticed a billboard on the far wall with upcoming events that he had never seen before. Slowing to a fast walk to take a look at this new discovery, he was quickly snapped out of it when Gabriel disappeared down the hall with a right turn at the water fountain.

Fourth one in from the left on the top level, 1 right, 9 left, 10 right, listen for the click, "Click," Gabriel's locker was opened with a muffled jerk on the latch. Reaching into the rectangular space behind a stack of books and a pair of sneakers, Gabriel pulled out a small canvas bag with several pockets all buckled down by hard plastic snaps. Pushing his arms through the shoulder straps, Gabriel adjusted the weight of the

ALICE bag by tightening the cam buckles down on his chest. Just that fast, he closed the locker and was again racing back down the hall to make his exit.

Outside the building and out of sight of the campus security, the boys found a place to rest at a well-lit gas station off the main highway. Unfolding the map and laying it on a table, Gabriel took a deep breath to collect his thoughts.

"Look here do you see how the bay on the map has no labels or names but the shoreline is an exact match for south Florida?"

The boys had spent hours over the previous weeks debating the maps location. Gabriel still believed Tampa was the port, as his departed friend had told him it was, but he couldn't disagree with Nathan's argument for Charlotte Harbor. The legend had always claimed that the treasure was in the Peace River which is a river that flows into Charlotte Harbor. Panther Key, the last known residence of Juan Gomez, was another fact that Nathan used to make his argument. It was a Key located about 40 miles south of Charlotte Harbor, a few hours by sailboat but at least a day away from Tampa Bay, which was another 50 miles to the North. Nathan had overlaid a current map of the southern Florida coasts with the treasure map. It was a perfect fit. The southern swamp of the Everglades was depicted by several exotic wildlife drawings on the map. Snakes, alligators, and other terrifying monsters covered the marsh landscape to the south. Below the bay, there was a large land area that jetted out into what they assumed to be the Gulf of Mexico. This land was a perfect fit for the current Cape Romano, just south of Naples FL, in Collier County.

Near a chain of islands that looked a lot like the Florida Keys, another land mass was unlabeled on the map that would be a perfect fit for Cape Sable. Cape Sable is the outer rim of Everglades National Park and it is again a striking match to the jetting land shape drawn onto the old map.

Charlotte Harbor is just south of Tampa Bay and if the points on both maps, current and old, do in fact line up together it makes perfect sense that the island with the "X" in it would be in Charlotte Harbor. Nathan had even jumped out of his chair when he had read that the barrier island to Charlotte Harbor was actually named Gasparilla Island. The island protected Gasparilla Sound and even had a state park named after Gasparilla on its southern end. Nathan was convinced the map was of Charlotte Harbor and the treasure was there on that island named after Gaspar himself but Gabriel still trusted the words of his old friend Jose. The map appears to be a drawing of the south west portion of Florida, the boys could both agree to that, but it was the treasure map's peculiar folding that Gabriel still struggled with explaining. A large folded square perfectly surrounding the entire harbor area and within it a small barrier island with a black "X" on it. It was his simple gut feeling, against all evidence, that Gabriel still wanted to believe was not Charlotte Harbor but in fact was Tampa Bay. Just as his old friend, Jose had told him.

Gabriel pointed to the harbor and the surrounding shorelines. "The map is folded so that this area is outlined from the rest of the map."

Nathan remembered when they had first found the map and amongst all the excitement surrounding it, Gabriel had made the comment about how it was folded. An odd observation that didn't make sense to him then and now Gabriel was talking about it again.

"Usually, you would fold a map this size over itself in thirds and then in half but not here. Here it is folded from the outside in causing four creases in a perfect square. It outlines the harbor."

Nathan could see the creased square but was still trying to grasp where Gabriel was going with this.

"We assume that this is Charlotte Harbor, but it is not labeled at all. Nothing is except for some depth markings."

Gabriel pointed to a series of tiny numbers around the small islands at the southern part of the bay opening. The number markings would tell sailors what depth the water was in those areas. Before electronic depth finders, sailors would tie a rope to a rock or some weight and drop it into the sea. They would measure these soundings in Fathom measurements to not let the ship run aground. A Fathom, in old English, meant the length of outstretched arms or about 6 feet. When the rock would hit the bottom, they could measure the depth in Fathoms along that rope and tell, through feel, if the bottom was sandy or rocky. If a burial at sea where ever required, the body would be wrapped and weighted down as it would be dropped into the water. A minimum of 6 Fathoms (36 feet) would be required to bury someone at sea giving rise to the phrase "deep six".

Gabriel circled the open water bay that was enclosed by the map folds with his finger. "This area should be Charlotte Harbor. Mariners of that time would surely be able to recognize these features so why not just label it?"

"I see what you're saying but what's your point?"

"It's not Charlotte Harbor. That's what Jose knew when he told me that my journey starts in Tampa. He knew the map was hiding the actual harbor."

"But how? How did he know that" Nathan interjected loudly. His assertiveness surprised himself. Frustration was setting in to the tired boy. He didn't mean to snap at Gabriel but he just couldn't understand what Gabriel saw.

Gabriel didn't flinch at the sharp response his eyes were just fixed on the map reading every word and straining his eyes to focus on even the fibers that made up the paper itself and then he saw it.

"That's it! Look here, at the journal the letters."

Gabriel pointed to the maps journal and traced the words with his fingers. "Do you see the letters? The ones that are darker? The ones that are in bold? Look to the section where he gives his bounty?" Nathan looked at the legend and began to read aloud.

"El día dos de abril, del año de Nuestro Señor 1812. Encontré mi redención en una fuente vibrante entre los nativos al norte de la gran bahía. Le di recompensa al gran **C**acique nativo con los respons**a**bles de veinte ocho. Para el pequeño rey de los jefes de siete, a la gente de las cuca**r**achas **l**as cabezas de cinco, y para la gente de las aguas turbulent**os** que le di las cabezas de tre**s**."

Nathan finished reading and Gabriel translated. I gave bounty to the great native cacique with the heads of

28. To the little king the heads of 7, to the people of cockroaches the heads of 5, and to the people of the turbulent waters I gave the heads of 3.

Nathan had to look closely but then he saw them too. He needed to step back a little to see the difference in letter color but there it was; "C-Cacique, A-responsables, R-cucarachas, L-las, O-turbulento, S-tres."

C-a-r-l-o-s

"Carlos?" Nathan questioned.

With a smile on his face, Gabriel replied, "That's exactly right. Carlos, Bahia Carlos, the Bay of Carlos or as it is known today-Charlotte Harbor."

"But you just told me it wasn't in Charlotte Harbor." Nathan was frustrated and confused. "It's not, but you asked me how Jose knew it was Tampa and not Charlotte right?" Nathan nodded. "You and your hawk eyes found it with the repeating letters on the ring. The letters that had no meaning. The letters that made no sense."

Nathan strained his head to think back to what Gabriel was talking about. "K,T,Z,X,D,A?" He stunned himself by remembering. "I still don't get it."

"Have you ever heard of the Vigenère Cipher?" "No, what is the Vigenère Cipher?" Nathan's head was about to explode with exhaustion. "Please just tell me!"

"It's an encryption method for a polyalphabetic code."

"What?"

"A secret code that 300 hundred years ago was almost impossible to crack but now is studied by every spy fan that has a library card. It was designed by Giovan Battista Bellaso in the 16th century but a few years later, while working for the French King Henry the III, Vigenère tweaked it some and ultimately got credit for it. So we now know it as the Vigenère Cipher."

"How does it work?" Nathan asked. "Well, basically you make a chart with the alphabet across the top and running down the first column. Then you just fill in the spaces with the letters of the alphabet but you are shifting in one more space each time all the way down for all 26 letters. Then you have coded text; in our case K,T,Z,X,D,A and finally you need a key word." Nathan looked at the map again.

"C-A-R-L-O-S."

Sulphur Springs Water Tower and gazebo. Tampa, FL

Steps up Philippe Park Mound. Safety Harbor, FL

The Tony Jannus Memorial. Tampa, FL

Historical Marker Downtown Tampa, FL. Near Fort Brook Garage. (Timuquan Indian Mound)

Florida Brewery-Ybor City, FL

Jose Gasparilla, Pirate Festival. Tampa, FL

Egmont Key at the mouth of Tampa Bay just West of Fort Desoto.

Chapter 47

Sitting outside a quiet gas station, swarms of months and other Florida flyers were dancing under the neon lights. Gabriel had found a pencil in his bag and was quickly writing out the chart in hopes of solving the Vigenère Cipher.

A	B	C	D	E	F	G	H	I	J	K	L	M	N	O	P	Q	R	S	T	U	V	W	X	Y	Z
B	C	D	E	F	G	H	I	J	K	L	M	N	O	P	Q	R	S	T	U	V	W	X	Y	Z	A
C	D	E	F	G	H	I	J	K	L	M	N	O	P	Q	R	S	T	U	V	W	X	Y	Z	A	B
D	E	F	G	H	I	J	K	L	M	N	O	P	Q	R	S	T	U	V	W	X	Y	Z	A	B	C
E	F	G	H	I	J	K	L	M	N	O	P	Q	R	S	T	U	V	W	X	Y	Z	A	B	C	D
F	G	H	I	J	K	L	M	N	O	P	Q	R	S	T	U	V	W	X	Y	Z	A	B	C	D	E
G	H	I	J	K	L	M	N	O	P	Q	R	S	T	U	V	W	X	Y	Z	A	B	C	D	E	F
H	I	J	K	L	M	N	O	P	Q	R	S	T	U	V	W	X	Y	Z	A	B	C	D	E	F	G
I	J	K	L	M	N	O	P	Q	R	S	T	U	V	W	X	Y	Z	A	B	C	D	E	F	G	H
J	K	L	M	N	O	P	Q	R	S	T	U	V	W	X	Y	Z	A	B	C	D	E	F	G	H	I
K	L	M	N	O	P	Q	R	S	T	U	V	W	X	Y	Z	A	B	C	D	E	F	G	H	I	J
L	M	N	O	P	Q	R	S	T	U	V	W	X	Y	Z	A	B	C	D	E	F	G	H	I	J	K
M	N	O	P	Q	R	S	T	U	V	W	X	Y	Z	A	B	C	D	E	F	G	H	I	J	K	L
N	O	P	Q	R	S	T	U	V	W	X	Y	Z	A	B	C	D	E	F	G	H	I	J	K	L	M
O	P	Q	R	S	T	U	V	W	X	Y	Z	A	B	C	D	E	F	G	H	I	J	K	L	M	N
P	Q	R	S	T	U	V	W	X	Y	Z	A	B	C	D	E	F	G	H	I	J	K	L	M	N	O
Q	R	S	T	U	V	W	X	Y	Z	A	B	C	D	E	F	G	H	I	J	K	L	M	N	O	P
R	S	T	U	V	W	X	Y	Z	A	B	C	D	E	F	G	H	I	J	K	L	M	N	O	P	Q
S	T	U	V	W	X	Y	Z	A	B	C	D	E	F	G	H	I	J	K	L	M	N	O	P	Q	R
T	U	V	W	X	Y	Z	A	B	C	D	E	F	G	H	I	J	K	L	M	N	O	P	Q	R	S
U	V	W	X	Y	Z	A	B	C	D	E	F	G	H	I	J	K	L	M	N	O	P	Q	R	S	T
V	W	X	Y	Z	A	B	C	D	E	F	G	H	I	J	K	L	M	N	O	P	Q	R	S	T	U
W	X	Y	Z	A	B	C	D	E	F	G	H	I	J	K	L	M	N	O	P	Q	R	S	T	U	V
X	Y	Z	A	B	C	D	E	F	G	H	I	J	K	L	M	N	O	P	Q	R	S	T	U	V	W
Y	Z	A	B	C	D	E	F	G	H	I	J	K	L	M	N	O	P	Q	R	S	T	U	V	W	X
Z	A	B	C	D	E	F	G	H	I	J	K	L	M	N	O	P	Q	R	S	T	U	V	W	X	Y

"Now you take your key word and find the first letter on your first column. Run your finger across the row until you find the first letter of your coded word and then look up at the top row."

Nathan read of the letters and Gabriel ran his fingers across the chart decoding it.

"C to K is **I**; A to T is **T**. R to Z is **I**…"

Continuing on, the boys read off the letters.

"I-T-I-M-P-I,"

"It must be another code." Nathan sounded deflated. He had hoped it would have been a better clue.

"No it's not. You know this. You've seen this word. It's Tocobagan." Gabriel claimed.

"You're right! It is a word. I remember now. ITIMPI was the misplaced Tocobagan name for Tampa. It was a reference to another village but early map makers mispronounced it and later wrote Tampa. Its translation means NEAR IT. But near what?" Nathan waited for an answer he knew the smiling Gabriel already had.

"Carlos Bay or as we know it Charlotte Harbor. It wasn't uncommon for early sailors sailing up the Gulf to get the harbors mixed up- Charlotte Harbor for Tampa or vice versa. Some of the early maps of the Spanish age didn't even have Charlotte on their maps they assumed it was all part of the Espirtu Santu or Bahia de Tampa and they would write the wrong name down. In those ancient times, the harbor drawings looked very similar."

Nathan disagreed, "You're reaching Gabriel, that article also said that Tampa was from another ancient word- Tanpa. Fire sticks or something like that."

"You're right, that is the Calusa word for Tampa given by Hernando de Escalante Fontaneda, a famous Spanish sailor who was shipwrecked and lived with the Calusas for years until he was rescued by the Explorer Pedro Menendez." Gabriel continued. "But at the time of Gaspar, the Tocobagans had previously lived in the Tampa area while the Calusas lived south in Charlotte. Only someone that had lived with and communicated with the local natives would be able to speak their different languages. So why would Gaspar use a Tocobagan word for near it in reference to the Bay of Carlos?"

Nathan's head was spinning trying to think of an answer but couldn't. "I don't know… I guess to tell us that the map is of Tampa Bay?" "That's right!" Gabriel couldn't stop smiling with excitement. Nathan on the other hand was mentally exhausted.

"But why was Itimpi mistaken for Tampa in the first place?" "I don't think it was. That was a theory that came about in a book from the 1940's. There is no other record of that being the case. Gaspar spoke Tocobagan and I think he was simply using it as a clue to anyone who may follow his footsteps."

Nathan thought about it for a moment and couldn't think of any other solution. He didn't have to believe it but it was the best option on the table so he decided to agree.

"Ok, so if the name for Tampa came from the Calusa why would they call this area fire sticks anyway?" Nathan questioned. "Fire sticks are a reference to lightning." Gabriel replied. Nathan now felt Gabriel was just teasing him. "I give up."

Gabriel smiled, "Do you know what city is called the lightning capital of the United States?" Nathan perked his head up and smiled, "I do. It's Tampa."

"The code that my friend Jose broke told him what body of water this was on the map. It was supposed to look like Charlotte Harbor. It is very close to it and often confused with it but it wasn't Charlotte it was Tampa."

Smiling at himself, Gabriel looked at the ring and remembered the words spoken to him from his old friend Jose- "the ring is the key." He was right. Gabriel wished his friend could be there with them on this adventure.

"But Juan Gomez had the map, ring, and Cross for years. He sailed with Gaspar, why was he living on Panther Key in Charlotte? You don't think he recognized that the harbors were different. He must have known those waters by heart?"

"He did." Gabriel snapped back. "Remember what Santos said? His great-great grandfather almost captured Juan once, where?"

Nathan had to think hard back to a conversation that seemed like years ago but was actually just a few hours ago. A conversation he had with a crazy man who was trying to kill him after he had just been bound and kidnapped off of the streets of Bayshore. A conversation that was like a distant nightmare from his childhood that he would rather not remember. But he needed to focus and he needed to face that fear and he needed to do it now.

"Long Key?" He surprised himself.

"Yes! In modern day Saint Petersburg beach, Pass-a-Grill to be exact, the story of Juan saving the stranded sailors by digging up water from an abandoned well. Juan must have been close when Raúl and his men finally caught up with him. What if he hid the stuff, the map, the Cross and the ring, in someplace safe before he got caught? Say perhaps an old deep freshwater well. A place he knew he could find if he had to come back."

"The Great Gale" Nathan added. "That's right. Just before they caught him he escaped in front of a massive hurricane that changed the landscape of that whole area. When he came back he had lost the well. It took him years to find it but when he did, he not only found his stash but it made news because he brought freshwater back to the area. The story about him helping those sailors missed the real reason he was there. He was trying to find his treasure."

"Unfortunately, the telling of that story also cost him his life to Raúl the second." Nathan added.

"It took years for Juan to find that well while at the same time hiding from Raúl. Juan assumed Raúl had to be dead or too old to still be looking for him when that story was published but he never expected Raúl's grandson to continue looking for him."

"The treasure is somewhere in Tampa. My friend Juan figured it out but he never wanted to risk Santos getting it first, so he decided to hide his identity for years until he found someone he could trust."

Nathan seemed pleased with Gabriel's theory. "Ok, I'm in. It's the best lead we have so far, I'll go find a cab. Where are we heading to?"

Gabriel looked down at the map and read the first line of its journal.

"On the 2nd day of April, the year of our Lord 1812. I found my redemption at a vibrant spring amongst the natives north of the great bay."

He placed his finger on the large mouth of a river at the upper end of the bay and began to trace it. He stopped on a small circle just off the river that seemed to be feeding into it. He smiled for a second and answered Nathan's question,

"Sulphur Springs."

Chapter 48

The cab ride was faster than Gabriel had expected. Sulphur Springs was only a few miles from their school and if you knew the backstreets like their cabby did, it was a quick inexpensive ride. Julio, from Port-a- Prince Haiti, was a tall muscular man who didn't talk much but was very pleasant. He had only lived in Tampa for a few years but already seemed to know every pothole to avoid and shortcut to take. His immaculately cleaned taxi cab rolled into a large parking lot next to a small water park and came to a stop.

"Your water spring is there." His thick accent was noticeable but still easy to understand. "No not a water park. We are looking for a spring." Nathan replied as he looked at the colorful water slides and diving boards. "Yes, your water spring is there." Julio answered more emphatically and pointed to the water slide.

Nathan decided not to argue when he watched Gabriel calmly get out of the car and reach into his back pocket for his wallet. Gabriel handed some money to Julio and said thank you. He then motioned for Nathan to get out of the car.

Pausing for a second, Nathan built up the courage to ask if he could borrow Julio's phone. Gabriel disapproved but since Nathan had lost his phone somewhere on the streets of Bayshore during their chase, he gave in and handed a few more dollars to Julio.

Nathan had to call his sister. He knew she would be worried sick, but he also knew she would call his Mom to let her know he was ok allowing him to avoid having to lie to his Mom. Julio provided his cell and Nathan punched in his sister's number.

The phone rang a few times and then went to the familiar greeting. "Hi this is Lisa. I'm sorry I missed your call but I'll get back to you just as soon as I can." Nathan apologized to her and left a message to please come pick them up as soon as possible.

"By the tall white medieval tower," Gabriel heard him say.

He knew that the tower would be a landmark she would obviously remember. The phone clicked off and was returned to Julio. The taxi taillights turned onto Bird Street and then quickly disappeared.

Sulphur Springs had once been called the "Coney Island of Tampa." But far from its glory days of 1912, it was now a vacant empty lot of its past glory. The vast parking lot rarely used as a spillover for the Greyhound dog track, that stands a few hundred yards away, covers over the once thriving shopping district.

The area was named for the mineral rich artesian spring that bubbled up from the ground and brought tourists and therapy seeking visitors by the droves in the early 1900's. A health spa and sanitarium was built to heal the sick with the pure natural water. A swimming pool with a large dive platform and toboggan ride was built around the spring to cool off the locals. An entrepreneur eventually built the first mall, Movie

Theater, and hotel in central Florida around that spring. It was one of the top tourist attractions in the state until the depression, and World War II put it on the financial ropes. But ultimately it was a broken dam from a power company that flooded out the area and set the spring into a financial downslide that it never recovered from.

Few of the old landmarks are left but there are still reminders of the area's once greatness. The white plastered dome gazebo is a timeless artifact from another era. Now sitting behind a no trespassing fence, the dome was placed on top of an ancient artesian well that used to flow up through a now missing fountain. The Cherub Angels that top the dome must have seen countless weddings, dances, and numerous other town events before they fell into disrepair. Locals believe that the three carved marble Angels still offer a blessing of great things to come for this historic place.

So rich in natural resources, the area around the springs was picked to be the location for the 1919 film "Birth of a Race." Funded by the great educator Booker T. Washington and his Tuskegee Institute, the film was one of the first ever African-American made films. Starting with the creation of man in the book of Genesis, the film depicts human history up until World War I. Filmed in response to the racially charged 1915 film "Birth of a Nation," "Birth of a Race" was truly a pioneer in early motion pictures as well as in the important Civil Rights' movement.

"The map said that Gaspar found his treasure at a vibrant spring north of the great bay. On the 2nd day of April, at a vibrant spring amongst the natives north of the great bay, along his return he stopped at several places to pay homage to the local Indian kings. He offered heads of 28 to the Cacique or king. And then he gave, 7 to the little king, 5 to the Cockroach people and 3 to the people of rough water right?" Gabriel was interrupted when Nathan asked. "When you say heads do you mean actual heads, heads?" "I'm not sure. It sounds like it. Maybe it was a sacrifice or something for the natives that had helped him."

Gabriel continued, "5 days later, 2 minutes before midnight, beneath the eyes of my beloved princess, I buried my great fortune where no man would return for fear of death."

The boys continued to walk around the water park's children's play area. It was a modern playground with slides, water guns, swings, and a lap pool but on the back side of the playground, Nathan finally saw the large open spring that gave the area its name. Wedged between the playground and just north of the river bank sat a large circular well about 40 feet across and what must have been hundreds of feet deep. The clear water flowed up at a chilly 76 degrees all year around just as it had done for millions of years. The clear freshwater poured over a concrete wall down into a holding area and then back into the Hillsborough River. They made their way past the spring and down towards the river edge. The wooden boardwalk that reached out over the river and around the spring was locked with a chain link gate so the boys made their way back towards the parking lot.

"Do you really think the beloved he wrote about on the map was the Princess Joseffa? The girl Gaspar beheaded." Nathan broke the silence. Gabriel paused to listen to his question. "The map said that he buried his beloved under the burnt stone by Useppa Island right?" Gabriel nodded. "Well then he says that he buried his treasure under the watchful eyes of his beloved princess. Do you think he may have buried the body in one place and then placed the head over the treasure in another?"

Gabriel stopped and had to think for a moment. "I hadn't really thought about that. I'm not sure. It's pretty twisted if that were the case but I guess it's possible. I don't know if I want to see a head covered treasure." Nathan responded. "The legend of the captured princess has always plagued Gaspar. The story goes that he loved Joseffa the Princess of Spain but when she didn't love him back-he killed her. Maybe he still loved her and felt that she was watching down on him from heaven. Protecting him? If he was infatuated with her maybe, I'm not quite sure. But does that sound better?" Nathan smiled, "It does. Let's go with that but if there is a head in the ground you can dig it out OK."
"Deal."

The boys had been walking the grounds for about 20 minutes and during that time Gabriel had been pushing his mind to its limit trying hard to put the mystery pieces in place. The puzzle was so close he could smell it but it was just out of reach. There was something missing and he couldn't find it.

Suddenly, headlights flooded the tall oaks that lined the river's edge. The boys held their hands up to block the light and were forced to squint to see Lisa's white Camry. However, the oval shapes of the headlights were wrong and they both knew it. The tall thin figure that was stepping out of the now open door was easily recognizable even through the piercing light that was blinding them.

"Run," Gabriel ordered. "Run now."

Chapter 49

A paved trail lined the edge of the riverbank away from the spring and towards the I-275 overpass; the boys were now on it and racing fast along its dark path. The curving sidewalk was great for leisurely scenic walks but the fastest way to a point is a straight line and the boys quickly found themselves bobbing and weaving between ancient grandfather oaks trying to make cover as fast as they could. Through a small clearing between the trees, where alligator pens used to hold hundreds of reptiles for curious tourists in the spring's golden age, the boys finally reached the wood planked boardwalk that ran underneath the Interstates' overpass. A quick dog leg bend in the bridge and the boys finally stopped when they reached the protective shelter of the overpass. Leaning on the boardwalk railing gasping for air, the boys tried to listen closely but the busy highway about 30 feet above their heads made it impossible to hear any foot noise behind them.

Hiding in shadows at the belly of the bridge, where it crossed over the Hillsborough River, Gabriel tried to ignore the cars racing over his head. As he peered into the darkness back along the river walk, it was a flash of light behind the oaks that caught his attention. Then a fraction of a second later, bits of stone and shrapnel erupted behind his left ear. Hitting the ground, Gabriel instinctively grabbed his ear and felt the back of his head. No blood just some dirt. It was close but could have been deadly this was only a warning shot.

"Was that a gun?" Nathan screamed from the shadows.

Getting to his feet and looking back down the path, Gabriel saw the thin man's silhouette step from the dark out into the open field.

"He's coming!" Nathan's shout confirmed Gabriel's shaken vision.

The boys turned and continued deeper into the tunnel. A bright light was coming from the other end of the overpass which gave some hope at first but when the boys ran out from the tunnel it quickly disappeared. The light was coming from several, large, up lit, spotlights that emblazoned a gigantic white tower standing alone in the middle of an open field. About 300 yards away, with no place for cover in between, the medieval looking tower at Water Tower Park was their only chance for protection and the Ghost was just a few yards behind them.

Like the watchtower in the legendary tale of Rapunzel, the Water Tower of Sulphur Springs was a breathtaking monument that has baffled Floridians for years. Standing 214 feet tall of stark white concrete and gothic battlements, that crown the top of the tower, it looks completely out of a different era and place compared to the modern Tampa skyline. However, built in 1927 it has become a beloved landmark of Tampa's diverse identity.

Racing across the vast open ground that was once a drive in theater, Gabriel hoped to reach cover before the Ghost could get another shot off. Looking back over his shoulder to find Nathan, he was pleased and somewhat surprised to see the tall lanky boy right on his tail and actually closing on him.

With less than 10 yards to go, white painted concrete exploded from the base of the souring tower. Gabriel's reaction was to lead Nathan to the ground behind one of the tower's fin-like concrete base supports. Diving to the ground, Nathan quickly followed. Gabriel soon took position behind the triangular support in order to look for the Ghost. He saw him about 100 yards away and closing.

"We can make it. The street is just a few more yards that way. We can get help." Nathan pleaded. "That shot wasn't a warning. He missed. He won't miss again."

Gabriel frantically scanned the tower for someplace to hide. He noticed a white painted wooden door behind the support fin at their back. Unsheathing his tomahawk from his belt loop, he began to hack and pry at the wood door. Ripping back the plywood, just as the Ghost was reaching the tower's base, the boys crawled through a concrete opening and slid through a second iron cutout that was on the inner core of the tower. Barely able to fit his broad shoulders through, Gabriel had to reach one arm into the black hole and then his head followed by his other arm. Nathan, who was already on the inside of the massive tube, had to pull him the rest of the way through. Slamming closed the metal hatch and locking the door from the inside with a rusty old lock, the boys knew it would hold but not for long.

Once inside the smell of neglect almost took their gasping breath away. Musty and damp, the only inhabitants inside the tower had been pigeons and Florida insects for decades. With over 70 years of bird droppings covering the walls and floors, the boys had to cover their mouths with their sweaty shirts to try to keep the rancid stench from their lungs. Crossing over a small catwalk that spanned across the historic water well that the tower was built on, Gabriel struggled to make out a shadow on the other side of the wall.

"A ladder," Gabriel whispered to Nathan and directed him towards it.

Shuffling their feet and sliding their hands across the slimy scum covered handrail, the boys made it past the rusty well pump and onto the rickety old ladder. The Ghost could be heard in the darkness banging on the metal door. Eventually the banging stopped and the chilling sound of a rusty hinge opening up sent panic up the boys' spines. He was in the tower and starting to climb into the tube.

Trying to be silent but moving up the ladder as fast as possible, Nathan, who was ahead of Gabriel, froze when a beam of light shot over his head. The Ghost had flicked on his flashlight and now the stream of light slashed across the tube, like a never ending light saber, below them. Holding his breath and moving up a few rungs Nathan made it to the second platform about 50 feet off the ground. The platform was just above Nathan's head with a small cutout to let the ladder continue up to the top of the tower. Gabriel was still stuck on the ladder unable to move for fear of making a sound. The light beam was moving in a sweeping pattern back and forth over sections of debris in the space getting closer and closer to the ladder.

With one of the passing arcs the light cast a glow on the roof just above Nathan's head. Nathan noticed that the roof seemed to be moving. His fear was confirmed when the next pass brought the light a little closer. The roof just above his head was crawling with cockroaches, thousands of them. They seemed to cover every inch of the iron landing as they began to scurry and drop with the awakening light. Holding back his desire to scream, Nathan bit his lip hard and tried to not move. Several of the insects had dropped into his hair and were now scurrying down his neck and onto his back. Looking down into the cavern at the rotating spotlight, he wondered which was the greater threat, the gun totting maniac or the million legs that were about to crawl over his body. Seeing Gabriel's figure begin to be illuminated, Nathan knew that the Ghost would see his friend on the next pass. He had to think of something quick.

Using his arm, he reached up above his head and flattened it across the moving roof. With a sweep of his arm he slid thousands of the tiny monsters off the roof and down into his shirt that was held out like a pouch with his other hand. Feeling the weight of his catch scurrying in the pregnant ball of his rolled shirt, he took one foot and his right hand off the ladder and leaned far out into the dark void to look for his target. Judging the angle and distance to the Ghost, he gave the heavy mass a one armed shove and let the critters fall. A second later, as the light was reaching Gabriel's foot, a scream came from the abyss and echoed throughout the iron tube.

Gabriel took advantage of the distraction and raced up the ladder to the platform above catching up to Nathan. Nathan shook off the last few hangers on and moved higher up the ladder to the next landing. Now protected by the metal landing below them and no longer needing to hide their location, the boys picked up their pace and continued to climb. Several landings and 150 feet later, they had reached the top. The Ghost was far below them but they knew he was coming, they knew he was mad, and they knew they had no place else to hide.

Sliding through a narrow window slit, the boys cherished the fresh air that poured into their lungs. They stepped out onto the ledge of the 20 story tower and paused at the stunning view that it provided. But the joy of fresh air and breathtaking views quickly came to an end when the cold realization hit them that they had nowhere to go and no way to get down.

Chapter 50

Nathan clung to the wall of the tower with all his might, almost willing his fingers to dig into the smooth concrete surface. In the meantime, Gabriel was racing around the narrow ledge glancing down each side looking for some miracle escape ladder to appear. The thought of tying their clothes together into a rope and climbing down raced through his mind, however he knew even if they had a 100 foot rope it wouldn't get them half way down. They couldn't run any more… it was time to get ready for a fight. This wasn't going to be a street fight. This Ghost was a trained killer with a gun and what did Gabriel have to his advantage? His tomahawk? Surprise? The answer to the map?

Gabriel heard the Ghost just on the other side of the wall. He removed his trusted tomahawk in his right hand and took position near the narrow window that they had just climbed through. As the Ghost got closer, Gabriel imagined the possible scenario in his mind. The Ghost would climb through the window. Gabriel could knock the gun away or do worse if he had to. At that point it would be a fist fight. Gabriel felt OK if he could get to hand to hand but getting rid of that gun would be the key. He waited as the muffled footsteps on the rusted ladder grew louder and louder. It would be the first strike that would matter. Gabriel hiding behind the wall had the advantage of surprise but he would get only one shot. Either try for the gun… or aim for a kill shot. The decision was agonizing for Gabriel as his pounding adrenaline pulsated through his veins.

A sudden thought struck him hard almost like a loud scream in his ears, don't fight-now is not the time. Use your mind. He instinctively backed away and started to change his strategy just as the footsteps were at their loudest. Putting the tomahawk back in its sheath up his back, he walked to the southern face of the tower and removed the golden cross from his pocket. Staring out into the darkness down into the vertigo inducing ground level, Gabriel started to judge the angle and distance to the river. It didn't take studying geometry to know that his arm wasn't strong enough to reach the river even from this height. But he knew that he would rather get rid of it into the darkness or even break it and lose the clues it kept before he would let it fall into the hands of Santos. Perhaps if the cross was gone, the Ghost would spare their young lives in hopes that they could replace the need for the cross with what they already knew. It was a long shot but right now he was all out of options.

Nathan had not moved from his wall clutching position for several moments but something seemed to be pulling him away from the wall out across the ledge and closer to the crumbling retainer wall. Just inches from falling down some 200 feet, Nathan leaned out over the railing and stared down on a new set of car headlights that had appeared in the parking lot.

Just then Gabriel heard a loud cell phone ring blasting through the narrow window with a clarity that had to be just on the other side of the tower wall. The

Ghost was already on the top platform just inches behind the boys. Nathan ignored the call and continued to squint into the darkness, straining his eyes all the way down to the tower parking lot. He was focusing on a figure that was now standing in the path of the car's headlights. Her blond hair seemed to give off an angelic glow as it reflected in the bright lights.

"Lisa!" Nathan gasped.

The cell phone ring that was heard through the window was now replaced with a hissing voice.

Hoping to find some sort of escape, Gabriel gazed across the park grounds at the large Greyhound track on the other side of Bird Street where the once great mall stood and then to the newly built Physician's clinic that had been built on the spot that once belonged to the gigantic arcade from the '20's. His gaze finally turned to stare into the frightened eyes of Nathan.

"It's Lisa. They have her."

Gabriel stepped beside Nathan and looked down towards the parking lot. His fears were confirmed. They did have Lisa. The limited choices that were racing through Gabriel's mind were now gone. There were no more choices. It was over. It was up to fate now.

The pasty white face of the Ghost with his dark sunk in lifeless eyes poked through the window opening first, almost tempting Gabriel to strike him. But with Lisa in their hands, that was no longer an option, and the Ghost knew it.

Now standing outside the inner tower on the ledge just feet from the boys, the yellow toothy grin of the Ghost seemed to shine through the night sky. Like a yellow crescent moon that would tell ancient mariners a storm was coming, Gabriel knew this was bad and indeed a storm was about to come.

"You boys have caused us a lot of troubles. I think it's time we call it a night and head back to Mr. Santos' house," the Ghost seemed to be whispering across the whipping wind.

"If we say no?" Gabriel questioned while still frantically trying to think of a solution.

"I only have room for 2 in my car. Since we have your sister I don't think we need you anymore." The Ghost pulled his revolver from his shoulder harness and leveled the gun at Nathan's chest. "If you come with me I can get your friend a seat in Mr. Santos' car. If you say no then I take you with the girl and your friend dies up here."

Nathan didn't say anything but Gabriel seemed to notice his friend stand up straighter with his chest out, almost leaning into the sights of the Ghost's gun. Don't do anything stupid Nathan, Gabriel thought, just give me another second. After a moment, Gabriel finally answered with a defeated

"OK."

Reaching back into his pocket he pulled out the golden Cross and held it up into the chilly air.

The Ghost's toothy grin returned as Nathan's lungs deflated in defeat. Gabriel had no choice, and he knew it was the right thing to do. But something suddenly struck him odd. The golden Cross in his outstretched hand began to spin. It had gotten tangled in his pocket and instead of hanging normally with the Cross in the upright position; the chain had been threaded through the cutout hole in the center of the

Cross. The Cross was now balanced and level lying flat as it dangled spinning in the opposite direction of the gusty breeze. The long end at the bottom of the Cross finally settled on its position perpendicular to the high altitude wind. Gabriel took a closer look at the markings that were spaced in between the jewels. He thought they were just a series of lines but he quickly realized they were in fact Roman numeral numbers.

No longer listening to what the Ghost was saying, Gabriel snapped his head to the right and stared at the rectangular 5 story building that was once a large bank but now just sat vacant in the middle of the parking lot.

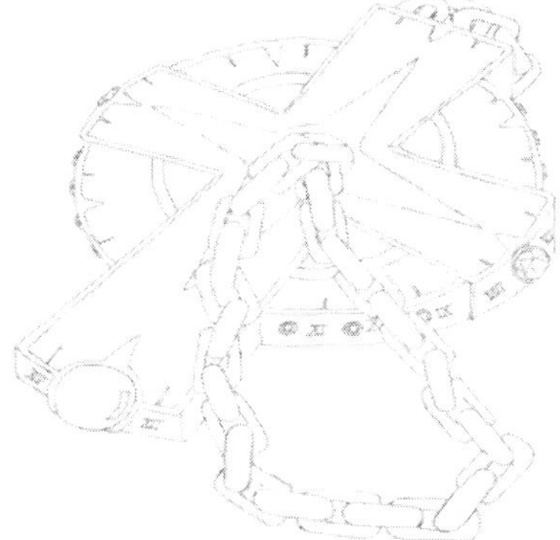

Gabriel remembered a story he had read about ancient Indians that had lived in this area-the article from the Tampa Museum by D.B. McKay? They built their village around the freshwater well and had built up burial mounds on the ground all around this area. Beneath the bank he was now staring at, under the Greyhound track, where the outdoor movie theater was, and even perhaps beneath the tower where he was standing now, the mounds had been organized in a fan like pattern that would inform the locals of the seasons much like a calendar would. The outer mounds on either end would be directly under the Sun on each solar equinox telling the natives when to start the planting and harvesting season. The middle mound would face east towards the rising sun and the largest of the mounds would face north. The same direction that the gold Cross in Gabriel's hand was now facing. The mounds were markers that would stand out amongst the ever changing forests or eroding sea shore and could give the people who knew about them the cardinal directions in any light or weather.

Interrupting the Ghost's orders, Gabriel snapped.

"I've got it. I can find the treasure!"

Nathan looked surprised but could tell by the enthusiastic sparkle in Gabriel's eyes that he seemed to be telling the truth.

"I know where the treasure is and I can find it but you need to let us go." "Don't take me for a fool boy. You are going nowhere." "Give me your phone." Gabriel now spoke with confidence and wasn't taking no for an answer.

Placing his phone into Gabriel's hand, the Ghost kept his other hand on his gun that was still pointed at Nathan's chest. Gabriel hit the redial button and began to speak into the phone receiver without addressing the heavy breath on the other end.

"I can get your treasure but you need to let us go."

A throaty "No," came back.

"I've cracked the code and can get you the treasure tonight. If you say no then good luck finding what your family couldn't for another 200 years. Let us go and I'll bring it to you tonight."

A cheap shot at his family's expense didn't please Santos but the possibility of holding the treasure tonight was pleasing to him. Waiting for his specialists to crack the code could take days possibly weeks, perhaps never, he could wait one more night to see if this boy was telling the truth. Worse case he would just kill the kids for wasting his time but then again he had already planned on that so he really didn't have anything to lose.

"I keep the girl," the voice on the phone answered. Nathan started to yell "No," but Gabriel agreed before he could get it out. "No harm comes to her or the deals off." "Of Course," the raspy voice agreed. "But you fail me and she becomes food for my pet gators; your fate will be much worse."

Gabriel knew Santos wouldn't let Lisa go until he had his gold so it wasn't worth wasting time arguing about it. Their only chance for survival was to find that treasure fast and time was short.

"One other thing, I'm going to need a car."

Chapter 51

Racing along Interstate 275, Nathan's hands were in a cold sweat at their 10 and 2 position on the steering wheel. He had driven a car before, Gabriel had not, but he had never driven on the interstate at night in a high performance Audi G6 at 90 mph to save his sister's life. It had been a crazy evening.

Gabriel sat in the leather bucket passenger seat next to him and was frantically looking over the map. Circling points along the coast line of the bay, with a chewed on pencil, Gabriel highlighted several points at the mouths of rivers that flowed into the bay. The map was roughly drawn in free hand with no labels or markings other than the legend that talked about finding the treasure and the hidden message that had been found by Juan Gomez many years before. But what were clearly defined on the map, were several wiggling lines that spread inland from the bay… rivers. Gabriel had highlighted Sulphur Springs at the head of one long line that flowed into a larger body of water that Gabriel labeled Tampa Bay.

"I don't get it," looking over into Gabriel's notes, "If that's Tampa Bay why doesn't the shoreline look like it?" "You're looking for Davis and Harbor Island aren't you?" "Yeah," Nathan pointed to a long winding line running up from the bay, "If this is the Hillsborough River where are the islands?"

"They didn't exist in 1820." Gabriel recalled from one of his late night study sessions of early Tampa history. "They were man-made in the 1920's when they dredged out the bay. In order to make the bay deeper and attract larger shipping vessels the bay needed to be dredged. All of that soil was piled up at the river mouth and later developed into a housing area. The islands you know as Davis and Harbor Island didn't exist back then."

Turning off onto Hillsborough Hwy, the black Audi was forced to slow down but was still moving faster than Nathan was comfortable with.

"I didn't know that. So then why are we going to Safety Harbor?" "According to the map," Gabriel spoke at a hurried pace, "After Gaspar found his treasure he headed north to pay tribute to the Cacique or king that gave him safe passage. At the time, the Tocobagan Indians ruled this area and their main temple was in Safety Harbor at Philippe Park."

"I don't understand why that makes sense to you. He paid tribute with the heads of people. How does that lead us to the treasure?"

Gabriel smiled to himself, "Those weren't heads of people. That legend was just a clue. They were heads from this."

Gabriel pulled out the gold Cross from his pants pocket. "This isn't just a precious religious symbol. It's a Lodestone Compass."

Pulling off of Hillsborough Hwy on to state road 580 and then hopping a curb to run on to the Philippe Parkway, the black Audi raced down the dark road until it slid to a stop at the park gate. Closed for the night, the boys would have to travel on foot. Backing the car into a palm tree covered parking space, the boys grabbed their gear and began to run across the darkened lot. The fence was no problem for Gabriel but Nathan tore part of his pants leg on the jagged fence top. No blood but his pants were ruined and Nathan knew he would need an explanation for his mother. He felt that there was something about kidnapping and buried treasure that he didn't think his Mom would want to hear so if they should make it home alive, he would need another answer for her.

Not sure where they were heading, Gabriel turned toward the water's edge and started running south.

"What are we looking for?" Nathan breathed heavy. "A mound, a large grass covered mound," Gabriel answered.

"A burial mound?" "Yes, a burial mound."

Along the water edge was a narrow pathway with a wood lined fence that kept tourists from walking into the water. It wasn't lit but the bright moonlight lit up the walkway and gave the boys some comfort. But Gabriel wasn't looking at the path ahead of him instead he seemed to run along the trail by instinct. His eyes were turned inland towards the dark tree covered area of the park that didn't allow the moonlight to enter. After a few moments of jogging and about 400 yards along the darkened path, Gabriel saw a pathway up into the darkness. Turning direction and increasing speed, Gabriel suddenly disappeared under the black canopy of night. Nathan paused for second unsure of following anymore and was suddenly left alone on the dark pathway. The pause was actually welcoming to the tired boy something about just the noise of lapping waves on the stone breakwater to his feet, gave him a moment of peace. A slight wind in his ears, some noisy crickets, and then off into the distance was the reassuring voice of Gabriel.

"Come on, it's up here." Gabriel's voice pierced the darkness and rang in Nathan's ears. Reassured there was life beyond the dark scary shadows, Nathan began running again. He was quickly surprised by the sudden inclining stairs that made his legs burn but a minute and 46 steps later, Nathan found himself on top of the great Philippe Park Indian Mound.

Sitting atop of the 45 ft. high hilltop, Nathan could look out at the entire Old Tampa bay waterside. A beautiful view with the wind blowing hard across his face, Nathan imagined the countless people that had stood on this mound over thousands of years since it was first built. Centuries of piled up shells, bones, and bodies, the large midgean began to grow in size and height around 500 B.C. until it would become the center point of the entire native village. An entire race of people the, Tocobagan Indian people would dominate this bay area for hundreds of years and this mound would have been their temple mount for their high king.

Walking to the center area of the mound and looking past a clearing of some over grown oak trees that now obstructed his view, Gabriel pulled out the gold Cross and strung the chain through the hole in the Cross's center. Just as it had done by accident on the top of the Sulphur Spring Tower the cross began to spin.

Reaching back into his bag he picked up a small pair of binoculars. Standing with his back to the wind to make sure it had no effect on the spinning compass; Gabriel held it up close to his eyes and read the faint numbers that surrounded the halo around the Cross's edge. Finally after a moment of settling, the bottom point of the cross pointed exactly to magnetic north just passed Gabriel's shoulder. He scanned the Roman numerals that were engraved on the beveled edge until his eyes focused in on the head of the numeral 28 in between two ruby jewels. With his binoculars, looking hard into the distance across the giant body of water, Gabriel spotted the faint sparkle of lights shining through the darkness several miles away.

"Land… we have our heading." Gabriel reached into his back pack and pulled out a small bronze lensatic field compass. "Hold this," he handed the gold Cross to Nathan. Gabriel flipped up the bronze sight line and lens on his pocket compass and lined up his compass with the gold Cross. Looking thru the lens and sight line his eyes focused in and tried to line up with the numeral 28. Looking between the numbers and on to the twinkling lights from the distant shore; Gabriel rotated the compass to line it up with magnetic north. He got a bearing of 150.

"Ok, let's go." Gabriel quickly tucked the gold Cross back into his back pack, packed up the rest of his gear and then took off back down the mound into the darkness, once again leaving Nathan alone in the woods. "What just happened?" Having no idea what Gabriel just did, Nathan huffed to himself and then began the long jog back down the hill and along the dark path after his friend.

Chapter 52

Back in the black Audi and again racing along the highway towards the interstate, the boys only had 5 hours until daylight and Nathan's knew his parents would soon realize that their children were not home. He knew how afraid they would be. He knew they would call the police. Then he knew he would have to explain the situation about Lisa and he knew the police would never find her. People like Santos have ways of making people disappear without a trace. People like Santos know people that he and Gabriel didn't. Who would the police believe? The thoughts ran thru his head at an alarming pace and his heart began to beat hard in his chest. They had to succeed he couldn't lose his sister. Sure she was annoying most times, but she had always been his best friend, she had always been there for him, and the pain his parents would face if she were to disappear would be too much for him to bear.

Given the situation, Nathan knew that their chances were pretty slim, the worst seemed inevitable, but he still wished that they could all make it home safe and sound before his parents woke up. He wished that this was all just a dream, but it was actually a nightmare. So much had happened to them in the last 12 hours that it finally hit Nathan like a sledgehammer. The tears started to flow, and he pulled the car over.

"What are you doing? What's wrong?" Gabriel asked.

"I just need a second to calm down."

Gabriel looked at his friend and understood his fears. He felt the same way as Nathan, but he had learned, at a young age, to control his fear. Years of abuse and violence had molded Gabriel into a devoutly faithful young man. He knew what he could control and what he could not. He knew there would be times when he would just rely on his faith and put it into God's hands. This was one of those times. He had learned to control his emotions, his adrenaline, and his fear thru Faith. Nathan had not.

Nathan was used to his warm bed and a loving family. When he was afraid, his parents were always a shout away from him. On those rainy thunder filled nights of his youth, a short walk down the hallway and into his parent's bed always made him feel better. He had never really been tested in life. He had never been pushed or forced to keep moving against all odds. In this situation there were no second place trophies. This is life or death and there can be no mistakes. He knew his sister was depending on him but for the first time in his life, he was forced to depend on himself.

"I don't think I can do it." Nathan wiped some tears from his eyes. "We need to call the police and get some help."

Gabriel paused carefully to think about his words.

"Your sister's life is at stake. If you want to call the police and you think that is the right thing to do then let's find a phone and call them right now. But let me say one thing first."

Nathan was turned towards the driver side window trying to hide his face from Gabriel, ashamed of his tears. He wished he was strong like Gabriel but right now he just can't find the courage.

"These guys are killers. They have a lot of money and a lot of power. They have been waiting for this moment for a long long time. They are capable of doing anything. Your sister means nothing to them and she is easy to get rid of. If we call the cops what will we tell them, a crazy story about a lost pirate treasure? We don't even know where Santos lives if that's even his real name. By the time the police even could get close, assuming they believe us, Santos would be long gone and your sister would be nowhere to be found. No trace, no evidence."

Nathan knew he was right. He turned back towards Gabriel. The color was washed from his face and he looked like he was about to get sick. Nathan's pale lips bit back the urge to puke, and he took a deep breath.

"Our only hope to end this is to find that treasure and then use it as a bargaining chip for your sister's life. I know how to find it. I can do it but I need your help. I can't do it alone. If you want to call the police that's fine but if you want to save your sister we've got to go and we have got to go now." Nathan, tearfully looked to Gabriel, "I'm scared." "I'm scared too. I don't know if this is the right thing to do but I know that this is something that we can do. A voice in my head tells me that this is what we must do and I've learned to trust that angelic voice in my head." There was a long silent pause until Gabriel spoke up again. "Do you know any prayers?" Nathan nodded his head. "I'll say them with you… but you need to start driving now."

A wave of emotion came out in one long deep breath then the center gear shift slapped into first, Nathan's foot came off the clutch and slammed on the gas. The wheels began to smoke in unison as the black Audi left two parallel streaks across the highway. Nathan was back in the game and he wasn't going to lose… even if it was the last thing he did. Which, he feared, it just might be.

Chapter 53

The smell of stale tobacco and aged cedar was mildly pleasant but the pungent damp humidity of the room gave Lisa an uneasy feeling. The room appeared to have been a storage space at one time but the moldy smelling dampness let Lisa know that this room had been long forgotten from its original purpose. Its new purpose, however, was far more frightening.

Sitting in the center of the room, on a wooden rocking chair, Lisa had her hands tied behind her back with plastic zip ties. She could barely see the opposite wall through the darkness but a slight ray of light bounced off the floor from under the door jamb. She could only make out shadows but between two tall bookshelves, a few feet apart, the wall appeared to have a pair of large chains hanging from it. Not sure of what she was seeing, the fear of the unknown began to get the best of her. Kidnapped at gunpoint and locked up in some basement dungeon, her brother was now racing around on some wild goose chase to save her life and just a few hours ago all she wanted to do was catch a movie.

A loud rattle at the door gave her a jolt, the giant wooden door swung open and the rush of cool air chilled the sweat on her legs. The flood of light stung her eyes.

Squinting hard she could barely make out the shadow of a man that was now walking behind her. A few seconds passed before the deep heavy breathing turned into a low heavy voice. "So what do you think of my humidor?" Santos asks.

Now able to see, Lisa was relieved to see that the two large bookshelves were actually humidors holding hundreds of layered resting cigars. The hanging chains that she once feared were merely old decorative leather horse stirrups hanging from a wall mirror.

"It's great… I guess. Why am I here? What do you want with me?" "I don't want to hurt you. I don't even want you here." His voice was warm on her neck. "Your perfume, although pleasant, is not good for my cigars and my cigars are my babies. They need love and someone to take care of them and your presence upsets them. They don't want you here." "You brought me here. If you don't want me here then why did you put me here?" His rancid breath was filling her nose.

"Because I need you,"

She swallowed hard as he leaned in closer.

"Your brother and his friend have something that I want and they are going to get it for me because you my beauty are my ace in the hole."

Santos' thick fingered stubby hands ran through her silky hair. He breathed in the fragrance from her head and she could feel him smile behind her.

"How do you know that they will get whatever it is you want?" Lisa tried to sound calm.

His face was now brushing up against her ear but she could still not see his face without making any sudden movement. "If they don't my dear, you will never see the light of day again."

She could feel him move back away from her and suddenly with the slamming of the large heavy door the room was black again. With him gone, she let out a gasp of relief. She could feel her heart pounding in her chest as tears swelled up in her eyes. It took a moment to collect her thoughts, but it was that instant, when the large man left the room, that her mood changed from fright to anger. She was no victim, she told herself, and whoever this man was that was keeping her hostage he was going to have his hands full with Lisa Gale.

As her eyes adjusted to the darkness, she started looking around the room again trying to remember what she had seen in the light. The fear of the unknown was now gone and her attention was focused on how she was going to escape. Sliding her rocking chair closer to the wall every inch taking all of her strength, she could almost reach the horse stirrups. The old and cracked leather stirrups hung from a wood framed mirror she remembered.

"Ok you jerk. You think I'm going to let you hurt me or my brother? You picked the wrong girl."

She stretched out her long left leg as far up the wall as she could. Thankful for all of those years of ballet and dance, her thigh began to twitch as it strained to pull her foot higher and higher up the wall. Almost vertical, finally her heel reached the leather wrapped wooden horse stirrup. Resting her heel on the stirrup tread she pulled down hard on her heel with all of her weight. Lifting her body up out of the chair with one leg extended to the wall, the stirrup suddenly came off of the wall bringing the tacky mirror with it.

Shards of glass bounced off the floor and the noise echoed throughout the room. Not waiting to see if anyone had heard her, Lisa quickly tipped her chair over and the weight of her body slammed hard against the cement floor. Reaching behind her back, she found a thick shard of broken glass and began to work on her plastic handcuffs. Slicing the sharp glass edge against the plastic ties, the angle hurt her hand and the finger cramping was painful but she had to keep trying. She had to fight the pain and the fear. She had to escape. She had to find her brother. She had to live.

Chapter 54

After a quick pit stop at an all-night Circle K gas station, Gabriel leaped into the Ghost's Audi and the two boys sped off down the highway. Gabriel reached into the paper bag and handed Nathan some Sweetarts for his blood sugar, he had been feeling a little dizzy and was starting to sweat. Usually, that was a sign that his blood sugar was getting low and he needed something to raise it back up. He desperately needed his glucometer to tell him where exactly his blood sugars were but he could tell thru experience that his levels were running low and some hard candy would make him feel better. The panic of traveling without his medicine was starting to frighten him but the fear for his sister was much more important. Stopping back at his house, over an hour away, for his backup medical supplies was out of the question. Meanwhile, Gabriel worried about his friend's health but felt that Nathan knew what he was doing and he honored his wishes to keep going.

Along with Nathan's necessary sugar, Gabriel needed to get his hands on a map of the Tampa Bay/St. Petersburg area. It wasn't great but it would work. Folding the map out on his lap, Gabriel placed his bronze field compass on the spot he designated as Phillip Mound. Lining up the spinning magnetic needle with the bezel mark he had rotated on top of the mound, Gabriel placed the compass on his starting point of Phillip Park. Using his Tomahawk Shrike handle as a straight edge, he followed the compass heading of 150 and drew a line from Phillip Park across the bay until he hit land. The line went right up into the Little Manatee River.

"Here, this is where we need to go." Gabriel smiled. "What is that?" Nathan asked. "I'm not sure exactly but 200 years ago. This used to be the location of an Indian tribe." "How do you know?"

"He said on the map." Gabriel pointed to the ancient parchment in his backpack. "Gaspar talked about paying homage to the natives that helped him. He had been searching throughout the Indian territories for his treasure. Once he found it, he went back to say thank you and pay homage. The Mound Hill at Philippe Park was just the starting point. That was the capital city of the Tocobagan tribe. The Chief that had helped Gaspar was there, and he wanted to say thank you."

"Thank him with what?" Nathan questioned. "I don't know. It doesn't really matter. But he needed to say thank you to the tribes that protected him. He also needed to leave a trail. Breadcrumbs if you will to retrace his steps in case he needed to dump his treasure and find it again later, or perhaps, if he couldn't have it someone else would find it."

"Why would he need to dump his treasure?" "Phillip Park, the capital of the ancient Indian tribe. Where is it located? Not the county, but the area is called what?"

After a moment Nathan answered, "Safety Harbor."

"Exactly! Safety Harbor. Do you know why they call it that?" Nathan shook his head keeping his eyes fixed on the road.

"In the old days, Conquistadors exploring Florida would seek safety from tropical storms and hurricanes in the northern waters of the Old Tampa Bay. The peninsula would offer some protection from the rough seas but they were also inhabited by natives. The natives and the Spanish didn't always get along and the Indians drove out the Spanish for many years. Sometime after those first explorers entered the bay, Pirates started sailing these waters. They also needed protection. Not just from storms but from the Spanish Navy and eventually the United States Navy. Those pirates became trading partners with the Indians. In return for the trade goods, the Indians of these waters would help protect the fleeing pirates. So they named this area of the bay, Safe Harbor."

"So Gaspar," Nathan questioned, "started at Mound Hill and then shot a bearing to another Indian city?" "Correct," Gabriel answered. "He needed to say thank you to the natives but we assume he also wanted to leave a trail, a code, to retrace his steps if he should need to drop his treasure for some reason." Nathan was still confused, "But if he had the aid of the local Indians, he could avoid the Spanish and U.S. Navy. Surely with his skill and experience, a Florida storm wouldn't frighten him. So what reason would he have to be concerned?"

Gabriel thought for a moment and then answered, "His ship, the Floriblanca. It would have been too big to sail up the Hillsborough River to Sulphur Springs so he must have left it somewhere and taken a landing party. He goes looking for the treasure and when he finds it he then has to return to his ship. He wrote about leaving the treasure where no man would dare risk looking for it." Gabriel remembered the quote, "Beneath the eyes of my beloved princess, I buried my great fortune where no man would return for fear of death."

"So when he found the treasure, for some reason, he felt that he couldn't bring it back to his ship." Nathan concluded. "Maybe he didn't trust his crew or just felt the timing wasn't right. So he needed to leave a trail on this map to find it again." Gabriel agreed. "I guess there is only one way to find out for sure and that is to find it for ourselves."

Nathan pointed at the circled river mouth with the pencil line drawn to it.

"That's the Little Manatee River in Ruskin. It's about 45 minutes away, but we will make it in 30."

The engine revved high when Nathan's foot pressed down on the gas. He dropped the clutch and slipped the gear shift up one. The red taillights of the speeding black Audi quickly disappeared into the darkness.

Chapter 55

Florida, 1812

The evening was unusually warm and humid even for Florida. The air was thick and there was no relief of a breeze anywhere. Underneath the weeping Spanish Moss covered trees a quiet river was broken up by a small boat gliding against its current. Using the traditional silent "J" paddle stroke, the two men skillfully beached the wooden canoe on the river bank with barely a sound. The older man in the back of the boat reached into the clear cool water and took a drink.

"No salt. We are close, we walk from here."

Enshrouded by giant oak trees along the river bank, the men find an opening and stow their boat in the thick sticky muck of the river bottom. Walking along the slippery steep bank working very hard to stay out of sight, the younger man notices the setting sun and addresses the older man.

"Captain, we don't have much time. The sun is setting, and it's not safe to be in the swamp at night. Bad things happen."

The Captain didn't respond. He just smiled and continued on along the river bank. The walk wasn't too far but it took several minutes to move throughout the wooded area in silence. A few snakes and raccoons were nothing to be concerned with but when a large 8 foot alligator began to hiss at the approaching men, the younger man had to be held at gunpoint to keep him from running.

"Captain please." He begged the old man, but the Captain didn't flinch. "Keep your voice down." He commanded.

Drawing his sword the Captain continued walking towards the wide mouthed dragon. Fearless, he was within inches of the beast when the gaping mouth closed and turned towards the water. In an instant the massive scaled tale was the last thing the men saw as it slithered into the river disappearing beneath the ripples. The Captain turned back towards his companion with a wide grin and then continued on his way.

The young man thought to himself about what he had just seen. The legends were true- this Gasparilla feared no man… nor beast. After another 100 yards, the two men heard a strange bird call, and they began to climb up the river bank. At the top of the climb they came face to face with a dark skinned muscular man with painted symbols on his face. Captain Gaspar shook the man's hand and then began to follow his Indian guide deep into the dense woods. At least it was dry land and not the miserable muck of the river bank, the young man thought to himself. But they were still far from danger and not just the animals, this was Spanish territory and they had patrols all over the area.

The sun was now almost gone and the only thing blacker then the swamp at dusk were the mosquitoes that were now feasting on the men's warm bodies. Dozens of them fed on every inch of bare flesh and sometimes even thru the covered areas. The young man noticed that the Indian guide was either oblivious to the stings of the bloodthirsty insects or the ferocious bugs seemed to avoid him. Either way, the young sailor wasn't as lucky as he smacked another one digging into his neck.

At a small clearing about a half mile from the river, they waited for what seemed like an eternity in the hellish swamp when suddenly the Captain ducked down behind a large tree trunk. Off in the distance, a small torch light danced its way through a narrow path amongst the trees. As it got closer, the Captain drew his sword and gave the signal to get ready. The young man hated to stop his mosquito swatting but had no choice, this is why they had come all of this way. He scratched his neck one more time before grabbing his sword as well as a small curved blade from his boot. The Indian drew back on his bow and aimed his stone carved arrow head directly at the man holding the torchlight.

The moment took forever. The pain searing into the young man's neck was excruciating. He welcomed for the battle to start because the cut of a sword had to be better than the stings of the blood thirsty winged devils buzzing in his ears. The pounding of his heart and the blood racing though his veins must have been like a dinner bell to the tiny vampires.

The Captain however never flinched, never shook, never took his eyes off of his target until his raised hand dropped. The "swoosh" of the guide's arrow took off into the darkness and struck with precision as the distant yelp of the torchbearer gave proof to the hit. Almost before the arrow struck its target, the Captain was racing after it along the blackened path. The young man by instinct alone followed his Captain into the pitch black battle. He wasn't sure how many men he would face or what type of battle he was racing towards. But he knew one thing, he knew he was being led by the ferocious Captain Gaspar and that meant he had a better chance of living than those the Captain was running towards.

Chapter 56

Tampa, FL-Present

Pulling off Interstate-75 on to south 41, the black Audi had made good time. One close call with a state trooper waiting on the other side of an overpass had made the boys a little nervous. However, Nathan had remembered his father getting a ticket at that very spot several years ago and had a feeling that he needed to slow down. He did just in time.

Down route 41 passed the local hardware store and the popular Showtime Café, a local hangout for retired carnival workers. Ruskin had a long rich history with the carnivals over the years, many junk yards contained old floats and train cars from the carnival's glory days. It was even common at the Café to see some of the old circus performers, like Lobster Boy and the Bearded Woman, sitting across from local patrons eating breakfast.

Turning down a few side roads and eventually coming to a stop on a dark gravel road between two open fields, the boys jumped out of the car, hopped a fence and began walking through some thick brush towards the Little Manatee River. Ducking under the sharp leaves of some Cabbage Palms and trying to avoid the unkempt branches of a Brazilian Pepper Tree, the boys made their way towards the river bank.

"Why a mound?" Nathan asked. "Why would Gaspar choose a shell burial mound for his map?"

Gabriel adjusted his back pack and picked up his pace as he started to jog.

"When you're shooting a bearing from a ship you look for landmarks."

Gabriel continued talking as he jumped over a half standing rusted chain link fence.

"You want something that you can see from a great distance and something that will be there for a long time. In those days there were no lighthouses or even stone buildings in this area. The shore line in Florida is soft and sandy, no rock cliffs or jetties, so one good hurricane could change the whole waterfront knocking down trees and washing out the beach. The only thing that Captain Gaspar would have counted on to shoot a bearing to would have been the giant shell mounds that the natives lived on. Some of these mounds were over 40 feet tall and had been there for centuries."

"Plus it would give him a higher advantage point to see further out because so much of the bay's shore is at sea level." Nathan added. "Now you're thinking like a sailor." Gabriel smiled.

They had to slow down because the brush was getting thicker as they got closer to the river and the soft sand was getting tougher to trudge through. But soon they came to a clearing where they spread out and began to sweep the area. Flashlights in hand and in a large open space, the boys could clearly see about 200 square yards around them but saw no giant mounds in the distance. Gabriel looked at the map again to double check his bearing confused as to where they could have gone wrong. Nathan took a moment to have a seat and catch his breath.

"It has to be here. The line cuts right thru here." Gabriel lamented. "Maybe we just need to keep looking. I'm sure we're on the right track." Nathan tried to sound positive.

Looking up at his friend, Gabriel spotted something odd. "Nathan what are you sitting on?"
"Some shells," he replied.

Gabriel looked at the small lip of white shells that were only a few inches off the ground but ran for several feet into the darkness. Picking up on Gabriel's thoughts, Nathan asked "Could this be what's left of it?"

"Of course! I remember know. It was called…" Gabriel shot into his backpack looking for his answer and after a few wrong selections removed a book written by I. Mac Perry. He flipped thru several pages until he found it. "Thomas Mound!"

"Who?" Nathan asked. "Not who but what? This land used to belong to a Captain Thomas." Gabriel continued scanning the book's paragraph. "And there used to be a large burial mound on this land but it was destroyed in the 50's when they dredged out this river. The author talks about looking for it but the mound was gone. However, he did find evidence that it was once here."

Nathan asks, "So we are on the right path but it's gone now what do we do?" Gabriel was running a pencil line across the map. He smiled to himself and then began packing his bag up. Throwing the bag over his shoulder, he turned and headed back thru the darkness.

"Let's go!"

"Go? Go where?" Nathan was still trying to catch his breath. "With no mound I can't get a bearing from here. We need to go to the next spot." "Where is that?" Nathan was now jogging to catch up. "In this book, there is a map of other mounds in the area. If we are systematic, as a sailor would be, to make our way out to the gulf we would use consecutive bearings. The next mound we should see will be Cockroach Key."

Nathan stopped in his tracks.

"The Cockroach People?"

Chapter 57

The drive was short, only a few miles down Hwy 41, when the boys turned onto Cockroach Bay Blvd. It was a long desolate road, but it was a clear night and the Moon was almost full. Even though there were no street lights for miles, they could see fine. They reached the end of the pavement and the sparkling moonlight bounced off the rolling incoming tide. The road ended at a sandy boat launch and a few moments later the boys were entering the frigid water.

Stomping through thick mud and slipping on submerged tree roots, occasionally the boys were forced to stop and pick each other up out of the sinking marsh bottom. Gabriel knew it would be easier to just swim across the channel but he couldn't risk ruining the map so he kept the bag over his head for most of the hike. Luckily the water never got above their chests, but the cold water was like daggers on their skin and often took their breath away.

Making his way across the channel, Nathan noticed swarms of fiddler crabs that seemed to make the very ground move. But their distraction was soon gone, and he began to focus again on his misery. Blood thirsty mosquitoes dined on his hot sweaty skin, the overall wretched low tide stench of the bay, and his complete exhaustion made him think to himself that this was quite possibly the most uncomfortable moment of his life.

But Gabriel never slowed down for second. He seemed oblivious to the surroundings and even appeared to be enjoying himself. Even when he stumbled on an oyster bed and almost completely went underwater, Gabriel reached up high in the air with his backpack keeping it dry while he fell head first into the freezing mud. A quick rinse in the deeper water to clear his eyes of the sticky muck, and he continued on barely skipping a beat. Not wanting to slow him down, Nathan found the strength to suck it up and ignore his own discomfort. The thought of his sister pushed him to not quit and keep moving but Gabriel made him move faster than he believed he could.

The key was finally at their feet but without a boat it was hard to see where the mound was from the shoreline. After about 10 minutes of climbing over and through the mangrove lined mud banks, Gabriel finally saw it. On the west side of the key about 500 yards from the bay, several trees were standing high above the rest on the muddy mangrove so he made his move inland.

"This is it." Gabriel beamed. "How do you know? It's covered with weeds and trees." Nathan replied. "Precisely, it's the only thing with enough soil to grow trees out here. Everything else is low mangroves soaked with tidal waters but this area is dry. Two hundred years ago this was a shell mound and there was probably a house or wooden temple right where we are now standing." Nathan was just excited to start climbing up the pile and out of the black cold water that he didn't really hear Gabriel's answer. His feet were heavy and his clothes were wet and filthy but he was happy to finally be on dry land. He looked down at his feet but all he could see were his expensive white Nike shoes now black and draining mud from the toes.

On top of the mound, looking northwest out across the bay, Gabriel took in a deep breath of sea air. For a moment he forgot about the task at hand and the dangers that they faced, instead he took in the salt air and imagined countless natives who for centuries stood here and looked up at those very same bright shining stars. A smile spread across his face as he imagined what it would have been like to live back then and the hardships they must have faced to survive. He took a second to rest and listen to the silence but soon the moment was over and realty set in. Gabriel reached into his bag and pulled out the compasses.

"Hold this."

Nathan stood up and took the pocket field compass and map from Gabriel. Gabriel lifted up the golden Cross and leveled it on its chain. The Cross began to spin as the lodestone picked up the magnetic field and then finally settled on the north heading. Looking on the bezel for the number 5 Gabriel found it and began to line up his shot. Looking out into the darkness of the bay he couldn't see anything but he knew it was there. Somehow he just knew it. He could feel it. No one had gotten this close before. This had to be the trail to the "Isla de Muerta." The trail to Gaspar's treasure was in their grasp.

"Come here and look at my arm." Nathan leveled off the pocket compass as he had done before and shot the bearing along Gabriel's arm. It was awkward because he wasn't shooting at anything but a big black void. He just tried to follow Gabriel's arm as best he could.

Gabriel glanced at the compass to give his approval and read off the bearing. "250 degrees west."

Gabriel dropped to ground and placed the Circle K map in front of him wiping some mud off of it. Lining up the field compass, as he had done before, he began to trace out the bearing from Cockroach bay. Drawing a line out through the open water and towards the mouth of the Gulf, Gabriel's heart began to race.

"There it is!" He could barely contain himself. "We found it!" "What is that?" Nathan strained his eyes through his steam fogged glasses to see Gabriel's dirty fingers pointing to a brown spot on the map.

Gabriel looked up at him with a wide grin, "the Island of Death."

Chapter 58

Florida, 1812

Standing at the edge of a large freshwater spring in the middle of a black swamp, four men peer over a wooden chest about the size of a shoe box. They were dressed in torn up dirty rags for clothes, but they stood straight and carried themselves as if they were anything but poor. One man lit up a pipe and muttered something under his breath as he swatted his neck.

"Blood thirsty devils,"

A dancing torchlight appeared down the path from them, they all turned and prepared for their scheduled meeting. The light came closer, so they lit their own torch as a signal to enter their camp. As the traveling light came closer the men shouted out to the three men on the path but there was no answer. The tension among the four men began to climb, an uneasy feeling raced through their bodies. One man reached under his coat, pulling out his flintlock gun and aimed it at the approaching trio. Finally, a reply came out from the approaching men.

"Put down your gun my friend. Do you not recognize the uniform of an American General," The gravelly voice of Jose Gaspar cut through the humid air.

The group of men, whose uniforms they were now wearing, had been ambushed earlier by the Captain. Taken by surprise with an arrow strike from the Indian scout, the General had fallen without ever seeing it coming. The remaining four soldiers in his platoon also fell but they at least put up a fight. Unfortunately, the element of surprise is a powerful advantage and they barely stood a chance. Two of the men were non-ranks and their uniforms were too short for the young first mate but the Sergeant's uniform fit him just fine. For the Captain's uniform however, he was forced to make some alterations. Being of short stature, Gaspar was swimming in the dead General's 6 foot 2 inch framed shirt and pants. He quickly cut off about 6 inches of his pants leg and stuffed them into his boots. He rolled up his wool sleeves, against protocol but in this humidity wouldn't be questioned, and folded almost half of his shirt into a tuck at his back. By pulling the General's leather satchel case strap across his chest, the Captain was able to cover the fatal arrow hole in his shirt and his transformation was now complete. The Indian scout refused to wear any clothes so the men just grabbed their gear and headed off down the path to their scheduled rendezvous with the men and the wooden box.

The gun man now lowered his flintlock but did not uncock the hammer. His uneasy feeling was still rolling in his gut.

"Why do you approach our camp?" A short heavy set man spoke English but was trying very hard to hide his thick French accent. "I am here for an exchange. You have something that I want and I have something that you need. It is no more complicated than that my friend."

After a moment to pause and think, the heavy set man agreed and opened the chest up for the travelers to observe. The iron hinge squeaked as the latch of the lock rotated and the wooden top swung open. Looking over the Captain's shoulder, the young First Mate was surprised when he looked into the wooden box.

"What is this," exclaimed the First Mate standing next to Gaspar. "Where is the gold?" "Gold… Monsieur? No Gold… only proof." The heavy set man replied.

Gaspar didn't make a sound as a large smile crossed his face.

"It is perfect my friend. You have upheld your end of the deal and I shall uphold mine." Gaspar reached into the fallen General's satchel while never taking his eyes off of the treasure box. "Captain what is the meaning of this?" The confused first mate asked. "Capitan? You wear the uniform of a General. You are not who you say you are." The heavy set man loudly shouted out a command in French and his companions all drew their weapons once again leveling them at Gaspar and his First Mate.

The Indian scout had been able to keep his distance from the group and was now managing to slip thru the darkness into the woods unnoticed with the confusion.

"Please put down your weapons." Gaspar requested. "We ask for no trouble. I have the papers you requested and I am happy to give them to you now."

Slowly pulling out from the leather satchel that was hanging below his left shoulder, Gaspar removed a rolled up parchment paper. "Your papers of land ownership are now yours my friend. You and your men are free to seek out your destiny in this new land of America. I hear Pennsylvania is quite nice this time of year." The rolled parchment paper was indeed a grant of land ownership signed by the now deceased General. Obviously, it was to be used as a bargaining chip for the trade of the treasure. Gaspar was just completing the transaction.

The young first mate pulled out his gun and saber and aimed both towards Captain Gaspar.

"You promised me fortune and wealth. Where is the gold Captain?" "It is here my friend. I have not lied to you. Your fortune lies in this chest and its value is beyond your wildest dreams." "You old fool," the young First Mate argued, "you have gone mad and you risk my life for nothing."

The heavy set French man glanced at the papers in his hand and turned to Gaspar. "If you are not who you say you are then these papers are worthless."

Gaspar pleaded, "My friend those papers are valid. I have not altered them at all and they carry the word of the man that signed them."

"But that man is not you, Monsieur. I cannot honor your word for you are an imposter." As the tension and confusion climbed, it was the First Mate that made the first move. He swung his musket towards the heavy set man, but before he could get a shot off, there was a loud bang and he was struck in the arm with a musket ball from his right.

Gaspar shouted, "No" but he could not stop it. He had to act fast because the guns were now turning towards him.

In a flash, he spun to his left and swung his sword from his waist. The blade slashed cleanly into the Frenchman with the graying beard. A howl came from the man's mouth as the blade dug deep into his flesh. Gaspar didn't hear the man's scream because with his other hand, he had fired a loud shot from his pistol into the heavy set leader of the group. The noise was deafening at such a close range. Gaspar's ears were ringing painfully and his eyes were straining to see after the bright muzzle flash of his gun.

With his ears still ringing and his eyes starting to clear, Gaspar saw the third man lying on his back lifeless with a wooden arrow sticking out of his ribcage. Remembering his hidden Indian friend hiding in the tree line, Gaspar would gladly pay that man extra for that shot. The last of the Frenchmen stood still with his hands up in the air and his empty pistol on the ground. He had gotten the first shot off and it had hit the First Mate's arm. But now the frightened man was falling to his knees and pleading for his life.

The First Mate was a little rattled but quickly realized that he would live and the man that had almost taken his life was now defenseless. Enraged the First Mate grabbed a nearby sword and began to swing on the helpless man when the Captain's command made him freeze. "Halt or Die!"

The frightened man pleaded, "Monsieur, I surrender. Please have mercy on me."

Gaspar smiled at the scared young soldier. "Seńor, I am not an evil man. Although, I am a pirate and a vicious one at that, let it be known that Captain Gaspar is also a man of honor. I shall let you live." He handed the kneeling man the rolled up land grant papers, "You no longer need to divide your fortune among 4. You alone shall have plenty of land in this new world."

"Bless you Monsieur; you truly are a great man…" Before the pleading man could finish his thanks, a strike to the back of his head knocked him unconscious on the ground. He was out cold. Gaspar's Indian friend had taken the butt end of an unused rifle to his skull.

"I said I would let you live but I also don't need you following us. I never trust the French."

The Captain picked up the treasure box with great reverence and began his journey back towards the river with the Indian scout at his side however the First Mate was slow to join. Fury was now burning in the Mate's eyes as he stared at the man that had deceived and used him, the man that had so much while others had so little, the so called great Captain Gaspar. He thought, it was time that the Captain got what he deserved and the young First Mate was just the man to do it.

Chapter 59

Tampa, FL-Present

The night sky was starting to turn to an early morning bluish tint as the moon was setting and the sun was beginning to crest. It had taken the two exhausted boys over an hour to find a small Jon boat and race the 25 hp. motor out along the mouth of the Tampa Bay. It was about 10 miles of open water and even though the water was fairly calm the small, flat bottom, single engine, boat bounced around horribly. Hanging on for dear life, Nathan had already vomited in his mouth twice and was struggling to hold back a third.

The green faced Nathan tried to calm his stomach by talking to Gabriel, who was steering the throttle handle to the small Mercury motor, but was temporarily distracted from his upset stomach as he looked up to the underneath of the majestic Sunshine Skyway Bridge.

The cable suspension bridge, built in 1987, is over 4 miles long and stands 431 feet tall. It is listed as one of the top ten bridges in the world and to the awestruck boys floating beneath it they could see why. The sheer size of it took their breath away as it spans across the entire mouth of Tampa Bay.

"Why was it called the Island of Death?" Nathan slurred as he points off to the distant island of Egmont Key. "This was the one place that pirates in that day would have feared the most, only the bravest and most connected pirate would ever come here. Look behind me." Gabriel pointed off the boat's stern. "You see that large island over there? That's Fort Desoto."

"I know that fort," Nathan answered, "it was a Confederate battery during the Civil War. I went there on a field trip once. But I don't think it was built until the 1840's. Why would that matter?"

"Egmont key was a strategic location to protect the mouth of the bay. America purchased the island from Spain in 1827. Spain had tried for years to build a fort on it but it was too difficult on the sandy shores. America eventually built a large battery on that point there and it became Fort Desoto. This area was crawling with patrolling ships for years,"

"I still don't get it."

"What do pirates fear the most?" Gabriel asked. Nathan thought for a second and then it clicked. "The Navy."

"That's right. The only ships that could put up a fight against piracy were the military vessels. These waters were crawling with them at that time. Spanish warships, the British Navy and the French Navy were patrolling these waters as well as the American cutters that were surveying and protecting shipping lanes. The French owned Louisiana. Spain controlled Florida. Britain was at war with America. It was deadly for any pirate to sail these waters."

A particularly large rolling wave hit the boys on their port side and sent Nathan sliding off his seat and onto the wet boat floor. Crashing with a hard thud that took his breath away, he quickly got back into his seat and tried to play it off as if his now wet butt wasn't sore. It was an uncomfortable, choppy, wet, ride for Nathan and land could not come fast enough.

"Are you ok?"

Nathan nodded his head but grimaced when Gabriel wasn't looking.

"The era of the pirate was at an end. Gaspar himself was called the last of the pirates. He would have had to leave his ship, the Floriblanca, someplace safe because it was too big to not be seen. He then had to rely on the protection and passage of the native Indians to move inland and search for his treasure. On his passage out he must have been forced to dump his treasure someplace safe for some reason where he knew no one would dare go after it. The crew of his ship must have known about the treasure and Gaspar knew that they would want to search for it. So he had to find a place that only the craziest pirate, who had the support of the local natives, would ever dare to search for it."

The engine was cut off and the bouncing boat slowed to a coast, eventually landing on the soft sand of Egmont Key. It couldn't come fast enough for the now white faced Nathan who leapt off the boat before it even came to a stop. Face down on all fours in the sand, Nathan took in several deep breaths to help settle his stomach and the spinning motion in his head. He soon felt the striding Gabriel walking past him up and over the island's sugar sand dunes. Gabriel never seemed to miss a beat, Nathan thought to himself as he struggled to hold back something burning in his throat.

"Come on land lobber, time is wasting."

Nathan looked up only to catch the last glimpse of Gabriel as he disappeared into the dark island sea grass. Struggling to his feet in the cold wet sand, Nathan found the strength to start walking after him. Even when he didn't think he could go any further-somehow he found the strength to keep moving. He had to… Lisa needed him to… He needed to. "Just keep moving," he said to himself. And he did.

Chapter 60

Florida, 1812

A small sailboat, not much bigger than a dingy, was tacking into an eastern breeze. Captain Gaspar was at the tiller and his First Mate was hauling in the sheets from the swinging boom. The thick wool Sergeant's overcoat was now on the boat floor with a small musket ball hole in the right sleeve. The First Mate had literally dodged a bullet when the musket shot from the scared Frenchman went too low and missed his flesh. A musket shot at that range would have taken the First Mate's forearm clean off but even a minor wound, with the filthy clothes and swamp conditions, could have led to a deadly infection. The First Mate was thankful to have made it out safely. He was thankful for the oversized coat. He was thankful for the missed shot and ultimate escape from the trade deal. But his anger towards the Captain and his greed for the Captain's treasure was festering and growing deep within him.

The shoe box size treasure chest was resting ever so close to Gaspar's foot on the deck of the boat. A wide smile spread across the old captain's sun tanned face. A final wave from his Tocobagan friends, whose help had made this voyage the most rewarding of his long life, was a sign of respect and thanks to the natives that had helped him. As the sailboat made its way out into the deep Gulf waters, the mound fires of the Tocobagans lit up the mouth of the bay with dancing light and high rising smoke columns. But the vast open waters were getting much darker as the vessel moved further away from the mound fires and into the black deep waters of the gulf.

Now in a pitch black darkness that only the night sea sky could provide, the Captain took a glance at his gold Cross and made a correction to the helm. With the bow now heading two points East by North, the First Mate knew their heading was wrong but chose not to question the Captain. The tension was already thick between them and he thought it would be wise to just stay quiet. He knew his time to face the Captain would come when they returned to the Floriblanca and the Captain would then face the surprise of his life. Until that time, the First Mate would bite his tongue and wait for his moment. Eventually, the First Mate noticed the splashing whitecaps of the surf and was forced to call out "Land Ho."

The sailboat had made its way across the racing currents of the great channel and landed on the large island at the mouth of Bay. After sometime, the two men hiked across the island through the bladelike sea grass and swarms of mosquitoes. The large slow moving family of tortoises that inhabited the island was a friendly distraction to the now exhausted men. After some time into their hike, the Captain glanced directly above his head into the starry sky and called for them to stop. With a small shovel in his bag, the Captain ordered the First Mate to start digging into the sandy soil.

After more than 30 min of digging, the dark hole in the ground measured about 6 feet deep and several feet wide.

"Captain it's such a small chest why must I keep digging?" the First Mate asked, barely able to stand up straight from exhaustion and the pain in his back. "You are right my friend. It is too deep for the chest alone." Gaspar removed his pistol and leveled it at the tired man inside the hole. "Captain what is this? Why have you turned your weapon on me?" "It was not I who turned his anger my friend. You think that you can conspire with the crew on my ship and not have me aware of it? Your time by my side washed away with that solemn word of mutiny. In time, I would have given you the Floriblanca to sail under my blessing but your haste and ambition has cost you your life. The crew that you worked so hard to turn against me these last few months will soon realize, with your death, that no man dares to rise up against Gasparilla."

A shout of horror was drowned by the sound of a blasting musket shot. The First Mate collapsed to the bottom of the hole that he had just finished digging. The Captain climbed down into the hole and placed the wooden treasure chest on the body. The Mate's hand suddenly grasped the Captain's arm in one last gasp of life but it was useless. The shot was fatal and the Mate's hand slowly slipped away. Gaspar stared into the man's eyes and watched as they slowly closed forever. The Captain then looked to the sky above him and blew a kiss to the stars.

Another hour to fill in the hole and make his way back across the island, Gaspar now tacked his small sailboat back into the wind and out to sea. His heading was south towards his beloved Floriblanca. He knew the crew on his ship would get the message but he also knew, like spoiled fruit, it only took one bad apple to ruin the bunch. His crew had been infected by the First Mate's ambition and it would only be a matter of time before they would challenge him and his wealth again. It would only be a matter of time before another disgruntled ambitious deckhand would again challenge the elderly extremely wealthy Captain. Most likely that slob of a deckhand, Raùl Vargas, Gaspar thought to himself but it could be anyone. Such is the life of a Pirate, he thought. But that life of piracy was soon to come to an end when he would return for his treasure as a new man, a free man, and his new life would bring him home again at last. He smiled at the thought; the great Captain Gaspar after all of these years would again one day soon be welcomed into the Spanish court where he belonged.

All the gold and all the wealth that he had plundered over the decades paled in comparison to what was now buried under the sand on that desolate island. He had to protect it until the time was right. He knew the crew would never stop searching for it. He knew the Tocobagans were on borrowed time as the Americans, Spanish, British and French battled over these waters and the inland shores. That island sat within cannon shot of the newly surveyed American fort that would eventually be placed on that Tocobagan shell mound with the dancing light. He knew that the highland of that very island would be an ideal place for a future military battery. That's why he placed the chest on the upper end of that island. Close enough to be too dangerous to search for but far enough away to never be found. A quiet spot on the island that no pirate would dare risk looking for no matter how filled with treasure lust they could be. An island so surrounded by dangers it was only fitting for him to label at as the island of death. La Isla de Muerta was definitely a safe place for his precious treasure no doubt. But what made it perfect for the Captain and why he chose it in the first place was that the island was directly located under the watchful eye of his beloved princess. It was fate, he believed. A beautiful omen, that his dreams would at last come true.

Chapter 61

On the north end of Egmont Key about 300 yards from the wall of the old battery, Gabriel stopped to check his map. Standing next to a large palm tree with saw grass all around his dirty legs, Gabriel laid his map on the ground and used his flashlight to light it up. He had drawn the bearing lines from his gold Cross compass across the map. There was a bearing of 150 degrees from the Philip Park Mound that lead directly to the Thomas Mound area. There was an approximate line Gabriel had drawn from there with a bearing of 248 degrees. That bearing, he assumed would be accurate, because it was in relation to the gold Cross bearing of 7 from the pile of shells that Nathan had been sitting on. With no mound to be precise it was a best guess. 250 degrees from the Cockroach Bay mound landed directly on Egmont Key's lower middle area. Unfortunately, that line crossed the entire island. The distance along that line was several hundred yards and digging it would take years. The line from the Thomas Mound bearing crossed the Cockroach Bay line right about where Gabriel was but it was still not precise enough. Just on degree off and they could be dozens of yards away from the treasure. So Gabriel added another line that would give him a good bearing to the mound for the king of the rough waters.

Gabriel knew he was close. He had two lines intersecting on the island but he had 3 bearings to plot. Using the gold Compass number of 3, Gabriel had to work backwards. On the opposing side of the Cross directly opposite of the number 3 was the number 17. He then retraced a back bearing by lining up the gold compass to the lensatic compass in his hand. This gave him a bearing of 120 degrees out from Egmont key. However when he drew a line of 120 degrees from his current location the bearing pointed to nothing on the map. There was no fixed point or landmark or mound that Gaspar would have shot a bearing to from back in those days. However when he decided to draw a parallel line using the same bearing just a few yards north of his location that line made his heart race. Running directly into Snead Island, at the mouth of the Manatee River, his new line ran over the very spot where the Portavant Temple Mound once stood.

The Portavant Temple Mound or Snead Island Mound is located in the Emerson Point Preserve on Snead Island. The island sits at the mouth of the Manatee River which flows into the Tampa Bay Harbor. Sitting within the preserve that has seen 5,000 years of habitants, the temple mound that was started around 700 A.D. and its multiple surrounding smaller mounds was the largest in the Tampa Area. The once thriving Indian culture that lived in this area found an abundance of natural resources as the large out flowing river collided with the salty deep waters of the gulf. The swirling currents and thermal changes formed a constant challenge to mariners even to this day but to the ancient Indians of the turbulent waters this was their home.

"Perfect, we are close! Both bearings line up with Indian mounds from this point. I've got two good bearings but the Thomas Mound bearing is throwing us off." Gabriel had guessed the location of the Thomas Mound location but it was about an inch away from the other two intersecting lines. With a discrepancy like that, he thought, their lost treasure could be anywhere within a 100 yard radius.

"Gaspar would have wanted something very precise. Most mariners rely on three or more bearings to get a good fix. He wouldn't want to waste time looking for his treasure he would want to get in fast and go. We need another crossing line to get a location fix or will have to dig up this whole island. Let's stop here and think for a second." Gabriel dropped to the ground and reached into his backpack.

Nathan, however, was frustrated and didn't want a break. He looked out at the rising sun and felt a sudden sense of urgency. Lisa was counting on him and he didn't want to take a break, there was no more time. "But the map doesn't give any other headings. We need to find that Thomas Mound location and try again we are running out of time." Nathan pleaded.

"I'm going to need a few minutes to work this out so just hold the light on me." "What are you doing?" Nathan questioned. "I've been thinking about something for a while now and I think I may have just figured out my hunch but I need to do some work."

Removing a massive book from his bag, Gabriel began flipping thru the pages. The book was about 3 inches thick and its reddish brown binding was worn bare from years of constant use. Noticing the faint gold lettering along the bind, Nathan spoke out.

"What is... Bowditch?"

"Who is Bowditch?" Gabriel corrected. "It's my light reading." Gabriel said with a sarcastic smile. "Nathaniel Bowditch was an amazing mathematician and sailor. He wrote this book some 200 years ago, and it's an encyclopedia for ancient mariners, their Bible in other words. Using this book, he taught sailors how to navigate the seas literally with their eyes closed. He could use tidal charts, solar lines, and in this case celestial lines to navigate anywhere in the world. He has a reduction chart in here that I need to find just give me a second." Gabriel continued to flip thru the pages when Nathan spoke up.

"Reduction chart for celestial lines?" Nathan asked.

Finally finding the page he was looking for, Gabriel showed the tiny lined number packed chart page to Nathan.

"Absolutely! Look, using math, I can plug into this sheet our statistics and eventually get a bearing that we can place on this map and it should cross this line and give us a fix on the buried treasure. It just might take a little while to work it out, I'm a little rusty."

"Hold on." Nathan ordered. "I don't know what you're talking about but I know there is a faster way."

Nathan pulled out the Ghost's cell phone and quickly started a search. A few seconds later and then a quick download of an app, he showed it to Gabriel.

"I don't think he will mind paying for this. Ok, what do I need to put in?"

Gabriel looked at the recently downloaded star chart application that Nathan had just found. What would have taken Gabriel close to 30 minutes and on his best day would be within 5 yards of the actual mark, was now reduced in seconds to within GPS precise inches.

"I need a bearing line for Andromeda using the time of 11:58pm and the date April 7th, 1812."

Nathan recognized the time and date from the treasure map's log. It was 5 days after the 2nd of April, the day Gaspar buried his treasure. But what was Andromeda he thought to himself as he continued to plug the information into the phone's app. He got his answer instantly.

"Ok, it says 015 degrees."

Gabriel started plotting the line on the Circle K map. He drew a line with a bearing of 015 degrees on the map and then slid it down until it crossed perfectly on top of the other two intersecting lines. A sudden shout pierced the silence and Nathan knew something good had just happened.

"YES!" Gabriel threw his arms up into the air. "We got it, just over there a few yards."

Quickly, he grabbed his gear and made several giant leaps over sharp sea grass about 20 yards to the south.

"What did we just get?" Nathan followed.

"On the map he wrote beneath my beloved princess right?" "Ok." "Well, what if he literally meant beneath the princess and not just a dead ghost looking down on him? When I saw the gold Cross spinning from the magnetic lodestone on top of the tower, I looked out to where the Indian mounds used to be. I remembered how they would line up the mounds with celestial markings like the winter solstice or the North Star."

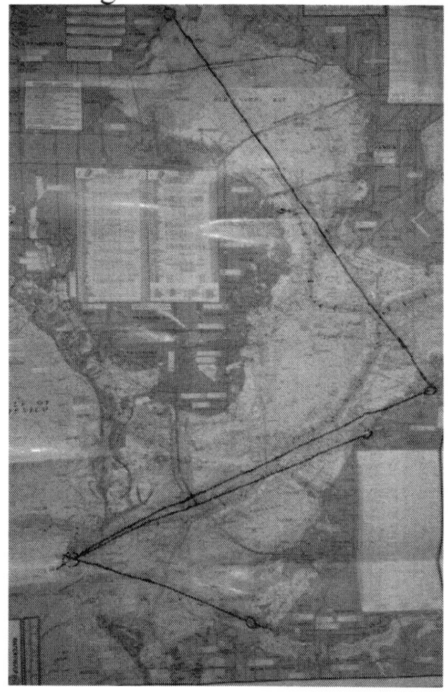

"I'm still not following you." "It just struck me how important the celestial markings were to sailors. They didn't have computers and apps like we have today. They didn't have street signs to tell them the way. They used the stars and land features to find their way. Captain Gaspar used Indian mounds to lay out a pathway for him to return when he could. But what if one of the mounds were destroyed in a storm or weather was bad and he couldn't see all of them? He would have wanted one more bearing line to be as precise as possible, a bearing that would mean something to him. This bearing would change every night and would be almost impossible to figure out unless you were educated in chart work. A celestial bearing line that only he would know to look for once he buried his treasure. On that day, at that time, at that location he looked up into the night sky and saw his beloved captured princess… Andromeda."

Nathan stared back blankly at Gabriel, "Now… who is Andromeda?"

Chapter 62

Still working on his chart plots, Gabriel doesn't look up to address Nathan. Instead he focuses on keeping his hand as straight as possible as it draws another bearing line across the Circle K map. "You never studied Greek mythology?" Nathan stared back at him for a moment and had to think of an answer. Not wanting to admit that he had studied it but never really paid attention, Nathan meekly answered.

"I did, but it was a long time ago and I'm a little foggy." "Well, according to Greek mythology, Andromeda was the beautiful princess of Cepheus. When Andromeda's mother, Cassiopeia, boasted about her daughter's unequalled beauty it offended Nereus and his daughters. Nereus asked the Greek god Poseidon to punish Cassiopeia and her kingdom. Poseidon, the brother of Zeus, was the god of the seas and he sent the legendary sea monster Cetas to bring havoc on Cassiopeia's kingdom. Are you following me so far?"

Nathan nodded but was really lost.

"With his kingdom nearly destroyed, Cepheus asked an oracle for an answer to save it from the monster. The oracle's answer was to have the king's daughter, Andromeda, chained to a rock and offered to the sea monster, Cetas, as a sacrifice. Forever to be known as the captured princess, Andromeda was saved by Perseus at the last possible moment. Perseus had slain the evil queen Medusa and used her head to turn the sea monster, Cetas, into stone. Andromeda and Perseus were married and they would go on to live forever together in the stars."

"How do you know all of that stuff?" Nathan asked. "With no one to play with, I had a lot of free time on my hands. Books of great stories can be wonderful friends." Gabriel answered but never broke his stride.

It was a difficult area to move around, off the beaten path of the traveling tourists and away from any type of clearing. The white sand path got them close but to reach their spot they had to tread through sharp palm branches and razor like saw grass leaves. Using his tomahawk to chop his way through some of the really dense brush, Gabriel had finally stopped where his lined crossed the map.

"Give me the compass." Nathan gladly handed Gabriel the dangling compass from his neck, the weight of it had been rubbing his skin raw. "I need to shoot a bearing back to our waypoints but I can't see them. I'm afraid this is as close as I can get."

"Stand back and let me at it." Nathan pushed his way past Gabriel. Using the Ghost's cell phone's GPS, Nathan located their exact location. "27.590° by -82.761°," Nathan read off the phone's screen. Gabriel plotted it on the Circle K map and they were standing on his bearing line.

"Ok, now find Andromeda again on April 7th, 1812 at 11:58pm."

Turning the cell phone up towards the early morning sky and running the star charter app, the phone began to sparkle with moving illuminating dots. Nathan typed in the date and time while the phone paused for a moment to load. Then there it was. Reaching up high into the sky with the cell phone directly above their heads in a virtual star filled sky from 200 years ago was the captured princess star-Andromeda.

"Centuries of nautical knowledge all at the push of a button on one little instant phone." Nathan stated with a smile. "I'm impressed Nathan, great job." "Don't thank me, thank Android." Nathan replied.

With a swift swoosh of air, Gabriel's tomahawk slashed into the sand and kicked up a large pile of powdery white Earth.

Meanwhile, on the other side of the bay, the Ghost was standing on the edge of a sea wall. Using a large night vision telescope, he looked through the greenish lens towards a dark island about 2 miles to the West. It had been a long time since the small motorized

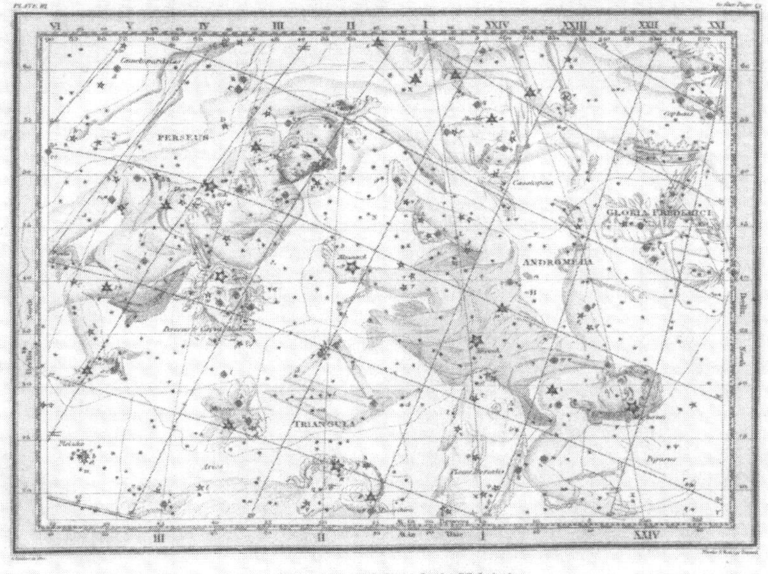

boat disappeared with the boys. Beached on that island, no one had arrived or left since then.

The pale thin fingers reached into his pocket and pulled out a new shiny black cell phone. Dialing his boss's number from memory, the gravelly voice answered.

"What have they found?" "I think they are onto something. They haven't left the island, and it's been almost two hours. I will keep watch but I suggest you get the boat," the Ghost hissed.

The deep raspy voice replied, "At last, after all of this time Gaspar's treasure is finally mine."

Chapter 63

The dig had been hard and long. Sugar sand is not easy to shovel with bare hands and a tomahawk but the boys had finally dug down to the cool damp soil that was making it easier to move thru. They continued on for some more time until Nathan let out a short yelp. "Ah, what is that?"

Nathan leaped out of the hole in one quick jump. Pulling the flashlight into the hole and crouching down for a better look, Gabriel noticed some torn fabric that looked to be a blue tint. Lifting the fabric up a bit a surge of fear raced through him as he saw what Nathan had grabbed and yelled at. Attached to the blue fabric was leathery dry skin covered bone. The small bone was lying next to a several other smaller white bones parallel to each other.

"It's a hand."

Nathan's adrenaline was at an all-time high. It was one thing to be chasing down a treasure map, even if you believe it's real, but to actually dig up a spot and find a 200 year old pirate was too much for him to handle. He started to hyperventilate.

"Nathan it's ok, go catch your breath. Do you need any sugar? I have some in my bag." All Nathan could do was shake his head "no."

"It looks like the hand is holding on to something." Gabriel brushed away some damp sand and noticed that the person's arm was covering something wooden while the other arm, still partially buried in sand, was reaching up over his head.

Clearing away some more of the soil the gruesome scene became more apparent.

"Is he holding it?" Nathan asked. "It looks like it. He must have been buried with it."

"Buried alive?"

"Yeah, it looks like he tried to dig out."

Nathan no longer in the hole suddenly found it necessary to wipe himself clean.

"It's cursed man, that treasure is cursed by him and we just let him out. That's not good Gabe, That's not good." "Relax; he's been dead for a long time. Besides, he would be happy that the truth can now be told. We did him a favor."

Stopping for a second to think about what Gabriel said, "I like that. I do. Did you hear that Mr. Dead Pirate? We are doing you a favor please don't haunt us."

"Are you done?"

"Maybe."

"Well get down here and help me dig this thing out."

It didn't take long to remove the chest from the pirate's clutch. As careful as the boys could be to not break apart the fragile bones, it only took a few moments to remove it and place it on the ground outside of the hole. But now time seemed to take forever as the boys stood above the chest wondering what could be locked inside it.

The chest was made of hard cedar wood but a couple hundred years underground in the damp sand and it was very brittle. Small holes and gaps could be seen through the outer wood shell but another wood lined interior seemed to be still intact. The hinge and lock were almost none existent. Rusted to almost nothing, they were still in place but about to fall off. Gabriel had to be very careful not to destroy the corroded metal.

"It's getting light out here," Noticing the rising sun, "Tourists will be arriving soon. Let's open this thing and get out of here." Nathan stated. "No let's not open it yet. We can go but I want Santos to open it."

Gabriel grabbed his bag, loaded his tomahawk, and with the small wooden chest in his hands started walking towards their boat.

"Leave the body there. Someone will report it and let the authorities deal with it. We don't have time to waste." Gabriel stated. "Why don't we open it?" Nathan was desperate to see the treasure.

"I want Santos to open it. He needs to see what's inside. If it's open first he may think we didn't give him everything and he would still hold your sister captive."

Nathan wanted so badly to open the chest and see what the treasure was but he knew Gabriel was right. He would have to wait.

The Jon boat was pushed off from the sandy shore and the motor fired up a high pitch whirl. Gabriel aimed the bow back towards the mouth of the bay and revved the engine to its limit. The rising Sun was now clear off the horizon and bright as could be. The Sun's rays were warm and felt good to the cold wet boys but it also meant that Nathan's parents were waking up soon. Imagining his parents' fear of not knowing where their kids were made Nathan feel his parent's pain. He couldn't wait to see them again, but only if his sister was with him as well. He wouldn't stop until he saved her. Holding a hand up to see through the blinding rays, Gabriel saw a massive yacht off in the distance turn directly towards them. He killed the engine when he saw it because he knew it was for them.

The giant white hulled super yacht, something you would only see on Lifestyles of the super wealthy, was speeding straight for them. Its hull was so high the boys couldn't see the upper decks from the water line of their tiny boat.

"It's coming right at as why did you stop the engine?" Nathan began to panic. "It's Santos."

"How do you know? He's going to run right over us." Nathan was full panic now as the massive yacht continued to barrel down on them. Gabriel stood up in the wobbly boat and held the wooden chest over his head.

The loud engines of the super yacht suddenly went quiet and the massive vessel began to slow down in a now eerie silence. The small Jon boat rose for what seemed like an eternity as it climbed up the massive yacht's bow swell and then came rushing down again. The tiny boat bobbed up and down in the shadow of the gigantic super yacht but thankfully, to some relief, it was now blocking out the blinding sun.

The boys sat and waited for Santos to come and get them. Not sure how they would make the climb up the towering hull on to the main deck, they waited for a ladder or something to be dropped. A loud “CLANK” and then a “THUD” seemed to come from the metal hull beside them. Suddenly with a long “HISS,” a large square section of the hull began to drop down at the waterline in a slow descend. It was a landing platform on the side of the ship that was large enough for the boy’s entire boat to easily slide onto. All they could do was watch and imagine what waited for them inside. The hull door finally stopped just above the waterline and seemed to be reaching out for the boys to climb on.

Stepping onto the platform, they thought it was almost as good as dry land. The ship was so big that it was barely moving in the choppy water. It was a welcomed change from the bone jarring bounce of the small Jon boat. But the pleasant change was soon gone when the raspy voice of Santos called out from inside the cavernous hull.

“Welcome to the Floriblanca II.”

Chapter 64

The massive floating fortress was a stunning sight to see. The sheer size of the ship seemed to make even the bay seem smaller. The boys had been bobbing across the vast water on a tiny float of a boat and now they were perfectly still on the gigantic mansion in the water. Its length was at least 200 feet long and over 50 feet wide. The twin Caterpillar generators turned the screws at over 7000 horsepower pushing the floating city upwards of 20 knots on the open sea. She had 4 decks that could be seen above the waterline and probably another one below the water. Taking in the grandeur for a moment, the boys forgot the danger they were in, but only for a moment.

The light colored maple was clean and bright in the lounge area. Wood trimmed walls with large open windows let in the morning sunlight that seemed to bathe the room in daylight. The leather covered couch was a comfortable seat for the tired boys as they were asked to sit down on it, but the situation was anything but relaxing.

"You have impressed me. I didn't think you had it in you." Santos' voice carried across the room. "If I thought we could work together there would be a place in my organization for you. We could use a young man like you." "I don't work for criminals." Gabriel responded. "I thought you would say that and I can respect your decision. However, in time I believe you will change your mind but for now, it will be your loss. Now… let me see my treasure."

The tall thin Ghost walked forward from the back of the room and reached out for the small wooden chest.

"So tell me." Santos' voice had a hint of glee to it. "The legend goes that Gaspar killed his First Mate and buried him with the treasure. Did you see him?" "Yes, he was buried alive while still holding the chest." Gabriel answered.

Santos erupted in excitement.

"Ha, the legend is true then. The First Mate that Gaspar placed so much faith in did get his punishment after all. The man, who never allowed my ancestor, Raùl, to move up the ranks and who was the real voice of mutiny on the ship was killed by the very Captain himself. Gaspar should have made Raùl the First Mate but he never did. Raùl would have been the Captain of the Floriblanca if Gaspar had not gone so crazy in his old age. That means that my family is the rightful owner of Gaspar's treasure, the treasure of the Floriblanca, and I am here to collect it."

Reaching his pale arms forward to hand over the chest into Santos' thick fingers, the ghost gave a pleasing nod to his boss at the exchange. Santos couldn't help but be a little surprised by the size and weight of the chest. It's smaller and much lighter than a fortune of gold should be, he thought.

A pair of bolt cutters was left unused on the table while Santo's massive hands did easy work on the large rusted padlock that had sat in the sand for 200 years. A collective deep breath was felt by everyone in the room as the latch was lifted. Even the boys who knew they were still in grave danger couldn't help but look towards the chest in anticipation and excitement.

The lid was lifted and the sudden expression of disappointment was obvious on Santos' face.

"This cannot be. What is this? Where is the gold?"

Santos removed an iron "T" shaped tool and tossed it on the couch next to Gabriel. Gabriel quickly bumped it with his knee to get a better look at the flat round bottom of the metal piece. He noticed an impression on the bottom of the item. An impression or logo of some kind he couldn't make it out but it appeared to be a stamp of some sort.

Santos then pulled out a brittle tan leather pouch from the bottom of the chest. Years of lying on the wood in damp conditions had fused the leather pouch to the wood bottom; it gave a tearing sound as Santos ripped the pouch from its perch. The careless regard for history sent a chill down Gabriel's spine as he heard the leather tear under Santo's meaty grip.

With the pouch now ripped in half, two metal objects fell and bounced around in the ancient wooden chest. They sounded heavy and landed with a thud but when they slid together and hit each other the metallic sound was unmistakable.

"Two coins! That's it. Two miserable gold doubloons. Something must be wrong. You have tricked me."

Santos turned his attention back to the boys.

"You switched them on me. How dare you take me for a fool?"

Nathan pleaded, "What do you mean? You opened the case we didn't. How could we have switched it?"

"I didn't spend my life looking for this worthless chest of two coins and a hunk of metal. It is still out there and it is mine to have. I will find it myself. Take them down below."

Gabriel had noticed a monitor on the wall just behind Santos' large frame when they walked into the lounge area. While he listened to Santos' go on and on, Gabriel had been eyeing the small navigational chart plotter on the wall behind Santos' head. It was a bright 36" LCD screen that had a color chart of the area and a small blue arrow sitting in the middle of the bay. The GPS tracker was positioning the massive yacht about a mile southwest of the Skyway Bridge. He had never seen an actual chart plotter before but he had seen plenty of charts in his studies and knew exactly what he was looking at. What interested him the most was a dark brown area to the port side of the blue arrow, a large sand bar about 2 miles away at the mouth of the bay.

The lounge room, they were sitting in, was just inside a sliding glass door that led to the Captain's chair. Santos dismissed the boys to the Ghost and then walked into the Bridge and sat down heavy in his chair. Gabriel watched the angry man slam his meaty fist down full on the chrome covered engine throttles. The roar of the engines could be felt through the floor as the ship hopped up on its plane with both propellers spinning at top speed. At this rate, Gabriel knew they would be past the sandbar and in open water in just moments. He had to do something, and he had to do it now.

The Ghost grabbed Nathan by the shoulder and started to move him towards a back stairwell that headed down into the main deck level.

“Wait stop. Where is my sister? We did our job you promised me I would see my sister.” Nathan yelled out. “You will see your sister; soon, in fact, you can spend all the time in the world at the bottom of the ocean-together.” The Ghost hissed.

Gabriel had stayed motionless on the couch during Nathan’s heated exchange. When the Ghost approached him he didn’t move right away. He sat waiting not moving, thinking, running everything through in his head. What would he do to get out of here? How could they escape? Then he saw the metal “T” on the couch next to him. He lost his train of thought for a second and soon his mind began to race on about the treasure instead. The stamp, the coins, the length Gaspar went thru to protect it, the value it must be worth… to him.

“I know what it is. I know the secret,” Gabriel blurted out. “Let go of Nathan and I’ll tell you.”

The meaty fist pulled back on the throttles, forcing the ship and everyone on it to lunge forward a bit. With a cold glance from Santos, the Ghost stopped in his tracks with his hand still on Nathan’s neck.

“Talk boy and it better be good."

Chapter 65

Still standing in the lounge of the gigantic ship, Gabriel watched as the Ghost squeezed Nathan's neck to the point where he thought Nathan's head might actually "pop" off. Santos was now facing Gabriel and didn't look happy. Gabriel thought to himself that he better be right or this could be it for them both.

"Look at the piece of iron on the couch. It has an impression on it doesn't it?" Gabriel stated. "And I bet it is the same impression as the one on those coins."

Gabriel glanced back at the LCD monitor on the wall. The ship was now just 100 yards off the sand bar.

"Look at it and tell me what you see."

Santos leaned over to pick up the gold coins from the bottom of the small chest. He looked at the impressions.

"I see the mark of Mexico on one side and the mark of… looks like France on the other."

"That's right. Now look at the iron tool or should I say stamp."

Gabriel watched Santos move towards the couch and lean down to pick up the iron "T" shaped stamp, he knew he had to make his move now. Gabriel turned his eyes towards Nathan to see his friend one last time before he risked their lives with an attempted escape. Gabriel's mind was racing to find an opportunity when he noticed Nathan was watching Gabriel and thinking the same thing. With a quick wink and an ever so slight smile, Nathan began to shake. He started to spit up and make noises as if he was having a seizure. His body shook violently, and he was so convincing that even Gabriel paused a second to wonder what was happening. But then he caught on to Nathan's plan.

"He's diabetic!" Gabriel yelled. "He's going into hypoglycemic shock. He needs his medicine." "Let him die" hissed the Ghost.

"He's going to vomit all over your ship and die right here on your leather couch if I don't get his Glucagon shot." Gabriel pleaded to Santos.

"Fine, give him the shot."

Gabriel raced to his bag and began digging through it pretending to look for Nathan's injector pen. As he continued to fumble around the bag, Nathan made his acting show even more dramatic by falling to the floor and shaking on the deck.

"Oh come on hurry up already." Santos barked as he continued to look at the rusted iron stamp, trying to see if he could figure out what Gabriel saw in a piece of iron junk. His distraction was just enough time for Gabriel to make his move. With the sheath still on, he was not able to get it off in time, Gabriel hoped that the tomahawk would be enough to knock out the massive Santos. He would have only one shot at this and he had to make it count.

Gabriel leaped toward Santos and swung the tomahawk with everything he had. The hit knocked Santos to the ground but the majority of the blow was on the metal handle and not the strike Gabriel had hoped for. Santos crumbled to the ground and Gabriel continued his momentum running past the Ghost in a flash. The pale man reached for him but he missed. Gabriel sprinted towards the spiral staircase near the back of the ship. Climbing up the staircase, Gabriel reached the Flying Bridge in about 4 leaping bounds.

The Flying Bridge was an open air area where the Captain could sit up high above the ship and get a 360° view of the ocean. It was the highest point on the ship with only one access point, the stairwell, but more importantly it also contained a complete set of ship controls.

The Ghost had followed closely behind Gabriel up the stairs with his gun drawn, leaving Nathan still curled up on the floor and shaking. As the Ghost climbed into the Flying Bridge, he reached his Glock 9mm thru the hatch and quickly fired two shots off in the direction where he knew Gabriel would most likely be- the Captain's chair.

He missed. Gabriel wasn't there. He stuck his head up further to get a better look when a massive blunt kick to his head came from behind. Gabriel was hiding behind the bridge's floor hatch. When the Ghost stuck his head up, Gabriel got a clear and open shot at the back of his skull and he made it count. With all of the weight and force Gabriel could launch he landed a devastating blow to the Ghost.

Never seeing it coming, the Ghost slammed his forehead into the deck and was out cold. His body slumped down and began to tumble backwards down the stairwell crashing in an awkward contortion on the stairwell base. Nathan, saw the Ghost fall down the stairs so he stopped acting sick and jumped up off the ground. He assumed his sister was below decks so he made his way towards the forward stairwell.

Santos was trying to shake off his dizzying head and was having a lot of trouble standing up. The lump on his skull was expanding to the point where the skin might actually burst open and the pain was intense.

Meanwhile, still up on the flying bridge and turning back towards the ship controls, Gabriel flipped on the override switch that allowed him to take manual control from the automatic pilot. The yacht engines began to scream at a deafening pace as Gabriel slammed the throttle handles forward. Twin 3,500 horsepower diesel Caterpillar engines roared as the entire ship once again rocketed through the choppy water.

Gabriel watched the RPM's climb and the ship's speed increase. The little blue arrow on the flying bridge GPS began to race faster along the chart screen. Gabriel watched the sand bar he had been looking at on the screen below race along the port side of the ship. He moved the helm to the right as he eased the ship out to sea when suddenly he spun the helm wheel back to the left forcing the ship and everything on it to list terribly out of control.

Glasses fell off the shelves, furniture flew across the decks, and everyone on board the massive vessel slammed hard against whatever they happened to be standing next too. Gabriel had braced himself thru the turn and now he was bracing himself for the impact. With the sandbar just yards off their bow, the yacht racing full speed towards it, Gabriel lay on the floor and positioned his legs forward with his feet up against the control panel wall. Any second now he thought to himself when suddenly, the yacht banked hard to the port side and the entire ship seemed to bounce out of the water.

Gabriel knew he must have lifted at least 3 feet of the deck because he slammed back down on the nonskid teak wood with a thud that took the wind from his lungs. It took a moment for him to catch his breath and get a sense for where he was but the ship was still upright. In fact the ship was still floating and the engines were still roaring except the ship was no longer moving with any power. She was still moving but slowly just drifting and now, over the hum of the engines, Gabriel began to hear the raspy shouts of Santos down below.

Chapter 66

Gabriel's plan, as ill prepared as it was, had not worked the way he had intended. He knew slamming a massive speeding yacht into a sandbar was never a good idea but he felt that a violent crash might be the only opportunity they had to escape. He really had no other choice, a fight with two armed men was not a good option but if he could alter the environment and set a new stage for battle, he felt the rules might be changed to his favor. A lesson he learned from The Art of War by Sun Tzu it was more light reading for Gabriel and one of his favorites.

Unfortunately, the ship didn't break apart in dramatic fashion and render the villains helpless. Instead, the ship seemed to be drifting smoothly in open water and a mad man with a gun was rapidly coming up the stairs after him.

No longer in the stairwell, Nathan picked himself up off the ground. The ship's collision had slammed him up against the galley bulkhead but he wasn't too badly hurt just a bit sore. He raced down the long hallway kicking in every door he could. Screaming out his sister's name but he heard nothing. Continuing down the hall he came to a stairwell that headed to the lower decks, he raced down the stairs skipping every other step on his way. Room after room, Nathan searched for his sister until he came to the last door on the lower third deck. It was a heavy metal door with three hinges and a rotating latch. He yelled to the other side but there was no response. His heart began to sink. He prayed that she was on the other side of the door as he began to turn the long white latch handle. With a hiss of hot air puffing out of the door jamb, Nathan slowly pulled the door further open and nervously stuck his head into the room.

Above on the Flying bridge, Santos had made his way up on the teak covered platform and was now scanning the entire ship for any sign of Gabriel.

Just before Santos made it up to the bridge, Gabriel had slid over the side railing and carefully moved down the side of the ship's tower. Using every inch of his body, Gabriel was pushing his arms, legs, face, and torso into the side of the ship. With barely a ledge to grasp on to with his fingernails, Gabriel almost willed his body to be a suction cup on the smooth fiberglass surface. Gabriel could look down some 40 feet below him and see the dark blue water splashing on the hull. He had made his way to the deck rail below about 8 feet from the flying bridge just as Santos began to look out over the vessel for him.

Gabriel dove back into the lounge room and took a second to take a deep breath. With his trusty tomahawk tucked into his back belt, Gabriel grabbed the gold coins that were lying on the floor, with everything else in room, and snatched the iron stamp as well. He stuffed the items back into his ALICE bag and ran towards the forward stairs to head downstairs and find his friends.

With the door wide open and light shining into the dark compartment, Nathan's prayers were answered. Tied to a chair with a rag stuffed into her mouth was Lisa. She let out a scream of joy but barely any sound could be heard until Nathan ripped the rag from her mouth. He wrapped his arms around his sister and kissed her forehead. They may argue a lot and there are times when Nathan can't stand his sister but they both knew that they loved each other. Unfortunately, it only took a life and death situation for them to finally admit it.

"How did you get here? What's going on? Get me out of here." Lisa cried. "We are still in danger so I can't explain but we have to move fast and find a weapon."

Nathan looked at the ropes that were tightly wrapped around his sister's wrists. The skin on her hands was raw. The rough rope had rubbed her flesh down to pink, sore, peeled, skin. Nathan could tell she had been struggling to escape, and the cold blueness in her hands told him he needed to hurry. "We need to find something sharp." "Here grab my hand." Lisa said.

Nathan palmed her hand and was taken back when her wet fingers were actually wet with blood. He moved around her seat to look closer at her hands and noticed a small pool of blood beneath them.

"You're bleeding," "I know. I've been trying to cut the ropes but I just couldn't get them. I have a piece of glass between my fingers."

Nathan pried open her sticky red fingers and found the shard of reflective mirror glass. She had hidden the glass between her fingers after she had pulled the horse covered mirror from Santos' wall. When the Ghost retied her hands with the hemp rope, he made sure to make them tight so she couldn't escape but he never thought to check between her fingers. Nathan frantically began chopping at the ropes with the sliver of glass. He looked around the room at what seemed to be the ship's rope locker or some sort of storage room. There were boxes of hemp rope on the floor and spools of various nylon ropes wound up along spools across the bulkhead. A few unmarked water pipes ran up and down the walls and ceiling but there were no tools or potential weapons that he could see.

A few moments went by and he was close to freeing Lisa when his heart suddenly stopped. He heard the latch to the door behind him begin to turn. Nathan turned quickly and leapt for the door but it opened before he could get to it. Reaching back with his arm over his right ear, Nathan got prepared to punch the intruder with everything he had. But just as he was about to swing, he stopped.

"Gabriel! Am I happy to see you? Lisa is here, and she's OK. I almost have her free. Where is Santos?" "Right behind me," Gabriel answered too calmly for Nathan's liking. "What? He is still coming?"

"Yes."

Gabriel slammed the hatch closed and began to tie the rotating handle with some Paracord line he found next to a crate by the door.

"I've got to lock us in here for a little bit." "But he's coming. He won't let us out if he has us trapped." Nathan argued.

Gabriel turned and looked at the brother and sister with panic over their faces. He hated to have more bad news for them but he had to tell them sooner or later.

"It's a lot worse than that."

It only took a second until the bangs came. Outside the metal hatch, a frantic Santos was banging against the door latch trying to get it to move. Gabriel's quick knot had held but soon the gunshots began.

Two shots made it through the metal hatch spraying the room with jagged shards of metal. A piece of the shrapnel struck Lisa's foot and caused a small tear in her flesh but she didn't seem to notice the pain. The third shot didn't make it through the bulkhead but the raised impression of the bullet's path left a small dent on the inside of the smooth metal door hatch. After the third shot rang out, a long eerie silence followed. It was so quiet that the kids began to miss the ear shattering blasts because at least they knew where their attacker was located. Now, the silence let their minds begin to race trying to figure out what evil Santos was up to.

"You said it was worse than that. What do you mean?" Lisa was the first to break the silence. "Give me a second to think." Gabriel replied. "I heard a loud crash, like a collision. It felt like the boat came out of the water." "I need a second to think. Please." Just then, the few thin remaining threads of her ropes started to stretch and then snapped from behind her back. Feeling the warmth of blood rush back into her cold hands, Lisa was thankful to be free at last. Rubbing her sore hands and wrists, she turned her attention back to Gabriel.

"We're sinking aren't we?" Lisa's question shot through Nathan's spine like jolt of lightning, his body went stone cold and his muscles froze to a stop.

Gabriel turned and faced the twins with as much confidence as he could muster, he had to answer them.

"When I came down the hall to this room the passage was filling with water."

"Oh my God!" Nathan exhaled.

"The collision damaged the propellers and the engine room. We are taking on water and the stern is beginning to sink. That's most likely why Santos left. By now, the hatch is probably underwater and so are we. We don't have a lot of time and I need every bit of it to think. So please be quite unless you have some suggestions, we are running out of time."

Chapter 67

It had been almost 10 agonizing minutes since Santos' last gunshot had slammed the hatch with a deafening "bang." The kids, still huddled in the rope locker room, were sitting on the aft bulkhead. The normally level deck was now almost vertical as the ship's stern was nearly full of water. Sitting on the wall staring at the floor which was now in front of them was a chillingly surreal moment for the kids.

The wait was becoming worse than any horror that was pending. The silence was interrupted by the occasional strange sounding creaks and clanks of bending metal and cracking wood. Faint sounds of items crashing off their shelves could be heard through the metal decks above them. Time seemed not to move as the kids sat together holding each other waiting for their fate. Water began to sweat on the walls as the heat from their bodies warmed up the room and hit the metal that was holding back the cold sea water.

"You didn't have to come back for us." Nathan spoke up. "You knew the boat was sinking. You could have made a run for it." Gabriel turned to his friend, "Would you have left me?" Nathan's eyes began to swell, "Of course not… I don't know… I'm sorry."

A smile came across Gabriel's face. "It's ok. I'm scared too." Gabriel stuck his hand out and offered it to

Nathan. Nathan shook his hand and forced a tearful smile. "But don't give up. There is always a chance and I have a plan."

Gabriel stood up and began to untie the Paracord line.

"What are you doing? What plan?" Nathan questioned. "I've been waiting for the ship to take on enough water and I think it's time to make our move." "Please tell me you called the Coast Guard and they are on their way." Lisa asked. "I didn't and I don't know but I doubt it. Besides, we can't wait any longer."

Gabriel swung his tomahawk hard and with a loud "clank" on a flat piece of ship metal. He used the sharp weapon to cut some nylon rope long enough for him to tie it around his waist and the twins.

"The ship has been taking on water in a violent way. To fight against it would have been suicide. The rush of water would have drowned us for sure. However, the ship has slowed down its rocking and I don't feel it sinking as fast anymore but make no mistake we are still sinking. Most of the ship is now under water but there are still pockets of trapped air slowing our descent. Basically, we are like a floating ice cube, a little on the surface but mostly underwater. When this room fills with water, we will have a few seconds to swim out of here before the ship completely goes down."

"Wait you're filling this room up with water?" Lisa snapped. "If we don't we will slowly continue sinking until we hit the bottom. The pressure could rupture the hatch and we would die on the bottom of the bay. Not to mention this room is air tight and it's getting hard to breathe in here already. We have no other choice and this is a good option. We can do this."

"I trust you Gabe. Tell us what we need to do." Nathan held his sister's hand and tried to reassure her.

"The ship has rotated on its side and it is now stern down with the bow up that means we need to swim along the walls towards the front of the boat. The roof will be underneath us. The main staircase is now below us and the small forward stair case will be our escape. The ship still has power so there are lights on but we will be under sea water so expect to be swimming mostly by touch and not sight."

Nathan finished tying the nylon rope around Lisa's waist.

"I got a pretty good look of the layout and I'm a strong swimmer. I'll go first, then Lisa and then Nathan. Nathan you carry the backpack. We are all tied together so if you go the wrong way or get stopped, we all go down. It should take about 2 minutes to get out so don't panic or you will waist oxygen. Stay calm and stay under control. Calm is smooth and smooth is fast. If you panic and try to race it, you'll make a mistake. Do not quit even when your lungs are hurting and you think you can't make it. We need to make it."

Lisa turned to hug her brother long and hard. She would have squeezed him into her if she could. Of course they didn't always like each other but they loved each other deeply. Lisa was only a few seconds older than her brother but she still had that older sibling desire to protect him. Even though he was taller and stronger, she wanted to make sure that she did all she could to keep him safe. Besides she thought, she was a much better swimmer than him.

Lisa began to untie Nathan's rope and removed the knot around her waist. "What are doing?" Nathan asked. "Don't argue with me or I'll scream in your face."

She continued to retie her knot around Nathan's waist and then she moved to the end of the line and wrapped it tight around herself.

"Someone has to push you slow poke." Lisa smiled. "You know I'm a much better swimmer."

Gabriel turned his attention back to the metal hatch on the wall.

"Ok when this door opens a rush of water will come in fast. Don't fight it just brace yourselves against the wall. As the room fills up, wait to take your breath at the last possible second. Once the room is completely filled then and only then will we leave. Is everybody ready?"

A hand grabbed Gabriel's shoulder and spun him around to face Lisa. She leaned in hard and pressed her lips against his. It was a startling surprise that quickly turned to a tingling sensation across his mouth. He flinched at first but then settled into the warmth of her soft lips. For Lisa, she had been waiting to kiss him from the moment she met him. Even now at their moment of life or death, it was worth the wait. All she could feel was the dizzying bliss of her feet light on the ground and her knees soft in their gentle bend. Their lips parted and after a moment she opened her eyes directly into his and could see her reflection in his sparkling bright eyes.

"For good luck," She whispered. "Now let's get out of here."

Chapter 68

Gabriel smiled and turned back towards the door. With a giant heave of his strong shoulders the latch popped and water began squirting through the hinge. Another quarter turn and suddenly a giant wave erupted thru the door slamming the kids against the back of the room.

"Hold on. Don't hold your breath yet! Let the room fill up." Gabriel screamed over the rush of water.

Lisa and Nathan held on to each other as Gabriel braced his legs against a steel beam. He thought it was Nathan's arm at first, when the hand struck his face, but how could it be in front of him, he thought. Suddenly, he realized it wasn't Nathan at all. It was the meaty dark haired arm of Santos.

Fearing for his life, Gabriel let out a primal roar and grabbed the man's throat. He quickly shifted his stance and tried to slam Santos into the metal beam above his head. Gabriel struggled against the weight of the man's large size in the rushing water but was surprised that Santos didn't seem to be fighting back. He was surprised until he looked into the man's face and saw that it was lifeless.

A small swollen red hole was directly between Santos' bushy eyebrows and his lifeless dark brown eyes cast a cold blank stare over his face. The third bullet, the one that didn't make it through the bulkhead, must have ricochet from the wall and struck him in the head. That's why he stopped attacking them. He accidently shot himself. Gabriel realized what had happened and was soon able to push the man off of him. He soon heard the rush of the water and the shouts of the twins again as he raced back into the moment. Lisa and Nathan were bracing their forearms up against the roof of the room. Their faces pressed hard against the sheet metal as the cold rushing water raced up their chests and took what little air they had out of their lungs. As the water reached their necks, the twins locked eyes on each other and watched as both their lives passed before them.

"I can't do it. I can't do it. Stop! Stop, the water!"

Lisa began to scream out. Nathan's hand grabbed her and pulled her closer to him. Staring at his sister's panicked eyes Nathan tried to calm her with a comforting smile. As she gasped for precious final gulps of air, Nathan could only smile at her and try to keep her calm. But it wasn't just for show, it was a genuine calm and he believed it. He believed they were going to make it. As everything around him suddenly slowed down, Nathan was convinced that they were going to make it. And for the first time since he could remember, he was confident, he was calm, he wasn't afraid, and he felt strong. The thin sound of air was suddenly replaced by the muffled heavy percussion of water filling their ear canals. One last deep breath and a final glance to his sister before his eyes began to sting from the salt sea water… then everything went silent.

The water was cold, and the salt stung Gabriel's eyes but it was his responsibility to lead the kids out of the sinking ship and no pain could be worse than failing. Down the hallway and to the right, debris was everywhere but the lower to the bottom they swam the clearer the water was. The lights were dim but the white paint on the ceiling, which was now below them, gave Gabriel a path to follow. Once at the stairs, they could use the steps as hand holds to pull their bodies through the water and save some energy. Gabriel could feel a slight pull on the rope around his waist but the twins were doing a good job staying with him.

Third deck and then second deck and then finally main deck, Gabriel pushed from the stair well out into the lounge area. He swam over the leather couch where he had sat and watched Santos open the treasure chest no more than 20 minutes ago but it now seemed like a lifetime had passed. Over to the open bay windows and out onto the ship's sundeck except now the sundeck was above them and pushing the kids down as the rest of the vessel was sinking fast into the dark blue sea. With every foot the ship sank, pressure was building in Gabriel's ears and a growing sharp pain was stabbing behind his eyes. From the intensity of the pain, Gabriel assumed they were at least 20 feet under the crushing weight of the ocean and dropping fast.

His lungs were painful, and he knew the twins must be in agony. The rope was tight around his waist and he knew they were falling behind. He dug his nails into anything he could grab on to and pulled himself across the sinking deck. At last, he reached the white painted metal railing and began to climb over it. The force of the sinking ship and his aching exhausted muscles made the climb harder than he expected. But after a long second, he was free and on the outside of the ship. Unfortunately, the line on his waist grew tight and kept pulling him down as the twins were still behind on the other side of the railing. The ship was sinking faster now and his ears were in piercing pain. Gabriel pulled on the line with everything he had but still could not see the twins. He could feel them on the rope but they seemed to be stuck on the deck of the ship and all the pulling, Gabriel feared, might snap the line. One last chance before time ran out. Gabriel had no choice, risk snapping the line or they all go down with the ship. His lungs burned and his eyes felt like they were already on the outside of his skull. He braced his feet on the railing and heaved back with all of his weight and strength that he could muster. Finally, the line came free and the tattered torn strands of the snapped line floated in front of Gabriel's eyes. "I snapped it," he thought to himself, "What have I done?"

A dozen small boats of local fishermen and some weekenders had pulled around the site to look for survivors. They didn't get too close to the gigantic yacht for fear of a possible explosion or perhaps it rocking back their direction and capsizing them. But as the ship began to sink they crept closer and closer until now they were nearly on top of the once magnificent yacht. The ship was now completely under water and sinking fast. All that was left of the once gigantic ship was now floating debris around the area.

It was a woman from Nebraska, visiting Florida for the first time with her family, who was the first boater to scream out. The woman had just seen a once in a lifetime mega yacht sink in front of her eyes when her shock turned to thrill with the sudden splash off her starboard side. "There over there…" she cried out. "Survivors!"

First there was the long blond haired girl that struck the surface and then up came a young boy. As they both gasped for air, they began scanning the area for someone else. The boaters quickly closed in on the twins when another boat captain shouted out. "Here over here. I found another one!"

During their escape off the sinking Floriblanca II, the twins had gotten their line stuck on a deck cleat. They tried to unfowl it but couldn't get it free when suddenly the line snapped and broke them loose from the ship. As they swam past the railing, Nathan caught a glance of Gabriel but lost him when they raced up to the surface.

Still floating in the bay just outside the reach of a small walkabout fishing vessel, it was the warm sun on his face and the bright light in his eyes that let Gabriel know he was alive. But it was the distant voices of his friends calling him by name that brought a smile to his face.

Chapter 69

It had been a couple of days since the kids escaped the Floriblanca II. The swim that was only took a few minutes made a lifetime of memories for the trio. A Coast Guard small boat took them to shore and gave them some food and blankets. Nathan was so impressed with the HU-60 Jay Hawk helicopter hovering over his head that the pilot eventually let him sit in the cockpit after he landed on the tarmac. The press came in droves however the kids, being under the age of 18, had their identities kept secret even though their story was a big one to tell.

Gabriel was a little nervous around Lisa after the rescue. He wasn't sure if the kiss in the ship was just for good luck or if it meant something more. It felt like something more to him but Lisa was very good at keeping him guessing so he would just have to live with some passing glances and awkward smiles. He would like to have it mean more but he would have to wait and see. He was OK with the wait; he thought to himself, she just may be worth it.

The Coast Guard did not find any other survivors even though they searched for almost two days. Santos was found still inside the vessel by a SCUBA team but the Ghost was nowhere to be found. Most likely he floated out to sea but not knowing for sure didn't sit very well with Gabriel. Unfortunately, there was nothing he could do about now, but the disturbing thought stayed with him that one day he may see the Ghost man again.

School started on Monday, just like always, but the first day back was different for the three kids. They had all gone through so much together. They went to class and opened their books just as they had done all their lives but something felt different… more precious. They had learned to trust each other and believe in each other. They didn't worry so much about the small little things that used to bug each of them. They knew the value of life because they had faced death. They learned the power of prayer because sometimes that's all that you have. They each had a new appreciation for history given that they had perhaps discovered one of the most valuable pieces of history the world had never known… and that's when Gabriel was pulled out of class by the man in the black suit.

Sitting in physics class, Gabriel was listening to Mr. Rosetta go on and on about circular motion and its relevance to everyday life when a knock came softly at the door.

"Mr. Fletcher would you step outside please?" Principal Stockard asked.

Gabriel walked past the whispers and snickers of his classmates. Outside in the hall, Principal Stockard introduced Gabriel to a man in a black suit.

"Gabriel this is Mr. Christopher Gadsden. He would like to talk to you."

Principal Stockard walked down the hall while the man in the suit led Gabriel in the opposite direction.

"Hello Mr. Gadsden. What can I do for you?"

"Call me Chris please. My friends don't call me by my last name."

"I just met you sir, so I prefer to call you by your last name if that's OK?" It was worded as a question but Gabriel already had his answer and wasn't changing his mind. The man in the suit was older than him and Gabriel was disciplined in courtesy. The man in the suit smiled and leaned over to whisper to Gabriel. "Just between you and me that's not my real last name." "Well then I doubt Christopher is your real first name either. Unless of course you're a 280 year old General of the Continental Army with a flair for designing yellow flags with coiled rattlesnakes on them. So don't tread on me, if you don't mind, sir. I would prefer to just keep calling you Mr. Gadsden."

A smile came across the man's face. Gabriel had picked up on his historical reference to the popular historical Gadsden Flag.

"What they say about you is true. You do know your history. I just like that flag," The man smiled at Gabriel.

"What can I do for you Mr. Gadsden?"

"Gabriel, I am the director of a group called SERNA (Search and Recovery of National Antiquities) a division of the State Department."

"I've never heard of it."

"No, unless you're a Senator on a very small budget committee, most people don't even know we exist. Do you have any idea of the hornet's nest you kicked up this weekend?"

"I have my theories."

"Let me hear them."

"Well, the iron stamp that was in the chest had the seal of Napoleon Bonaparte on it. The same seal that was on one side of the coins in the chest except the other side of the coin had the seal of Spain."

"Go on." Mr. Gadsden seemed pleased.

"It doesn't take a genius to know that France had recently purchased the territory of Louisiana from Spain, in 1800 during the Treaty of San Idelfonso. Napoleon had his eyes on Florida as well. But war, revolution, and the ever rapidly growing Americans, put a stop to that by the early 1800's. Andrew Jackson started the first Seminole War in 1817 and he put a stop to Spain's control of Florida. However, somewhere in there around 1810, France lost interest in Florida or perhaps lost something. I can only assume that France had purchased Louisiana with some or maybe all counterfeit money. They were acquiring gold from the area, most likely pirated Spanish Galleon's or perhaps from Spanish controlled Mexico, and they were re-stamping the gold with the seal of Bonaparte. When the seal was lost and proof of their forgery was out, they pulled out of the area and gave up Florida. They couldn't afford it anymore."

"Interesting theory. But why would a pirate like Gaspar steal it and go to such lengths to protect it?" Gadsden asked.

"I believe Jose Gaspar was looking for treasure but ultimately he wanted to be redeemed. He wrote about his redemption on his map. I think he found that when he discovered France's scam. He discovered proof in that chest. He had been outcast from his mother country for 30 years. He had dishonored his homeland, and he wanted to be forgiven. He searched for the fountain of youth, the Espiritu Santu, for years never finding it. He collected massive hordes of money and wealth but it wasn't enough. He never felt he could redeem himself with Spain. But then one day, he discovers that France had purchased the Louisiana territory and its vital ports from Spain with their own gold. Bonaparte was now working on a deal to buy la Isla de Flores, the island of flowers, Spanish held Florida right out from under Spain's nose with their own gold. Spain was fighting America and running out of money because France was stealing it. They eventually lost Florida to America and the rest is history. This was the proof that Gaspar had. Finally, he had something that he could return to Spain with and earn his place in the Spanish court. But he never made it."

"I'm impressed that's quite a theory." Mr. Gadsden smiled. "Am I right?" The tall man continued to walk across the school court yard. "Am I right? Please, Mr. Gadsden, I want to know am I right?"

Finally, after a few more steps, the man in the black suit turned back to Gabriel.

"The historical and political ramifications of three powerful countries claiming the same land is a complicated and delicate issue. It is a debate that will probably go on for many years, amongst people with much higher pay grades then you or me. My job is to acquire that historical proof and return it to the powers to be so that they can make those decisions. I appreciate all that you have done and would like to offer you this check from a non disclosed account that I assure you is credible."

"Wait I don't won't your money." "Oh I assure you. You want this money."

Grabbing the check from Mr. Gadsden and ripping it up to pieces, Gabriel furiously shouted back.

"Those items belong in a museum. Where are they now?" "They will, in time, be placed into a museum but for now they are being cared for by the top professionals in this field." "I don't believe you. I gave the police that map and the items from the chest for their investigation but I expected them to be placed in a museum. But I can see that you're going to lock them up and they will never be seen again. Right?"

A smile crossed Mr. Gadsden's face, not a smile of smug arrogance but a smile of respect and admiration.

"You have great instincts kid. I have a feeling you and I will meet again someday but this is out of yours and my control. Please let it go."

Gabriel didn't like the answer. However, he believed the man's sincerity. He would let it go but he would never forget it.

"If there is anything I can do for you, just let me know." Mr. Gadsden tried to ease the boy's anger.

Disgusted, Gabriel replied, "I told you that I don't want anything from you."

"You have already applied several times to the Naval Academy haven't you? A little early for a high school sophomore, don't you think?" "How did you know that?" "You need a Congressional Appointment to be selected to go there you know? Do you know any Congressmen?"

"No Sir," Gabriel answered.

With a smile and a nod, Mr. Gadsden replied, "I do."

With that the man in the black suit turned and walked away leaving Gabriel alone in the school courtyard. After a long quiet moment, a smile came to Gabriel's face. He had a feeling that wasn't the last he would ever see of Mr. Christopher Gadsden.

Chapter 70

Still standing in the courtyard as the class bell rang, Gabriel quickly found himself swallowed up by the sea of high schoolers. He didn't move but stood still thinking about the mysterious Mr. Gadsden as kids raced around him. The noise of school kids is at a jet engine level but there is always a word that seems to carry over any volume of noise that every high schooler recognizes and reacts to instantly.

"FIGHT."

Behind the cafeteria, Lisa was trying to talk with Roger Woods. But his red flushed face was proof of his escalating anger.

"You're breaking up with me? Who do you think you are? I'm Roger Woods. You don't break up with me I'm the reason you are anything at this school. Don't you forget you chased after me?"

Roger put his hands on Lisa's arm and pushed her back towards the cafeteria stone wall.

"I was doing you a favor by going out with you and you treat me like this? I could have dated so many other girls if I wasn't wasting my time with you. You don't break up with me. I dump you, you ugly…"

"Enough!" The shout came from behind the gathering crowd of youthful spectators. Nathan pushed his way through the crowd. "Leave her along you jerk."

Roger swung his head around and pounced on Nathan before Nathan knew what hit him.

"I've been wanting to do this to you for two years." Roger began to choke Nathan.

"You just won't shut up will you-you punk. Talk to a senior like that I'm going to knock you out."

Lisa tried to pull on Roger's shirt in an attempt to get him off of Nathan. But the 6 foot 2, 230 pound athlete was too strong for her to pull back. Nathan was trying to get Roger's hands off of his throat but the grip was too tight. He couldn't break the hold. Lisa got her hands on Roger's ears and began to tear them back finally forcing him to release her brother.

"What is wrong with you? Leave him alone." She screamed.

A slap came across Lisa's face sending her to the ground. She could feel the salty metallic taste of blood begin to fill up her mouth. She spit the burgundy colored fluid into the dirt and tried to shake the stars from her head.

Nathan was up again and landed two solid shots on Roger, one to the ribs and the second to the base of his neck. Roger winced in pain but didn't stop. Two of Roger's teammates jumped out from the crowd and grabbed Nathan from behind holding him defenseless. Roger swung his elbow backwards and landed it right on Nathan's cheek. Nathan had barely hit the ground when Roger was on top of him pounding down on him like a crazy person.

Gabriel arrived at the crowd and slid between two freshmen. He dropped to his knees to help Lisa.

Holding her face in his hands, "Are you ok?" he asked. She nodded "yes."

"Help Nathan, Roger will kill him." She pleaded.

Gabriel raced over to Roger who was now on top of Nathan and in one motion lifted the star ball player off of his friend and tossed him several feet into the crowd.

"Stop it!"

Roger, a little stunned, stood up and pushed back on the crowd of people that he had just landed on. "I thought you would show up, so I brought some help this time."

The crowd moved back and 7 more large teammates stepped forward surrounding Gabriel forming a ring around him.

"You're getting smarter." Gabriel addressed Roger. "You brought more than 4 this time. But do you guys really want to spend the rest of the year on crutches like his other buddies?"

The players paused and looked at each other with a sense of concern. They liked Roger, but they weren't necessarily ready to risk their season for him.

"Even if you beat me, most of you guys are going to miss the season and a few will never play again I promise you." "Get him!" Roger called out to his teammates. "I have another offer." Gabriel stopped them in their tracks. "I'll let you have Nathan. But it's going to be a fair fight. Keep your boys off of him and I'll stay off of you." "What?" Lisa grabbed Gabriel. "Are you crazy?"

He ignored her and walked over to Nathan. Kneeling down to help his friend up, Gabriel stared into his face and began to pump him up.

"Is this all that you have? After everything you have done, everything you have been through, you're going to let him beat you. I don't accept that. You're better than that. You're better than him. You don't go down. You fight. You take everything he's got. You take the punishment because you can. He can't break you and when he has nothing left you unleash on him. Do you understand?"

Nathan believed his friend. He knew he was right. He knew he had more fight left in him. He knew he could do this… He had to do this. He pushed Gabriel aside and waved to Roger.

"Come on."

The two squared off and began exchanging punches. Lisa looked at Gabriel with confused horror. Gabriel stared at her for a second and then turned back to watch Nathan.

The fight started out even but a quick jab to Nathan's eye sent him stumbling back. Roger didn't let up he kept hitting the staggering young boy. The sound of bare slapping flesh gave Lisa chills. Nathan was about to stumble when he braced his back foot and managed to shove Roger off of him for a second.

Lisa began to run to her brother's aid when Gabriel grabbed her and held her in place.

"Wait. Watch him, he's not done." Gabriel whispered into her ear.

Roger got his balance and charged at Nathan with all of his fury. His right arm was high in the air with his fist clenched for that final knockout blow. Nathan was wobbling and Roger knew this was it for him. But as the upper right hook started to come down, Nathan dropped his chin and squared his forehead directly into the fists path.

The cracks could be heard a dozen yards away as the metacarpal bones in Roger's hand shattered. His wrist folded in on itself forcing a piece of jagged bone to pierce through the skin. Roger's screams were anything but macho. He doubled over in agony as his hand went limp like a sand bag.

Nathan shook off the bright lights in his head and then charged at Roger. In 30 seconds Nathan had taken out 2 years' worth of anger on the bully and left the team Captain crying in a rolled up ball on the ground.

"Stop, stop, Please stop. I give up." The senior cried out.

Nathan listened and eventually backed off, he was the bigger man and there was no need to keep fighting. It was over. Roger was done. Lisa ran over to hug her brother and Gabriel slapped him on the back.

"I knew you had it in you, buddy."

Gabriel put his arm around his friend and helped carry him away through the now cheering crowd. Lisa never looked back at Roger, who was still crying in pain on the ground. She would never fall for a weasel like Roger Woods again. She wanted to meet a good guy that would be good to her and would be true to her. Someone she could trust. She smiled at the thought, maybe a guy like Gabriel.

Nathan had never felt so confident in his life. His head hurt and his body ached but all of that pain was nothing compared to the pride he was now feeling. It had been too long since he was proud of himself and didn't feel like the lesser sibling to his popular sister. Kids all around the courtyard and hallways were talking about the sophomore that just took out the most popular senior in school. A bright new future was in store for him and for the first time in a long time, he actually began to believe it.

Gabriel looked to his right at the twins and smiled to them. This felt good. It felt right. For the boy that had been a lone for so long he felt like he was now a part of a family. He knew he had a buddy in Nathan that he could trust with his life and he would do the same. The brother that he had always wanted was now smiling with a bloody lip and swollen eye. Perhaps telling for future adventures to come of the two boys and that would be fine for Gabriel. He didn't know what to think about Lisa. The kiss they shared seemed real and passionate but only time would tell of things to come. He didn't want to make things awkward or confusing right now he was happy to just have her as a friend. However, she was definitely the best looking friend he had ever had that was pretty cool too.

A smile crossed his face, a genuine smile that felt good to him. It had been a wild and exciting adventure, an adventure that started with a gift from his beloved friend Juan just a few months ago. So much had changed since then. He still missed his friend, but he felt good that his story and legacy was discovered and would be eventually told. He had a strange sense of trust with the man in the suit, Mr. Gadsden. He felt confident that one day he would see him again. And even though the secret of Jose Gaspar may never be truly told, at least Gabriel knew the tale. And if he ever forgot, he had a little something to remind him of it.

Reaching into his pocket, Gabriel pulled out the heavy gold ring and placed it on his finger. He had given the treasure and the map to the authorities but some things are just too valuable to be left in other's hands. A gift from an old friend should never be given away and who knows perhaps it holds more secrets that still need to be discovered.

The End.

Prologue.

Afghanistan Mountains.

Deep inside a cold dark cave high up the Kabul mountain side. A group of Taliban soldiers come in after a long patrol to warm their hands in a nearby fire. They pull out some meal rations of lamb meat and potatoes and begin to eat like they've been starving for days. Barely a morsel is left when they are done. The few scraps of bones with their grizzle and fat are collected and placed on a tray.

The short beardless soldier, no more than 13 years old, has the duty. He takes the tray of meat scraps and potatoes and starts to walk deeper into the dark damp cave. A simple flashlight shines the way but he has walked it so many times before he doesn't need it. He comes up to a metal door with wrought iron bars and thick wooden baseboards. Sliding the tray under a small space at the threshold, the tray skips to a stop and tosses the food scraps all across the filthy cave floor.

Behind the door, scuffled sounds of movement begin as the food is heard slapping the stone floor. Dirty, black covered, hands from every direction reach out from the darkness and begin to pick up the scraps.

One pair of hands is noticeable cleaner than the others. They belong to a young Texas man with an olive green jumpsuit on and an American flag patch on his shoulder. As he begins to bring the food up to his mouth a voice booms out from across the room.

"New guy, wait. We have rules here." "I'm sorry. I didn't know." The Texas man replied. "First we say prayers then we offer the best pieces to the sickest and that would be the old man." "I'm sorry. I was just captured last night. I didn't know. I'm Lieutenant..." "Rank means nothing in here." Another voice came from another direction. "In here it's all about surviving. And to survive we need to follow the rules."

A small ray of light, coming from the card game outside, pierced through a break in the wood panels of the door. It bounced off the wet floor and cast a slight glow to the room. After sitting in total darkness for hours if not days, the slightest faint light seemed like a Mac truck's high beams to the tired captives.

The Texas man moved closer to the light in hopes of seeing his surroundings better or maybe subconsciously trying to feel some warmth for his freezing hands.

"Can I see you? How many of you are here." Tex asked. "Four now. Used to be 6 but with you now we're 4." "How long have you been here?"

The sliding sound of fabric came from the dark and then suddenly a face appeared right in front of the Texas man.

"My God." Tex gasped.

The face was covered in hair and dirt. It looked to be a hundred years old and the very sockets of his skull could be seen around his eyes. The cheek bones on his face were pronounced as the fat of his cheeks were sunk into his jaw. Wasted and starved the man could barely lift his head but there was a kindness still in his eyes that brought comfort to the Texan.

"I'm sorry Sir; I didn't mean to be rude." "That's OK. You're a bit of shock to me too. I forgot what life looked like."

Noticing the faint gold markings on the man's shirt, that was now just rags, the Texan snapped a salute.

"Commander Sir, Lieutenant Joe…" The Commander feebly returned the salute with what strength he could muster. It wasn't a common practice in the cave anymore. The common military display of seniority acknowledgment had lost its meaning in the cold harshness of the prison, but had originally found its roots on the battlefields of honor. When medieval knights would acknowledge each other out of respect, they would lift the face shields of their helmets to see who they were addressing. This action continued down thru the generations as the military salute. Even though their bodies were broken and formal ranks no longer mattered, these men still had pride and respect needed to be acknowledged. To the Commander, like a long lost friend returning home, it did feel good to once again be acknowledged as a man of honor. And for the first time in a long time a slight smile spread across his thin lips.

"I told you no ranks son." "Yes sir. Sorry sir." "You can call me James," the Commander replied.

"Sir, my name is Joe Carroll from Austin, Texas sir. I'm an F-15 pilot that was shot down yesterday on patrol sir. I tried to hoof it out, but they picked me up a few hours after I crashed."

"Nice to meet you son." "Sir… James… do you mind if I ask you?" "How long I've been here?" "Yes sir."

"What's the date?"

"February 2nd, sir."

"What year?" Tex was taken back a bit by the question. How could this man not know the year? He thought to himself and then quietly answered.

"2014."

"Did you hear that men? 2014." The Commander spoke out loudly.

A few muffled coughs and chuckles sounded out from the shadows.

"I've been here for almost 3 years." "Three years!" Tex gasped as he glanced around the dark cave and took in their conditions. "How have you survived?"

"Rules son, we have rules. We pray before each meal. We don't complain. We give the most to the worst of us. And we never use rank."

"I got it sir. Earlier, you mentioned the old man. Who is that?"

"The old man is the old man. We give him the most food because he's the worst off of us. He's been here longer than any of us. None of us would be alive if it weren't for him. He started the rules and took care of each of us as we came in even when he should have fed himself he cared for us. A lot of us haven't made it but somehow he keeps breathing. He's over there."

The skin covered finger of the Commander pointed to a shadowy heap against the back wall. The shape was hard to make out but by best guess it looked like a very skinny man laying on his right side with his back to the room.

"How long has he been here?" Tex whispered, not wanting to be heard talking about the strange man.

"If it's 2014 that would put him at just about 10 years."

"My God. That poor man. How… How has he lived in this hell room for so long?"

An unfamiliar voice suddenly spoke out from the back of the room. It was a youthful sounding voice with a slight northern accent but it was faint-weak-almost not audible.

"You want to survive you need to focus. Focus on the one thing that you love the most. The one thing that you will live for, for as long as you can live. No amount of pain or suffering will ever take that vision from you and that vision will feed you, clean you, and keep you warm."

"Sir, if you don't mind me asking, what has kept you going all this time?" Tex asked gingerly.

The old man rolled over to face the young pilot. His face was sunken in and his eyes were tired, so very tired. But he seemed to light up when he started to speak, "The one thing that I love the most, the one thing that I have lost, the one thing that I will see again… my son."

References

Barton, David. The truth about Thomas Jefferson and the First Amendment,
Perry, I. Mac. Indian Mounds you can visit: 165 Aboriginal Sites on Florida's west coast
World's First Scheduled Commercial Airline: The Historical Marker Database (HMdb.org)
Jose Gasparilla, an 18th Century West Indiaman: Historical Marker Database (HMdb.org)
Timuquan Indian Mound, Historical Marker Database (HMdb.org)
Old Fort Brooke Municipal Parking Lot, Historical Marker Database (HMdb.org)

www.TrailofFloridasIndianHeritage.org
www.tampapix.com/watertower
www.Wikipedia.org
www.JoseGaspar.net
www.Gasparillapiratefest.com
www.treasurelore.com/florida/gasparilla.
-Demystifying the lives of Juan Gomez: from Pirate to Pilot, by Carrie Caignet 2006. (HI 390 H Privateers and Pirates in the Americas, Dr. Catherine Griggs.)
-Arnade, Charles W. Three Early Spanish Tampa Bay Maps.
-Gonzalez, Thomas A. "The last Florida Pirate" The Caloosahatchee: Miscellaneous writings concerning the history of the Caloosahatchee River and the city of Fort Meyers, Florida
-Stewart, George R. Names on the land: an historical account of place-naming in the United States.
Photo images: provided by Google Image
Gasparilla Pirate ship- www.destination360.com
Egmont key –www.Gulfster.com

To all the wonderful people at the Tampa History Museum and the Florida State Park employees that helped me make this happen- Thank you.

Stay tuned for the upcoming sequels in the;

Americana Adventures series

And follow the ongoing adventures of Gabriel Fletcher and his companions as they discover and explore new and forgotten treasures of American history.

If you enjoyed this book please recommend it to your friends and "like it" on Kindle.

They can also find it at Amazon.com

Thank you for your time. I hope you enjoyed the story. Now go out and discover America.